A STARTING LINE

They are called the "We."

As in, "We the people who were here first." Yes, they claim that right over all of humanity, over all of us. They have a ranking system, a hierarchy divided by seven levels of power they were born to. Each level indicates how much power they can hold. However, even the most minor level, a level one, carries enough magic to reinforce their claim.

So they are called the We. Secretly they share our sidewalks, shop in our grocery stores, walk their dogs in the same green parks where our children play. Throughout our history, they have peaked and fallen, having both ruled and been hunted. But how did they come here? How did it happen?

You must understand the We lived before the world began, up there, in that higher plane with the Creator. Long before there were angels, before there were demons, before Earth, Heaven and Hell, there was the We.

Up there, the We shared the same space, living with one another in joy and bliss while euphoria and ethereal power ran through their lungs, filling the air and their hearts. Every spoken word hummed and tingled with energy so raw and real it couldn't be denied. Pure electric joy coated every kiss, every hug, and every handshake. Each heartbeat they experienced was filled with laughter and love.

That was the cosmos the We were created within. That was their start: a space of love, community and magic filling their souls to capacity.

Then Earth was created, and the unseen war started. The war between Heaven and Hell.

When the We were forced to choose sides and forever become angels or demons, the ones who came to Earth requested a different path. They claimed then that war had no place in their hearts, and they wished to stay separate.

Perhaps at the time they made the request, they under-stood the consequences of leaving a perfect world filled with euphoria and gave up an endless supply of ethereal magic. Perhaps they understood they were leaving it all behind but for the small amount they could carry inside.

And so the We came . . . and they have been here ever since.

For some, avoiding the unseen war led to their own personal corruption, while for others, the choice was their salvation.

Maybe that should have been it. Fallen "angels" coming to Earth by the hundreds, living in secret, without wings, struggling with the burden of time. However, they didn't come empty-handed. Riding within each soul was the magic they were born to. Known as ethereal energy up there and the magic of creation down here. However, when this magic slipped from the higher plane to ours, the rules that governed our perfect world changed.

Now, with ethereal magic reverberating on Earth, a rare human can be born with this incredible gift. But this rare human finds him- or herself thrust into a world amongst the We, with little to protect them from being killed and having their fresh magic taken. Their only chance is to find allies amongst the We and protect each other as they discover a power within that has untold possibilities.

Welcome to the world of Alice and Owen.

HARMONY
OF FIRE

BRIAN FEEHAN

JOVE
New York

A JOVE BOOK
Published by Berkley
An imprint of Penguin Random House LLC
penguinrandomhouse.com

Copyright © 2022 by Brian Feehan
Excerpt from *Harmony of Lies* copyright © 2022 by Brian Feehan

A JOVE BOOK, BERKLEY, and the BERKLEY & B colophon
are registered trademarks of Penguin Random House LLC.

ISBN: 9780593440537

First Edition: June 2022

Printed in the United States of America
1 3 5 7 9 10 8 6 4 2

Book design by George Towne

I dedicate this novel to Michelle Greene,
whose grace and heart are far greater than my own.
I will forever be thankful for who you are and the
endless support you have given to our family and me.

Chapter One

Truth is ever to be seen in the contrast of choices. Oftentimes, truth comes in cool and comforting, easing the body and even soothing the soul. Just as often, truth enters with a crash so loud, so bright, only the brave cannot turn away, forcing all others to cower and hide. More often than not, the magnitude of a truth, its mass and gravity, crushes those who witness its awesome power, breaking them to dust under a heavy and unbending force. But like the phoenix, through truth's destructive and giving burden, the strong, the brave and the willing can rise again, higher and higher, leaving those who are too afraid to accept truth's embrace far, far behind and unaware.

MONTHS BEFORE A+O

Owen Brown pulled his old green truck to a stop across the street from the roadhouse just outside Columbus, Ohio. Hardly surprising for a Saturday night, even at this early hour, the parking lot was packed full of trucks and a few random cars. It was a good thing. Tim and Aurei had been kind to him and his, and the two owners could use the business after a long off-season.

Owen slipped from the old truck, his boots landing on uneven ground yet holding firm. Well muscled with experience beyond his twenty-six years, he moved to the back of the covered bed.

Owen turned and pulled open the shell over his truck's long bed. The tinted glass flipped up and out of his way. The tailgate fell open with a familiar rocking clang. Owen moved with a fast, practiced motion, sliding the long white cooler, heavy with a fresh load of ice, from the bed of the truck. It took effort, but after years tending bar and lugging endless musical equipment, coupled with a life always in motion, the ice and cooler were light work.

Setting the cooler on the ground, closing the tailgate, closing the shell, Owen didn't bother to lock up the bed. There wasn't anything in the back anyone would want. He picked up his load of ice and headed across the street.

He was not fast, wasn't slow, in making his climb around back of the semiremote roadhouse. He moved to the screen door without problems, the weight of the large cooler filled to the brim with heavy ice a burden but one he had accepted when he told Tim he could make the run to collect the much-needed supply for the current patrons.

Young Max had offered to join him. The twenty-two-year-old was good company at times, but as of late, the kid had started to talk a little too much. Max also enjoyed practicing his card tricks. Tonight, with the bar filling up, Owen had been wanting some quiet time before the long night of serving drinks and dealing with drunken customers.

Owen's booted foot caught the aluminum border of the screen frame that didn't sit perfectly flush any longer. He shifted the white cooler as he opened the door and walked in.

The difference in sound from outside to in was noticeable and grated on his nerves as he passed into the back of the kitchen. The roadhouse was a twenty-four-hour bar with its OPEN sign never turning off, and that was a good thing for Owen and his crew. But it also meant there was a fair amount of work to be done, and customers always came first.

"You got the ice," Daphne greeted with cheer. "Good thing. We're getting slammed out there. Aurei will need some up front. She's getting low. I heard her asking Tim when you would be back when I went up there last."

Owen saw the faint flush of her cheeks and couldn't help the tingle of fear as Daphne forced herself to look away. The innocent crush was fading but not gone. Not yet.

"Got it, thanks. How is everything going back here?" Owen asked, trying to keep the question innocent, neutral.

The difference in age wasn't huge, and yet the difference in life and maturity was vast. He'd hoped her crush would have faded by now. Daphne was young, only seventeen, and vulnerable on more than one level. On weekends and nights, he always tried to keep her in the back, where she was safe, and that meant she was the permanent dishwasher for as long as his people stayed here or until she turned eighteen.

Not that eighteen was too far away, thank the Lord. Daphne had only been with his group for a couple of months, and she was fitting in nicely. She didn't cause problems and was willing to throw in a helpful hand. If only she would stop blushing every time he walked into the room.

At least she isn't trying to flirt with you anymore . . .

"Oh, you know, dishes come in dirty, they leave clean. Same old, same old. I have no idea how Aurei and Tim managed this place on nights like this before us. It's crazy out there. I think there might even be a line outside," Daphne said.

Setting the cooler down, Owen snatched the empty, clean, white plastic ice-cream container and began shoveling fresh ice into the old brown ice machine. Its cooler still worked, so the ice he was putting in wouldn't melt. Maybe tomorrow he could find time to see if he could fix the water pump so trips to the twenty-four-hour gas station were no longer necessary.

"No line outside, not yet. Based on the number of trucks, we will have to start holding people back soon."

Owen looked up and couldn't help but notice Daphne was far too skinny. She wore skinny black jeans around a too-small waist, and the material was starting to look loose. Basic white sneakers she somehow kept clean and a deep red, almost burgundy sweater that was cut to ribbons in the back. The black tank underneath thankfully didn't allow for much skin to show whenever she walked into a room. His concern grew as she continued to wash. She was smart and talented, but for some reason, she would forget to eat. It had taken him far too long to notice the habit as he had tried to let her crush dissipate. Now her lack of eating was another concern on his list that never seemed to stop growing.

"Are we going to have enough food? The fridge froze yesterday," Daphne said.

"I already fixed the fridge, and we restocked. It's all good now."

"I am just saying that Tim and Aurei could use more than one or two things working around here."

The words she was thinking were clear in the space between them. *This is a temporary arrangement. What are Aurei and Tim going to do when we all leave? When we have to go because it is no longer safe, because of me.*

"Don't worry about a place like this. Tim and Aurei had it long before we got here. Everything will keep working long after we're gone."

"Yeah, I know, Owen, but they are good people," Daphne said, with the sound of soapy water and sponge hard at work behind her words.

"They are at that."

The cooler of ice was almost half empty. Seeing it as such, Owen judged he had taken enough for now. Setting the makeshift ice scooper to the side, he shut the lid to both cooler and ice machine, picking up the white cooler once more.

"Okay Daphne, wish me luck. I'm going in."

"Yeah, like you need luck out there." She rolled her eyes like a sister might, and Owen found it was nice to see.

"Hey, Tim. Hey, Max," Owen said while passing down the hall.

Owen looked to his right as he carried the cooler past the opening to the kitchen, Tim and Max both hard at work over the long grill and deep fryer. The grease fans and a box fan were both on high, competing with the sounds of sizzling grease and music coming from the bar.

"Hey, Owen!" Max said while flipping out two plates and loading them up with burgers and fries.

Both older man and younger worked in unison, even as their appearance was in contrast. Max was coming close to six feet at twenty-two years of age and still growing, but his body was long and lanky, like it didn't belong to him. Tim, on the other hand, was even taller and built like a mountain, with a personality to match: slow to rise, with a gravity that could only be described as grounding.

Tim gave him a small nod and, without a word, went back to working his grill. The silent nod was more than what the half owner of the roadhouse normally said. Owen took the gesture as friendly.

Working together over the last month, he and Tim had come to a quick understanding between the two of them, even sharing a couple of beers after work on occasion. There wasn't conversation so much, but that wasn't what mattered with a guy like Tim.

Owen respected Tim's calm control and easy nature. And Tim, it seemed to him, had needed to see Owen was more than just a pretty face. All the work and effort around the bar, coupled with keeping his own people in line, had helped to win the bigger man over.

Leaving Tim and Max to their work, Owen made his way farther down the well-worn hall, getting closer and closer to the heart of the night's event. People's voices mixed with those of the latest band rolling through that had made a quick contract with Aurei to play tonight.

"Ice coming in!" Owen announced over the noise as he pushed the long cooler through the Wild West–style doors. They swung open for him, the hinges squeaking as he made his way into the action.

The bar was packed full with people ranging from twenty-one to early sixties. The patrons were dressed in every type of outfit, from the well-groomed to the motley. People wanting any number of drinks, food and shots were crammed in like peanuts in a long row and several deep, trying to get the attention of the three people tending bar.

Owen ignored the looks that came his way as he moved the ice chest to Aurei's side on the left, where she was slinging drinks and warding off friendly attention in equal measure.

Aurei, early fifties and still a fox with short black hair and a wicked smile, was on his left. Her butt was tight, and she carried a painted sleeve of a dragon sleeping in a sea of daisies on her left arm. The ink work was solid and hadn't begun to fade.

She was the kind of woman who could throw a punch as easily as she could place a gentle hand on your back, depending on what was needed. Owen couldn't help but like her, as they all did. With her demeanor, it wasn't any wonder this place reminded him of home. A home he hadn't seen in a very long time.

On his right were the remaining two of his people. Smooth and steady Jessie, and working beside him, the continually moving and oftentimes over-the-top Clover. Both two years his junior at twenty-four years old.

The first worked with a smooth, no-nonsense rhythm. The latter was bouncing and bopping as she moved, gliding and even twirling at times, as if she were always in a hurry to make drinks, flirt and take in cash. Both were attractive—Jessie with his long lines and solid good looks and calming demeanor. But Clover, well, even he had to admit Clover held an internal music that never turned off or down.

"Oh good, you're here. I'm almost out," Aurei said, indicating the ice and signaling him over, the tight quarters causing their bodies to squeeze together as he went past. Her smile he found genuine.

He could feel the low-lying pull of chemistry between them. Nothing to act on, not that she ever would, but just a small zip up the spine that made for a smile. Seven years ago, back when he was still in Miami, he would have tried to ride that chemistry to something greater. But that was before the long road alone, back when he had thought he had nothing to lose.

Jessie gave him a small nod over his shoulder from the other end of the bar. At the same time, he opened two bottles of beer using only his hands. With a gentle, easy motion, Jessie tossed the metal caps over his shoulder five feet into the trash without looking. His patrons made a noise of appreciation in reaction. The bottles hadn't been twist-offs and Jessie hadn't used a bartender's tool, making it look like magic.

Owen gave a hard nod in return.

"Ice machine is already half filled in the back," he said to Aurei. "You want me to make another trip right now?" Owen spoke loudly. Between the band playing and the crowd, there wasn't much of a choice if he wanted to be heard.

"No, that's okay. The grill closes in another hour. I can send Tim for ice then. I need a hand with drinks. We just got another wave, and as they say, time is money."

"No problem." Owen made quick work of transferring ice using the clear scooper that was already there for just such a reason.

Working to fill the front icebox, Owen stayed in close to the cooler while waiting for Aurei to count out change. The moment she was done, he stood, scooping out some ice for a set of four drinks. Working in tandem was second nature, hardly surprising after being raised in a busy club.

"Aurei, by any chance, did you see if Daphne ate something before the crowd got here?"

"Tim made her some food. She ate with us."

"Okay. Thanks." He felt relief and mentally crossed it off the list of things he needed to get done. He wanted to have a sit-down with Daphne, but the flush of her cheeks said it still wasn't time.

"Yeah, no problem. What do you think of the band? They're pretty hot right now. They came in with twenty of their own people." Aurei's hands were moving as she poured three beers at once from the row of taps and deftly snatched a twenty out of an offered hand.

Owen didn't need to listen or take a moment. An extra compartment in his brain was already running a commentary.

Their bass player isn't in time with their drummer; he keeps getting pulled off. And their lead guitarist's fourth string is starting to slip out of tune. He needs to adjust. Their sound guy should soften the vocals and heighten the pitch. And their keyboarder should take up knitting instead of doing whatever the hell he thinks he is doing. He can't decide what sounds he wants, and by the time he does, the band has moved on.

"The band is good. The crowd is liking it," Owen said instead, while doing his best to close the doors on the subject.

"I should have believed you about people coming here and the uptick in customers. I am sorry I didn't, but Tim and I are thankful."

You should have, he thought. *My kind always attracts a crowd. It's why we have to keep moving, and why I need them to stay hidden within sanctuaries until Daphne turns eighteen.*

"All's good. It's a win-win." Owen didn't say the words *for now*, but he could see she felt the inevitable.

He couldn't stay for too long, as each member of his group needed to create music and fill that music with magic.

It was a primal need to release the growing pressure of ethereal power from within. A busy night like this helped take some of the edge off. But they all needed to create with magic, with the power inside. Each of his people were feeling "the itch"—a common name for what was by all accounts a nasty by-product that grew the longer they waited to bleed off the power building inside. The longer they held back, held in, the worse the itch, the more reckless each would become.

The greater the power, the higher the intensity, the more the itch could climb into their skin and bones. There were stories throughout history of more than one etherealist having gone insane because of the itch. More often than not, it led to terrible decisions in which etherealists chose to create or simply go far beyond their limits.

Maybe eight weeks more. I'll have to watch Clover for signs of going crazy. Jessie too. Maybe that long. We can find somewhere to play off the beaten path where we can't be tracked, then run from it.

He was almost finished with the ice on Aurei's side.

"Hey, did you know Daphne doesn't eat meat?" Aurei spoke as she moved past him, grabbing two bottles off a high shelf as he continued filling the icebox.

"What?" Owen said in confusion.

"Daphne. She doesn't eat meat. Tim and I didn't know that. We were kind of shocked when we found out. We've been making you all dinner, and we didn't know."

He stood up once more, helping her by handing out a set of bottled beers, using the bartender's tool to pop the top on each. The caps he dropped in the trash without any of the flair Jessie, his piano man, preferred. He took the recipients' beer money without even a glance in their direction.

"Daphne isn't a vegetarian. She eats meat. I've seen her." Hell, they always ate sandwiches, and the sandwiches always had meat.

The idea was shocking.

Daphne was his responsibility—they were all his responsibility. She was the newest, only joining his group as they were leaving Philadelphia before traveling through Pennsylvania, until they arrived here in Columbus.

"I think she didn't want to complain to you. She asked Tim if he had any veggie burgers around when we started up the grill. She ended up eating two. It kind of reminded me of a starving animal or, you know, Max."

Owen's body contained the little shock that ran through him as he tried to wrap his head around it.

How could I not have known? How could I have missed this?

Because she has had a crush on you since the first day she met you, and the last thing you wanted to do is break some kid's heart.

"That can't be. I've seen her eat burgers. Real burgers, not a patty made out of black beans. We practically live on burgers." It was true, during all the travel, the other roadhouses they worked. "Hey, Jessie," he called to get the man's attention. "Hey! You have seen Daphne eat meat, right?" Owen asked across the bar.

"What are you talking about, Owen? We all eat meat. We live off the three B's."

"Jessie," Owen warned, knowing his humor could push boundaries at times.

"Burgers, beer and brains. That's us, buddy. It's what fuels our music. Just yesterday Daphne and I shared a burger and fries out back, and we talked about how much we love the three B's." Jessie's voice was low but carried under the sounds of everyone else. It was like he was a major league pitcher, but instead of a baseball, he was able to use his voice like a curveball, sending it right under the swing of the bat. Or in this case, the sound coming from the other side of the bar, making it really easy to hear his voice without any apparent effort on his part.

"Did she eat the fries or the burger?" Aurei asked loud

enough to be heard over the sound coming from the other side of the bar.

Jessie suddenly stopped what he was doing, and it seemed like the clients at the bar focused on him, as if the simple act of not moving was a betrayal to their entire being. "She ate the fries. I can't believe it. She only ate the fries. I even ate her burger. Daphne can't be a vegetarian! Vegetarians are not rock and roll."

Clover chose this moment to chime in. "Peace and love and save the animals, guys. It's the new age order. Get your heads out of the past and into the California sand. Organic veggies rule, and you two dumbasses need to get with the times or be left behind." She gave a smile to Aurei that said, *Boys will always be dumber*, as she continued. "Slaughtering animals just because they taste good, and we have been doing it for thousands of years, is not love. It's not life."

"Clover, you love a rib eye. You talk about it all the time," Jessie countered.

"A girl can indulge in cravings, but it doesn't mean I am not aware of the cruelty." Clover spun, taking two bottles with her. The way she turned her back, it was clear she was no longer in the conversation.

Owen shared a look with Jessie like the world was far too crazy a thing to control. "All right, Aurei, you are full of ice here. When I am done topping off their side, I'll come back and give you a hand," Owen said.

"Actually, do you mind holding for a minute? I have three orders for food waiting, and Jessie has five. I need to get to Tim in the kitchen."

You just want to see your man. Your kind always do. No reason to point out the ice and cooler are taking up half the bar.

"No problem. I have this," he said over his shoulder, already pointing to a man wearing a blue-and-red Cubs hat in front of the bar, who Owen understood to be next.

"Thanks, Owen," Aurei said, picking up a light gray

plastic container filled to the brim with dirty glasses and thin, pressed silverware, presumably to bring back for Daphne to wash.

The Wild West doors sang their customary squeal as Aurei disappeared behind them.

"Hey, you! Hey, you there! Give me the stamp. I need the stamp!"

Warning bells flitted through Owen's mind as a long, skinny arm wearing a simple black-and-gold leather watch knocked down hard on top of the bar. The clasp to the watch faced up, veins and tendons in the wrist creating lines and valleys for his eyes to follow.

He is freaking out! The thought hit him and reverberated through Owen's body like a siren going off. *He is freaking out. Is this where it starts?*

"I need the stamp! Wait! What are you? What the hell are you? You're not one of the owners? I don't care. I need protection. Where is the owner?" His voice was fast and drove in like a ram's horns, twisting Owen's gut.

The stranger's hand reversed from pressing flat and open into a tightened fist, demanding satisfaction. Owen looked from the fist to the stranger's face.

A sea of humans enjoying the music, atmosphere, or simply wanting drinks framed the new customer. Air in motion stilled as Owen looked, examined, studied. Owen made mental notes of the creature speaking in case he ever might have a need to find him again.

Five foot eight, on the thin side, black hair parted to the left, wrinkles around the eyes, oval face, nose slightly long, not overly bulbous. Asian American, most likely. Well dressed, in a gray suit, open-collar white shirt, expensive material. Appearance ruffled, sweat around the rim of his hair.

Blue underglow shading just beneath the right eye, as well as along the right jawline. A level two and very frightened.

One of the creatures before Earth. One of the We who had celebrated with God before their choice between going to war or staying here . . . One of the We.

Frightened always means deadly when it comes to the We. He doesn't know who I am. I have to give him something he can hold on to. Be the bartender.

"Hello, sir. Aurei is one of the owners, and she just went to the back. She will be out in a moment, and she can help you with what you are looking for. My name is Owen. How about while you wait, I get you a drink, something cold? You look thirsty."

A patron to the We's left spoke up. "Hey, I have been waiting for like ten minutes, and this guy just walks in here, and you're going to help him? This is bull. I have girls waiting on me. I was next."

"Quiet, you fool!" the level two commanded, striking out by infusing his voice with ethereal energy.

Owen watched the wave of words fan out, slamming hard into the patron who had spoken, like a blow to the throat. Instantly the patron's windpipe closed, but the choking didn't make a sound. The wave of spoken power rippled past like a stone in a pond, silencing those gathered nearest as well.

The power shattered against Owen's own protection. Like the itch, the protection was a by-product of ethereal energy stored within, and Owen had more than most.

I hate level twos. They don't know their ass from their elbow.

Owen's right hand moved out to the side, with the message *Hold. I have this.* A clear sign for both Clover and Jessie, who were looking his way.

The release of power in the air was like a foghorn going off to anyone with ethereal power inside the building.

Using the white cooler, Owen stepped up and, in one smooth motion, leaped over the bar, one hand touching the thick, polished wood for balance as he slipped himself into the small gap that had formed.

The maneuver created reactions, but Owen ignored them all, focusing on the thin We with the specs and the human patron who could no longer breathe.

With a quick double tap to the gagging man's back, Owen broke the influence of the command. As the gagging could suddenly be heard, Owen twisted, slipping in close to the level two. The skinny We tried to move back, but Owen moved faster, coming in closer, tightly even, so his right hand could rest on the lower part of the creature's spine. Beneath his fingers he felt the tingle of the level two's stored ethereal power. The well of magic.

To a human man or woman, this could be intimate. To one of the We, it was the equivalent of wrapping your hand around his shaft and starting to squeeze. Not pain, not yet. More sensation, but with it a promise of absolute destruction.

"Friend, you will get a stamp from Aurei when she comes through those doors any second. However, if you cause another problem in here, I'll drain the little that remains of your power and end you for all eternity. Decide right now." Owen whispered the words, but each was spoken openly and honestly, the threat unmistakable to a creature that could hear the truth.

Owen let some of the mask he wore slip for just a moment, for just a breath. The handsome, friendly bartender slipped away to reveal the man beneath.

The level two didn't speak. Like the gagging human who was now pulling in fresh air, the We didn't have the breath to respond. The Wild West doors squeaked again, and Owen didn't need to look to know Aurei was there.

With a small push, Owen guided the level two We in Aurei's direction before turning back toward the recovering patron, once more the helpful bartender.

CHAPTER TWO

Alice, age twenty-six, an etherealist, looked to her left, past Father Patrick, who was driving the SUV down Main Street in Denver, Colorado, and spotted the elementary school she had attended as a child. Memories distorted by time played in her mind as she watched the stone building. Father Patrick continued to drive down the street, and Alice shifted in her seat so she could keep watching, until finally she was forced to turn back. There, following the cement path, were children and parents on their way to school holding hands, just as she once had.

She watched as buildings changed from one size to another. Alice held her breath, frozen in place as she watched and remembered. Sixteen years had passed since she had been here last. A lifetime, another life.

All because of that single day when she was nine years old. Alice's body trembled as she remembered the song she had been forced to sing with the monster known as Kerogen.

A level six We who wanted power and her free will. It was the first day she had learned she was something different. That she had power. And Kerogen had done his best to take it from her.

A stoplight turned red, and there it was. Grace Cathedral stood with all its old and timeless glory. As she looked, she could see the ghost of her nine-year-old self holding her mother's hand, walking up the stairs and opening the doors to the stained glass, pulpit and pews. A much younger Father Patrick had offered to help her practice her solo, for she was to sing for the visiting cardinals.

She felt Father Patrick's stare at the grand old church he once watched over, and his concentration matched her own. This was ground zero, this church. Three lives had been lost. Father Patrick's, her own, and that of an elderly priest who gave his life so she and Father Patrick could flee. Within those doors, it had happened—the bonding between her and Kerogen. Sixteen years of being away, and they still couldn't go back.

Father Patrick was late to the green light, his attention and thoughts deep within.

"Father, you're up, it's green," Alice said.

This has to be just as hard for him as it is for me, Alice thought to herself.

"Of course," he said in a muted but steady voice.

The SUV moved through the intersection, even as they both tracked the holy building.

They drove in silence, each needing their space. Twenty minutes later, they turned off the highway and entered the ungated housing development on Jessup Street. A left turn, then a right and four blocks beyond that before Alice spoke up.

"Pull over here, and, Father, please take your collar off. We don't want anyone to recognize you," Alice said with a gentle grip of resolve as she scanned the street up ahead.

No one will recognize me. I haven't been here for what

feels like an eternity. I was just an innocent child then.
Even so, Alice wore a blue baseball hat, dark shades and
kept her window up.

Attuned to the only person she was close with, Alice felt
the stress in the breath Father Patrick released as he pulled
the black-tinted SUV to the side of the street. The vehicle
smoothly came to a stop, and the priest reached up with two
hands and carefully unbuttoned the white collar from
around his black clergy shirt. With the ease of companions,
Alice opened the glove box with her right hand as her left
opened the center console that sat between them. She lifted
the silenced Beretta out of the center console and transferred it into the glove box, where it lay beside three black
columns of ammunition prepped and ready to go.

Father Patrick didn't blink at the weapon, nor did he
miss the rhythm of her movements as he slipped the white
collar down and safely away. In sync, he was handing her a
tube of lotion while closing the lid of the console with his
elbow. Neither had taken their eyes off the street and the
cookie cutter houses up ahead. This was too important, too
vital.

"Is that the house? Blue door, gray trim, up on the right,
with the red mailbox out front?" Father Patrick asked.

"Yes, it is."

Alice knew her words were clipped, but there wasn't
much she could do about that right then.

Leaving the glove box open with the silenced weapon on
display, Alice put lotion on her hands, then offered some to
the father. She liked the lotion because gun oil was hell on
the skin, but Alice thought Father Patrick liked it because
of the smell. Honey blossom. When his dark-skinned hand
extended, she placed a small dollop in his palm, then screwed
the cap back on and set it beside the deadly Beretta in the
open glove box.

Rubbing her hands in a circular motion, she scanned
the street, the houses, the cars, and every shadow and any

obstructed viewpoint she could find. They were looking down a quiet cul-de-sac in a typical middle-class housing development in Denver, Colorado. It was autumn, and the mature trees were losing their color in preparation for winter, showcasing a bouquet of reds and oranges and even some purple above in the limbs and below on the short cut grass that lined the cement sidewalks.

Alice bent her neck to one side, then the other as stress took its toll—every sense on high alert.

"I don't see anything out of the ordinary. Can we get closer? I see a spot across from the house," Father Patrick said.

"No, we stay right here," Alice said, quick and fast. She didn't want anyone to spot them, be it friend or foe.

One silent minute ticked by, then five minutes, and then ten. Together they scanned, watched and listened.

After fifteen minutes of not speaking and seeing nothing out of the ordinary, Alice moved the dark jacket off her lap and tossed the baseball cap she was wearing onto the front dash. Father Patrick accepted the jacket and offered up a hand, his own body turning in the seat to assist her with leverage. She moved fast, climbing from the front passenger seat to the row behind. One of Alice's legs bent like a gymnast's as she made her move up and over the console.

Up front, she had been exposed, but back here with the dark glass, the world was her own and concealed. With fast, efficient hands, she folded the first row of seats down and climbed farther into the back. The modified M16, with silencer and green laser sight, was in her hand as she lay prone. Gently Alice tucked her right eye behind the tactical scope. Her world split as she kept both eyes open. With her left eye, she watched the world through the windshield and spied on the distant collection of homes as a whole.

But with her right eye, Alice's world became the white house with soft gray trim and a blue front door. The house was almost the last in the line, right off the open circle. The red dot of the military-grade scope drifted over the gold knocker, a brass beetle that lay still and unmoving. For a single moment, Alice let herself hope. For one single breath, she let herself feel it, both fear and joy, and a whole lot of regret as she imagined the front door opening—her father and mother, whom she hadn't seen in person in over sixteen years, stepping out and into her view.

Like a slap to the face, her training kicked in and she continued to scan for threats, for inconsistencies and for vulnerable points that could hide monsters.

"You see anything? Any We?" Father Patrick asked.

The We. Father Patrick was asking about them, the seven levels of fallen creatures who hadn't been in God's plan. Those creatures that had come down to Earth, still holding their ethereal power. The same ethereal magic that lived within her own body.

"I don't, but it doesn't mean Kerogen hasn't planted someone in the neighborhood."

"Typically, the We don't do suburbia. They tend to like large gatherings and action, places where they can be themselves."

"I don't think Kerogen has any real friends, but it doesn't mean he can't threaten or pay others to do his dirty work. I just need to make sure before I start hunting him again."

"Alice, do you really believe Kerogen would come for them?" Father Patrick's voice lowered and changed from slow to quick. "Four houses down on our side of the street, there's a dog and a woman on the steps. Do you see her?"

Alice was already moving the weapon and the scope. The red dot slipped over the forehead of the woman. "I have her, keep watching the street and shadows," she warned.

Alice's mind moved and tracked several things at once. But first and foremost, she checked the face for the telltale signs that the woman was one of the We: blue underglow around the cheeks and ears. This woman was clean of underglow—just a normal everyday human.

"No underglow, she's fine. She's crossing the street now, most likely headed for the park. We're fine," Alice said again when the woman continued moving away from them.

Alice went back to searching from one house to the next, looking for anything outside of the ordinary.

"Alice, you didn't answer me. Why, after all this time, would Kerogen target your parents? Just because he's back in the United States doesn't mean he's coming here. You always said it was between you and him."

A tingle on her face distracted her, but she held still, focused and unmoving as she watched through the cracks in the curtains of a light blue house. Through the small gap, Alice was looking for signs of surveillance equipment.

"I don't think Kerogen is coming here. Kerogen doesn't really care that I'm not on his leash. In his mind, he owns me no matter where I am in the world. Because he does." Her voice was flat as she swallowed. "But he could have someone watching the house. Keeping an eye out in case I decided to come back. We just need to make sure."

"You've been hunting him outright for just over seven years. You don't think he came back to the United States because of your parents, because of you?"

Alice thought about what she was going to say. It was hard to explain the relationship she held with Kerogen. The forced bond between them when she was only nine years old made their connection special and horrifying. After all, the We was a madman and an asshole. Her own personal demon, and yet through the bond, she had gotten glimpses of who he was inside. The core of the man.

"I don't know why he came back to the United States. But he's not tired of me hunting him. In many ways, Kerogen loves that I am hunting him. Revels in the idea. Despite the rage he carries, both sides of his mind love that right now I am holding a gun and looking through a scope searching for him. Because with me, he matters." Alice went on. "You know the history we have on him."

She paused in her search as her scope stopped once more on the front door of her parents' home. A tightness came to her throat as she moved the scope slowly over the large brick-framed window. The curtains were closed. Nothing moved, nothing gave a sign that her mother and father and new baby sister were home, and yet Alice thought she could feel them within. Perhaps to distract herself, she continued talking.

"He was a king, worshiped back then by thousands of people in so many ways. He had parties, and people bowed and sang his name. And Kerogen can still remember what it was like before he and his wife were dethroned. And now, no one cares. No one cares where he goes, who he kills, or what he does. But for me . . ." Alice paused, and Father Patrick stayed silent.

After so many years spent together, she knew the man was trying to get her to continue. He liked her to share what was on her mind. After all, confession was good for the soul. Or so they say.

"No one in the world cares about him, not even his wife, who I understand hasn't seen him in over five hundred years." Alice waited, then added, "Kerogen thinks of me as the same nine-year-old child he bonded seventeen years ago. Despite my skill as a hunter, even though my power and abilities are still growing, he doesn't think of me as a threat. I'm more like a small pet that bites. He won't be coming here. He won't even think of it." The last point she said with conviction, to the point her body lost some of the tension she had been feeling since she boarded the plane back to the United States four days ago.

Regardless of her own words and knowing they were right, Alice continued to look at the house; she couldn't enter until Kerogen was dead.

"Alice, listen to me." Father Patrick abandoned his search of the street and turned around in the driver's seat to look back at her. "You and I can go into that house right now, your parents' home. We can simply scoop them up and then disappear."

Never taking her right eye away from the scope, Alice's left eye focused on him. Father Patrick had been in his midthirties when he served Grace Cathedral, not more than a few miles from where they were now. He held scars on all ten of his fingers from the day that had changed both of their lives forever. And for seventeen years, despite being a pacifist, Father Patrick had never abandoned her. They had traveled most of the world together, so when he spoke, she felt the weight in the question like it was a building coming down over her heart.

"We have the skills, and the contacts, to take you and your family out of this country. We walk in there, convince your mother, your father and your little sister to get in this car, right now, and we go. You can have your family back. You don't have to kill Kerogen. The relic you wear keeps the bond covered, and the rest is simply outsmarting him. As you said, he doesn't have friends to help find you, and the world is a vast space. We can do it. You can have your mother and father back today, now. Right now."

Alice stared at the good father as every muscle and cell in her body shouted out with pain and ice. It hurt. Hurt more than the pain she had come to live with. It hurt in a way that crushed her soul into small pieces.

"Oh, Alice, it's okay. We can do this," Father Patrick said as he opened the center console, pulling out a fresh white tissue. "Here, you're crying." He reached as far back as he could.

It hurt to move, even as Alice set down the lethal weapon and gathered her will. One hand wiped away the tears that had slid down to her chin. Then she reached forward and took the tissue from his weathered, scarred hand. The white cloth smashed in between hers and his.

"I can't. I can't do it. Father, they had a service and buried me, and you know it. Right now, they aren't in danger.

But if I take them. If I change their lives like my life has been changed, then all three of them will be hunted forever. Because, if I stop going after Kerogen, I know beyond a doubt, Kerogen will come after me. He will never stop because he owns me." Alice's left hand touched her collarbone and slid across the faint crisscrossed lines that lay there. "Kerogen has a plan once my power stops growing. He will need everything I have to give if he wants his soul to break into Heaven, and we both know it. He won't ever stop or let me go."

Alice held his gaze. The depth of his blue eyes held the weight of the Earth.

Can't you see, they buried me years ago, they had to let me go and start over. You're asking me to go in there and break them just as he broke me. I can't offer them anything but pain.

"Alice, you can have it all. A simple life in a fishing village, or live on a mountaintop. You could meet a man and start your own family." Father Patrick stopped talking as Alice let go, the white tissue still in his hand, taking on a symbol of surrender she could never accept.

"I'm broken, Father. Kerogen broke me on that day when we sang together; he tied our souls in a way I can't escape. I don't get to have a family, a husband and partner I call my own. I'll never be a princess with a normal life. I don't even understand what that would look like anymore. I just need to fix what he did to me. Break the bond and send his ass to Hell. Just look around. I don't belong in this place. There is no little white cottage for me. No ivory tower, no picket fence. Father, you did your best to save my soul, but I'm broken, and I won't stop until Kerogen is dead."

Alice's tears no longer fell freely, but she watched as fresh drops manifested on the good father's beautiful face.

She looked into his deep blue eyes and owned the weight and pain of each tear as a lashing over her soul that she would have to answer for. Those tears, his tears, were on her.

There were words within her. Trapped inside her heart and chest that for so long, she had simply never been strong enough to tell him. To whisper or even admit. But now, with her parents' home before her and the long journey up to this point behind her, she found the strength.

"Father, Kerogen isn't hunting you. You're not on his radar. Even after all that you have done for me. You are free. You can go back to your old life. Speak to your contacts within the church, and they will protect you. I'm old enough and skilled enough now to do this on my own."

All the vulnerability she held solidified and hardened before she spoke. It was the only reason she could keep still as his eyebrows raised, and the weight of what she had just said climbed back atop her shoulders ten thousandfold.

For the first time in sixteen long years, she watched the good father's eyes harden to steel. Then he sat back in the driver's seat so she could only see the back of his head.

Alice swallowed, then looked around the street again as she forced her mind back to the task at hand.

"You know, Alice, there have been times that I have asked God why he has sent me on this journey. A challenge. To be ripped from my home, and ripped from what I thought was my path, and set into the chaos of his design. Do you know what the Holy Ghost whispers to me when I ask? She whispers that I have always been on this path and that you need me because you are a terrible listener."

"Father, was that supposed to be a joke?" He didn't answer, so she went on. "I mean it. I don't believe you're in danger. You can go home. You can go back."

Their eyes met in the reflecting glass of the rearview mirror.

"We started this a long time ago, you and I. And I am not going anywhere. This is the last time we will speak of it. Do you understand me, Alice?"

I do.

Alice couldn't speak. She simply nodded, and he nodded in return.

For the slightest moment, she remembered the monastery in Northern Italy where the secret sect of the church and Father Alton had trained her. She remembered the other kids, now most of whom would be adults, hunters in their own right, working together under the watchful eye and power of that secret sect rather than alone, as she was. She remembered Kerogen coming for her then, and the trap she had helped set for him. Father Patrick had refused to leave then too.

CHAPTER THREE

Jessie, our things? Did you get them all loaded up in the van?"

"Yes! All but your acoustic guitar and Clover's violin, like you said. I got the rest in there, but don't blame me for the packing job. I had to move fast," Jessie whispered low and slightly out of breath, worry and tension in each word.

Owen couldn't blame him. At two thirty in the morning, the crowd was down to a small fraction of the number it once had been. But with every minute that passed, it seemed there were more humans going home and more of the We coming in. By last count, the We were up to thirty-seven. Each and every one of the We recognizable to Owen and his people with their own display of underglow around the face and the edges of the ears.

By far, the lone level five was the most dangerous. He hadn't even approached the bar, let alone taken the stamp. And by not taking the stamp, it was a bold statement saying he did not require the protection the stamp offered or accept the authority of the sanctuary. A statement that said he refused to play by the rules. On a night like this, he might as well be a living flame hanging out by the pumps of a gas station.

The level five was wearing soft-toned clothes, all blues and whites, but it mattered little. The energy that radiated off him felt like it could power a small town. Owen made sure his senses always knew where the level five was. On the other side of the spectrum, the level ones he practically ignored, despite their larger numbers. They were here for safety and finding music and humans to interact with. Naturally the level ones had joined the party, tossing their meager influence into the band and patrons. It was rare that a level one was ever a threat. They were more like flies that, every once in a while, would turn into a mosquito.

"What is the gas situation with the van? My truck has three-quarters of a tank," Owen said.

"The van's good. Filled her up two days ago when I took the girls into town. Do we know why they've all come here? Is it you, all of us, or something else?" Jessie said, missing some of the calm he normally had.

Owen couldn't blame him. The vibe in the air was one of unrest. And unrest with ethereal power meant danger. Lots of danger.

"If they were here for me, they wouldn't have taken the house stamp. It gives too much of their power to the roadhouse and Tim and Aurei, who are on our side as long as we stay smart."

Clover bopped in from the bar and made her way straight for his group, who had gathered in the back by the dishwashing station.

"Poor girl. Daphne looks miserable. Tim has her in the kitchen peeling potatoes with her back against the wall, while Max cleans out the grease traps. Meanwhile Tim is cutting onions. The smell in there is nasty. Are we going to split soon? Three more of the We just came in, including a strong level four who didn't take the stamp. Though he can wear a pair of jeans."

"Tim is doing us a favor and giving us extra protection. As for Daphne, she can take a little discomfort right now. Is the level five still by the stage?" Though Owen could sense the We, it still was unnerving not to be able to see the creature.

"His name is Butch, and some of the We are whispering about him. Apparently, he's an asshole and a badass. No, he hasn't moved. Just sits in the corner to the left of the stage, staring back here. And I have to tell you, he is not looking at me. I know, I checked. He is freaky strong. And the way he keeps looking around, I swear, I think he is ready to tear the house down."

"He is just a level five. It's not like he is a level six," Jessie said.

"Jessie, man, don't even say something like that. A level five is plenty scary. Without the stamp, neither Aurei nor Tim can directly control his power," Owen put in.

"Yes, but Tim and Aurei are both practically glowing at this point with all the power that is being siphoned off so many. They can take this Butch, and inside their house, it will be easy. Damn, that would be a show," Jessie said.

It was true. Each time the stamp/contract was made, the power of the recipient was siphoned off into the two owners and, if rumor was to be believed, into the building itself. Owen believed the rumors. Such power helped strengthen the rules and the power of the roadhouse, granting sanctuary during bad times. Creating a safe place for We and etherealists who had reached the age of eighteen.

To everyone else, this was just an off-color bar. But to anyone touching the ethereal, a twenty-four-hour road-house was a sanctuary, provided they took the stamp and spoke the words.

"Nothing easy about a level five. Besides, he's not alone. If this turns into a fight of any kind, Aurei and Tim will be the only ones on our side." Owen hoped. The We were not human, and although Aurei was human, she had chosen to willingly bond with Tim, one of the We. It made her something else, meaning she too played by a different set of rules.

Owen had to stretch his arms. They tingled with all the power in the building. One thing was not up for debate: they couldn't stay. There were simply too many of them at one time, and Daphne was still seventeen and unbound. Far better they find safer waters.

"I'll talk to Tim, but we are leaving. Jessie, you're step one. I want you in the van first with Max. Get the engine running. I'll watch from the doorway. Is the shotgun out there loaded?"

"It is, along with the forty-five under the passenger seat," Jessie said.

"When you and Max are in and the engine is running, give the signal, and we will come out. Step two, I want that shotgun in your hand, Jessie, with Max already in the back of the van with the gear. Clover and I will escort Daphne between us. I'll ask if Tim will be willing to help us leave."

Owen looked from Jessie to Clover, seeing the resolve in both.

"Clover, once Jessie gives the go-ahead, you get Daphne into the van. Keep her between us, get her head down. Clover, that forty-five is yours. Be ready to pull the trigger on my say. I don't trust anyone here to play nice with us tonight. There is just something in the air."

His body pulsed, as if in anticipation of action.

"When everyone is in—step three—you all get out. I'll stay and watch to make sure you leave safely. Once I know you're gone, I'll get my truck on my own. Anything goes wrong, we fight like hell. Hopefully everything will be fine. Otherwise, we will have to rely on the stamps' protection for the four of you. Stay together and watch each other's backs until I get there," Owen said, making sure his people understood this was as serious as it came.

The original idea of the stamps on the wrist was to allow you enough time to get away from the roadhouse safely. Say, for example, if someone happened to follow you out into the parking lot. It was a type of body armor against magic attacks. Of course, the protection of the sanctuary did have limitations.

He understood the stamp was a last line of defense, one he wasn't planning on relying on. His people needed to leave and find another sanctuary where it was calm. A place relatively unused, where Daphne could turn eighteen. And they needed to do so now.

"Owen, man. I don't like leaving you. You didn't take the protection like the rest of us did. We can't just drive off and leave you," Jessie said.

Ethereal magic could be sensed by other users unless purposely twisted, concealed. But that was rare, because to do so slowly drained ethereal power. Like leaving the lights on when no one was home. You could do it, but there was a cost, and We never wasted ethereal energy. Etherealists, on the other hand, wasted it all the time.

"I didn't take the stamp for a good reason, and you know it. Just drive north. When I know we are in the clear, I'll tell you where we are going next. You got the new phone number and know where to meet up if things go really bad?"

"I have it, Owen," Jessie said, all business. "I still don't like leaving you behind. We could leave your truck, come back for it in a month or two. I am sure Tim wouldn't mind."

"I'll be fine. Nobody is going to hurt me. We need to get Daphne out—she's the biggest risk. Once she is out of here, everything calms back down."

Jessie and Clover nodded their heads in acceptance. Until Daphne turned eighteen, she was at risk for a bonding from any level three or higher. Daphne needed to make it to her eighteenth birthday unchained. To be bound was to have your soul and well of power tied to a We and, with it, your free will stripped from you. It was still possible to be bonded after one turned eighteen of course, but it was much, much more difficult. So far, all of Owen's crew had stayed unbound. And he would be damned if that was going to change tonight.

Clover couldn't hold back anymore. She and Owen had joined forces many years ago. If anyone understood the risk and the danger they were in, it was her.

"Owen, come on. We can at least drive you to the truck. It is just on the other side of the lot and across the street. The lot should be mostly empty by now. I'm with Jessie—I don't like leaving you behind and just driving off. That's not what we do. We haven't seen this many We come in like this. Not since some tried to make a run to the fourth gate over in Austin."

"I'll be fine." His skin was itching as the edge of an invisible cliff sang in his bones for him to join in with the gathering. To lose himself in wild winds of creation and the pure joy of being alive.

It wasn't a new feeling. In truth, it had been with him his entire life. The edge, the call, the Devil's itch, some called it. Whatever the name, it was the need to reach in two directions at once and to, for a time, live in the space between. The music of the other side.

Owen knew it for what it was. Not the Devil but the music of both Heaven and Hell. His fingers, his voice longed to reach further. His soul craved the other side, and right now, such a thing would get them all brutally killed. Or worse, enslaved.

Aurei poked her head back in from the bar, seeing them huddled. She spoke quickly, understanding the situation. It was easy to see the underglow surrounding her skin. Soft blues and greens. Odd for a human, but it was all part of the contract with the owner (and their companion) for a sanctuary filled with We. All juiced up on power.

"You guys need to get going. I finally got one of the twos to let me in on what is going on. If Tim had gone out, I am sure he would have found out a lot sooner."

"What's happening, Aurei? Why are so many here? It can't be us. We haven't even played in this town yet. Nobody knows who we are." Owen double-checked Clover and Jessie to make sure he was telling the truth. If either had played with power, it would have left a signature in the air. Such a thing could be tracked.

It was a difficult thing not to play for a full month. Each had their own ways of dealing with it. But the looks on both Jessie's and Clover's faces were clean of guilt, instead holding a touch of anger at being questioned.

"No, it's not you. There are hunters over in the city. Apparently, they set a trap and ended up killing twelve of the We, including two level fours. The whole community is in an uproar. By tomorrow night, I imagine this room will be filled, and Tim and I will be turning humans away. You guys need to get Daphne out of here."

Hunters were bad news. They didn't negotiate, they normally didn't speak unless they had to, and they acted as judge and jury, killing anything and everything that stood between them and the We. Little to no regard for any human that stood in their way. They were a death squad, one Owen had no desire to tangle with.

"I have cash. You guys did great work. I'm sorry I never heard you play. Come back when the dust settles." Aurei handed over a small stack of twenties and fives. It was a lot, possibly too much, even with the large crowd. She was feeling guilty for them being forced out on such terms.

Owen didn't argue. Instead he snatched the cash before she could change her mind. If it wasn't for his people, he probably would have cut it in half. But such things were for people with far less responsibility than what was currently on his shoulders. "What kind of trap did the hunters use?" Owen asked, already knowing the answer.

She looked to him, her eyes shifting, soft and pleading. "There was an underage etherealist girl who snuck into the Old Spoon and Bucket. She got onstage and somehow started singing. While she sang, she used ethereal magic, ensnaring most of the crowd's attention. And then the hunters started killing."

"Poop sticks," Clover said as understanding became clear.

Owen felt the lump drop in his stomach as Clover looked to him.

"Oh, we are screwed," Jessie said as he caught on just a touch behind. Owen could feel Jessie focus on him for guidance as well.

It wasn't just murder but a violation of an unspoken code between etherealist and We.

"Is anyone out there going to believe it wasn't Daphne who got up onstage?" Jessie asked.

"No," both Clover and Aurei said at the same time.

"We have to go. Now. Right now," Owen commanded.

CHAPTER FOUR

SEVEN YEARS BEFORE A+O

Kerogen found himself looking out toward the square monastery in Northern Italy with a casual, almost lazy disinterest.

"The child is inside the walls. Just right there." He pointed a finger to mark the location. "Finally," he said to himself. After being alive as long as he had, speaking to himself was the most normal thing he could do in a day.

Kerogen breathed in the air as if it were spring water. After all these years, Alice was finally going to be his once more. The child he had bonded years before in Denver, Colorado, only to be swept away and out of his reach, by a priest of the church.

"Yes, yes, but this is no time to be simple. It is a trap the church has set for us. And yet they are fools." Once again one side of his mind spoke to the other.

Anger rose within him and traveled all the way up to the bridge of his nose.

"Fools enough to keep her from you for so many years? Fools enough to escape from us the first time? These are your fools. Our fools. Do not underestimate them."

Kerogen let the discrepancy of self go as he continued the two-sided conversation.

"They don't remember me, even in their protected archives. They don't remember what I can bring to bear."

Kerogen stared over the valley of long grass in the direction of the old monastery, with its dust-covered walls and single high bell tower.

"You could break the ground they reside upon. Our power has grown so much further than I ever believed possible. The bonded child is special. Her will, her gift. Get to her, and remind the fools of their betrayal."

"Shut up," Kerogen said, tired for once of his own voice. The excitement of the child's connection no longer being blocked had been a very real thing for the last three days. A sensation that took an effort to dampen. But now something else was growing within his heart.

"Disgust for those who have taken her from us."

"And a deep rage." He puzzled.

A predatory smile crossed Kerogen's face as he understood his own mind, his own soul. With a twisted joy forming, he started the long hike toward the monastery. His ethereal power and will surrounded his body before he folded back the energy, causing him to disappear from the visual spectrum.

Any sign of the demon?" Father Alton asked into a hand-held radio.

Five voices took turns answering back from the radio's speaker. They were the spotters, Alice Davis knew. Each was set up on a different wall of the monastery, and a fifth was set up in the bell tower. All had rifles of one sort or another.

Alice stayed calm. After all, it wasn't the first time Alton had asked the question. It happened about every twenty minutes, going on now for hours. There were more of Alton's priests inside the building, hiding and ready just inside the walls, prepared to spring forward the moment Kerogen showed.

"Are you getting anything, girl?" Alton asked.

Alice checked inside, where the connection to Kerogen was in her mind. The connection was fuzzy, as it had been for the last five hours. "No, nothing. The connection is the same as before, but I know Kerogen is nearby. I just can't connect with him."

"Don't fear, child. We will kill your demon tonight. God is watching and is on our side."

Alice let the statement fall away. She was nineteen and knew better than to try to have a discussion with Father Alton. After all, God had been in the church where Kerogen had bonded her ten years before when she had been torn from her family. As far as she believed, God intended her to fight her own battles. And she was ready; whether this was all part of God's plan for her or something else was up for interpretation. However, Alice doubted Father Alton would agree.

Needing to stretch out the growing tension inside her, she started a fighting routine. The courtyard was empty except for the small round table and chair Father Patrick had placed off to one side. She missed the others. Sandy and Josh were her friends, if a bit younger. But they were good company and decent sparring partners. Josh was strong, if not as fast. Sandy was younger by three years, with a welcome smile.

Alice moved low and with balance as she had been instructed, her body harnessing the stored ethereal power to cover more ground. She flowed like water over the entire courtyard. Using ethereal energy was amazing. Magical, even. Alice could move faster than normally possible, with far less effort.

Her hands snapped out in punches and blocks. Her feet whipped high, then low, as she pictured Kerogen's head and knee. On she moved across the open ground, the stars above drowned out by the floodlights highlighting her actions in the center of the courtyard. She came close to a wall and improvised by running up the side, her feet finding purchase as energy helped seal her footing on the pale stucco. One, two, three steps, and she backflipped off, going high into the air so she didn't need to tuck, instead staying straight like a pencil, watching the courtyard as her perspective changed from floor to ceiling and back again. Her hands itched for the knives tucked under her arms and on her back.

Feet flipping down, she twisted at the last second so her back was facing the direction of her momentum. She rolled backward, pushing with hips and hands, lifting into the air. Picturing Kerogen's face clearly in her mind, Alice imagined launching all four knives into his chest.

Demons looked human to all but those that could hold ethereal power. More importantly, she had been assured they could be killed like a human. As long as you did the job quickly and didn't give them time to heal. She landed again, this time her feet sliding across the pebbled ground.

One look at Father Patrick, and it was clear how uncomfortable he had become with what was about to happen.

A thud like a sack of something wet and heavy hit the ground hard not more than fifteen feet away. She, along with Father Patrick and Father Alton, and the four other dark-clad priests within the square, turned to see the dead scout who had been watching up in the bell tower. Alice looked up, as did everyone else.

"Kerogen. He is here," Alice whispered as her resolve hardened. A small shudder passed over her skin. Ten years of hard work, ten years of never speaking to her parents in fear Kerogen would go back to the home he had stolen her from. And finally, he was here. Now, after all this time. And she was ready.

Kerogen moved with a hunger he hadn't felt in a long time. Violence. It welcomed him like a hot campfire in the cold of night. Violence held another type of energy, another source of power. It crawled inside his chest, vibrated through his skin and flared deep in his soul.

"Isn't this better?" he asked as the dead man's body fluttered for a brief moment before splattering within the well-lit courtyard. "We could have torn down the walls and building, forcing stone into rubble. Alice is a bonded ethe-realist. She would have survived, and we could have simply plucked her from the wreckage. But this! This is far better. Feel it. Take it in and hold on. Revenge, one dead body at a time? No, we shall not give this up. Look at them. Look at the way they squirm like insects below our eyes. Let us crush them now. Let us feel their bones snap in our hands like the dried sticks that they are."

Kerogen leaned out over the edge, the night air like wings on his back. "You are acting indulgent. You want to taste their lives as they drain away?"

Slowly, Kerogen shifted his body back. "A job well done is a task we can enjoy."

Together both sides of his mind shared a chuckle.

"Vengeance and violence then. Let us be free of hiding so they can remember again their ultimate mistake. And we can take back the child once and for all."

Pulling on a stream of ethereal power, Kerogen's mind and will shaped the ethereal power into a weapon. An ability made easier now with the depth of his ethereal well, thanks to the child and bond. The tentacle vibrated before the end caught the moonlight with a wicked gleam. A living spear at his disposal. Satisfaction rippled through his soul as he looked up toward the pulley system beside the large bell that held a unique black vine of metal that was currently catching the light and shone despite the dark hour. A bell that was made to keep his kind out of such a place as this.

Like a phantom, Kerogen moved away from the disabled bell, swiftly speeding through the compound. He ran the outer walls, encouraging each victim to scream before snapping the neck. One body he left dead in the night air atop the old crumbling wall where the priest had been patrolling. The following two priests, he tossed their dead bodies over the wall to land hard out of sight, forgotten. With each kill, with each scream, Kerogen felt the weight over his heart lift in a pure, pumping joy.

CHAPTER FIVE

MONTHS BEFORE A+O

We had nothing to do with what happened at the Old Spoon and Bucket. My people and I were here all night. I say this with an open heart. Hear me—we had nothing to do with the hunters and your dead friends!" Owen shouted to the crowd of We that had swarmed out of the front entrance.

The level five, Butch, led the pack of We that had come out the main door, spilling in numbers into the parking lot. Owen's crew were safe in the van, but a cord of black ethereal power from Butch's hand had forced the van into a hard, swerving stop.

"If I thought for a moment you had anything to do with the attack this night, I would have already torn you to pieces, and your bones would be in a fire of my own making," Butch called out over the black paved lot with a horde of We at his back.

Owen took another step to the side, placing more of

himself between the mob of We and the back of the van that contained his people. "Then let us leave and no one needs to die tonight," Owen called.

"An unbound girl is a prize not easily passed by. Do you really expect me to let her leave?"

Owen felt the crowd of We inch closer. "If you don't let her leave, I'll kill you before you ever have the chance to sing with her. My word on it." He watched as the anger flashed in the level five. Owen took notice as two thick black strands of ethereal power fanned out behind Butch, both cords rippling in frustration, reminding Owen of two tentacles made of living oil. The other We gathered close to Butch, taking a few cautious steps away.

Owen watched them all, preparing, the familiar weight of the acoustic guitar on his back. It wasn't the weapon he wanted just then—like bringing a seat cushion to hold back a pride of lions. But it was better than nothing, he supposed.

"She was not at the Old Spoon and Bucket. She is not with any hunter. This child is with me, under my protection, and anyone wanting to get to her will need to go through me first," Owen declared, loud and clear.

The crowd rippled as his words settled in. Promises mattered to the We. They could smell a lie like one smelled rotten eggs. Moreover, they could feel the truth.

Even so, Owen doubted his words would be anywhere near enough to stop and settle them this night. There was blood in the air. A price unpaid for what the hunters had taken.

"I know of you. You're the mortal that was given a gift, one of our gifts. You are not such a common thing for me to forget one such as you." The five's underglow shimmered and moved, as if the possibility of inaction was a foreign thing to him.

The level fours had split to either side of Butch and looked eager for conflict. Ironically there were four of them, one on the right and three moving on the left. The rest of the We who had come outside were all like dogs, ready to follow the command and influence of the stronger. Eager for scraps and favor, if any was to be found.

A blast fired loud into the air to Owen's left, stealing the attention of some, but Butch's clear blue eyes never moved away. Never broke contact with Owen's own.

It was Tim's loud voice that shouted over the rest, shotgun pointed up into the air.

"Owen's crew has taken my stamp and been good to my house. This establishment, this sanctuary. The child and his members have each taken the contract and therefore have my protection. You know the truth of my words. I give my word she was in my kitchen all night, when the attack took place. She is innocent. Anyone who wishes to get to her will need to face me and my house first."

Tim let his power flare, and even looking forward, Owen was impressed with the strength of the glow coming from the side. So many tonight had taken the stamp; so much ethereal power was at his disposal.

The crowd seemed to shrink in the shine of his power. A few of the lesser We even moved out of the gathering, slipping back into the bar. Back to safety. But too many held their position.

"Oh, Timothy, has joining with your human allowed you to forget your place within our people? The child's gift is not her own. It was given to us so we may grow in power, in life. You know the strength she will grant, the ethereal energy to be harvested. Utilized by us, for us. Step aside."

"No, Butch. She has my protection and has made no violation. She is free to safely leave." To drive home his point, he aimed the shotgun straight at the level five's chest.

Butch started to chuckle, the power inside him rising to the threat. The air in front of Butch shifted, changing as it expanded forward, thick with ethereal influence. But Owen was focused on something else, something far more important. It was the feel of the crowd. The feel, the sense of who they were. Butch wanted violence. The more powerful normally did. But the rest were scared. Fearful. They needed security, perhaps more than his own people.

"Owen?" He heard Jessie call from the window of the van, where he too held his own shotgun, ready to fire.

The level fours, riding along the edges of Butch's influence, started to creep forward like hyenas sensing a meal. The tip of Tim's gun started to rust—as if it were in a movie and someone had just pressed the fast-forward button on time, orange and red flecks falling away like rain. The corruption Butch was sending forth crawled toward Tim's hand. In a few moments Tim wouldn't be able to pull the trigger without the weapon blowing up altogether.

For all Tim's quiet demeanor, he knew what he was doing as he held steady and spared a single glance that said, *God help us all*, in Owen's direction.

Owen didn't have time to swear. Didn't have time to think about the consequences any longer. If Tim pulled the trigger, it was going to be an all-out fight right here, right now, and the odds that all of his people would survive were thin. There were just too many against them.

His quick hand reached up to his collar, slipping under his shirt. In the same moment Owen shook his head to Tim. The look he sent said it all: *This isn't your fight; it's mine.*

Owen's hand found the silver chain, which was not a chain. It was pure ethereal essence. Something rare, forged out of love, devotion and protection given, to form a substance made of raw, connected power. A contract much like the bands around Aurei's and Tim's fingers. Only this was old, very old, and it was his to keep and protect.

The chain separated without any fight, moving on his will. Owen used a tendril of ethereal power to snap the shoulder strap on his acoustic guitar so it could fall away freely. Before the guitar had dropped halfway, Owen rushed forward, ethereal power lending his muscles speed and strength as he charged into the opening before him.

Butch's smile fell away as he came in. But the evil tentacles of ethereal influence Butch was exuding couldn't touch Owen. They were nothing compared to the vast reservoir he now held in his fingertips.

No longer hidden behind a weave of concealment, he allowed both his own significantly large well of ethereal power and the well of power contained within the chain's essence to be seen and felt by all. To the We, it was like pulling back the curtain on a blacked-out room, all in full view of the sun.

Butch, the level five, had called him a gatekeeper, and he was right. Now he let Tim and the rest see what he was keeping as he came in.

The level fours held their place, surprised but not afraid of the sudden turn of events. With a snap of the wrist and concentration of will, Owen used the chain as a whip, slicing through the black cords of energy.

The raw essence whip obeying his command, Owen continued his strike, the chain reaching out and wrapping several times around Butch's neck before the level five could take more than a single step back in retreat.

Owen didn't stop moving. Instead he came in hot and punched Butch straight in the face.

"My people are leaving!" Owen said to the crowd as he punched the level five We again and then again.

The influence bubble of the level five broke as the power of the chain locked the creature's power within his own body. Owen didn't let up, couldn't let up. Not with a five and not with the crowd ready to collapse in on him. Weakness would be remembered. And each of his people were on the line.

Again and again his fist connected, pounding in, using the chain to pull Butch toward him as the five tried to backpedal in surprise and defense.

"My people are leaving now. If you are hungry, you can

try for my power. But they leave." Each word was accented as he broke the five's face with his fist. The fours started to surround him, but none were ready to stand out from the crowd. Influence and leadership were the same in these things. His childhood had showcased this truth: take down the biggest and you have a chance.

Butch's fist came in from the right side, and Owen could feel the massive amount of power in the swing. Butch wasn't done. Wasn't out of the fight.

Owen didn't let the incoming punch connect, instead letting it swing by harmlessly. But he followed it up with three shots to the body and one hard shot under the jaw with his right hand. The hand that still held the chain wrapped over the knuckles.

Butch hit the ground, and Owen dove atop his chest and set to work. He needed it to be bloody, needed those gathered to feel the truth of his resolve.

One, two, three, four hard shots to Butch's face with power and muscle as blood sprayed his hands, his clothes and even his face.

He could feel the power inside the We growing, ready to roar for release. Two hands snaked up like vipers, catching Owen's hands around the wrists. Pain erupted just under his hands where the five tried to crush bone.

"Fool gatekeeper." Butch spoke out of a bloody mouth and matching face. "You fight with flesh instead of the power you so desperately hold. Now it will be mine. Now your people will be mine."

Owen answered the best way he knew how. His head slammed forward, and he felt the crunch as Butch's nose broke under the impact.

"You want power," he whispered in the creature's ear, tired of hiding. "You want a piece of me? I am fire. I am the storm. And you cannot have what is mine. What is in me." He spoke from his soul so the five could understand, so everyone who heard his words would understand. He was not prey. Would never be the prey to these We or to anyone else.

His wrists still burning with pain, Owen surprised the crowd and the five by breaking both grips and slamming his hands down hard on Butch's chest. Blue ethereal light swept out from the sides as he moved forward. Not another attack, as much as ethereal power was used to grant momentum. Owen used the small burst of power to shoot forward into a rolling dive, taking the chain in his hands and pushing up to his feet.

The chain pulled taut while Owen stood, the thin metal glowing with power as it slid over his shoulder. And using both hands, he pulled hard, forward and down. Butch, tethered by the neck on the other end, had little choice but to follow him up.

Owen pulled with muscles infused with ethereal power, angling his back as he lifted Butch onto his toes. And using his voice like the weapon it was born to be, he spoke to the crowd. He wasn't gentle. This wasn't the time or the place for the meek.

"You all see me now. You are starting to understand who I am. What I am. I am giving each of you a choice. It's a simple choice." At his back he could feel the five as he struggled to breathe, struggled to find purchase. For all Butch's power, his body was still that of a human. Owen looked into the eyes of the crowd. Most of the We didn't believe in sides or violence. Those who chose to come down had mostly been entertainers, those who claimed to be lovers of life. If they were anything else, they would have chosen to be conscripted into the heavenly war between Heaven and Hell, the war each had chosen to avoid.

What he saw was hunger and fear in equal amounts.

"One option, you and I fight. You and I, now and forever. You become my enemy, and I will hunt you down to my last breath. My people have taken the oath of protection, but none of you have. Therefore, nothing will stand in my way as I bring you down like wheat."

He turned his attention to the level fours, who were a hairbreadth away from coming in on him, their expressions unreadable. The biggest and strongest amongst them—a Black man wearing a leather jacket with a thick collar, stylish jeans and boots—seemed to suddenly stand out from the others. Owen locked him down with a look.

"Or you let my people leave now, safe, unfollowed and unbound. And in return, I will play for you. Together we will see the light of the first arch of Heaven. I will take your soul on a run." The way Owen said "you," it was clear he meant everyone in earshot.

A stillness came across the gathering. Even Tim's glow dampened at the mention of the first silver gate. The level fours all broke their passive expressions, looking back and forth, unsure for the first time.

"However, this one—" Owen squeezed harder on the chain and arched his back slightly, Butch's feet slipping completely off the pavement of the parking lot. The sound of his choking increased. "This one dies tonight, either by my hand or yours. It is your choice. We are on the same side, or we are not. Choose now and choose quickly."

With a twist and a burst of power, Owen dislodged the five from his back. He used a well-placed kick to break Butch's knee so it couldn't hold his weight, even as he commanded the chain to shorten once more. The thin, polished strands of silver retracted back to him as he stepped away from the very much alive and vengeful level five.

Owen continued his backward steps toward the van, the fours letting him pass from their circle. Each step he took was a signature of strength as raw ethereal power sang in his blood and bones. Owen watched the crowd, watched the fours particularly. After Butch, one of them was the most

likely to lead. His money, if he was to bet, was on the biggest of the level fours. The man with the thick-collared
jacket.

The glances back and forth solidified as Butch made
strangled sounds from the ground. Owen saw the calcula-
tion as the tall level four accepted the mantle of responsibility for the pack.

The man looked once across the gathering as Butch tried
to rise and struggled with the broken knee. Owen knew it
wouldn't last—the reservoir of ethereal power within Butch
was already healing the broken bones, much as his own reservoir of power had already begun to heal his wrists.

"Fool, you should have killed me. This has come to an
end," Butch said from the ground.

Owen watched as the four checked in with a skinny
woman wearing a long summer dress and blue high heel
shoes. She was a level three, but Owen had already pegged
her as the strongest of that level. He watched as she gave a
small nod of acceptance and a smile that was all predator.

This time, as Butch started to rise back to his feet, a loud
crunch snapped into place as bones realigned and the five's
broken knee held his weight once again. The exterior lights
dimmed as Butch called forth more and more of his power.

"Now, gatekeeper, I shall personally deliver you to the
river of souls. Right after I drain your power and take what
is no longer yours."

In answer, Owen gently wrapped the steel chain around
his left wrist in a wide circle, once, twice, three times. Between his fingers, he felt the chain slowly retract to a more
manageable length.

The leader of the fours spoke, pulling the attention of all.

"The third arch this night, gatekeeper. All of us can see
how much this matters to you."

Owen knew what the man wanted. He knew the cost too.
Perhaps more so than everyone else. The third arch before
Heaven was impossible for him on his own, even with so

many willing to lend their power. Even if Tim, with all his current energy, was willing to anchor him. It wasn't a possibility, even if he was willing to give his own life for the run.

"I give my word to try for the second arch." *Even if it kills me.* He hadn't used big words or big promises, hadn't needed to worry about nuances. The others, the We listening, would feel the truth, all of the truth within his words. *My people need to be safe. They need to be free and alive.*

Power like a black storm billowed out of Butch's hands, threatening to eat Owen whole as it crossed the ten feet of dusty parking lot. Owen's wrist flared blue, and his body tingled as he called on the power he held stored to shield him against the attack.

The gathering of We in front of him disappeared as Butch's boiling black tendrils of evil covered them from view, blocking out everything before him. Power, clean and beautiful, coated his skin in blue and green as he set his feet, preparing his defenses and counterstroke.

A snap, loud and thick, reverberated through Owen's body as it filled the air.

Even though Owen had been waiting for it, the violence came as a surprise.

The black sea of ethereal tendrils before him fell away as ash, dissolving in a breeze that wasn't real to this plane. The leader of the level fours stood tall and foreboding, his hand around the back of Butch's neck, with Butch's head hanging awkwardly to the side, dead and lifeless, spine clearly broken.

Owen looked on as the three remaining level fours descended like a pack of animals, eager for the store of ethereal magic. Glowing hands plunged into Butch's corpse with no regard for the dead.

Animals and humans prefer a pack in time of crisis, Owen thought. *The higher the stakes, the thicker the cluster. Control the leader, control the many behind the leader. An old lesson from an old teacher.*

Owen watched as the leader of the level threes, the woman in the sundress and boots, strode forward and away from the rest. Without hesitation, she drove her hand into Butch's back just below the neck. Shockingly, the level fours already feeding made room for her, the rest of the rabble taking a step back as the leader of the fours dared anyone else to come forward.

Owen, still glowing blue and green with power, moved to his right, keeping himself between the mob and the van. One hand tapped the side of the old metal frame, and he didn't care that he left a dent as the van roared to life on his influence.

"Get out of here, Jessie," he commanded with a voice that would take no nonsense.

Thankfully, Jessie understood the stakes and put the van in reverse. Owen moved to the side in time with the van's motion. Tim came over in case there was a need.

Owen's back to the van, they walked as one. The van, forced to pull back and then forward, slowly made its way through the parking lot. Owen watched and was ready for anything, his eyes scanning the crowd, the feeders and all the darker shadows.

No one moved to interfere.

Unexpected red brake lights had Owen's head swiveling to check on the van as he heard the loud telltale creak of the passenger door opening and then closing.

A mixed bag of emotions swelled as the van pulled away, leaving a very serious Clover standing there with her violin and bow in one hand, her instrument's case in the other.

CHAPTER SIX

Father Patrick stood up, climbing out of the outdoor metal chair, snatching his Bible to his chest. *I have to do something. I have to try again.*

He had refused every weapon both Alice and Father Alton had tried to give him. Killing was not what he stood for.

He heard the screams as priests died in the distance. One, two, then three—each man dying without a single shot fired. The fourth man's death scream was coming. They all knew it. Could feel it in the air. Patrick and his Bible moved closer to Alice, and therefore Father Alton.

I have to try once more before it is too late, he thought. *I have to.*

"The relic, she needs to put it on! We need to get Alice out of here before Kerogen can get his hands on her! Father Alton, you have to see my logic now. Kerogen is here like you wanted, but now we must protect the child." He tried to be as clear as he could.

Another loud snap of bone reverberated out into the night, this one without the scream.

"You three get up into the bell tower and be prepared to ring the bell as soon as you get my signal," Father Alton said to three of the four priests he had been standing with.

"Father Alton, the relic. Alice needs to put it on so she can leave," Patrick urged.

"Calm down, Father Patrick. We always knew there could be casualties."

"Kerogen went straight for the bell tower. He probably disabled it. How do you know they can even get it working again?" Patrick asked.

"Really, Father, I thought you would have far more faith than this. We are on God's side. He will protect us," Alton said.

"God's side and God's plan do not always let people live. They are not always the same thing. Alice is not ready to face him. You know it and I know it. We need to get her out of here now. She is only nineteen."

"It was never the plan to have Alice bring the demon to its knees." Father Alton produced something from inside his robe that chilled Patrick to his bones.

The item he produced was small, black and square, close to the size of a garage door opener, only it had a red cover over a silver switch.

"What is that?" he asked, already knowing and yet fearing the answer.

"This is the detonator to the C-4 that I concealed above the bell tower. One way or another, the bell is going to ring. When it does, the demon will fall to his knees, and either we shoot him until he stops moving, or I plunge this knife into his body, and we take him back with us. Either way, the acolyte is safe, and you can go back to your life. Now stay out of my way. And for all that is sacred, keep your mouth shut, or I shall do it for you."

* * *

Kerogen let his laughter echo into the night air, his gleeful humor slipping under old wooden doors and driving into small openings only to rebound off walls. *Mortals. Humans. These priests are far worse than all the rest.*

He had spoken truth to them once, thinking their kind could have a place at the same table as he. Once, long ago, his kind had shared openly and honestly who they were and where they had come from.

When they had come from. Secrets were for the weak of mind and spirit, after all. Instead of opening arms and minds, the church created their secret sects and hunted his kind down. When they could have joined in the celebration.

There can be no partnership. Just look at them, standing there in wait of me. For us. Three humans, with rifles. They cannot know me, know us. How small they are. How false. You disgust me, he thought while looking down from above, his presence concealed within a folded weave of power.

Kerogen chose his first target out of the three priests who hid within the room. Cloaked in power he dropped, attacking fast, plunging his hand into and through the spine of a priest before the man even knew he was beside him. The dying man's weapon started firing, splattering the ground and inside wall, just below the window that led to the open courtyard.

The other two priests swiveled away from the window, shocked by gunfire so close, their weapons coming up protectively.

Kerogen let his laughter play out through the compound as both weapons roared to life. Shaped steel, hot and deadly, tore through his last kill. But he was already gone.

Yes! He watched once again from the ceiling above, his ethereal power hiding his presence even as he clung to the flat roof like a spider.

Play with them, mock their very existence. Demonstrate the folly of standing before you.

The dead priest's body jolted this way and that, like a marionette, before falling to the ground, spent shells continuing to fly into the air along with stucco and steel.

Yes, I had contempt for this world. Yes, I regret not joining in the unseen war. Anything is better than this filth. Everything is better than spending time with these lesser creatures.

With an extension of ethereal power, he formed a black shadow in the doorway, and the gunfire changed direction to its location. A priest coming in to help from the hall was just in time to catch four bullets to the chest.

"Delicious," Kerogen said as he descended, his left hand snapping the neck of a priest as his right hand caught the barrel of the remaining priest's weapon. "Violence begets violence," Kerogen mocked. The heat of the weapon could not compare to the flames that danced and celebrated inside his soul.

One hard yank, and the weapon flew across the room, the priest opening his mouth in shock, revealing a hidden and gruesome sight—his tongue had been taken out.

"You're still doing that, I see. Beautiful, undeniably beautiful." His words were whispered as he moved in close to get a better look, smelling the man's stale breath.

The priest didn't respond as he tried for a knife at his side, but Kerogen had seen enough. He plunged his hand in through the chest to the spine where he knew the priest's small well of ethereal power was held.

His hands closed around the rough bone as sensation filled his body and mind, and Kerogen drank the magic in. "An ethereal priest. How lovely. If only you had not forsaken your birthright, you just might have stood a chance. But probably not."

The priest opened his mouth once more, revealing the

gruesome space. His scream of pain came out garbled, creating an awful sound.

Kerogen's power-infused hand crunched bone and veins alike, destroying what remained of the life within.

Kerogen, facing the door, covered his body in power once more and reversed it, slipping from the eyes of mortals, walking slowly, knowing the sound of gunfire would bring more priests.

Something in the air changed and he had just enough time to dodge to the side.

A thin black blade spun by where his heart had been, but he didn't have time to think on it as a kick with the force of a speeding dump truck hit him hard in the chest. More out of luck than will, he flew hard through the open doorway. The power covering his body took the brunt of the force before shattering away.

Kerogen crunched into the wall of the long hall and bounced off. Gunfire flew in his direction as two priests unleashed destruction with their semiautomatic rifles down the hallway.

Having only one other option, Kerogen dove back into the bloody room he had just been evicted from.

He came up fast, smiling as he saw her for the first time. Alice, the child, his gift from the heavens. She was on him inside a heartbeat, still small and thin. How old was she—Sixteen? Nineteen? He blocked two kicks, each reinforced with ethereal power, swinging his body to the side of both slashes she made with long steel knives.

"Look at you shine, my dear. My doe," he declared.

This close, the power—her power—was a lovely thing. It was kismet, her and him. All the power between them a living connection with the bond he had forced. All of it now resonating between them like kinetic energy. And after so many years apart.

He blocked another set of kicks, dodged a series of

slashes, and slapped one knife out of her hand, sending it harmlessly off a bloody wall.

"Hello, Alice. It's been too long." He backed off, refusing to engage.

She rolled through the air, a spinning blade coming in at his chest, so he had to turn his body. Somehow she brought a foot out and connected it to the side of his face.

Snap. His mind went hazy as he flew against a wall covered in bullet holes and blood.

Kerogen knew what was coming before it happened. He had seen her, felt her. She wanted to kill him, and surprisingly, he didn't mind. At least with her, she had a reason. A true and honest purpose.

Pushing off the wall, he avoided her next strikes, each with another set of knives.

"We aren't going to kill each other, Alice. Our story is just beginning."

Alice let out a shout with power infusing her voice. He felt it build a fraction before a wall of ethereal power came at him like a speeding train. His power increased in front, and it took everything he had within to endure the onslaught. Even so, he slid four feet back.

In response, Kerogen opened up the bond he had formed with her. It had been necessary to cover over the connection so she couldn't inform the priest of his whereabouts, but now . . . Now it was time for Alice to understand the truth of her situation.

With will and focus, he released the cover over the bond, and instantly everything became more intense. Her rage, her fear, her need to kill him was so strong it flooded his senses. She was a storm, a torrent of focused will that refused to break or be swept to the side.

She came at him again. Her last remaining knives, the ones she had purposely set as her last defense—her favorites—flashed through the air. It wasn't what he had expected. The shock of the connection should have caused her to stall, should have made her pause. But instead she used the uncovered bond to pull energy from him as she came in close.

"Glorious. So strong of will, mind and power."

Lazily he blocked one attack, smacking her hand out to the side while he accepted a slice to his arm. It mattered little.

"Child, they didn't even give you a proper weapon," he observed as she tried for a killing blow.

It was time. Only a few seconds had passed since she had entered the room and surprised him. But now was time for Alice to understand what it meant to be bonded to the likes of him.

CHAPTER SEVEN

MONTHS BEFORE A+O

Clover was a killer—not in the human sense of the word. You might call it self-defense. But here, in this world, the world they lived in, she and Owen had killed level ones, twos, threes and even fours together. Not because they wanted to, but because it had been the only way to survive. The only way to stay alive. The only way to leave.

A price that had come with being born connected to both worlds. Human and the We. To being born with a living well of ethereal power and wanting to be free. Together they had more scrapes and scars than either would like to account for. After all, these creatures weren't human and didn't play by human laws or boundaries besides those of their own making.

Clover shook out her hair and walked forward like somehow the mass of people had created a runway just for her and her violin. Blue energy sprang to her hands and lips, and red, raw power coated Clover's silhouette in an eye-catching declaration, screaming, *I am here, and you cannot hold me!*

O wen set his acoustic guitar against the customer side of the bar, back inside the roadhouse. The acoustic had survived the fall outside. Butch hadn't, and Owen wasn't sure if he and Clover had either. Time would confirm their fate.

"Aurei?" Owen said like a man looking up at a mountain full of small stairs and knowing he had to climb.

He accepted the offered rag, using it to wipe some of the blood off his face and hands. Owen took his time, knowing the blood wasn't his own.

"Whiskey or water?" Aurei asked from behind the bar.

Clover set her violin on the old polished wood beside him, the others giving her a wide berth.

"Whiskey, six shot glasses and orange slices to match," Clover said.

Her demeanor was far different than all night and most of the last month. The carefree, dancing-on-the-wind mask she always wore when her violin wasn't in reach was gone.

This Clover was the Clover he played music with. This was his soldier willing to run into the fires of Hell, if and when he asked her to. This was his Clover, the one the world didn't get to see, to understand, until just before her bow was placed to string.

A woman who had pulled him back out through the gates of Heaven while a thousand hands had tried to hold him in. She had been there for too many of his mistakes and knew he would make more. And still she stayed. Clover's soul was older than her age. She was older than anyone could understand.

Together they had survived, and, God willing, they could do it one more time. One more time, they could pull off the impossible. The improbable. A thin margin to slip between and back out from again, to cheat the rules of Heaven and the blue flames that held the grieving souls within the river of Hell.

Owen turned his back on the bar and looked over the crowd as Aurei continued working to fill Clover's order. There were a few humans still here. Mostly those remaining were incredibly drunk.

His eyes continued to scan the room, seeing many of the We as they looked back. Word had already spread to those who hadn't followed Butch outside.

Gone were the looks of anger and destruction. Even with all the blue underglow shading their faces, he could easily read the excitement and friendly expressions. For the moment, Clover and he were now on their side. And Daphne, Max and even Jessie were no longer a concern. It was a drastic change that only one who truly understood the We could be comfortable with.

"Do you play?" He didn't single out the man who was now on his right, the same high level four from outside who had snapped Butch's neck. Even so, it was clear who he was talking to.

"All of us play."

"I know, but just because you can hold an instrument doesn't mean you can make a run for the arches. Can you play?" Owen insisted.

"My name is Ethan, by the way. And no, but Sage over there can." He pointed to the level three in charge of her group, the woman wearing the sundress and blue high-heeled shoes. "She can sing, and rumor has it she has made the trip before."

Owen wanted to ask if any etherealist she sang with was still alive or if they had burned away. He wanted to ask the question exactly as much as he didn't want the answer.

"Anyone else, Ethan?" Owen asked, his voice detached as the room tried not to stare at him.

"Devin is out helping to get rid of the body. He can play drums. He's good, if a bit young."

"Does he remember who he is?"

Owen had never truly understood the cycle of a We. How they aged or why they looked the way they looked. To his understanding, We didn't like to talk about it. He knew that some were new, some were young and some were old, and it might have to do with running out of ethereal magic. His own theory was that when a We ran out of magic, they lost a part of themselves and became new. The problem with making a run with someone new, was that they didn't always remember their full past. And that could be a problem onstage.

"He does remember."

"All right, Devin on drums if he is willing, Clover and I, and the girl, if she is willing. I can't promise any protection for any of us. You understand that, right, Ethan? I'll do my best to keep us alive, but Devin and the girl—Sage," he corrected, "they might both burn in the fire. I haven't prepared properly and neither have they. And the second arch is a long trip with two sets of stairs to climb."

Sage walked over like a woman who was born for a stage. Her smile was wide and bright, and she walked forward high on newly acquired ethereal energy, having just fed well outside. Sage slipped between Ethan and himself. Her hand reached behind Owen's back and stroked his spine, then dove farther down to squeeze his butt. He could see the lust in her face as easily as one could see a lone stop sign on an abandoned road. He was half sure Sage was also in the process of giving Ethan's butt a similar groping.

"I do love the bold. It makes this life far more interesting than everything else," she said, sparing both men a glance. "You are cute and deadly. Now there is a cocktail a woman can enjoy."

Owen let the words play over and past.

"Shots are up," Aurei called from behind him.

In answer, Owen turned back toward the bar, ignoring the second squeeze of his ass, and took the offered shot glass from Aurei.

Even though it was a double, he couldn't help but think it didn't hold nearly enough whiskey for his liking.

Ethan reached out, taking two of the remaining four shots, sliding one over for Sage. The other he kept for himself.

Aurei claimed the fifth, and Tim, keeping the rusted shotgun in hand but concealed under the bar, took the sixth.

"To making a successful run," Aurei said, all diplomatic as she held up her tall shot glass to the others.

"To being brain-dead stupid," Clover said.

"Fuck it," Owen said before anyone else could chime in. He clinked the other glasses nearest him and didn't waste time but tossed the brown contents back. The burn and flavor felt like home as it washed down.

The others followed suit, Ethan and Sage repeating his own words before downing the contents.

He bit into the orange slice—one of Clover's ideas from a couple years back that had become tradition. It wasn't his thing, but "in for a penny . . ." made him bite deeply, the fruit juice cutting the lasting taste in his mouth.

Owen grabbed the bottle of whiskey before Aurei could and started to pour another round for everyone.

The night was going to get far, far worse before it ever got better. Moreover, he could feel the door to his control starting to slip. There was a part of him that wanted to make this run. Needing this run to go fast and reckless like a sailor turning his sails before the wind, he wanted to feel the power and snap as he changed direction from unbending control to letting it all go into the wild force of being alive.

There had been a moment outside when he stopped pretending. A moment when he let his mask fall away, and he was free.

Owen didn't raise his second shot high again or even

pass out the others that he poured, but he pounded his without a second thought. Clover's hand caught the bottle before he could take it up again, her soft hand falling over his own.

She smiled a smile that was more family than any he had known in recent years. *Let's you and I do it again*, her smile said, bright and clear.

Owen tried to relax as he pulled his hand away. They were family, not lovers. There was touching, and then there was holding hands.

Clover started pouring as the others matched suit.

Owen let out his breath and tried to remember he had done one thing right: Daphne was safe. With luck, Jessie and Max could get her to her eighteenth birthday without him and Clover, if it came to that.

Clover leaned in close and asked the question into his ear. "Are you going to get her out?"

He knew it was coming, knew she couldn't help but ask.

"Might be a riot if I do," he answered, uncaring about everyone else listening in.

She was asking about his guitar. His real guitar, the one in the secret compartment under the back bench seat of his truck. The only thing between those four tires that mattered at all to him.

Owen accepted the double shot of whiskey she offered him.

"Your acoustic, how far have you ever gone with her?" Clover casually asked, but the question was like asking about a friend's sex life. You could ask, but most people didn't.

"Clover."

"No, for real, tell me. How close? I know you tried to make a small run on your own with it. When I went out to visit my sister. How far did it take you?"

Owen remembered the woods and a bonfire. He remembered the sound of the flames, the swish of the trees to either side while he had tried something very, very stupid.

"She didn't make it very far at all, before I had to turn back."

He shared a glance with Aurei, who clearly was listening in on their conversation, before he interrupted the connection by tossing back another shot.

"Do you know," Clover started, "I have been thinking a lot about why we are so good at this."

"Clover, that kind of talk is sure to get us both killed. And I for one don't actually want to turn into a human torch onstage."

"No, shut up. Listen. I think I puzzled out the truth of why we have pulled off all that we have done. When so many have died before even making a real attempt. It is simple. It is so basic I missed it for the longest time."

Owen set the glass down, enjoying the feel of the thick weight touching polished wood. He left his hand on the shot glass. Clover's own glass touched his, and she poured, uncaring about everyone else. So despite being surrounded on all sides by the We, with everyone listening in, it was suddenly just her and him, like countless times before.

"Okay, I'll bite. Why, Clover?"

"Because we seriously rock! I mean, like, rock on a heavenly scale. Now stop being an appetizer when you're a main course, and go get your real guitar."

Owen stared into Clover's beautiful face as he thought about what she had just said and then let out a chuckle. It was small and fast, like popping a balloon, but damn him if right then it didn't feel good.

Clover smiled in response. "You like that?" she asked.

"I do, yeah."

"Good. Me too. Tim, we are going to need some burgers. It's going to be a long night. You can't make a run on an empty stomach. I am sure that is a law of some kind."

"You got it, honey." Tim gave a serious nod before changing direction and heading back into the kitchens, the half-rusted shotgun he still carried moving along with him.

"Did he actually smile at me? I think Tim smiled. Aurei, did you know Tim can smile?"

CHAPTER EIGHT

SEVEN YEARS BEFORE A+O

Alice came into the fight knowing she had to kill Kerogen as quickly as she could. The priest had been clear on what a true bond with the demon would mean and do to her. She had to kill Kerogen now or she never would.

She attacked hard and straight, leaving him no room to back away, no room to slip to the side. She called on all her power. All the power she could take from him. Her entire ethereal well. Kerogen had to die.

Her skin bloomed with life energy. Her favorite knives glowed with power and burned with heat. Her muscles infused with magic propelled her faster than she had ever moved.

Alice distracted with the knives, knowing he would watch them. Her hand, circling, moved toward his face as she charged. His hands made to strike out and block as he had done already. And Alice knew, knew she had him.

It only took one moment, one mistake to kill a demon.

One single moment where they made a mistake and you hit your target. That was what the priest had been teaching her for seven long years away from her family. This moment was hers.

She shifted her weight to her left leg in a flash, her right knee folding up to snap a kick under the jaw, and then she would fall on him with both weapons. The timing and power were perfect.

But something dark and oily filled her mind, and then all her energy, her power, even her momentum disappeared as if it had never been, bringing her to a perfect stop. Both knives flew to the side as Kerogen's strikes connected, and she could hardly stay upright. All the wind was taken from her. Stolen, swept away, as everything she had was pulled through the connection, out of her and into the demon.

She set her foot down, and the simple act had her almost falling over. It wasn't real, couldn't be real. Shock and frailty stripped Alice's identity away as she stared, horrified, at what she was looking at.

Kerogen stood before her, waves of energy and color swelling from him in such a dazzling display it took her too long to understand she was looking at her own power as well as his.

"Yes, my doe. Now you see the truth."

She made to say something but didn't have words. She couldn't think, couldn't breathe. All her work, all her power, and she was useless. A paper doll before a living flame.

Something moved behind her in the window where she had dived in from the courtyard, and yet it didn't matter. He was here. Kerogen was right before her and she could do nothing. Nothing.

The room filled with blackness in a single heartbeat as she felt the demon's arms wrap around her and lift her off the ground. Her body flew with his while he moved up high, using his power to cling to the ceiling, like monkey bars. Together they moved fast as he flung himself from one corner to another, gunfire bright and loud covering the room, walls, floor and ceiling in a calculating manner designed to kill everything and anything, including her.

Her body and neck were rocked this way and that as Kerogen moved with blinding speed, staying just ahead of the lethal spray of bullets. She could feel Kerogen's body and energy surge as he moved from one side of the room to the other, her body no longer able to adjust to the overwhelming forces. Pain filled her senses so deeply it was all she could do to keep her eyes open and her mouth shut.

The gunfire was all around her; however, only the muzzle flashes could be seen poking in from the large square window where three priests rained death and destruction.

Father Alton? She watched the white of the muzzle flash.

She felt Kerogen shifting her body within his grip, his right hand suddenly pressing hard, pinning her to the wall just above the gunfire. So close that she stared down into the bright flashes and could smell the burn of gunpowder. The heat and noise were nothing compared to the fear that choked her as she understood she was about to be dropped in front of an active firing squad.

Don't they know I am in here?

She fought the fear with her limited strength, was even able to place one hand against Kerogen's while the other hand tried to find the rim of the window. Her nails scratched into the wall but found no purchase.

Time slowed as she focused on the three muzzle flashes surrounded by an unholy darkness.

A loud, desperate scream cried out. And for the briefest of moments, Alice thought it was her own scream finally free.

Instead she made out the silhouette of a man as he was yanked through the window and into the room. A hard crunch ended the scream just as Kerogen seized a second priest and likewise launched him into the room, across the open space, to smack hard into the adjoining wall.

The third gunman was late in releasing the trigger of his weapon, so the continuous sound of bullets hitting mortar was suddenly changed as Kerogen's latest victims found themselves in the path of the firing weapon. In Alice's mind she pictured the two priests catching the last of the gunfire before falling dead to the ground.

Kerogen's laughter filled the air once more, directionless as always and all the more evil for it.

Alice tried to pull on her well of ethereal power, to re-energize her body as she had done a thousand times before. Nothing happened. She felt tears build up in her body as she tried again. Nothing happened. Helpless and weak. Hardly able to lift her own hands and arms. She wasn't even sure if she could walk.

Once more she was powerless against the demon. Though she had sworn over and over it would never happen again.

Her body was half pulled, half caught as Kerogen unpinned her and moved her up and over like an insect carrying its food.

She bobbed and swayed as he held her tight against his body. Keeping away from the open window, he moved to the top corner of the room.

"Unholy demon! Face me. Face me now, you vile, rotted perversion of God's will."

Alice knew that voice. And even though she had never cared for Father Alton, his commitment to the cause was suddenly a source of strength.

She ran her hands desperately over the arm that held her secure, trying to find a weakness, something, anything that might get him to release her. Again nothing happened. Her strength was so drained she could hardly ruffle the clothing covering his arm.

"Demon! Face me now and meet your end. Face me, and

I shall end your suffering on this plane for all time!" Alton's shouted words slipped in from the courtyard.

Kerogen's voice was smooth and clear as he whispered so low she thought he might have meant the words only for himself, if he hadn't been whispering in her ear.

"Fool. I have killed almost all of his men in less than a half hour, and he still believes his God will protect him. I can no longer suffer fools, my doe."

"Demon! Do not hide, face me in the light. Face me now. I command you."

Alice was being moved, and far more gently than she would have ever expected. Careful and silent, she was placed down onto the floor of the room.

"Now stay here, and stay quiet. The priest will not think twice before shooting into this room again. I won't be long." His hand pressed her shoulders back against the corner.

She felt him move away, both through the connection and because of the way the air drifted over her skin.

Father Patrick looked on in horror from the ground of the courtyard, not more than ten feet from the two priests and Father Alton as they raised their rifles and fired into the room Alice had dived into only moments before. The sound of Alice fighting Kerogen had slowed his heart, but now it froze with fear as he lay on the ground helpless, watching three rifles unload death upon the small room filled with an unnatural darkness.

Registering the pain in his hands and hip was nothing compared to the pain coming from his mouth, where Father Alton had hit him hard in the face with the butt of the rifle, sending him to the ground for interfering.

Even so, none of that mattered as he looked on in terror. Alice was in there. In that room. And the priests were shooting over and over again. It was like the world was upside down. She was just a child, and now they were willing to kill her. She was on their side! It didn't make any sense.

Patrick started to get to his feet, preparing his mind and body to tackle at least one of the priests. Even understanding he would probably be killed for it. And yet he was determined that it was the right thing to do.

One of the priests was suddenly yanked into the blacked-out room, followed shortly by the second robed priest. Leaving only Father Alton holding the remaining live weapon.

He watched, stunned, as Father Alton stopped firing and backed away in a frantic hurry, an empty magazine hitting the ground as the priest reloaded.

CHAPTER NINE

Well fed with Tim's burgers and well lubricated with whiskey, Owen placed one foot on the small wooden platform the roadhouse had for a stage. It was time. The sun still had a couple hours before it would rise, and they had done everything that needed to be done. It was time to do what he had promised to do.

The burn of the whiskey matched his mood, its dulling effects helping to center his determination. His heart was steady as he looked at the musical equipment set up. Devin was behind the drums, tuning and checking the placement of his cymbals. Sage stood to the side, speaking with Ethan, the strongest of the level fours. And Clover. Clover was speaking softly to her violin, uncaring who was looking or listening.

Owen looked to the case just to his left, the black, worn edges masking or perhaps hinting at the treasure that lay beneath.

Clover was right. He should use her—the instrument was made for this sort of run. An unprepared run. To be stupid and reckless. To dive into the fire and blow on the flames.

He would normally never offer to take himself and a group of We he had never spent time with to the first silver arch and more. Bloody more. He had given his word he would try for the second arch. In the moment he had known it was the price that was needed. The price required for the We who were killed by hunters earlier in the night, and letting an unbound Daphne leave. It was the right price then . . .

Only an hour had passed, but it felt like a lifetime.

When Owen had made the promise, he'd understood the stakes, understood what was needed to get Daphne, Max, Jessie and all out safely. It was worth a frantic unplanned run, an unprepared attempt to do the impossible. He was prepared then to accept the flames and the price of them leaving safely. They were his responsibility.

One hour ago, was it really so different?

He pushed his weight into the wood, feeling the strength of the old stage as it held firm. His eyes were still on the guitar case and the beast hiding beneath.

Clover didn't fully understand, though he knew she could feel it. She didn't understand the pull and demand of the instrument locked behind two simple brass clips. His guitar had been a gift, an instrument passed down over time from one special musician to another. This guitar had a soul, and that soul's single purpose was to push further than anyone ever has. In the case or in his hands it was a wild mustang, always and forever pounding its hooves, demanding the wild run of freedom.

His fingers clenched and unclenched as he stood on a precipice. Every time he played her, Owen inwardly swore he wouldn't play her again.

Every time, Owen knew without a doubt he was a liar. And now here he was, once more onstage with her at his feet. *Did I somehow manipulate this to happen, just so I could be right here? Ready to pick you up again?*

"Hey, Owen, you ready to do this thing or what?" Clover called.

He looked to her, disregarding the rest of the crowd and the other members onstage. He felt the air around him, knowing what he'd always understood. *This is just where I belong.*

"Next time, you stay in the van." He moved onto the stage, letting the persona he normally carried for everyone else fall away.

"Not a chance, boss. If we are going to burn, we burn bright and burn together. Rock-and-roll style," Clover said with a smile that lit the room.

He felt the squeak of wood underfoot as he moved onstage. The weight of the whiskey bottle in his hand was cold and comforting. The booze helped soften the impact of what was to come next. It wasn't necessary, but it helped with the transition in. It helped lift the weight of the other side and reduced the burn of the fumes.

"Let's see what we are working with. Clover, start him out," he ordered.

Devin snapped his head over, looking up from the drum he was locking down. A fit, athletically built man with clear eyes and a tight haircut, there was a will behind his eyes that made Owen think Ethan had spoken truly when he said Devin could play.

Clover turned her back on the crowd, who were wavering between nervous excitement and quiet anticipation. It was understandable. What was to happen, be it success or failure, would be quite a show. Success meant touching the other side, and a plethora of euphoria and ethereal energy for everyone. Failure meant watching those onstage burn to death.

"Okay, Devin, you and me. Let's start this out nice and slow. The road is long and wide. Just stay with me."

Clover's violin came up to her chin as she locked eyes with the young drummer. Owen felt her rhythm, could feel her intent as she breathed in. She was so familiar, so open, he didn't have to work to know her. Devin, on the other hand, held his rhythm in close behind a wall, his pulse of life concealed.

So much so, for the briefest moment Owen thought Devin might not be up to the task.

Clover placed her bow to strings in one smooth motion, a single perfect note humming through the air and silencing the crowd as she started to play.

Owen watched, calculating and living each note. Devin's walls bloomed open like a timid flower to the sun just twelve heartbeats before he picked up his cue and joined in Clover's soft melody. The pressure of the sticks on drums was easy and fluid, the harmony moving as one as Clover grew her song. All the while, Clover stared and studied Devin, as he did her. It was a dance between them, small touches as they learned to move together.

Devin stayed with her, his sound one with her own as they felt each other's edges.

The gathered onlookers had their own heartbeats. Each was there in the background, part of the scenery at the moment. Like willing musicians in their own right, ready to get their signal to come in and play, half eager and half terrified. Everyone understanding the risk.

The song grew, and Devin stayed on point even as Clover started to push his skill this way and that, even going so far as to release a fraction of ethereal energy into her song. It was a trickle, almost nothing, but to him and the room filled with the We, it might as well be a bear horn going off indoors.

There was and would always be a small difference to the ethereal energy coming from a human. When one of the We like Devin used their well, it always held a tinge of the stored. Like food preserved in a barrel. However, when a human, an etherealist, could power their sound with ethereal energy as Clover was doing now, it was fresh, new, clean like a mountain spring.

"Devin is good. I have never heard him play. Your girl Clover, I heard about her. Now that we know who you are, the stories are coming out," Sage whispered in his ear. She had a way of moving up on him that reminded him of a snake. In this case, a very beautiful and flirtatious snake. With long legs and a rocking body to match.

Owen ignored the rest, concentrating on the drummer. "Devin has an opportunity with that skill. He's good. But you and I, on the other hand, how we get along up here is undecided."

Sage looked at him, just a glance, as he watched and listened to Clover and Devin playing. "For all the stories, you look younger than I expected. How old are you?" she asked.

Owen turned, still listening but wanting to face her. There could be only one leader onstage. He understood that with every fiber of his being. And Sage was clearly a leader in her own right. "That is the wrong question. The right question is will I keep you alive when we go in. Will I bring you out when we leave. Can I? But before you ask me, allow me to ask you this."

He let the tension between them tighten like a note that refused to die.

"Are you prepared to burn in the pure white light? When the flames are touching your face, are you willing to lean into the eternal power of holy will, the vast ocean of energy that protects the gates of Heaven? Are you ready to be reduced to ash for what we are about to do? You know the risk, Sage. We don't belong up there. You know the price for thinning the veil, for going. Are you willing to pay?"

He had known the answer before she had come to him. He had already felt what happened the last time Sage had made a run. Sage had seen the gate and in that moment had failed, leaving her band to burn as they had gone beyond without her. He knew it as only one with his experience would. The signs had all been there—the hidden glances, the flutter around the edges. The mask in the face of what they were up against.

She had come back to the We as a hero who was capable of making a run, but a hero with a black stain on her soul.

Owen had recognized the stain. She wasn't the only one sporting black marks that could never—would never be scrubbed clean.

For the first time, the confidence and flirtation fell away from her. Like water running down a window, the truth was revealed. "I didn't mean to stop. I didn't mean to jump off-stage."

Owen could feel her heartbeat as she let her truth be spoken aloud.

"We were good and strong and had prepared. But I was new, and the gates . . . just the journey getting to them—" She cut off before starting again. "I can't tell you what it took from all of us, and then to see and feel it again . . ."

"You remembered the other side. You remembered your life before you came here. Before the choice God gave you to stay out of his war? And the weight of the memory froze you in place," Owen supplied.

And in that mistake, your band died.

Her expression was genuine, real and filled with sorrow. "It was perfect, I was perfect in a way that can't be described . . . and then they were all dead." Her voice trailed off.

"You aren't the only one to lose members on a run. How many?" Owen could feel for her. It was a hard thing to know people so well you could make a run only to feel the fire on their skin, breathe in the fumes of their flesh burning, knowing there was nothing you could do for them.

"There were eight of us."

He didn't need to ask if she was the only survivor. It was there between them. Seven other souls, seven other bodies, and most likely some of the crowd all burned alive.

In truth, it was simple luck Sage had made it out at all.

"I'll bring you back when we get there. I will bring you back. I am the first in and the last out. You understand me? I decide when we go in, and when I say to leave, you leave."

Their souls were open, and he knew she could hear the truth and power of his words, but he needed her to believe them. To count on them beyond everything else. A singer didn't have an instrument to help take on some of the burden and weight of the journey—their voice was the instrument. It meant there was nothing to shield them from the dangers. As the leader who would hold the group, command the group, it was up to him.

"Okay," Sage said.

In response, he held up the whiskey bottle as an offering, both as an olive branch and as reconciliation for the wound he had torn open.

She smiled, and her eyes quickly changed from shame and vulnerability to, well, to a woman who was preparing to follow him into the gates of the hereafter.

She accepted the bottle and pulled deeply, a small sigh escaping her before her smile returned in full as she took a quick second pull of whiskey.

Sage surprised him, coming in fast and hot. Her full, soft lips came down on his own, the kiss crushing, the smell of whiskey wafting in like warm wildfire a second before she pressed half the shot she had taken into his mouth. She was cinnamon and spice with energy as ripe and full as any fruit. Sage leaned into the kiss, refusing to let him get away, giving him just enough time to be lost in the feeling before she pulled back and he swallowed down the burning liquid.

"Damn, you're hot. All these layers over layers. Remind

me to do that properly when all this is over," Sage said. There was heat in her words that would be impossible for a deaf man to miss.

Owen didn't bother responding.

Sage moved away, taking the bottle with her.

Clover's song dipped down, and he could feel it start its slow rise. *Beautiful Clover*, he thought. *You have come so far from the crappy little backwater shack I found you in.*

Her need to play had grown so deep in the month since they had come to this sanctuary. It was nice to see and feel and hear as she let some of the itch out. Within her song there was hunger, dark and demanding in the heart that was almost akin to his own.

A change in the sound, in the vibe radiating over the stage, had Owen turning, facing the drums.

Don't do it, Owen thought. *Come on, Devin, come on. Don't do it.*

Devin pushed the sound, his hands moving in circling motions as he pressed his will into the song.

Son of a pig ass!

Vaguely he watched Clover close her eyes as she had to change course, drifting back to allow the drummer his moment of fame. *It's always someone*, Owen thought. *Always one in the group who thinks he is important. Why, oh why, is it always one who never gets the message?* All you had to do was pay attention.

Devin didn't disappoint, and in his defense, he didn't showcase, but he used his imagination and know-how to bring the song up, fueling it with some of his own power in the same way Clover was doing. Together, the song changed, widening as his sticks took on more and more speed in order to keep up with the demand. Owen listened as the song ran away from Devin for just a single moment.

"Wrong. You just killed us all." Owen spoke up to be heard over the combination of drums and violin.

"What?" Devin shouted, his sticks continuing to move.

"Don't stop!" Owen ordered as he made his way around and behind the drum set, closer to Devin's side.

His eyes didn't follow the sticks; he didn't need to. He knew where they were, where they were going to be because of the sound, because of the music.

Owen came in close, much as Sage had to him.

Owen could feel the discomfort coming off the drummer like a tidal wave as he leaned closer still.

"Keep going, you're good," Owen soothed. "I can see it, and I can hear it. But if we were making a run just then, you would have killed us all when you fell out. I won't be able to pull you back in if you leave my space like you just did to Clover. Where we are going, you're dead if you think for a moment it's about you. It's never about you, never about her, or her, or me or anyone; it is about all of us and the here and now."

"What are you talking about?" Devin asked.

"Just shut up and keep listening to my voice or get off my stage. This isn't a concert. This isn't any kind of song you hear on the radio. It's not storytelling or singing the blues. There is no headliner or fanfare. This is the thinning of our world and the space between here and the hereafter. When we play, we play open. We play a song not of our choosing, a song that is a combination of us in the when, the now and the after. We have to find it, and you can't push it, ask it or plead for it. No matter what you feel inside or out, you need to play the song. We can only play it when we are together."

Owen watched for any sign of Devin not being able to understand.

"Now keep going. Clover sent you down this road so we could see you, so I could see you. When we play, we play with our souls. It's not about the sticks and the skin. It's not about power or volume. It's about keys and locks. It's about opening doors inside and out. This is about being one in space and time. By playing together, we can open the way to the other side and come back out again."

Owen knew his voice held power, and he was using it to manipulate.

"You have to let go of indecision when we are up there. You have to trust we are with you. You can't guess where to go. You have to become us. Feel her, feel Clover in the sound, feel her in each pull of the string, each press of the flesh. Feel her heart and soul as your sound blends and becomes the same as hers."

Owen waited and listened.

"Better," he said. "Much better."

As if they were old friends, Owen tapped Devin on the shoulder.

"Now, open up. Open up that space inside that no one is allowed to see. Let Clover in so she can feel you. Fear is for the living, and where we are going, we need to be more than alive. Let the walls you are keeping up fall away so she can see your soul. So she can take a piece of you into her mind. Remember, we aren't people or strangers, not up here. Up here, we are all members of the same whole. But you have to open the doors. When it gets thick, like you might choke on the pressure, you have to open your heart to each of us. To all of us."

He listened as Devin's playing drifted down, away from indecision and fear into clarity, and finally, into a surety. This close, Owen couldn't miss the pull and desire to play, to walk the road of the dead and back up to where all things truly started.

Clover smiled as she allowed her fingers to dance over the strings in first position, creating a melody that was far more suitable to the combination of her soul and Devin's than the one they had been playing earlier.

Owen slowly shared Clover's smile, backing up carefully, wanting—no, needing—Devin to have time in the pocket of space he was in so they all might survive this run.

His speeches to both Devin and Sage were the first steps in a whole series he would normally have taken with a band that was preparing for a run over the first three steps and to the first arch. Let alone the second arch, and the accompanying stairs. But he didn't have time to prepare. He had given his word.

Owen looked to Clover, knowing she would understand. It took a moment, as she was deep into the song she and Devin were creating, their power commingling and adding a thin line of ethereal energy into the air.

Her eyes looked to him, and they were a soft blue, springing with life. They shared a conversation in that look about the probability of failure and stupid choices that had led them both to this point. Clover finished it with a look that said it all: *Let's do this! Right now, and let the fires decide our fate.*

Devin is ready. Sage is ready. Clover is ready. Owen let out his breath and glanced once more at the guitar case that sat still and lifeless just there on the end of the stage. Black ragged edges and scratched brass clips.

CHAPTER TEN

SEVEN YEARS BEFORE A+O

Kerogen, having left Alice in the corner of the blacked-out room where she would be safe now that he was pulling all her energy, exited out the same door she had kicked him through.

No reason to rush now.

"And this feels good."

Kerogen strolled as would a king, making his way through the corridor and continuing on, moving through a set of rooms. His gait shifted, like that of a king approaching his throne. *She is only a child, and look what she can give me*, he thought. *Not yet come into full power. How much growth is left?*

His soul felt outright relief, and with it a sense of calm joy.

"Oh, what music we shall sing together, my little doe," he whispered, unable to keep his joy contained any longer. Ethereal power pulsed, and the walls to both sides and the ceiling behind him cracked, chunks of mortar dropping to the tile floor.

"Demon, I command you to face me now. I shall rid this world of your evil taint and send you back through the gates of Hell," the priest called out again.

Kerogen looked at the curved opening to the courtyard just ahead. Angling his voice to announce his location, he spoke, walking forward out of the hall. Each step, each intake of breath, each word spoken shifted into a savoring of violence to come.

"Do you know I knew your Devil back before the choice? Can I tell you a truth I have only just now realized? Right at the point when you ordered the others to fire in on the child and myself did I come to understand." He paused as he looked at the fanatical priest robed in soft browns. "Your Devil has it right. You are not the creatures God wishes you to be. Your souls are dark and corrupt, and now so is mine. *Hate* is a word none of us knew before humans. True destructive hate only came when God made you. But now it lives in me too. I hate you. I do. I hate you down to my toes. There is no redemption for your kind. I have seen it all. And each and every one of you are liars. You can't even contemplate what it means to be pure. Your minds refuse to be true."

Kerogen's head snapped to the left as he heard the breath of sound before the first words were spoken.

"You are wrong! We are flawed, but every day we can strive to be better than our own limitations. It is in the struggle to be more than ourselves that God's plan is brightest. It's not too late for you. Let her go and end this madness. You still have a choice. You still have free will. Use it," Father Patrick said.

"Father Patrick? What a welcome surprise. It has been too long, old friend. Have your organ skills gotten any better since the last time you played for me?" Using a cord of black ethereal power, he hit the priest, sending him sprawling to fall hard on the ground. "Simpleton," Kerogen said as he focused on the last priest who stood in his way. The only remaining priest who threatened what was his.

The courtyard was large and square. There was only the smallest outline of a large circle in the center, where Kerogen guessed a statue or a fountain had once stood. A thin, wiry tree with two old metal chairs and a small round table stood empty and alone in the corner and to the left.

Across the open space, the last priest claimed his attention as he drew his rifle up to take aim.

Ethereal power coursed through Kerogen's body and soul. The power to build worlds, the same power that had been used to breathe life. The power of a different space and time. And now, pulling through the bond he held with Alice, he held more ethereal power than at any other time. It was glorious. One hand reached out as tendrils of black swam behind him. Focusing his will and soul, he twisted the power to do his bidding.

The priest's weapon fired in a quick, tight, three-bullet burst. Kerogen smiled large, showing perfect white teeth as each bullet disintegrated into red dust ten feet in front of him.

Unperturbed and already sensing the feel of the priest's spine in his hand, Kerogen continued his slow stalk across the square. The steady crunch of pebbles beneath each step reminded him of bones breaking. With fear and a soft panic shaking his aim, the remaining zealot fired again.

"Now you understand, don't you? Now you know your failure. Now you can see the truth of your order. We are not equals. You are not the hand of God, because God never fails. But he does like to watch fools die."

The rifle rang empty, the priest tossing it to the side. Quick hands pulled out a small handgun. The fresh gun roared its protest, but Kerogen hardly noticed, so wrapped in protective power. Instead he savored the struggle in the lone priest's eyes.

Ten feet still between them, and the handgun rang empty. The priest tossed the gun straight forward in anger. Kerogen watched as the weapon was caught by the thick influence of power he was shaping. In a fraction of a second, the weapon rusted over, then fell apart as if it had never been.

Understanding crossed between them, as there was nothing left but open space and death. Kerogen almost shivered with the joy of something so true. It was real, more real than the ground he walked on. Death was between them.

Ethereal power thick and strong answered Kerogen's call, forming out from behind his shoulder like a living appendage. The priest reached for the radio on his hip, bringing it up to his mouth while his other hand reached inside his cloak.

"Now, now, now!" The dead man yelled into the radio with a sense of triumph.

Kerogen struck, sweeping his cord of power from left to right. Like a scythe shearing wheat. His aim was true and snapped out fast and quick; however, pain radiated up his arm, shoulder and spine as the priest pulled out a knife with inlaid polished gems, cutting the cord of power as if it was nothing more than air.

The lone priest came in fast and quick. Kerogen just laughed at the futility and the gumption. Shaking off the pain, he backed up just out of reach of the weapon designed to kill his people. The priest struck at his face and stomach but never came anywhere close to making contact.

"Fool. That knife was never made for you to wield. You should have given that weapon to the child. She might have had a chance."

"The bell, ring the bell!" Alton shouted again into his radio.

"Oh, the men you sent up to the bell tower died before they even made the door to the stairs. Now I am done with you."

It was time to end this farce. Kerogen attacked from four sides, his power launching out over his shoulders and under his arms as he moved with blinding speed. The priest's knife, which was made up of pure ethereal essence, a remnant of old, cut through the first tendril and the second. Each connection the blade had with the shaped ethereal power sent pain running through Kerogen's body. But this time, he was expecting it, so it mattered little wrapped in the overwhelming power.

Kerogen let the pain wash through and beyond as he landed a series of small strikes, then hit hard with his own fist. Joy filled his spirit as he felt ribs break like thin wooden chopsticks.

Catching the priest's hand that held the deadly weapon, he looked deep into opaque, hate-filled eyes. Tendrils of his ethereal power encased the priest, holding him firm like an insect caught in the web of a spider.

"Now, priest, you see. Your people should never have left my protection. Your kind should never have betrayed me all those years ago and taken away my crown. We were beautiful once. Your people and I. Musicians and singers filled with ethereal power traveled across the world to sing before me. And in exchange we helped you build and bind humans so you might spread God's word. However, you broke your word to us. You lied and now call us demons. The arrogance. The smallness. The falseness. The lie."

He watched as the priest made to speak, but he had heard enough. He drove his hand in through broken ribs, past organs and clamped his hand around the spine. Power thick and demanding granted strength to his hand and forearm. There was no power here for him to take in. The priest was a normal human, no ethereal well for him to drink.

The priest managed a loud scream that echoed off the walls and reached up into the night sky.

Kerogen's hand crushed the spine to powder, shredding veins and bones as easily as one might crumple a piece of paper. The scream cut off as the pain reached new heights. Suddenly Kerogen's enjoyment disappeared, perhaps as quickly as it had come. He couldn't be sure. But the fight was over. There was no one truly left besides the girl and Father Patrick. Neither were of consequence. Neither could stand against him. Neither would be in his way.

Using two tendrils of power, he broke the neck, ending what remained of the priest's life and flinging the dead body to the side. With a snap of his arm, he sent the vast majority of blood clinging to his hand down to the ground.

A high-pitched scream broke his victory, cutting through his joy and triumph. The scream was so clear and pure it sent a shiver down his own spine. He turned toward the blacked-out window where he had left Alice. Before he could move, before he could think, pain racked his own body, curling his fingers and snapping his wrist down. His arms moved instinctually, slamming hard against his chest, and his legs suddenly became weak.

His pain vocalized, matching Alice's own as he landed roughly on his knees. Vaguely he noticed the tendrils of power disappear as he lost all control.

Raw pain he had no chance of blocking vibrated through his body, so strong it was as if he was being tied down and lashed a thousand times. The skin over his arms and back broke open in tiny slices, in a tight, crisscrossing pattern that burned as if salt were being pressed into each individual wound. The pain was so great he couldn't think, couldn't breathe. It was too much, too big, too intense a pain to endure.

Alice could feel Kerogen move away from her as he left her helpless and weak in the corner of a room filled with a blackness she couldn't possibly see through. Her mind was slow, like the time she had gone too long without eating.

She wasn't the only one in the room. She knew there were dead men scattered across the floor. She couldn't see them, but she knew their bodies were there. Three or four, maybe more.

Her mind was soft, and she struggled to focus. If she could move to one of them and get a weapon . . .

She leaned forward, reaching both hands out to catch her body so she might crawl toward them. The space between her hands and the floor shouldn't be far; she calculated as she leaned farther and farther until her body finally gave in to gravity's constant pull.

Fingers pulling back for protection, hands forward, Alice fell only a handspan, but as her palms made contact with the cold floor, she understood her mistake.

Arms too weak to hold her gave out. Alice's face hit the ground hard. Tiny pebbles, probably debris from the bullets tearing into the wall, dug into her skin, and something wet coated her cheek.

Alice took in a big breath, ignoring everything else. *Get up, Alice*, she said to herself as most of the pain dissipated. *Get up. You have to get up and get out of here.*

She breathed out and struggled to pull in air. Face still pressed hard against the floor, she fought as big flakes of dust caked in her mouth.

Doing her best to stifle a cough, Alice turned her head enough to move her lips away from the floor. She was so weak, so bone-weary tired. Everything hurt, but that was nothing compared to the fact he had done it again. Kerogen had made her helpless. Helpless to do his bidding. How was it possible? She had been so strong. So determined. She was the strongest hunter the order had ever had. The other kids were children compared to her power and skill. She had done everything they asked—learned with everything she had—and now she had failed again. Failed to get back to her mother and father. Failed to stand up to him.

No, come on. She breathed. *I won't lose. I won't stop.*

Come on, Alice. There was one play left, one chance Father Alton had given her. The relic. The relic that could block the bond. The guns on the ground weren't a real option, not with how weak she was, but the relic could slow him down and perhaps give her strength back.

Desperately she fought the fatigue, moving far too slowly.

Ignoring Kerogen's laughter and Father Alton's call, she used every ounce of strength she had to reach the small flat leather pocket she had on her belt. She had to half roll to get the right angle to unbutton the leather clasp. Her fingers were so sensitive to the soft material it was like a cool balm as she brushed it with her fingertips.

Time moved faster than she could as she tried to pull out the old cloth relic.

It seemed far too delicate, a thin, almost translucent rectangular cloth. Compared to the solid feel of the brass cross before, the new relic was dainty, leaving her unsure of its effectiveness, yet she had no choice but to try.

Her fingers worked the material out far enough that her thumb and forefinger could just pull free the shroud.

Alice had to stop so she could breathe. It was so difficult.

Kerogen is taking all of your energy. All of your ethereal power. You are being drained dry.

Rolling back, she pulled as hard as she could, taking the folded relic with her. Something was happening out in the courtyard, as Kerogen spoke, but she ignored it. Only one thing mattered. One single ray of light was her only chance. Relics were special; they weren't like plugging something in. You had to find the On switch.

With the brass cross she had worn for over ten years, it was simple: a thumb rubbed across the center and mental concentration directed toward the relic. And abracadabra, it worked. But the shawl? The shawl was something much more difficult. For two days, she'd had to kneel before it, her mind tuned and focused for an hour at sunup and sunset. For two days, she had looked to find a connection in her mind. Last night it had been there, and yet she hadn't activated it. She hadn't called on its ability to block the bond and hide her. The reason was clear then: she had feared Kerogen might not come. Now this shawl, this tiny fabric in her fingers, was her only chance.

Slowly she got her hands in front of her. Still she was facedown, but there was nothing to be done about it. Carefully she unfolded the thin material. Doing her best to spread it out, uncaring about the dirt and debris. It wasn't as if she could see any of it anyway.

Her hands spread, touching rough stone and a thick liquid that clung to her fingertips in such a way that she knew it could only be one thing.

When the cloth was unfolded and spread out as far as she could manage, Alice forced her body to move. With strength that was too thin, too small and too fractured, she fought hard, shaking to pull herself back up onto her feet.

Pain flooded her body, and she wasn't sure if she was going to cry or fall flat again.

With all the strength she could muster, Alice was able to once more get her legs underneath her so she was kneeling with her forehead balancing her on the hard, wet ground. Chest pumping, with a scream of both triumph and despair sticking in her throat, she concentrated hard on what she needed to do next.

CHAPTER ELEVEN

MONTHS BEFORE A+O

Clover and Devin's song finished in the background as Owen walked over and stood above the case of his guitar.

The crowd gave a cheer for Clover and Devin, but it was new and soft compared to the gravity of what was to come.

Staring down, Owen had the familiar feeling of the crowd focusing on him. The room quieting. Clover, too, as she stood off to the side, watching and waiting.

"Here we go, one more time," Owen said into the silence, wanting to break some of the tension. His words came short of their mark.

There was a look between Sage and Clover.

He looked back down to the case as it sat still, lifeless even, on the end of the old, worn stage.

With a snap of ethereal magic, he opened the locks, much like Jessie preferred to do with bottles of beer. The brass clasps flipped up and vibrated ever so softly as the case started to open.

I want you with every fiber of my soul. God protect us both.

Owen couldn't take his eyes off the case's slow open.

He watched the case as the lid lifted up and back. Perhaps to any normal human, it was a guitar without strings. Just another guitar amongst millions. Perhaps.

Owen's body tingled, heart rising high in his chest as he looked to her long black neck and frame. Stringless and guardless. Instead of either, a small worn patch of paint was the only thing that spoke of this guitar being well used. For it shined bright; it reflected the lights above like it was freshly polished. Even where it was worn by the ones who had come before him, it shined.

It shined with the oil of the men and women who had poured their hearts and souls into the instrument. Three knobs and a bar, and she was cradled on old blue felt that held a promise of a time forgotten. He could almost smell the history, just as he had the very first time he had ever opened the case.

Owen's heart throbbed as he stared, the conversation drifting away. Owen could feel the call of the bones of the guitar. The pulse of it, wide open before him, her spirit ready for him to pick up and ride.

Owen's left hand reached down, and he felt the essence around his wrist disconnect as it unspooled, dropping down toward the guitar.

Owen moved slowly, prolonging the feeling. Guiding his hand just above the body, where the strings needed to be anchored. Glowing white and gold tendrils flayed open as the essence slipped inside and fell away off his arm.

You need your strings so you can sing. Come dance with me, come fly with me, oh, my scary beast.

As he watched, the essence half crawled, half fell forward over the neck of the guitar and up to the head.

A twinge in his neck and just behind his ears tingled as the essence splayed into six long strings returning home.

There was a history to her, a long and beautiful and terrible history that he could feel in every fiber. A history he respected and could understand. His life, his own love and pain and choices were only to be a small bump in her long and dirty road.

With ethereal energy, she lifted up, Owen bending down. Owen's left hand firmly took the neck as he smoothly slipped the black strap over his head. Sensation raced through his body as he accepted the weight and power of her.

Snapping back with a ruthlessness, his open hand used the power he was born with to pluck the cable that sat spooled in front of the amp. The black cord flew forward, its male brass end landing hard in the palm of his hand. Owen slipped the cable in and let go of what had been building inside.

Owen's fingers danced as he shut down all other sound in the room.

His hand picked the strings made of pure raw essence as his other hand half strangled, half massaged the strings to sing his sound, bright and loud, sweeping it over the room. He wanted more, needed more. Needed to let his frustrations out. Only his need was not alone.

She, the guitar that he held in his hands, had her own need. Her own will blended with his as he struck chords in a fast flurry and power, letting some notes hang as others fought each other in mad, fierce finger-work, all the while building his song.

This wasn't a run to the gates of Heaven. No, this was his fury, his storm, fire and brimstone. He wanted to go to the only place he had ever found sanity. His song scratched his skin, tickled his tongue as he let it loose into the air around him. The power inside coating his aura as he let the Devil have his gold.

Owen played. Owen played for the power, he played for the frustration of not playing all these days and nights. He played for the injustice of being born into this world. He played for the will to go forward. He played for it all in a quick, hot tempest that dared to defy all laws.

His hands moved faster and drove deeper as he played with a feeling that was too powerful for words, an understanding that filled his fingers, his arms, his chest as the song coalesced into a beautiful, warring journey of sound and skill.

His song wasn't a master thief sneaking into a bank vault. His song was explosive, all TNT and broadsword. He was the battering ram refusing to be small, simple, meek. He wanted the power of the sun, the loneliness of the moon and the depth of the ocean. He wanted it all. Demanding his due, his own price. Without forgiveness or regrets as he went deeper and deeper.

I was not made to be simple.

Clover watched. They all watched and listened. His power infused the music, ethereal energy resonating out into the air as he refused to stop, refused to hold back any longer. His fingers stroked and blurred up and down as he fought to scream inside. The message, a single vibrating word . . .

Higher.

Owen let it out. As he felt the blue flames of hellfire, an ice-cold evil heat that threatened to both burn and freeze his skin at the same time. A second later he saw the blue flames just on the edge of his vision.

He was in; he had gone too far. If it was anyone else, it would be called an accident. But Owen knew where the edges were, understood the line. When ethereal power and music could touch the other side.

Just as he knew where he had gone. The blue river of trapped souls that led to the Devil's bridge. This wasn't a place to stay for long, and even so, his soul demanded he play on. He wouldn't give in, wouldn't back down, needing to be free.

There was awe as the crowd felt his choice, felt the resolve and understanding of what tonight was going to be.

Blue flames, thick and wide, blurred on the sides of his vision, and he refused to give in. Refused to be intimidated. Owen's sound built in his chest, in his mind, and resonated in his ears as he splashed into the shallow waters of the blue flames.

Poor, tortured souls trapped and locked in the depth of the flames started shouting to be heard. Owen shifted his sound, catching the cries and slipping their call into his song.

He played and felt the Devil's blue rivers of fire coat his hands, the power of the guitar and his own power protecting him from being burned alive. His song refused to be quieted. He would be heard; the souls trapped in the rivers leading to Hell would hear his frustration. Hear his voice.

He played on until he had breathed it all out. Until his own internal fire could finally burn back down to deep, hot embers.

His song changed as he backed away. Until the flames left his skin and vision became normal once more.

Of course, it wasn't that easy. The souls in the river, the cold of the twisted flames, were a powerful drug, demanding he continue forward, continue on. Stroking his soul, making promises if he stayed, if he continued. Even so, Owen backed away, stepping out as he delivered his last, longing notes.

The room was silent as the absence of sound finished his song, its lasting note speaking of the dying and the dead.

Owen became aware of the room again just before the applause of the We, and those few remaining humans. He looked around the room as the gathered clapped and shouted. Vaguely he noticed more had come in. He wasn't surprised.

"Damn, Owen. I think you just gave me an orgasm," Sage said as she handed over the bottle she had taken earlier.

He ignored her words. Far too filled with the need to

play, too consumed with the Devil's itch to answer the call. Owen did take the bottle, however. He pulled hard. He spared a look at Clover, who held a half smile that was calling him a show-off.

Someone was moving, coming up onstage from the left, and it drew his attention.

To his surprise, it was Tim, the owner. The way he was holding himself, it was clear he had something to say.

Owen felt the whiskey go down bright and hot as he turned away from the gathered.

Tim's eyes were wide and alive. The tint of power was still bright around his body.

"Tim? What's up?" Owen asked.

"I wanted to see your guitar."

Owen raised an eyebrow but couldn't see the harm in it. Leaving the guitar on, he held the instrument up to the light so Tim could get a better look.

Tim didn't take much time before examining it. All the while, Owen watched the way Tim's eyes ran up and down. But it was the vibe Owen was getting off the older We that was the most interesting. As if a great weight had settled over the other's chest.

Owen didn't think Tim had taken the incident outside as seriously as he was taking the revelation of the guitar.

"You have seen her before, I take it?" Owen asked.

"I have. It's been a while," Tim answered, still looking at her.

"Did you ever play her?"

The question had Tim looking up. "No," he answered.

"Probably a good thing," Owen said gently and with too much truth.

"A good thing? Owen, a good thing is not cutting off your own hand in the kitchen. A good thing is not accidentally running over your wife. Son, not playing that guitar was the smartest decision I ever made. How long have you had her?"

Owen could feel him then, all of him, just as he did the members onstage. "Long enough."

"I imagine that's right. You know she won't stop until she goes all the way or you're dead, right?" He paused, but it was clear he had more to say.

"She is made for greater things than me, but that's not what we are doing today."

"Okay, I know you just made a run into the river without any help or even anyone with you. But if you are going to try for the second arch, as you said, I'll anchor you this once."

Hope for the first time bloomed in Owen's chest. Before Tim could change his mind, Owen spoke. "I accept."

And without preamble, Owen reached up, grabbing Tim behind the back of his head. For a heartbeat, he stood there looking into the deep brown of Tim's eyes.

Tim whispered something in another language that even Owen, with his exceptional hearing, couldn't make out. Even so, Owen was nothing but grateful as Tim wrapped a hand on the back of his neck, leaning in until their foreheads could meet.

Forehead to forehead, they pressed into one another, each staring into the other's eyes. It was quick and fast as a temporary bonding snapped strong between them. Tim would be his lighthouse in the storm. His anchor to follow back when the waves threatened to batter him from side to side.

CHAPTER TWELVE

SEVEN YEARS BEFORE A+O

Alice's screams silenced the pain and terror Father Patrick was enduring. He sat helplessly on the ground where Kerogen had left him, listening to Alice's torment. Her voice was always sweet, but now it was distorted as if she were being tortured from the inside out. His heart broke, shattering at the sound, reminding him far too much of the first time Kerogen had come.

Patrick swiveled his head toward Alice's window, which was filled with an impenetrable black substance, as Kerogen let out his own scream, forcing the priest to turn back toward the monster.

The large, twisting blackness of power that had been fanning out behind Kerogen dissolved like black confetti, then disappeared altogether, revealing Kerogen on his knees in utter torment. The scream didn't break for air as the creature's head tilted skyward.

Vaguely Father Patrick understood there was no pleasure even here, but then something twisted in his gut as he understood Alice's ongoing scream was somehow harmonizing with Kerogen's, shaping the two sounds into the most macabre harmony he had ever heard . . . except for one other time.

Rising to his feet as fast as he could, Patrick looked back to the window where the oily blackness that filled the small room Alice was within was likewise dissipating. He moved as fast as he could toward the opening, toward the child, the small stones under his feet sliding as he ran. Coming in sight of her shattered what remained of his heart and soul.

Not the five dead priests who had been focused on killing a demon. Not the blood on the walls. But the child kneeling in the corner, covered with blood, her head raising up to the ceiling while she screamed in a sea of tortured agony.

The tiles beneath her were soaked in blood, like a pool made for a forsaken being, instead of the young girl he knew Alice to be.

Unsure, broken with his own inaction, Patrick glanced back to Kerogen on his knees. The demon who had enslaved the child and just killed a dozen priests, including Father Alton, seemed vulnerable for the first time. The first time since the church and the small bell. Since the day that had changed everything.

His own body shook with fear, heart racing as he was torn in two directions. He needed to get to her, to help Alice, but Kerogen was there, vulnerable. An opportunity to end Alice's monster once and for all.

Patrick understood what Father Alton would do, just as he understood what Alice would want him to do.

All people are children of God. The words never left his lips but were firm in his mind, just like a thousand prayers he had given. Asking for guidance, asking for courage, asking for God's protection.

Knowing time was running out, Patrick moved. He ran

as fast as he could to Father Alton's broken body, which lay more like a pile of meat than any sleeping man.

Patrick's hands raced, searching and probing the body. Blood was everywhere, covering his hands as he pushed the body to the side. Inside his head and heart, his mind screamed at him that this was wrong, undignified for a man of God, for any man. Only resolve and his love for Alice kept him from hesitating.

Alice and Kerogen were right there, still screaming together, and time was running out. Something sharp and straight cut him beneath the tangled robes of Alton, and he pulled his hand back to do a quick exam, yet the wound was far too covered in Alton's blood to make out.

Briskly he found the knife with a jeweled handle that Father Alton had possessed so reverently. Setting it to the side, he went back to searching, using his dull fingertips, pressing and pulling until something solid and square brought the search to an end. At first he thought it might be the radio, but it was too small.

Retrieving both the small box and the sacred knife, Father Patrick glanced one last time at Kerogen, kneeling and crumpled in agony as he screamed with ethereal power toward the night sky. Looking at the man who was proclaimed as a living demon, he should have felt more—more compassion for someone in pain or more anger for revenge. The realization that he held neither hit him like a cold bucket of ice water as he pushed off the ground and started to run back.

Kerogen only mattered in as much as Alice needed to get as far away from him as she could. God would take care of the rest.

Something bright and true built in his chest as he closed the distance to the window. He hopped over and through the square opening with ease, ignoring what his shoes stepped in.

With the blackness gone, the room illuminated by the light on the walls, he looked to Alice. Her back was to him as she continued her scream in the corner. The sound she was making shook his body. But what he was witnessing was far, far worse.

His first thought was to pick her up and run. To sweep her up and run as fast as he could with her. But stepping over the half wall and through the window revealed the source of her torment.

As fascinating as it was terrible.

A milky white and translucent cloth, glowing with a golden hue, was set over her shoulders and back. Even as he watched, blood oozed out through it, as the relic cut deeper into her skin, having already made its way through her jacket and dress. Thin, crisscrossing wounds bled through, covering the material and sealing it to her skin. Alice was being skinned alive.

"Come on, you have to do this. Come on, Alice. You can do it," Alice whispered against the wet tile floor.

She needed to finish, had to. But she was so tired. And it was going to hurt. The priest had told her. The sensation the relic gave every time she touched it practically promised it would hurt, and hurt bad. Not that it wasn't soft and silky, but there was something evil living inside. Purifying was what they said it was designed for.

Holding the material with both hands, concentrating so she wouldn't mess up, she breathed, trying to gather her remaining energy. She moved, and her body hurt as she flung the shawl around her shoulders, laying it over her neck and back. She cried out, small and pathetic, as everything hurt. *You're not done*, she thought as she struggled.

Surface area—the shawl needed to be wrapped around her body. Using one hand, then the other, she tried to wrap it over her chest and tuck it under her arm. Her jacket didn't make it easy, but it was done.

She felt the connection to her mind just as she felt her connection to Kerogen. Only where his was a deep, dark tunnel, the shawl was a burning bright light in her mind. Closing her eyes, she pushed the white light over Kerogen's connection as she held the material against her with one hand. *Please, please. Please work*, she thought as she concentrated.

Goosebumps covered her skin, followed by the hair on the back of her neck standing up.

Alice let out her breath in one easy effort. The single breath opened up her lungs, as if a weight had been lifted off her chest, and she felt strength coming back.

"It worked. It freaking works." Alice started to lift her head off the ground as her body strength started to trickle back, no longer being sucked away. She was careful to hold the shroud against her as she came up to her knees. "Ouch!" she said, her right hand moving toward the back of her neck in instinct. "Aw, no. Oh God, please."

Pain erupted through her mind and body as the relic from another age shimmered and vibrated. The smooth surface glowed softly as it burned and cut its way through denim and into her skin, the crisscross pattern slicing into her.

Her hand met blood as she tried not to scream out, her fingers pressing into a wide stream on the back of her neck. She felt the rough edges of what seemed to be crisscrossing razor blades, shaking ever so slightly.

Indecision plagued her mind as the relic was her only hope, but it hurt horribly—to the point she thought it might kill her.

Her vision went brilliantly, blindingly white as she was swept away by truly agonizing, primal agony. Fire and Hell lived inside her as the torment surged through her body and soul in one solid, never-ending stream.

Without control, Alice was no longer capable of thought as mind-bending pain racked her body. Time stilled or stretched or stopped. She could not be sure of anything as pain on a scale never known to her pulsed and built higher and higher.

She screamed without relief even as Kerogen's own scream followed suit.

Her mind was a white ball of fire, burning and bleeding inside, and Alice couldn't look away from above as agony swallowed her soul. Her body became a distant thing as white, bone-crunching pain became everything.

Alice lost her identity as the white torment refused to relent. Refused to diminish. On and on it continued. Stripping her away.

Alice's body hit the ground hard for a second time.

"Alice. Alice, come on. We have to go. We have to get out of here."

Tears fell from her eyes, and something wet ran like a river down the side of her back, but she didn't care. She couldn't care. The pain was everything.

"Alice, we have to go now. Kerogen stopped screaming. Come on, child, I know it hurts, but we have to go."

She felt something cover her back, and pain, bright and pure, washed over her anew. It was different from the torture of before but hurt all the same. Alice cried out but didn't have any fight left in her.

CHAPTER THIRTEEN

MONTHS BEFORE A+O

Owen wasn't crazy. Wasn't suicidal or even stupid. No, none of that. He had needed to let some of the frustration out, sort of like warming up an arm before the game by throwing hard.

Owen smiled and tossed the open bottle of whiskey over to Clover, who, quick as a tiger, switched the bow to her left hand even though it held her violin and caught the whiskey bottle without letting the alcohol slosh up and out.

"You ready to have some fun?" he asked.

Before she could answer, his finger drew across the strings. His song was bold, strong in spirit, but with a question that tickled the skin. He let the strings vibrate long into the atmosphere of the crowd. It was like reeling in a fish. For this run, he would need them. He would need them all. His upper hand clamped down over another set of chords, and he filled his song with power as he let it call out into the night. There onstage, he felt each of those willing souls who were to make the run with him. Through training, he took them into his mind and heart.

"On me, one! One. One. One, two, three," Owen called.

Devin came in right on time, as did Clover. Sage clapped a hand against her thigh as they began.

Seven hours later, Tim held the roadhouse door open. Owen and Clover were holding on to each other with their instruments safely in their cases. Both were worn to the bone, but their spirits were at an all-time high, calls of the We shouting at their backs for them to stay, to celebrate, to bask and to live in the bliss of success and the hereafter.

Clover didn't quite judge the opening of the door correctly, so she hit it, rebounding off, Owen working to keep her going in the right direction. Two souls deep in the intoxication of a purer kind.

The journey to the second arch and back had taken everything they had contained, and now here they were, free, breathing in air, without the golden flames from Heaven.

Of course, the alcohol had left both their systems hours earlier, a side effect of making a successful run. Tim muttered something about etherealists before shutting the door behind them. He had his hands full, taking care of a crowd fully fed and high on ethereal energy. Word would spread, and the party would grow. So much energy in one place was like throwing birdseed down in Central Park. The pigeons would come and celebrate the feast.

Owen looked across the bright parking lot. It was late morning to the rest of the world, he thought through the haze of euphoria.

Clover laughed for no reason, her unbalanced steps pulling at him as they clung to each other. *It always takes a piece, doesn't it? A piece, a price. And the deeper you go, the higher the toll.*

"Why did you park so far away?" she asked.

"This is easy, girl. Just one step at a time."

He moved in a rough line, each step taken a comfort, knowing they were on the right track. Of course, they could have stayed. Owen had done so in the past. But it was dangerous, and his people were still out there unprotected. No, better they leave now, while they could. Hit the road and find someplace safe to hole up until Daphne turned eighteen.

The country highway was empty as they crossed, the old green truck at a slight tilt from where he had parked partly in the dirt.

As he pulled on a trickle of power, the locks to the doors, both front and back, popped up at his command.

"Did you see it, Owen, the other side? I can never remember what it looks like, but it touches me every time. I can't describe the feeling, but man, I feel good. And Sage. I can't believe Sage. Did you hear her sing? We should meet up with her again. She was really good."

"All right girl, in you go," he said as he set his guitar case on the uneven ground.

"I'm going. Here, hold my Betsy." She handed him her case as she held herself up with the car door.

Owen smiled as Clover tried to puzzle out the best way to climb in through the driver's side. "Come on, in you go. You can do it," he urged.

"Of course I can. Don't rush me! Did you see me in there?" she said, turning back around to face him. "I was amazing. Betsy and I rocked the cabasa."

"The cabasa?" He held back a laugh. "You mean you rocked the Casbah," he corrected.

"You know what I mean, shut up. Why are you always so serious? It doesn't make any sense when you are that good-looking. You are supposed to be fun," Clover said.

"Get in the truck and stop poking at me."

Clover wrinkled her forehead. Her face spoke of too much and nothing at all. "Fine, Mr. Serious, but only because you played well tonight. Did I really make out with Sage?"

Owen's silence was rewarded with watching Clover use the steering wheel to pull herself in. He watched one very toned butt climb past the wheel and settle into the passenger seat.

Satisfied she was in and safe, he moved to the rear door and opened it up. A quick set of hidden locks, and he stored his stringless guitar in the secret compartment under the bench seat. He left Betsy on top. Sometimes Clover enjoyed playing while they were on the road.

Getting behind the wheel, he took a moment to take stock of how close they had come. The flames of the path and power of the arches not meant for mortals had been a mountain range of danger around them. Blue and white. He remembered the flames coating the band's skin and instruments. The song and ethereal magic were the only things that kept them safe. He looked Clover over as she nestled up to a rolled blanket she had set between herself and the window. Her bare feet were tucked in tight up on the bench.

He let out his breath as he smelled the burned hair and fabric covering each of them. Her pants had streaks of missing material, and her top was now missing a shoulder and a few random spots where the flames had eaten them away. His own clothing hadn't come out much better. A run could be hell on the wardrobe.

Something changed, and his body went as tense as a viper. Slipping his hand under the old seat, he found the familiar comfort of a heavy wooden handle.

Fast as he could, Owen drew the old revolver out and pressed it to the window, pulling the hammer back.

He turned his head slowly, already knowing that Ethan, level four, was standing on the other side of the glass. Tension built as Owen looked on, watching and sensing no one else in the area.

Ethan's hands climbed high and steady in surrender, an

upside-down cowboy hat in one hand and a familiar jean jacket in the other.

Gently, taking his time, Owen rolled down the window, uncaring if he was being rude as he kept the revolver on Ethan's center of mass. A gatekeeper and an etherealist as talented as Clover were always a prize at any time.

"What do you want, Ethan?"

"Peace, Owen. I mean you and yours no harm."

Owen listened for a lie, for the feel of any untruth. Gently he lowered the hammer back and set the weapon on his lap yet kept the grip in his hand.

"What are you doing out here?" Owen asked.

"You left so quickly. Aurei asked me to give you your coat." He held up the old blue denim coat Owen had forgotten.

"And what is that in the other hand?" Owen asked.

"You know, you are a very serious guy."

"I have people counting on me for their protection. It's a very serious responsibility."

"I know. I can feel that in the way you play. In the way you moved up there. Might be the most remarkable performance I have ever witnessed. A one-of-a-kind performance, and yet between you and me? I don't think that it will be your last. Am I right? You're going to make another run. It's just a matter of time. It's okay. You don't have to answer. I don't think there is a soul in that room or any room who can't see it, feel it, once they really see you. Besides, you don't owe me anything. You fulfilled your word. Here, I took up a quick collection for you and her," he said, pointing the cowboy hat toward Clover, who had already fallen asleep.

Owen had already guessed there was cash in the hat. It was a common gift after making a successful run. He accepted the hat and hardly took notice of the stray bills as they mixed with full clips and folded cash, along with different types of jewelry, from watches and rings to necklaces and earrings. The We could be extremely generous at times.

Setting the hat on the bench in between himself and Clover's feet, he didn't take his eyes off the We. Owen then reached out and took the offered jacket, setting it over both feet and hat. Clover continued sleeping undisturbed.

"Thanks," Owen said.

"Thank you." Ethan didn't back away, just remained standing and staring.

"Something else on your mind?" Owen asked with an edge.

Ethan nodded his head slightly in the affirmative, and Owen watched as he slipped a hand into his pocket and produced a cigarette. Using ethereal power, he lit the cancer stick. One long pull and release came and went before Ethan spoke. "It's an honorable thing, what you did. What you are doing for the girl. The etherealist child who left here safe. Keeping her unbound. You were willing to die for her twice. Once if we rushed you, and the second time in making an unprepared run all the way to the gates."

It wasn't a full run, Owen thought, but kept this to himself, needing to see where Ethan was taking this conversation.

"We're not all bad, you know. Just fractions of what we once were before we were forced out."

A truth, and a balance within Owen pulled for him to respond. To speak up. "I know you're not all bad. I have made a lot of friends within the We. The way I see it, you are all just trying to make it work here, same as anyone." Owen thought about earlier, before the run, when this man had made a deal with him. Sealing the deal with Butch's death. "I don't hold grudges, not with humans or your kind. It's a waste of energy, and besides, I can't see it doing anyone any good. Let's all just live and do our best to do our best."

Ethan pulled on his cigarette again, letting the smoke

drift into the late morning air. "That's fair. I can't say I would do the same in your shoes."

Owen could feel the tension inside the man and couldn't understand where it was coming from. The deal they had made was completed. The handshake inside the bar after the run had confirmed it earlier.

"You were doing an honorable thing," Ethan went on. "I thought during the run you would let Devin or Sage burn in retaliation. Most likely both. I thought you would be more . . . human."

Owen felt the pieces slip into place. At any time, it was true he could have pressed either Sage or Devin or both out, letting the fires burn them to a crisp. If either of them burned, the second arch wouldn't have been an option. And the risk to Clover and him would have been significantly less. The deal would have been honored because Owen had only agreed to try.

"That's not who I am. We had a deal, and I keep my word. Don't worry about the rest, it's all in the past. We made it to the second gate and out again. It was a good run."

Understanding the level four was just feeling guilty, Owen started the truck up. He had to give it a little gas, as the truck was old and thirsty.

The roar of the V-8 was loud and comforting compared to the tension and guilt.

Ethan came forward, laying a hand over the door. "You did an honorable thing, Owen. Twice you did, and I asked you to do something dishonorable. You see, I knew the third gate would kill you. I thought the second gate would kill you. To be honest, I thought you making a run to the first gate, unprepared and alone, would turn your body into a pyre of flames." Anger and frustration fountained through Ethan's words.

"You lose some friends last night at the Old Spoon and Bucket?" Owen waited for the guess to be confirmed before going on. "I have lost friends before too. It's all good, man.

Let it go. We're good. We're alive, still here, and that is enough for today."

"Owen Brown, you and yours are now in my protection. If you need safety at any time or any place, find me. Contact me and I shall provide it." Ethan held out a thin white business card with his name and number clearly printed on it.

Owen nodded his head, understanding the weight of the offer. When it came to the We, such a promise of protection was not given lightly. He reached his hand out of the window for Ethan to shake it again, for the first time knowing without a doubt the revolver would not be needed.

Ethan's hand was both strong and smooth as he gave a heavy-handed shake before passing over the business card.

Slipping the truck into first gear, Owen let out the clutch, pulling away.

A mile down the road, he opened up the glove box and tossed the card onto a small pile of similar cards. The revolver he left in his lap as he turned on the radio. Miles Davis came through the worn speakers, and Owen couldn't help but let out some of the tension as he softly started to hum along.

CHAPTER FOURTEEN

SEVEN YEARS BEFORE A+O

Father Patrick took one look at Alice wrapped with a relic made to purify the damned and understood what it meant for a heart to bleed with compassion.

Alice was covered in blood from halfway up her spine, over both shoulders and, he guessed from what he could see from his angle, her chest as well. The remains of her jacket were on the ground, and her dress had been cut in half. The torn fabric was shaved down to only a pile of loose fibers, soaked in blood.

Alice's scream stopped so suddenly the silence had him pausing in his rush to get to her. He watched just out of reach as she fell hard, away from him, smacking the ground without a complaint.

God protect us, Patrick whispered in his mind as he rushed forward. *It's going to be okay, it's going to be okay. Lord help her. I'm here now.*

His own jacket he slipped off and draped over Alice's

bloody back. The sound that escaped came closer to that of
a hurt animal than any human sound.

"I know it hurts, child, but we have to go. We have to get
you out of here."

He didn't wait for a response. Carefully he slipped Alton's jeweled knife into his pocket, hoping a little that the
weapon would fall out before he could cut himself again.

Being as gentle as he could, he picked Alice up. Each
cry, each whimper drove spikes of pain into his chest.

For all her strength and fighting skills, she was still
small, still so young and light. "Hush now, we are getting
you out of here," he said as she made a small, broken sound,
cradled in his arms.

Stepping over a dead body he couldn't avoid somehow
seemed small compared to the girl he now carried.

The door open and hall empty, Patrick moved deeper
into the compound, away from Kerogen and the bloody
room, Alice secured against his chest as tightly as he dared.

He tried to move faster, but she pulled on his arm, holding him tight as small whimpers continued to break the
silence, causing him to slow. So he ended up moving at a
fast walk instead. Patrick had never hoped for someone else
to suffer, for a child of God to be in pain, not in his entire
adult life. But he hoped for it now. He hoped Kerogen was
still twisted and broken back in the courtyard. He silently
prayed the monster that caused each of Alice's whimpers
was paying for his own damnation here on Earth.

And if his hoping was to doom his soul, he would gladly
pay the price.

Deeper Patrick moved down the hall and to the right, turning a corner only to find the three priests Father Alton had
sent back up to the bell tower. Their bodies were broken and
bloody, and in the tight confines of the hallway, he had to pick
his footing; otherwise, he might fall, taking Alice with him.

A rifle caught his eye. It was lying past the bodies, useless on the floor. Its black glossy frame stole his attention

as if someone had somehow spared the weapon just for him. A gift, a sign or a test?

He moved past the weapon, using one awkward hand to pull up on the steel latch of the closed door as he used his shoulder to gently ram the old wood open. Alice let out a protest so low he doubted she even understood she had made a sound. The square room was wider than the others, with a set of stairs leading up to a small landing that housed an open doorframe.

Over the last seven years, Alice had been moved six times, but for the last year, this had been their home. He had climbed those stairs and the stairs inside the room above as they led up to the bell tower.

Just as he also knew where the closed door ahead led. The door with a carved cross inlaid in the wood.

Taking Alice, he moved into the room, heading for the door.

He moved as fast as he could, hoping the door to his escape wouldn't be locked.

His hand on the handle, he felt a fraction of relief for a single heartbeat as the door opened the first few inches.

"Father Patrick. You have something that belongs to me." Kerogen's voice was sure, confident, even graceful.

Patrick didn't turn to face Kerogen, not at first. He couldn't. He was so close to getting Alice out safely. But in the end, fear forced him to look back, taking his responsibility with him.

Kerogen looked clean and elegant as he stood in the doorway, a calm, deadly expression covering his face. It was impossible and true.

Despite the small amount of dirt over the knees where Kerogen had knelt outside and the blood soaking his arm and no doubt covering his black suit, the man looked regal and perfectly put together, as if a blood-covered hand were the latest fashion trend.

"She is something, isn't she?" Kerogen said, taking a single step into the room and looking toward Alice.

"You should let her go, Kerogen. She is a child and good. Break the bond and let her go." Patrick had to fight for the words, his breath ragged.

"Don't be thin-minded, Father Patrick. I know your life is small and tiny and your years are short, but at least try to use your whole mind before speaking to me."

Patrick made to respond, but the sudden sight of two thick cords of ethereal power swarming up from behind Kerogen like thick, hungry snakes forced a swallowing of his response instead.

"Alice's power has grown so much since we first sang to each other. Beautiful. Pure. Strong of will. She has so much capacity still to gain. Oh, Father, you have no idea how many years I have waited and watched and listened to find one such as her. And then you took her from me, hid her from me and brought her to those I hate most in this world."

Patrick shifted his grip ever so slightly, not wanting anything more to happen to Alice.

"Oh my," Kerogen said, seeing a portion of Alice's exposed, blood-covered skin. "A shroud of tears. Not since the sixteen hundreds have I seen such a thing in use. If I would have known she had one, I would have saved her from it. It hurts far more when our bond is active, and I must say, I was being greedy when she placed the shroud over her shoulders. Now, Father, if you would wish to take it off her, rather than I, I see no reason why that cannot be. Surprised I am not such a monster? You think I wish to cause the child more harm for harm's sake? Not who we are, though you will see once the relic is embedded beneath the skin, it is not so easily detached." He smiled with a humor Patrick would never be able to understand.

Fearing any reply would give something away, Patrick started to kneel, taking the child with him. All the while keeping his eyes on Kerogen. Twenty-five feet separated them, and it wasn't nearly enough to feel safe.

Carefully Patrick set Alice's weight down on the floor, one last look at the monster who had ruined the brightness of the world for Alice, her family. A demon who had just killed fourteen priests and whose hunger for violence still wasn't sated. Patrick bent his head down toward Alice in humility and in hope.

With a loud voice that echoed off the walls, Patrick called out, "Lord almighty, humbly I ask you to protect Alice and myself in our greatest hour of need. Oh, Lord, grant me mercy and strength."

"Fool . . ." Kerogen's next words melted away.

Patrick's hand, low to the ground, hidden by the jacket covering Alice, shook ever so slightly as his finger flipped up the cover protecting the metal switch upon the small plastic box no larger than a garage door opener. Father Alton's remote detonator to the bomb hidden over the bell tower. The thick, large and ancient bell, once placed to protect this monastery from any of Kerogen's kind, was currently located five stories up, just over their heads.

Tightness built in his bones, strengthening his resolve.

A quick pull with a single fingertip and Patrick was already lifting Alice, as a loud, earsplitting explosion erupted above. It rocked the settlement down to the foundation, and with it came a ringing the likes of which he had never heard.

Even so, Patrick had just enough time to see Kerogen as the creature looked up above as if he could see past the ceiling and the next room and higher still to the source of the explosion.

Patrick lifted, pushing with his legs, back and arms, Alice once again in his keeping as he came to his feet.

Kerogen's hands flung up to his head, and the black ethereal power shattered with the ringing of the falling bell.

Father Patrick didn't have time to fear, didn't have a

chance to weigh risk or rethink his decision. With every fiber of his being, he turned away from Kerogen while the sound of the bell crashing down split his ears. One hand caught the ring of the old wooden door, inlaid with a carving of a cross surrounded by a sea of roses. He pulled hard even as he angled to get Alice's head in through the opening. One step, two, and five stories of stone and wood and one very large bell crashed in behind him as he dove through. His hands and body did their best to protect the child.

They hit the floor hard, and he had one last moment to cover Alice's soft head as the room turned black. Rubble, wood and stone crashed in from behind and sealed them inside the escape tunnel.

CHAPTER FIFTEEN

HOURS BEFORE A+O

Owen polished another bar with a red rag. The wood held the color of deep wine, the grain running the long length, framed in on the far side by a shiny, round brass rod that gleamed with the mix of sunlight through the windows and low lights overhead. The jukebox was silent in the far corner, so Owen listened to a local station on an old-school radio the owners, Jack and Benn, kept high up above a cluttered shelf.

There was an odd sad and warm comfort to an empty space that was designed for people to share. Owen was currently in the process of enjoying it. For a little while, at least.

His people were all out hitting the laundromat and doing a bit of shopping. Even Daphne had been allowed out, with Clover's insistence that both she and Jessie would stay on either side of the kid.

He circled the rag once, twice over a spot on the polished wood that held just a touch of resistance. He liked the mundane at times. The repetitive motion of something simple in a long, empty room. A man could think or calm or just be at times like this.

Absently Owen looked to the stage, past round tables that still held upside-down chairs from when Max had swept the floor clean two hours back. The stage here was nicer than Tim and Aurei's bar. This roadhouse was in the heart of Saint Louis, the original foundation dating back to before the city had grown up around it.

Owen had known the owners, Jack and Benn, for four years now, and thought, with Daphne's eighteenth birthday only two months away, it would be a safe place to stay until then.

Maybe we'll all head west after this. Utah, Park City, and the snow sounds like fun. Then on to Vegas. Have to tie Max to a chair, but it would be nice to let loose. Then on to California. I haven't been to San Diego. Maybe head there first, then go north by way of the coast. Or skip it and go straight to San Francisco, keep going until we hit Oregon. Keep moving. Safer for everyone if we keep moving.

Jessie talked about Oregon a couple of times. He would be down to go. There is a fresh vibe for musicians there, with plenty of places to play. Daphne only has two months, and then when she's no longer bondable, we can play openly, as long as we keep moving and don't take on any more strays.

The leather-padded front door, sporting a round porthole window, just to the left of Owen, swung open, and three girls hardly old enough to be allowed in came through carrying shopping bags on their arms.

"Ladies, can I help you?" Owen asked.

"Oh wow, look at you!" said the second girl through the door, who was sporting long blond hair and juggling two large shopping bags and a tiny designer purse.

Owen smiled politely in response.

"Um, do you have a restroom we can use?" the first girl asked, a little shy.

"Sure, it's right over there." He pointed, and the three girls marched together as the blonde made a point of thanking him.

Owen went back to polishing. A few minutes went by, and he thought he could hear giggling coming from behind the bathroom door.

Something out of tune in the air had his head shifting back to the porthole of the main entrance. Through the round glass, he spotted Clover, followed by Jessie. Everything screamed trouble, as they should have come in from the back.

"Owen, it happened again," Clover said as she came in.

Max and Daphne were close behind, Jessie having held the door. By the look of them, they were in a hurry and flustered by something.

"What happened?" Owen asked, not wasting time.

Jessie spoke first, his voice as always smooth and easy. "Clover received word the Black Mamba just cleared out. We and humans alike are dead or injured. Cops on their way."

"Hunters?" Owen asked, already knowing the answer but needing to hear it.

"Yes, hunters," Clover said. "Who else could it be? Paul, you remember the cool level three, with the body of a nine I was talking with two nights back? He just let me know about the attack. Said the hunters did the same thing as before. A young, unbound girl sang onstage with ethereal power, ensnaring many of the We, and then the hunters just started killing everyone. He said the place turned into a butcher's kitchen."

The three normal girls came out of the bathroom. The blond one was still fixing her hair, the other reaching into her purse. The last was talking about a jacket she was thinking about going back and buying. All three were smiling with what he took to be a "not a care in the world" attitude.

"Oh hey, is the bar open?" the jacket-wanting one asked.

Owen shifted attention, his mind racing as he spoke from a script in his mind. "This is a twenty-four-hour road-house. We are always open. Max here will make you whatever you want."

He gave a little nod to Max to jump behind the bar and take over as he pulled his phone out of his pocket. He could feel Jessie's cool, calculating gaze, Clover's still resolve and Daphne's nervous fear.

"Benn, hey, have you heard about the attack at the Black Mamba?" Owen asked as the line was answered.

It wasn't Benn who answered. Instead it was Benn's partner, Jack. "Owen! Yes, we know. I can't believe those assholes, with their holier-than-thou complex. I want to find them. Killing in the name of God—it's all bullshit and lies. We need to find them, chop off their nutsacks and feed them to them with hot sauce."

Owen could just make out Benn's smooth, soothing voice shifting in.

"Jack, I know, we will find them. Let me talk to Owen. Here, talk to Marcie for me." Owen heard the phone shift hands. "Owen?"

"Benn. We heard it was the same hunters as in Ohio and Virginia?"

"That's what we are being told. Like the two times before, they used a kid to get onstage and sing before they started slaughtering. Your luck doesn't seem to be holding."

"No kidding. We weren't in Virginia when they hit there last month, but I don't like this. It's too close. Do you know how many hunters? Besides the girl who got onstage?" Owen needed as much information as he could get his hands on.

"Unconfirmed. At this point, all we know is a lot of good people are dead."

"I am sorry, Benn. I know some of them will be close friends of yours. Did Billy and Doll get out?"

"I don't know, but they are not answering their phones. It might be they are on lockdown." Billy and Doll were the We owners of the Black Mamba and longtime friends of Benn.

Clover shifted impatiently, wanting to know the answer. He gave her a shrug, hoping it said, *I don't know.*

"Benn, I am sorry. Everyone over here is praying they got out safe."

"They are both strong and smart. If anyone had a chance to survive the attack, it would be them. Are you leaving?" Benn asked.

"As soon as I hang up, we are gone. We can't stay. It's not safe for us." As he spoke the words, he gave his crew a hard look. "How far out are you?"

"Ten minutes, at best. If you need cash, take whatever is in the register. You and yours are welcome back anytime. Tell Daphne both Jack and I wish her a safe and happy birthday."

"Thanks, Benn. Again, I am sorry for your loss."

"Good luck, Owen, and keep your people safe. This might get worse before it gets better." The line went dead.

"Are we leaving?" Daphne asked.

"We can't stay. Any second, the We in this city will pour through that door, and we can't be here. Not again. Get your stuff and let's go, right now."

"What about the three customers and the bar?" Daphne asked.

"It's a roadhouse. No one tending it for ten minutes won't matter at all. It's made of thicker stuff. Now let's go."

It took a couple minutes to put everything in the van and his truck, but they were gone before Benn showed. As Owen was driving away, he spotted a group of level twos walking in a rush in the direction of the sanctuary. Relief and fear touched him in equal parts as the light ahead turned green.

"You made the right call," Clover said beside him. Max was in the back seat. Leaving just the three of them in his truck. Jessie had Daphne in the van right behind.

"This time. We need to get out of this state. I can't believe the hunters are in this city. That's three attacks, and two were a stone's throw from us. We don't want anything to do with these hunters or the growing mob of We looking for retribution."

"What about going off-grid until Daphne's birthday? We can hit the mountains or a lake somewhere and just hole up out of sight in a cabin," Max said from the back seat.

It was a thought spoken about in passing after the wild run Clover and he had made at Tim and Aurei's place. Owen wasn't surprised to hear it brought up again.

"We are going south," Owen said, deep in thought as he checked to make sure Jessie's van was following right behind.

Daphne was in the back of the van, so even if someone was looking in through the glass, she would be safely out of sight.

"South, Owen?" Clover asked, her tone far more grave than he would have liked.

The South, thick with history and music as well as high-level We who had never liked to leave. Old We. Opportunity-seeking We.

"Let's find out if Mara will let me through the doors."

"Oh, come on, Owen! You told me she threatened to shoot you. In the chest," she added when he didn't respond.

"That is what family does." He accented his voice, pulling the words out and rounding them off.

"Who is Mara?" Max asked from behind.

"She is his aunt, who told him if he ever came into her bar again, she would kill him."

"The one in Miami?" Max asked with a combination of awe and excitement.

"She is not my aunt. She only calls herself my aunt. She's just family."

Clover noticed the way he shifted the leather cuff made of ethereal essence on his wrist.

"It's a long story," Owen said. "Besides, we need a secure place, and I can't think of any better. It's a sanctuary of a kind, and she will look after Daphne."

"After she kills you, you mean," Clover said.

"Wait, guys. Why don't we just go off-grid if your aunt is such a bad idea?" Max pressed.

Owen did his best to ignore Clover's comments. She didn't know Mara the way he did. There was history there. Old history. Painful history, but history all the same. He had been eighteen when Mara's adopted son, David, had died. Eight years now. It was a long time.

"Max, you have to run it through. Where are all these We going to go if they don't go to a sanctuary? Where is the safest place for them?" Owen checked the side mirror as they moved out onto the highway. If Jessie was surprised in his choice of direction, there was no indication in his driving.

"Now, Max, you know the stronger the We, the more they can feel our ethereal power and search us out. Like a polar bear can sniff out a meal. Do you have any idea how strong a smell we give off as a whole? It's why we keep going to the more friendly roadhouses and hiding within. It masks our vibe. And right now, all the We on this side of the country will have their senses wide open. If we were found isolated in a cabin somewhere, the outcome would probably end horribly for all of us."

"We could take out a single backpacking We in the middle of nowhere . . . Or you can, at least." Owen could feel the pride rolling off Max from behind his seat.

"And, Max, what happens if that one single backpacker sends out the word to other We? What if he waits outside while his friends come for Daphne? For all of us? It's happened to other etherealists before. Other groups before. We would be sitting ducks ready to be plucked. No, we need to keep her safe until her birthday, then life can get back to normal. At least our normal. But for now, we need a safe place with the firepower to take on any threat. And that now includes these hunters. I don't like the idea that we all might be on the wrong side of the old saying 'third time's the charm.' We need help, we need protection and we need a place even the hunters and those We looking for retribution won't screw with."

"You know something you haven't told us?" Clover said.

He glanced at her and couldn't keep his worry in. "It's just a feeling I've had ever since we made the run. Maybe before. Something in the air tells me to get ready for a fight because someone is coming."

The cab of the truck went silent. He wasn't a voodoo kind of guy, not one to look at shaped clouds and make life predictions. But every once in a while, the world would tip on its end, and if you weren't holding on to something, you would fall right off. Now just felt like one of those times.

"So, Mara's?" Clover asked with a slow resolve.

"Mara's, and with her place, Damon and Cornelius," Owen said.

"You won't mind if I place a bet with Jessie that Mara shoots you, right? It just seems like easy money after everything you told me about her."

"Seriously, how come I have never heard of her?" Max asked.

"She is not going to shoot me. Let it go, Clover."

"Really, Owen? Really?" Clover's voice was dripping with sarcasm.

"Mara won't shoot me. Well, she . . ." A fancy black

sports car passed them on the inside lane, moving at breakneck speed with a performance engine and hard, tight suspension. They watched it weave through cars and trucks as it sped along. While it glided out of view, in a low voice, Owen finished: "She might."

CHAPTER SIXTEEN

After almost twenty straight hours of being on the road, Owen pulled the truck to a final stop in front of the Golden Horn, an old club located in downtown Miami, Florida. Owen took stock of his situation as he shifted the truck into park, checking to watch Jessie, who had driven the van throughout the night, as he pulled into the space right behind the truck and settled into park.

His mind was fuzzy from the lack of sleep, the long drive and too much sugar, as the latest candy Max had purchased for both of them actually tasted better than it had looked. The truck now held a nest of wrappers that hadn't quite made it into the brown bag Clover had crumpled to form a makeshift trash can several stops previous.

Inside also lay remnants of fast food and energy drinks. Max was asleep beside him, as Clover, two gas stops back, had decided to ride in the van with Jessie and Daphne. Owen felt weary. He needed to brush his teeth and take a shower, but there wasn't time. Mara would know he was in her city in a matter of hours, if not seconds. She had a way of knowing the city like no other.

He looked through the windshield at the hanging sign for the Golden Horn, a landmark in the city that understood its long history. The building was far more than it seemed. A building with actual roots of a kind. The building behind the hanging sign was as much a precious item as his own guitar and the essence that came with it. This was not a roadhouse. It wasn't a sanctuary to all. This was something older. Something deeper. Between Uncle Damon's private sound studio in the back and the underground tunnels and chambers, along with the connected buildings to either side and behind, the bar was far more than what it seemed from the outside, the wooden sign of a yellow horn a simplistic definition of what lay inside.

Owen slipped the large revolver out from under the seat, and before he could rethink his actions, he emptied all but one bullet. A snap, followed shortly by a click, and the revolver was ready to fire. Opening the truck door with more force than was necessary, he made to exit, his body groaning as he forced himself out. Max moaned a good morning, but Owen shut the door before the kid could finish.

Once again his people needed him to do the impossible. His hand scrubbed his face. He needed fresh energy. He didn't dare pull on ethereal energy. Not here, not yet. He moved to the rear door of the truck, opening it with ease, and stripped off his shirt, uncaring of the pedestrians walking by or the cars that moved behind him.

A clean black tee slipped over his head. The V-neck held a small pocket in the left corner. A fresh shot of antiperspirant was the best he could do for now before he slipped the revolver into his back waistband. Handle to his right side for a fast quick draw.

Max spoke again, but Owen was lost in his own head as he shut the door.

Every time they had stopped before, Jessie and the others had gotten out of the van by now, whether it had been at a gas station or for fast food. But this time was different. This time Clover, Jessie and Daphne stayed inside. He looked back once, a last glimpse of Clover and Jessie staring back before they disappeared out of his sight.

The outside of the building held new paint, a deep red reminding him of fresh blood, framing a caged-in window that held a basic black-and-white sign that said CLOSED. Hardly a surprise, as it was still early, and on a weekday during the off-season. He hadn't expected any different.

Home after all these years, and it is just the same. Maybe eight years wasn't enough, not nearly enough for a place that doesn't age.

Stepping up onto the sidewalk, Owen couldn't help but remember the times he'd walked through the front door as a child. Then as a young man. And the last time he'd walked out.

How he hadn't been bonded was as much a mystery as to why he had been chosen as keeper of the guitar on his eighteenth birthday.

Pulling hard, he opened the front door despite its reinforced weight of thick steel. He wasn't surprised about the CLOSED sign, nor that the front door wasn't locked.

The Golden Horn was what one might call a social den. Others might think of it like an old gangsters' bar. The latter might be more accurate. The CLOSED sign was only for some people. If you had to ask, the sign was for you.

Owen was hit with the slightest scent of burned tobacco and expensive cigars. Yet in between, he could smell lilac and roses. The lilac was used for cleaning; the roses were Mara's favorite. *Perhaps I should have brought her some.* The late idea passed through his thoughts, and he knew it would have been a mistake. No amount of flowers would make amends for what had happened.

He stepped out of the sun and into the old room that had

been his home. Where he had begun to master his sound and his skills.

To his right was the main bar, shining with bottles of booze from all across the world as they caught the light and gleamed in an invitation to anyone foolish enough to walk in.

To his left was unscratched wallpaper, unmarred by time. From just below shoulder height, the wallpaper of little polo men riding horseback, wearing black helmets as they reached down with long mallets, ran all the way up to the high ceiling above.

Dark wood ran from the floor up to meet the seam of the green wallpaper. He himself had never seen a polo match. But he knew the constant back-and-forth that ran the entirety of this room like he knew the back of his own hand.

Thick, comfortable low-lying chairs sat pristinely positioned at gold-rimmed tables. All empty. All perfectly set into the same place they had been when he had left. In the low light, they sparkled as if even common dust knew better than to settle here.

His breath felt heavy with history and what was to come as he started his walk toward the muffled voice coming from deep inside.

Owen knew where they would be. Like characters trapped in a painting. Mara, Cornelius and Damon.

The old club was built like one long shaped L, the stage that could easily sit nine players in the center of the turn. He moved slowly but without hesitation toward the empty stage. Toward the sound coming from around the corner.

This was a place for predators. Like a pride of lions living inside a fence, pretending to be cats. He had never truly belonged, and yet it was home.

Instruments aplenty gleamed from hooks on the wall over the stage as he made his way closer. Deeper.

Heading toward the sounds coming from the back of the establishment.

Owen passed the empty stage as the room opened up

anew on his right. The small bar, more tables with soft chairs, and still on the left were high-backed booths. But only one table buried deep in the shadow of the furthest corner held life.

Six men and one woman were playing cards. Mara's back and her shiny hair, tight in crisscrossing braids that ran long, caught and held his attention. An old buried sorrow and love bubbled up from a place he had thought was no longer a part of him. It threatened to choke his voice from the inside as he stared, as he drank in an old, familiar sight.

Not a single person looked in his direction. Not even the woman with the braids who had her back to him turned to see who had just entered. Even though they all knew he was there.

Owen breathed it all in. The shiny bar, the low light, the old gold trim and the weight of history and power, both personal and ethereal. He took a few more steps closer, judging the gap between him and his family sufficient.

Poker chips from another era were pushed forward and cards dropped down flat so everyone could see who the winner was. He saw the glance, the recognition and the acceptance in less than a heartbeat from Damon. The level five looked as if he hadn't aged a bit in eight long years, the last time Owen had seen him.

Black skin, deep brown eyes, thick eyebrows and a sense of wisdom and power that was steady, calm and old—Damon was one of the scariest yet most levelheaded gentlemen Owen had ever come to know. They were friends of a kind. Kindred souls, Damon would say. Owen wasn't quite so sure.

Two other We took notice as the cards no longer held their appeal. Neither We did Owen recognize, but it was easy enough to see they were both level fives in their own right.

Another card player did turn to look. His movement was

fast, even sly. Cornelius. Owen smiled despite the danger he was in. Despite what he was feeling, despite the weight in the air.

Cornelius smiled in return, the blue around the under-glow proclaiming the long acquaintance as a level four. The strongest level four Owen had ever encountered.

Owen watched as Cornelius gave a small nod and then touched the hand of the only woman at the table. Mara.

Everything in Owen told him to turn his body to the side, to make himself into a smaller target as Mara turned to regard him. Instead he held himself firm, solid and un-relenting.

"Owen, are you ready to die? It's the only reason you would come back here after I gave you my word."

"Not the only reason, Mara," he said while Mara turned her back, having seen enough.

"We had a promise, you and I," she said.

"Yes, we do. You made it very clear. But before you pull the trigger, I'm not here to play her."

"Bullshit. I know you, Owen. There isn't a storm on this planet that can match the force inside your soul. If you're here, so is your storm. It's only a matter of time, and I won't have it in my club, in my city."

"You also know I am not one for tricks."

The room went silent as she thought before speaking. "You can't give her up. I can smell that guitar on you, and anything else I simply don't care about. Leave before I put a bullet in you and make a mess inside my place."

Owen took a breath like a man sealing his fate. Know-ing what he had to say would force her hand.

"Mara, I have a seventeen-year-old girl. Daphne is an unbound etherealist just outside who is under my protec-tion. If you kill me, my last request is for you to keep her safe until she turns eighteen."

Fury, bright and raw, burned through the room as Mara slammed her chair back, sending it flying ten feet to topple to the ground as she stood. The others at the table barely leaned away, as if they didn't have a care in the world despite the revelation of what he had just confessed.

He was ready as Mara turned, and so Owen timed it, using ethereal speed, reaching behind his back. His hand covered over the hilt and he drew. He saw in her hand the sawed-off shotgun she kept under the card table. Just as she saw his gun was going to get to her first. Her eyes went wide even as they promised destruction and retribution.

His gun hand came up in one fluid motion, pointing at her heart, and he released.

Not the destructive power of burning gunpowder in a confined location. No, not that. Mara had once meant the world to him. This old bar, and even its patrons, had been more of a home to him than any other he had ever had. She was right—he didn't belong here. Clover was right too. He shouldn't have come back. But then, what choice did he really have? There was a stone in his chest that said this time he needed help. He needed real help. A real shelter.

Besides, he was always going to come back. Owen opened his hand, releasing the weapon into the air.

The revolver flew fast and straight as her shotgun came up level to his chest. Mara's reflexes were some of the best he had ever seen, and she didn't disappoint.

Mara's right hand tightened around the shotgun, her left hand leaving the stock, catching the revolver perfectly and flipping it around to point right back at him, as smooth and as elegant as any exotic serpent.

Out of nowhere, an idea stuck as he stared at the two guns held by the woman who had sheltered and clothed him from the age of eleven until two weeks after his eighteenth birthday.

Someone could balance two dimes right there, one on each weapon. Damn, she is good. Steady. David, you would be so proud.

"Nice catch." Owen spoke with insight into what she

was feeling. Like his words, she was clean and clear for him to read. Right then they could sing together, blend and harmonize with little to no effort, if she didn't want to hurt him so badly.

To accent his words, Owen let the ethereal power he was holding fade away so only the man was left standing before her.

His revolver, the one she held pointed at him, roared with an angry rage, slamming him to the side and back so he spun, hitting the ground hard.

Pain erupted through his body, and he accepted it as cleanly as if he were a starving man and the pain was his first meal.

Unpaid debt rolled over and over in his mind as he lay flat down on the floor of the Golden Horn bleeding, one hand covering his right shoulder in an attempt to stem the tide.

"Owen, you asshole, why the hell did you come back? All that you had to do was stay away." Her voice was filled with pain, deep and old. The pain spoke of love and loss. "I let you go. Did you really think I would just let you come back?"

Gritting his teeth, he attempted to stand, but in doing so, he tried to use his right arm, and his world washed white for a second as new pain erupted. He fought the need to cry out and was only half successful.

Through it all, he heard her.

"Get up, Owen, so I can shoot you again. Come on, boy. Get up. I know you have it in you. You're not done until I say you're done. Get up."

Owen knew the answer. It was there, right there. Ethereal power. It could and would block the pain. Ethereal power would stop the bleeding and even begin to rebuild the bone that was fractured in his shoulder. If she wanted to fight, he could use the essence on his wrist like a weapon. He could fight back, heal and stand. He wouldn't win, not in her home. There wasn't even a chance, but he could make a show. One last show before he went on his way to the great beyond.

But then, this wasn't his fight. He had already lost this battle long ago.

His untapped reservoir of ethereal power called to him, the essence pulsed with power, and he shut it down, shut both sources away, leaving it all where it belonged. A moment between just her and him.

Marshaling his will, a groan slipped through as Owen got to his feet and turned to face her.

"I did everything I could," he said to her pain.

Mara came forward, pressing the black shotgun just under his rib cage and angled up. Owen refused to step back.

A single squeeze, and it wouldn't take much, would send his organs all over the far wall. For a time washing the little polo players in red.

Wouldn't be the first time, nor the last time someone's blood and innards had to be cleaned up in this room. Oh, Mara.

"I did everything I could to bring him back. David wouldn't leave," he said.

"You should never have made the run. You knew him. You knew David wanted more than this world, more than me. You should never have accepted that bloody guitar. Owen, you had no right to make that run with him."

"I didn't know about David."

"Shut up. Yes, you did. Yes, you did," she repeated. "You two were as close as brothers, and you let him go. Without you and that damn guitar, my David would have never gone in that far. He's dead because of you."

"Mara, I didn't know." It was all he could say.

In his mind he could see David's face as he shared in the euphoria of seeing the third arch for the first time. David had been older by four years, but it mattered little. White-gold flames danced over their skin, covering their hair and instruments as they played for a full house in a back corner alley off Third Street. Ethereal power coursed through their bones like electricity through a gold medalist Olympian doing her beam routine on the third rail. Raw, ethereal power sang into and through them, lifting everyone who could hear into new heights. But it was time to turn back, to leave, and make their way out.

David instead winked with glee as he surrendered to the power, to the euphoria. His body and possibly his spirit burning as he simply stopped playing.

"I didn't know," Owen said again, trying to allow the truth to be in his words.

"You knew he wanted more, that he was unsatisfied with the here and now. With his own skill."

"We were brothers," Owen said into her anger.

She cut him off before he could say more, jamming the shotgun into his center, forcing him to take a step back. "My David wasn't as strong as you. You knew it, I knew it. Everyone within a hundred miles knew it, including him. Don't lie to me and talk about what you didn't know. I should kill you right now and erase that guitar."

If some of the others in the room had any objections to what she was saying, Owen wasn't aware of it. It was only her and him.

"Mara," he pleaded.

"No, no. You don't get to say any more. He's gone and it's because of you."

Something ripped in his soul as he spoke words he didn't know he held. "I thought I was enough." His head nodded a trembling yes. Whether it was yes for her to pull the trigger or to reinforce his words so she knew he was telling the truth, he couldn't be sure. Perhaps both.

"What?"

"Mara, I thought I knew him, but I didn't. I thought the storm within me was enough for him too. I thought it was enough for him to anchor the storm inside himself. David was my brother, and it was our own need for freedom that bonded us. Mine is greater, larger, and more terrible than his ever could be. I thought he knew he could have shelter inside the eye. All he had to do was stay close. Stay beside me."

"It was your soul, Owen, that let him do more than he could do on his own. My David knew what was inside you. I knew what was inside you. You should have known it too."

You should have. It was the first time she had not fully blamed him for David's death. It was a single, tiny crack in the wall.

"I did everything I could to bring him out alive. I am so sorry, Mara. I am. He was my brother. David was my brother." Owen felt two small tears fall as he let some of the pain that he held tight be free. Tears that he had never allowed to fall before.

"You son of a bitch, you killed him." Her voice dropped, and for the first time, her words rang false. No longer reinforced by her anger, her own truth.

"I tried to bring him out, I swear I did. I didn't know what he was planning. He kept it from me. Mara, he did! Somehow he kept it from me."

For the first time, her eyes shifted.

"I was stupid and young, and he kept it from me. That isn't an excuse, but I didn't know."

"Oh, shut up, Owen." As the revolver dropped to the floor, her arms wrapped around him in a tight hug that had his vision turning white as fresh, hot pain ran through his body.

"Mara," he whispered into her hair, "I am so sorry."

"Just shut up."

He couldn't stop. His heart had broken and never healed. "I didn't know. I would never have brought him with me on a run if I'd known. I never would have tried or pushed . . . I never. He didn't tell me. Not once, not a single time. David hid it from me. We were brothers."

"Hush." Her hand stroked his hair as the other wrapped around his good shoulder, pulling him in closer. The shotgun, forgotten and still, lay flat against his back while her tears wet his cheek.

"We were brothers."

Tears fell, joining Mara's own as she soothed him. It wasn't the plan Owen had held as he stepped into the bar. This wasn't how it was supposed to go. But then, it hadn't been his show to run.

CHAPTER SEVENTEEN

*It is well documented that there are spiders that use
large, dangerous storms to fly. Without control or purpose of direction and utterly without seat belts or
health insurance, tiny spiders use high winds to cross
miles in the sky. What will it take for me to be like the
small spider with the will to do the impossible?*

A+O

Alice checked her throwing knives. The familiar feel of
worn black leather holding each deadly weapon in place
was always reassuring. Two forty-five handguns slid in
next, each with a green mounted laser sight. Soft fingers
brushed the extra clips while she turned her head to the side
and back again.

Tension. What she had come to think of as *go-tension*
relaxed as she worked more life into muscles eager with
anticipation.

Seven years had passed since the trap for Kerogen at the
monastery had turned nightmare. Seven years of wearing
the shroud of tears just beneath her skin. Life had started
anew upon the old relic, a soul-cutting pain she had struggled to crawl out of only to be sucked back into each time
her well of ethereal energy ran empty. But seven years had

hardened her, reinforcing her will to kill Kerogen. Seven years on his trail.

Alice moved her shoulders back and forth, preparing herself as she always did before going into a den. Her right hand touched the shiny gold buckle that sparkled with small green stones. A tingling sensation ran up her hand as the ethereal essence that was Alton's knife, now *her* knife, responded to her touch. Tonight was just like every other night, her single priority over all else: Where was Kerogen? Where in this world was the monster that had stolen a part of her soul? Until his death, nothing else mattered. Could matter.

The connection she and Kerogen shared was smothered, blocked by the shroud's ability, blocking his location and influence just as it protected her location. A wall that at every moment separated her from her goal.

And yet, if there had been one overlying lesson from the night of the massacre in Italy, it had been that letting Kerogen know where she was, was a terrible, terrible idea.

The second lesson that had come in the days that followed was that this hunt was to be hers, and perhaps Father Patrick's. The secret sect of the church that had trained her couldn't be trusted.

Alice sent out a quick message to Father Patrick.

Any change?

No change. Your parents are safe, and I will keep watching them. Are you?

I am following the lead, about to go into the Golden Horn.

God be with you, Alice.

Staying crouched as she got to her feet, she moved off the makeshift cot in the green van she had used to travel from Denver to Miami. Bought with cash, the van worked well enough for her needs, as she had left the black SUV with the good father. The door opened for her with an easy glide as she stepped onto the sidewalk across from where she had it on good authority there was a very old and well-known level five We within.

Beneath the tactical vest, she wore a black cotton T-shirt. Donning an overly large sweater with its attached dark green hood, Alice zipped it closed and placed her hands in her pockets. Her weapons were hidden well enough to get past the front door. The fact that she looked a little bulky with so much hardware underneath mattered not at all to her.

Power coursed through her bones and muscles, as her well of ethereal power was mostly full. A walking meditation and Alice reversed her ethereal presence, bringing it in, containing it so she wouldn't be detected as an ethereal-ist. Let alone one who was ready for combat.

One of the We on this side of the world knew where Kerogen was. Her contact said that he was here in this nightclub. Getting her hands on him meant she was one step closer to killing Kerogen. It was that simple. Step one, step two. Her search had brought her all through Europe and then Asia, staying on the heels of Kerogen, always just out of reach. She had almost had him, twice—once in Prague and a second time in Bangkok, Thailand. The third encounter had been a trap she had barely survived, as Kerogen brought down the entire building she had been standing in. Only a long, desperate leap through a window and a lucky grab had saved her from the demon. So life went on as both continued to play at hunted and hunter.

The trail had now taken her all the way back to the United States, where it had started long ago.

still don't like this," Jessie said to Owen inside the Golden Horn, as they couldn't be overheard. "There are three level fives in the building. In the building, Owen. And there are level fours, and I swear to you, man, Cornelius shouldn't even be one of them because his power is radiating out of him, he's so filled with magic. I have never seen anything like it. The man is wicked scary, and he likes to smile at me, and he even made a joke. I don't know what the hell we are doing here."

"Just relax, Jessie. This is Miami. Everything is a little different down here. The We in this area are old and live by a code. Keep in mind I grew up here," Owen said.

"Man, the whole point was to run to safety and away from danger. Never stay in one spot too long. Your first rule. The second rule, keep away from higher-level We! And what about the stamp? This isn't a sanctuary. We don't have any protection here, Owen."

"We are under protection. You and I are safer here. Daphne is safer here than anywhere else in the world. You have to trust me."

It had taken seven hours for Jessie to corner Owen away from everyone since he'd come out of the bar with a gunshot wound to the shoulder, bandaged if still slightly bleeding. Seven hours after he had explained to his people that Mara was willing to take on the responsibility of keeping Daphne unbound until her birthday, granting them all safe haven until then.

"Jessie, you need to understand that Miami is older than you know. The We here recognize Mara as the owner of this place, and with it comes promises made over lifetimes. When Mara takes someone under her wing, her people likewise take on her responsibility. Those level fives and fours are old. Like seriously old. They won't break their word over an unbound etherealist. It's all part of who they are, what makes them. I am not saying we aren't in danger in this city, but in this place . . ." Owen struggled to find what he wanted to say. "Anyone coming at us will have to get through them. As long as we stay smart, and respectful."

"She shot you, Owen."

"Yes, but only in the shoulder. And believe me, she could

have done a lot more. Besides, I'm already healing." The look Jessie sent his way said more than Owen was comfortable with. "Relax, man, and get some sleep. Oh, and whatever you do, don't play cards with anyone here whatsoever. That table has its own rules, and most of them are to take advantage of anyone dumb enough to sit down for the first time."

"I play music, I play women, and I play with the ethereal. I don't play cards."

"Seriously, you drove all night after being up all day. Go get some sleep, because what you just said was really lame."

"Yeah, you know, I thought the same thing as it came out of my mouth. Oh?" Jessie said as something new came to his mind. "How are you going to keep Max from sitting down at that table?"

Max's love of cards was undeniable, and they both knew it. "I have absolutely no idea. I was thinking of getting a nail gun and some straps, secure him to a wall, maybe? If you have any better ideas, don't keep them to yourself."

"Right, I'm going to bed." Jessie gave him one last look, the expression asking, *Are you sure about everyone's safety?*

"This is the safest place any of us could be right now. We're good. Go to bed, that's an order. We can figure out our next move tomorrow."

"Okay, boss." Owen accepted the light punch on his good arm.

Taking in a deep breath, Owen let the ethereal energy wash over him. His shoulder had been bad. Mara knew what she was aiming for, and the message had been clear. *If your arm can't hold itself up, neither can you play that forsaken guitar.* Not one bone but several had fractured and split off, tearing muscles and soft tissue. Thankfully now that Mara and he had reunited, he could pour ethereal power into the wound. The side effect being that he was seriously amped up. Like being in the middle of a hardcore concert and wanting to outjump everyone around him.

Power coursed into and through his body, stealing all fatigue from his mind and bones.

The bouncer outside the door to the Golden Horn was a normal human, with thick arms, wearing a red shirt and shades. He didn't even check her ID, simply waving Alice in as she approached. Power built in Alice's chest, ready to be used. A den of demons was no small feat to take by oneself. The priests who had trained her had told her all about it before she had left them. That was, of course, before the fall of the monastery. Since then she had avoided anything to do with any priest but Father Patrick.

After all, she would never be able to forget their betrayal as Alton and the others had turned their automatic rifles in her direction while she was in the room with Kerogen.

She had trusted them, and in return they had been willing to sacrifice her for practically nothing. Not even a sure kill. It was a betrayal that revealed the truth of their secret order. What her worth was to them. If it hadn't been for the demon Kerogen, she would be dead right now.

A debt to the monster she would never pay back.

After the attack, both she and Father Patrick had decided to stay in hiding from the church. Just as much if not more than they had from Kerogen himself.

Father Patrick wasn't a fighter, didn't have a soul for violence. Didn't believe in the necessity of it. She respected him for it, even though it was the opposite of her life. But Patrick had stood between her and death too many times to call him a coward.

And so on she went, not for the first time, into a den of demons who housed a level five she needed to have a hard chat with. The plan was simple: locate the five, shut down every person or We between her and her target, and then get this Damon to tell her where in the United States Kerogen was currently hiding.

Are you ready to have some fun, Alice? she asked herself while passing through the opening of the Golden Horn. *Never go back, only forward.*

Even early, the club was alive with activity. The main room was long and stretched out to her left, the main bar on the right by the entrance. A small three-person jazz band had pulled out the piano and were setting the mood for drinks and conversation.

"Excuse me. I'm on my way," a girl in her midtwenties said as she held up a round serving tray filled with drinks while squeezing herself in between Alice and a tall patron wearing too much cologne and showing too much interest.

Alice allowed her to pass by, turning her head away so she wouldn't be seen as easily. Casually Alice drew more energy into her body. She filed past tables filled with all manner of customers. Some young, some old, most well dressed in their midthirties, having an evening drink and making small talk.

Moving away from the entrance, making her way deeper, she felt people trying to see under her hood, men and women alike following her progress. It didn't matter. They would know who she was soon enough. She just needed to get to the back of the room. Level fives were like big bears, always going deep into a cave.

There was a smell to the place unlike anything she had ever smelled before. The hair on the back of her neck tingled, bringing every warning instinct on high alert.

There were We, of course. Level twos and level threes and ones, not that they would matter tonight. She avoided looking, marking targets. When you placed a green dot on someone, you wanted the shot to go straight in. Otherwise, you were likely to miss. One target, one hit. And right now her single dot was on the level five, this Damon. She had come here for him alone.

She moved to the wall, a clear path in the direction of the band in the corner, and tilted her head down as not to draw attention. The rhythm of the song was strong and smooth but was without ethereal energy. The band members were each normal humans. She could feel the weight of the vibrating strings as it mixed with the singer's shady voice.

The room was shaped like a large L, doglegging to her right. She took note of the second, smaller bar that stood against the inside wall. A few men and women were standing, waiting to be served.

This back section held far more round tables and chairs, but here they were shaded in by the dark alcoves, dim lights and hushed conversations, creating a side of the club that might as well be a different place than the front. It was more than just the difference between light and shadow. Alice could feel the difference between the two sides of the room. *Cave* was the right description of what lay ahead and across. A stone in her gut dropped, and just then, she was sure the We she was looking for was going to turn out to be anything but nice.

Good times, Alice, are go times, she reminded herself.

O wen gingerly stretched out his right arm. A small pain, like an internal buzzing, said that he had just torn some of the softer new growth while stretching out the muscles. It was nothing big, just newly made flesh that needed to be told what was expected.

With an easy hand, he removed the cloth wrap that had held his arm stable while the ethereal energy had fixed all the damage. Setting the sling in an old wooden case in Mara's small office he and Jessie had been talking in, Owen stepped out to go check on his people.

By sound alone, he could tell the club was filling up, but there was no rush here. The Golden Horn held old roots, didn't attract the hip crowd, thank the world. No, Mara's bar was for a clientele that wanted something more concrete, a place with gravity and danger stitched into the carpet and walls, a place to get a drink outside the everyday world that pretended to be made up of hugs and handshakes.

Max was currently sleeping in the back room, where three cots had been set up for the guys. Despite his nap in the car, the kid was still tired. With Jessie now going to bed, it left only Daphne and Clover to check on. The girls were to share David's old room, which still held two beds.

Owen moved down the side hall, taking the back route to the far side of the club. Here the light was low as he passed doors to restrooms and storage. A small water dispenser with fruit within was set up on one side wall, small square-cut glasses stacked and waiting. The sound of the jazz band grew with each step as he moved into the deepest section of the club.

Just to his left was the small bar with Jones, a trusted level three We, attending a few standing customers. Across the way, running almost the length of the room, were small rows of booths, high and deep, granting enough privacy for muted conversation for parties up to six. A small red light illuminated the patrons—some We, some not. In between the bar and booths were more round tables spaced with thick, matching chairs like those from the front. Half were full. Humans tended to stay toward the front of the bar.

Owen settled himself against the wall, scanning the crowd as he listened to the singer's voice. She was good, the players were tight and the instruments well maintained. He tracked back from the band, all the way to the deepest part of the building, to the main table off to his right in the corner. Mara laughed as she sipped a clear martini, and Daphne smiled slightly, turning pink as she did so.

He couldn't help but stare as Mara continued to laugh. She had a laugh that could curl inside someone. A laugh that could wipe away the horror of the world and set a child back on his feet. It was good to hear it again.

Damon was at the table, of course, the old sax player with his face full of lines and his eyes missing nothing as he laughed at Mara's no doubt crude humor. Cornelius was there as well, perhaps more relaxed than everyone else as he sort of sprawled back in his chair chuckling, then leaning in, the group listening then laughing some more.

Owen watched it all, taking it all in. How he had survived here without one of these We binding his soul to their own was impossible. He should be dead. He should be chained and bound. *Jessie was right. This is the thieves' den, the pit of doom for an unbound child, and yet I brought Daphne here. To the most dangerous place I know. Why?*

The answer came as easily as the question. This was home. Despite those three being We, he knew them as he knew himself. Mara believed in freedom . . . in innocence. In children. Her heart was bigger than even her anger. Damon had a wild soul, one that might very well tear down the heavens, but it was his burden and his alone. It had been over a hundred years since Damon had made a run with anyone, and even then, it had been more of a drunken field trip than anything real. No, the old sax player believed his will, his fight, was made just for him, and everything else was simply secondary.

He could be kind. Damon could be kind to a young teenager who had more fire and vinegar than sense. Owen could still feel the level five's large hand as it brushed his hair back and forth with shaking fingers. The weight of that hand. *He could have crushed me like a bug. Taken my power as his own how many times? How many opportunities did Damon have?*

Why did I bring Daphne here? Owen thought again to himself, answering his own question just as fast. *Because I trust in their word. I trust Mara as she sits there watching over Daphne and proclaiming to the city, "This unbound child is under my protection. You will have to get through me to get to her." And the others sit beside her as they always have, proclaiming the same.*

There was more, so much more on the tip of his mind, pressing to come forth as he watched them laugh together.

His right hand itched with the need to be free, and Owen took it for the sign it was. He wanted to play. Wanted to let go of so much weight. He wanted to release it and let it out into the night. During the road trip here, none of them had bled off the building energy, as it could have been tracked. Even releasing enough ethereal energy to fix his shoulder wasn't enough. He needed sound and danger. He needed to let go of this world and taste the other side.

Of course, if I go anywhere near that stage on my first night, Mara will kill me.

He looked away, spotting Clover setting drinks down in front of two older men, more engaged in their conversation than her. His scan moved just to her right, to the stage and the instruments on the wall that were there, waiting to be played.

A pull of force so strong it hurt to look away.

I can play them all, he thought. *Each of you that lie lifeless and hanging on the wall, right there. I am back, and I still remember how to give you breath, life. To run into the flames of Heaven.*

He had grown up doing just that. In between polishing and sweeping, he had learned to play each instrument here in this home.

His focus moved back almost absently, his gaze settling on a lone woman who stood in a shadow just to the left of the band. He was unable to see her face, her profile lost within a deep green hood. But there was something there. A force, an energy that was calling . . . Something more, something that separated her from everyone else.

An unseen spark snapped between him and the lone woman. It tingled and pulled hard in his chest, rooting him to the floor despite the forty or so feet separating them. Something hot and wild stroked up his spine as he tried to penetrate the shadows of her hood.

Owen tasted a change in the air as she seemed to still. He held that stillness and raised an eye before a slight sparkle of green stones on her belt attracted his attention, the bottom of the jeweled buckle just visible beneath her sweater.

His essence around his wrist buzzed with life, with a warning, sending every instinct he had on high alert.

Information clicked into place. A lone woman. Perhaps not a woman but a child. An unbound child gets onstage to sing and the hunter comes out. The hunter and the child.

They are here! The hunters are here. Somehow we were followed!

Alice took a moment to study the main table tucked deep into the farthest darkened corner of the club. Spotting her target and those sitting at the table beside him, she zeroed in on his face, confirming the description.

Damon Alfrez, get ready to sing like a canary. Because you will be telling me where Kerogen is hiding.

An internal warning had her glancing away from Damon and his table, looking instead off to the side, just past the small bar before the opening to a back passageway.

Thick black hair cut short, black T-shirt and blue jeans. The stranger's face was sharp and just a touch serious, but with a beauty that bordered on the dangerous. A pretty face that was more than smooth skin over a sharp jawline. Everything about him said *casual*, but the eyes—the intensity said *fire*. A promise of heat and storms. That mysterious sensation that raced into her blood had her pausing, had her heart skipping a beat as she held still.

For a single second Alice was sure the stranger could

see her. Could see all of her. Despite the distance, the shadows and the concealment of her hood.

Alice's breath quickened as if the battle had already started, a single electric sensation passing through her body, bumps running over her arms. A response inside tingled as she held his gaze from the safety of her shadowed hood.

Snap out of it, Alice. He is only a man, she reprimanded. *And I don't have time for men. Kerogen is all there is time for.*

As she looked on, two things became clear at the same time. First, the stranger with the face made for dark nights was one hell of a good-looking man. With shoulders and arms that said he took care of himself. And two, the stranger with a face sculpted for secrets was holding a crap ton of ethereal power!

The essence covering her belt buckle reacted, creating a sensation the likes of which she had never felt before and causing her skin to buzz with agitation.

She saw him break from the wall first at an incredible, ethereal-enhanced speed, pushing off with one hand while the other snapped down in a way that warned of a weapon.

Not sure what it could be, Alice casually unzipped her sweater.

Too bad. There was something about you.

Owen pulled on more power from his waiting well, both his own and the essence trusted into his keeping. He moved with the speed of a mountain cat, taking five long strides before leaping over a half-empty table. He hit the ground in stride. His thinking became as clear and simple as live or die. Zero or one.

Daphne will be protected by everyone at the table, including Mara.

Max and Jessie are presumably safe and away from the danger, but Clover is only two tables from the stage, from the intruder. In the very center.

What were the chances the unseen hunter would be far from the child by the stage? His eyes scanned the deeper shadows looking for signs of a hunter masking his presence. A ripple in light, a distortion of grays or color, a feeling, a sense of danger from either side. Anything just . . . off.

Owen was looking for it all as he ran to get between what was coming and his best friend. He watched the girl while she casually unzipped her green sweater, thought he saw tactical gear beneath.

Clover is too close. She is right in the heart of it. Where are the hunters?

The raw essence snapped down off his wrist into his hand as his heart climbed in his chest. The girl pulled back her hood, catching his attention once more.

She was beautiful. Striking, even, in a kind of light perfection he had only ever heard described as raw beauty.

Her skin was a perfect creamy white, with thick, full lips. Her nose matched her chin, not too small but perfectly proportioned to the rest of her face. But it was the wide, deep green eyes that sparkled bright in the shadows of the light. The force behind them declaring she was unafraid and unflinching.

She pierced him, held him even as he ran forward in a desperate attempt to be there in time to save Clover.

Behind it all was black hair, cut short in a hard angle down and forward, leaving a no-nonsense look about her that was anything but childlike.

Instincts shifted to certainty as he watched a knife snap up in her fingers only to rapidly be flung straight forward. The speed was lightning fast, blurring so the blade disappeared before his eyes, backed by ethereal power as it was.

Owen's body moved more out of preservation than any real thought. A single black cord of ethereal power of his own shot out of his hand and shoved the spinning weapon to the side. A patron was hit with force, but there wasn't any time left to be concerned.

"Clover, get down, get down!"

Clover, having seen his charge late, was in the process of turning around toward the intruder. Another blade was already in her hands.

Alice was surprised she had missed. This wasn't her first den, not by a long shot, and when she threw, she normally hit what she was aiming at. All the same, she took a step forward, closer to the real target in the back. Another throwing knife she drew free. "Come on in, honey," she said as the man continued his charge.

"Clover, get down, get down!"

Alice saw the recognition in the waitress's eyes as they went wide with understanding.

So there is a connection between this one and the etherealist coming at me. How sweet.

She watched as the waitress started to drop down, moving on his command, and Alice couldn't help but take advantage of the situation. A small step angled to the side as she threw sidearm, the blade spinning in line with the dropping girl, using her body as cover. She watched the path as the knife slipped just high enough to miss the waitress's descending head.

To Alice's surprise, a white whip of ethereal raw essence snatched the flying weapon out of the air, narrowly avoiding the woman and scorching the metal blade while flinging it harmlessly over the piano.

Well, that was impressive. The room erupted, and she let her sweater fall to the ground.

Too damn close. Owen's ethereal essence flung the blade to the side before it could hit Clover. It was all the time he had left.

Still charging, he snapped the energy whip back, off to his left side as the attacker came forward to engage.

He saw her right hand slide across her belt and he only had a breath before he knew he would be fighting against someone who also had an ethereal weapon. A first for him.

His whip cracked forward, striking at the chest, but impossibly she moved even faster, sidestepping the attack. A long, serrated knife made of raw essence formed in her hand. He pulled back the whip for defense against the weapon but was too late.

Owen dodged to the side, the blade scoring a shallow cut across his stomach. Pain was slow in coming, so filled with power, but she wasn't done with him.

Light and fast on her feet, she followed the dodge to the side, slicing across and up, narrowly missing his arm and neck before a hard, snapping kick sent him flying across the room toward the front exit. He hit a group of fleeing customers, smashing into them, taking the majority with him over a table loaded with drinks, and two chairs.

CHAPTER EIGHTEEN

A+O

Alice watched the etherealist guard as he flew from view.
The crowd of patrons erupted into full chaos. Men and
women screamed in kind as they trampled out the door for
their lives. Even some of the demons were in the process of
fleeing like deer from a forest fire.

Alice looked down to her right, where the waitress was
pulling ethereal power. A single shared look was a clear
understanding between two souls. Alice held the woman's
life in her hands. This close, if she wanted, the waitress
might as well already be six feet under.

A small nod to get out of here had the woman scrambling.
With a little luck, she would take her defender with her.

Alice gave the same indication to the band, who were
trapped in the corner between her and any exit. No, her
fight wasn't with them. She knew where the real fight was.
She looked past some of the We who had climbed out of the
dark booths to stand like sentinels.

She looked past the bartender who held a shotgun at the ready while standing guard behind the small bar. Looking deeper into the shadowed corner, she saw Damon standing with six others, a teenager now tucked back behind the table.

The enchanted blade morphed into a bracelet, decking Alice's wrist in green jewels just before she vanished from view. Ethereal magic covered her body, bending light and reshaping, so she was concealed from sight. Alice didn't stay still, couldn't stay still, and instead moved to her right in a burst of speed.

Some of the closest We on the left side lashed out with their ethereal energy, tossing tables and chairs to where she had been. The bartender's shotgun didn't fire, and she had only a second to think about it before she watched it tossed across the room with ethereal enhanced strength into the waiting hand of a level four We who stood in front of Damon.

Alice moved fast, going straight in at the closest We standing guard on the right by the small bar side. Her fist, covered by ethereal essence, punched in, the essence cutting right through any protection the level four had. Her fist met face, and the level four went airborne. The clarity in his eyes went soft and dull before he made a ninety-degree rotation in the air to land hard, out of the fight.

Taking a page out of Kerogen's book long ago, Alice went up, clinging to the ceiling, then moving across to land between two level threes.

More chairs and tables smashed down where she had been, but none came close.

Alice hit the closest level three in the back of the head, sending him crashing into an alcove and across its table. *Lights out.* Before the other one could even move, Alice hit him hard in the face, sending him sprawling out flat to the floor.

Three down and just getting started. Keep moving. Don't stop.

Needing to keep the attack going before Damon and his We could get a plan, Alice ran by a table while crisscrossing the room. Using just her left hand, filled with ethereal power, she tossed the heavy table in the opposite direction, causing one of the three by the left wall to have to move or be hit. It was only a distraction.

Alice came in low, half sliding to the right as she whipped a foot around, sweeping the legs of a level three and hitting his throat, crushing his windpipe. She heard the gargle of choking as he struggled for air. He would live—his ethereal power would already be at work healing the wound—but he was out of the fight for at least ten minutes. More than enough time for her to get what she needed.

Owen had to work to detangle himself from the fleeing patrons he had taken down in his crash. Coming to his feet, he watched as Clover took off running in his direction. Behind her he watched as the assailant allowed the band to go, to escape. His ribs hurt and his head rang a little, but he wasn't out. He wasn't done despite the several cuts to his body.

"Owen, thank God," Clover said as she rushed to him.

"I'm okay. Get to Jessie and Max. They're in their room. And then get them out of here. Take them out the back."

"I can't leave you and Daphne. You're bleeding all over."

"No, it's fine. You have to get them out before the other hunters show themselves. I'll get Daphne."

"Owen, there isn't any other hunter. She's the hunter. I saw the guns."

"No, she's just the distraction." Owen looked to the woman with sharp black hair and a face too beautiful. As Owen watched, the woman simply disappeared from view.

Seeing her disappear confirmed Clover's words.

"Oh, hell!" Owen said, knowing he had been wrong. "Go. Clover, go now. That's an order. I'll get Daphne out."

Owen felt his heart climb in his chest as the world narrowed. He had to get Daphne out of this, along with protecting Mara and the others if he could. Inside, he felt his resolve harden.

Alice took a moment. Something was off. No gunfire, no serious attack in response to her besides some punches in the air and thrown tables and chairs?

She spared a confirming glance at the main table, where the pack of high-level We were standing before her. That was, all but Damon, who stood behind the table, body in front of the teenage girl. *A bonded teenage girl, perhaps? His bonded?*

Fury built in her chest as the idea grabbed hold, and it took all she had not to cave in the bartender's head as she slammed him face-first into the flat of the bar. Using strength and power, Alice pulled the bartender over the bar and flung him across the room like a heavy stuffed animal.

Her ethereal scream followed right behind the flying man, a wave of ethereal power reinforced with focus and years of practice. Tables and chairs went airborne, glasses of drinks shattering and being flung as tiny shrapnel, all moving at explosion-level speed toward the main table.

Everything before her was moving in one fast, roaring wave directed toward the We gathered not more than thirty feet away.

Scatter them, break them up. Take them down one or two at a time.

The We on the right side of the table, the one who had caught the tossed shotgun earlier, moved at a blinding speed, taking one step toward the blast. His hair was flecked with gray on both sides, but his eyes were bright with joy as he made a fast slashing motion with his right hand and arm.

She watched as something new happened. Her wave

split in two, rolling out to either side, somehow taking all
the debris with it. Avoiding the main table altogether. The
We on the left wall were slammed back and up; however,
the main table was unaffected. Not even their hair was
ruffled by the moving air in the room.

Tables and chairs caught by her wave of power hit the
wall hard on the left, crashing and breaking, but there was
no one left on that side to be affected.

The female demon in the group—tall, with dark hair—
held a sawed-off shotgun in her hands. She spoke with a
voice that stole Alice's momentum. "Impressive, child. But
messy. Very messy."

Her words curled inside Alice's chest, stealing an ounce
of her will as she pushed to attack once more.

Alice twisted back, her hand snapping up in reaction as
an attack came from behind.

D amn, she was fast. The amount of destruction and violence that had passed on this side of the room had taken
only moments, and already the house was almost wiped out.

*And yet so far, it doesn't look as if anyone is dead.
That's different.*

Owen didn't have time to think about the revelation as
the attacker smashed Jones's head hard against the bar and
then flung his body like a missile across the entire room.

Owen was in motion, coming at her from behind, as the
ethereal wave rocked the room ahead. The giant shock
wave of power flung everything between the hunter and the
corner table end over end. Owen had his essence in hand as
he closed more of the distance separating him and the
hunter. He watched as Cornelius stepped up and somehow
separated the wave. At any other time, Owen would have
said such a thing was impossible. Because Cornelius didn't
just block or break the wave—he separated the massive
force in two, directing each half to the side. Poor Jones and

some of the other We still on the left side took the hit as they lay on the floor. But Mara, Daphne, and the rest remained safe, unfazed.

Mara spoke, and hearing her voice dripping with ethereal energy, Owen knew now was the time. "Impressive, child. But messy. Very messy."

Owen understood what that voice could do to a normal. Knew what that voice could do to a low-level We. He had even seen her use it against a high-powered We. His raw essence, shaped like a thin metal whip, snapped out, going for the hunter's neck. His aim was true, the essence reaching across the six and a half feet. The hunter's hand interposed itself as the essence attempted to wrap twice around her neck as it had with Butch in his last fight. Only her hand miraculously slid itself in between, allowing her to breathe.

Her invisibility disappeared even as she yanked back hard on the chain. He was ready, his feet planted and reinforced with ethereal power, as the move was commonplace. Even so, the force of the pull was tremendous. And then it disappeared while she reversed the pull and attacked, one hand still caught up by the whip, the other producing a throwing knife.

Owen's feet braced for a tug-of-war-like competition— now he was suddenly off-balance. Owen twisted his body to the side as the knife flew through the air before driving into his recently repaired right shoulder.

Another knife was in the hunter's hand, and he twisted out of the first slash, even while retracting the essence.

Owen dove backward, full out. Needing to change the game. He had just enough time to see her eyes going wide as understanding clicked in.

The essence around her neck and hand literally tied her own body to his. As he dove with a shortened leash, she had no choice but to follow.

She came off her feet as he flew back. Owen's boots caught her hard in the stomach, as if she were a child wanting to fly. He accepted a slash to the left leg for his troubles while using the momentum to send her ass on her way, over and behind.

Owen moved his head just out of the way, narrowly avoiding the knife's blade as she flew past.

Instantly, Owen pulled hard on the essence, needing to lock her down and keep her off-balance until he could find an opening.

Flipping up to his feet, Owen wrenched once more with reinforced muscles, but the essence slipped free of her neck as she used the flight and fall to unspool the whip.

Damn, she is fast.

Never before had he gone up against anyone with such skill. Heart pumping with ethereal energy, he slashed out with the whip, keeping her at bay. The tip went hot, scorching the air and leaving an orange line where her face had been.

"Get Daphne out of here. I'll hold her!" he called as he broke the air between him and the hunter with the tip of the whip.

"You should have run." The voice came in low, twisting his gut in reaction. The words rang true to his ears.

Owen made to speak, but the attack came.

Before Owen could even think about it, he punched down behind the attack, his fist connecting hard into the hunter's left eye before he had to fling himself back or take a knife to the side of the head.

Alice judged the whip, calling on her own essence to crawl up into her right hand, the serrated knife once more firm in her palm. Trusting its power to deflect the whip, she bounded to the side, using the flat of the blade like a small shield as the whip came in.

Her bell was rung, but she didn't shake it off. Instead her temper flared, pushing through the chaos of the hit.

You will pay for that.

"Get Daphne out of here!" he yelled again.

Alice started another attack but had to stop her charge as the whip struck the air just before her. She watched the young girl behind Damon try to move out toward the side exit, but Damon's right arm held her back.

I am running out of time. I need this to be done and done now. If this guy is only here because of the child, then maybe there is an opportunity.

"Which demon is the child bonded to? Together we can end her suffering, or if you don't have the stomach, stand aside, and I will do this myself."

His whip struck out, snapping a fiery orange line in the air between them.

"She isn't bonded, and right now the only danger she's in is from you. Leave now, and never come back here."

Too bad, Alice thought.

She attacked, flipping high into the air, two blades striking out at his chest midroll. She didn't see that he blocked both but could feel it in the way he backpedaled and swung the essence in defense. Alice came forward even while landing. She rolled the dice and went low, guessing he would go for center mass with his whip as he had done several times already.

The whip sang just over her head as she swept his legs. Fingers sticking to the ground as easily as they had the ceiling, Alice angled her body and kicked him with all the force she could muster. Both his arms blocked, but it mattered little as his body flew back across the floor.

"Drop the weapons, or I drop both of you," Alice said, sliding up to her feet and pulling her guns, pressing the laser sight to show her commitment as she leveled one on each of the We standing between her and Damon. "You have seen what I can do without these. With them, I will end each of you if you do not comply."

"You came here for something, child. What is it?" the demon with the raised shotgun asked. Her voice was intoxicating, delving into Alice like a cool drink on a hot, sunny day.

"Kerogen. He's an asshole, and I want his location. And I want it now," Alice said, directing it to Damon and then the gathering.

"Kerogen? That man is a . . . Well, let's just say he is something this world can do without. You're the one he bonded, I'm guessing," Damon said as the standoff between shotguns and pistols continued.

"Kerogen. Where is he?" Alice repeated once more.

"I don't know, but I can try and find out, if you want to lower those weapons of yours," Damon said.

"Not a chance. I need his location now. Give it to me, or I start shooting."

"Doesn't work that way. You see, I'll send out the word I'm looking for him. Word will come back. Could be one day, could be two, could be five. Could be he walks through that door himself. Kerogen is old, and the old can be a bit cagey when they want to be," Damon said.

Fear filled her bones, and she shifted the green lasers so they both were on him. "I have two guns pointed right at your chest, Damon. I want his location. I think you already know what I am capable of. Tell me where Kerogen is, or the bullets start flying, and then we have this conversation all over again." She watched him, the teenage girl behind. She was ready for the two We with shotguns in front, as well as the etherealist who was still on the floor not far from her feet and who was, even now, ready to spring back into action.

"No, child, you have two forty-fives in your hand." Damon spoke slowly. "Each is filled with small, measured explosives. However, only the last two are pointed at my chest." His hand wiped the air, causing the two green dots to shift from his shirt to his hands and back again. As if he could simply brush the light away.

Alice was trying to puzzle out what he was saying when

two thin vines of ethereal power, so tiny she didn't see them at first, for they looked thinner than a single speck of dust, shot straight forward, through the barrels, and dove down into the hilts of the weapons, causing them to instantly blaze hot in her hands.

She felt the remaining We build shields as one, black ethereal power coating their skin, then coursing out to the side to intertwine with each other, blocking her in. Even the etherealist who had interfered was layering power over his skin.

She let go of the weapons as they each shifted to scorching hot, terrified of what was about to happen. She took a step back as they hung suspended in the air by the thinnest cords of power Alice had ever seen.

She was out of time and knew it. Two of the We stepped behind her, their power-coated skin trapping her inside a ring.

"Down, get down," the etherealist she had been fighting with called as he waved her in his direction on the floor.

Out of time and without any other choice, she went with it, calling on her own power for protection but knowing she was far too late.

Alice dove into the only space available, hitting the ground hard. His body covered hers a split second before the guns exploded, sending heated shrapnel in all directions. The force of the explosion pounded his body into hers so she was suddenly squeezed tight on all sides as the room was rocked with the blast.

The etherealist's body was lean and well muscled, and before she could even toss an elbow into his face, his arms wrapped around her, pinning her to the ground. A thin gold vine of ethereal essence snaked around, stealing and shutting down her ethereal power from external use. It was different than the way Kerogen had sucked her dry, but it might as well be the same. She still had energy and fight

left, but one hard pull from him told her the struggle would
be a mistake.

Owen let out his breath when he was sure the hunter
couldn't get away from him.

"Don't try anything. Your life is in their hands now."

He whispered the warning, unsure why he had.

"What are we going to with her?" Owen asked the
question, already knowing the probability of what was
about to happen and not liking the way something in his
stomach turned over at the idea.

He spared a look at Daphne, who gave him a nod she
was okay. Though her eyes were wide and she had a little
shake of adrenaline in her.

Some looked to Damon for the answer, but Damon
looked to Mara. "Your house, your call," he said.

"Very well. Get her up, Owen."

Victor, a level four, one of Cornelius's group, moved in
to help. He was a bit bloody from broken glass but otherwise was fine. Victor wasn't rough but wasn't gentle either.
Together, Owen and the level four got the hunter to her feet.
Besides a small bruise over one cheek, she was relatively
unhurt, or at least she appeared to be.

Mara took her time as she moved closer, taking a good
long look. "Who gave you Damon's name?"

"Does it matter? You demons are all the same."

"Demons, are we now? Look around, hunter. You just
busted up my club, hurt my friends and customers, and you
want to talk about demons. I should feed you to one."
Mara's voice was flat then cold, and for all Owen knew, she
was telling the truth. If anyone could feed a person to an
actual demon, Owen believed this group could.

"Give me Kerogen's location, or I swear I will tear
this—"

Mara's fist slammed into the hunter's jaw, silencing the woman. Blood hit the floor and sprayed over Owen's arm. "You made a mess of my place. Now I have made a mess of your face." Mara's hand slipped forward, and thin fingers withdrew two throwing knives from where they were secured to the woman's vest. "I'll keep these as a memento to give to Kerogen if ever I see him again. Damon, I have already handled one problem today." Mara's simple glance indicated Owen. "I give this problem back to you. I am sure you can take care of it in a proper manner."

"As you wish, Mara."

"Daphne, you are still with me, child. We are going to have a drink at the other bar. You are old enough to join me, I think, before we deal with the cleanup and the cops. I truly hate hunters. Might be the only thing I hate more than that forsaken guitar."

Daphne didn't say a word as she moved out from behind the table. With wide eyes, she glanced at Owen in passing but gave him and the hunter a wide berth. He gave her the smallest of nods to go with Mara.

"Now I guess it is my turn to mess you up," Damon said as he came in, rounding out from behind the table and coming up close. "I'll tell you what, I'll make you a deal. Right here, right now. If you can tell me who gave you my name, then I will tell you where Kerogen is."

The woman started to speak, but Jones the bartender struck the hunter hard in the back of the head, knocking her out cold. It was so unexpected Owen almost lost his grip as her weight went limp and lifeless.

Owen cursed, as he had to work hard to keep her upright. If Victor hadn't held her other side firm, the woman would have gone down.

"You could have warned me," Owen said.

"It's been a long time, Owen. Some of our signs have changed. Besides, if this woman really is Kerogen-bonded, and I am inclined to think she is, your safe place for your crew just became complicated," Damon said.

"Who is Kerogen?" Owen asked.

"Oh, he's the same as everyone. You know, an ego with an asshole." His laughter was soft and deep. Perhaps contagious, if he hadn't turned back, moving toward his usual seat in the corner as if this was just another night.

CHAPTER NINETEEN

Alice woke with a start, her body snapping awake.

"Oh, holy hell!" she said as the back of her head hit a stone wall. A light pain mixed in with confusion as she blinked both away.

Where am I?

Cold black cut stone that seemed to absorb light more than reflect it was beneath her and behind. A single sconce was no more than twenty feet down the wall, the only light that appeared to be in the pure darkness that surrounded her.

Moving gingerly, Alice made to explore the back of her head, where the pain was throbbing. Her hands stopped halfway up as thick steel chains clattered, breaking the silence. Everything came back clear—each moment of the fight, all of it. Even Damon's face as he distracted her, offering a deal before the lights had all gone out.

Examining the chains revealed the links were thick and black, with a peculiar thin silver line cast into each. Seeing them locked tight to her wrist, a small child's voice inside started screaming, *Not again. This can't happen again.*

"Stop it. You will get out of this, you will be free." *You are no longer a child. Think, damn you.*

Alice said more—had to say more to stay sane. Finally she looked around while reaching back and carefully exploring the bump on the back of her head. The room was long, no telling how wide. All but her immediate surroundings were shrouded in darkness, hardly surprising, as the stones she was sitting on were deep black. As for her head, no blood matted her hair, and that was a good thing.

Alice froze still as a possibility clarified in her mind—

"No!"

Uncaring about chains, foreign rooms and the bump on the back of her head, Alice panicked as both hands flew to check the skin over her collarbone. Fear so thick it threatened to choke and blind her had her looking down, unable to interpret what she was feeling.

It's there. The same small, childlike voice spoke in her mind. "It's still there." She breathed in relief.

Alice's fingers, having run just under the collar of her shirt, were moving back and forth, exploring the odd feel of the shroud of tears's crisscrossing pattern buried deep beneath her skin. Still safely hidden. She let out a frightened breath as she followed the pattern up over one shoulder.

The idea of Kerogen having her again was too much.

The ethereal knife? If I have the shroud, I might still have the ethereal knife, she thought with a glimmer of hope. Alice checked her wrist, but even manacled, she knew it wasn't there. She checked her belt, but it wasn't there either. The essence was gone.

New light, bright and clear, poured in from her right, stinging her eyes, but not before Alice was able to glimpse that the room was far longer than she had first thought. Even so, the darkness drank the light, giving the sense of being left in a long hole.

Alice climbed to her feet, unable to endure the idea of sitting as the silhouette of four people came forward.

Two large doors shut without a sound behind them, and the room once more descended into the low light of the single sconce.

Her head snapped to her left as another matching sconce farther down the wall but behind her suddenly turned on, illuminating another coal-black section and another set of chains far out of her reach.

Yep, I'm in a dungeon. The sound of her captors' footsteps echoed off the stones.

"Good morning, Alice. While you were sleeping, we found out more about you." Damon's voice was deep and rich. He wore a blue pinstriped suit with an open collar and matching suede shoes. Everything about him said old-world polish. And yet there was something almost basset hound about him. Something soft and lazy, or perhaps simply unmoving.

The tall woman who had punched her in the face was currently looking at her as if she was an insect about to be squashed. Then there was the high level four who had cut the ethereal scream, the one with black hair dusted with a silver gray, sharp eyes and a small crinkle to his nose. He looked far more dangerous now dressed in black slacks, a blue shirt and a black vest.

And last, the only human in the group was the etherealist who had first attacked her. She spotted the leather cuff on his wrist and could see it for what it truly was, ethereal essence. She looked at him and somehow thought he was worse than the other three combined. *A human with power turned demon puppet.*

Owen watched the woman chained to the wall. How he could have thought her a kid because of her smaller size was simply ridiculous. Nothing about her said *child*. Everything said *warrior*. Even now, trapped, shackled at Mara and Damon's mercy, it was clear she would refuse to back down. If that wasn't the true meaning of a woman, he didn't know what was.

Last night he had helped deposit Alice here. Watched as Victor had efficiently and professionally stripped her of weapons, including the ethereal knife. Discovering the strange pattern that ran up the back of her neck, Mara, Damon and Cornelius had all been called down to take a look. A blocking relic. An old instrument to separate a bonded etherealist from their captor. A relic, embedded under the skin.

In the end, it was decided to leave the old thing right where it was. It had also been decided to give her drugs to ensure she didn't wake until morning. Owen had stood and watched it all last night, until it was clear the hunter wasn't going to be waking up.

He wasn't sure what he had expected to see now. But it wasn't this. How could it be? Chained and defeated, the woman still looked ready to tear the shackles off the wall and go on a killing spree. Far different than the soft woman he had carried in his arms the night before. For a moment Owen thought about Clover and the conversation they had exchanged that morning.

This woman hadn't acted like a true hunter. It was clear when you added in all the evidence from her attack. First, hunters killed, and they were all good at it. Second, true hunters almost never worked alone, and last night not a single person had died. That wasn't just luck. Alice was too skilled, too deadly. She was a killer, undoubtedly. But, it seemed, one with a purpose. It made the woman in chains staring with pure defiance something else. The idea was too akin to his own situation to be comfortable as he stood there watching her.

A contradiction, a note out of place, and yet perhaps in harmony with a tune he had yet to hear.

* * *

"Oh, honey. You can take that stance if you wish, but we have had a lot stronger and tougher things than you in those chains. The only chance you have of getting out of here alive is with our grace, and your full cooperation. After last night, that won't be easy."

The woman's voice was calm, unlike the night before. *Mara, was it?* Alice played back the small bit of conversation from the fight.

Alice watched as Mara reached into her pocket and produced a thin, dark cigarette. It lit as she pulled, the smoke leaving a small trail as she made a circle while speaking.

"Now, let's start this over and leave out the pissing match. I'm Mara, and the club upstairs is mine. This here is Cornelius." She indicated the high level four with black hair peppered with silver and gray. "You already know Damon, and look at that, he was the one you wanted to speak with anyway. And then beside him is Owen. Now that we are all acquainted, let's get this over with, shall we? I still have some cleaning upstairs to oversee."

Alice looked them all over, revulsion in her gut.

When they finally understood she wasn't about to back down by speaking, Damon spoke.

"Alice, it is eleven in the morning. The pinprick in the corner of your elbow is where we administered a sleeping agent. A woman comes in the bar looking to harm me, it doesn't take long to find out about her, particularly when she left her van across the street. So let's cut through the fog. You were bonded at age nine, in Denver, Colorado, by Kerogen. But you escaped and were whisked away by the church to become a hunter. Now you're after the We who did the bonding. You are after Kerogen. We have a few questions, and based on your answers, we might let you go. Hear me when I tell you there is an avenue for you to be released, but it requires you to be honest with us."

In response, Alice pulled on ethereal power. She pulled as much from her massive well as she could at one time. Despite the chains designed to block such a thing. Fire raced through her body, but it was only heat and pain. She could take both. Something in her head felt like it was splitting, but still she pulled harder, her intent to crush the cuffs around her wrists. To be free or die trying.

The level four didn't even step back as she made a sound and raised her arms as her body shook with the effort. The black cuffs, almost three inches long, grew heavy, and she smelled her flesh burning as the metal turned a fiery red, resisting the magnitude of her power.

She had just enough time to see the human called Owen move toward her as the pain turned her vision white, then black.

Owen's heart beat fast in his chest as the woman pulled on a well of power so deep and strong it shook him to the bone. He watched as the pain drove through her and she refused to relent even an inch. Destructive. Heartbreaking. And in a way that was nothing short of beautiful.

The shiver up her spine called to him. He moved as her eyes opened wide with the pain and the focus dimmed and then shut down. For the third time in under twenty-four hours, he held Alice, catching her body before she could fall hard to the stone ground.

"Impressive," Cornelius softly announced as Mara pulled on her thin cigarette.

"She isn't a musician," Damon said, as if everything else in the world were to be held to such a standard, and therefore Alice was beneath his care.

"True, she is not. But it's been a while since someone fought so hard against the chains. Reminds me of older days," Mara said with a chime to her voice.

"Thinking about singing again? We could bring down

the piano. Open a big bottle of champagne," Damon said in his low, mocking voice.

"I don't drink champagne anymore, you know that. Lights please, Jones."

Jones, who had been standing in the dark like one of the many pillars throughout the room, touched a control pad, and the room lit softly, dim lights growing into brilliant bright.

The room was enormous, far bigger than any one structure above it. It was old, so old Owen couldn't put an age to it. He knew some of the stories, even knew some of the myths. Back behind him and above were large crystal chandeliers, twelve modernized, twelve still holding candles and wax. The ceiling was high, reaching twenty feet around the edges, creating a natural outer box for fourteen feet in before shifting, angling up and climbing far higher into a dome painted with a master's hand. Each stroke of the brush a work of art, depicting the heavens before the fall. Before the creation of Earth and man. Before the We were forced to choose between the unseen war or life here on Earth.

When Owen was a child, this room had been David's and his own secret palace. Now it made him feel small. Even so, Owen couldn't help but notice the desire to play music once more grew within, the need vibrating through him as he glanced around.

Owen set Alice down gently. She, like the room, seemed to be a contradiction. In one light, she was unbreakable. In this light, something softer.

"Thank you, Jones. Did she say anything?" Mara asked.

"Nothing of consequence. Swore a few times. I think she was very worried about the relic still being in place under her skin."

"As she should be. As we all should be. That little harlot has placed us in deep water. If Kerogen gets word she is here, or if the hunters find out we have her, they will come. It will be like the old days," Mara said.

"If it is going to be like the old days, should we throw a party?" Cornelius's lighter voice made it clear the idea intrigued him.

Mara laughed, real and bright, breaking the stress she had been carrying since Owen had walked back in. "You think we should throw a party now, after all these years? Cornelius, there are times I think you are one of the craziest men I have ever known." Mara's eyes sparkled with delight.

"It could be fun. Look at this place, Mara. It's been a long time. And not even Kerogen would come at you while you are wearing a dress."

"The hunter had it right. Kerogen is an evil asshole . . ." Damon paused as he thought about something. Everyone stared, waiting as Damon cocked his head to the side as if he were listening to something only he could hear.

Owen paused too, his own body going still as he looked up toward the older man.

Recognition crystalized. It wasn't the first time Damon had heard a tune in the air. A tune that mixed power and air, heartbeats and creation. The rotation of the Earth with the vibration of the stones over their heads. Damon was, to Owen's thinking, a one-of-a-kind musician. And perhaps one of the scariest mothers when he had his saxophone in hand.

"Damon?" Mara asked in good cheer.

"If you throw a party, I'll play with the kid."

Owen took the words like a punch to the gut. It was the sort of declaration the likes of which he had never expected to hear. To play with Damon . . . The consequences? The journey itself would be . . . or could be . . . unfathomable. They would make it all the way to the Devil's bridge. Or the fourth gate of Heaven?

Mara flicked her cigarette at Damon's face as her eyes went as hot and deadly as a flash fire. Damon's head tilted just enough so the burning stick narrowly missed.

The itch to play within Owen intensified fivefold as the idea sank deeper and deeper, fanning an ember that had been within him all his life.

"Get the fuck out of my house!" Mara screamed.

Damon laughed as his head stayed tilted, listening to a sound only he could hear.

It has been said, and shall be said again, that the space separating a musician from society and the powers governing the stars are not far apart. For a musician, life is one of rotating loneliness amongst a sea of people they can only reach for but never touch. Mercy and kindness are only words in a life so vast and so utterly alone.

It's been two weeks, Owen. You're not going down there again, are you? Maybe we should leave," Clover said, not for the first time since the attack on the club.

"It's fine. We are still safer here than anywhere else. Six weeks and Daphne is eighteen. After that, we can go."

Clover kept her voice low, not wanting to be overheard. "Mara and Damon are going to pull this place down around us if we don't get out of here. Why won't you tell me what's going on? Mara won't even go to his side of the club anymore. Seriously, Owen, the vibe in here is so intense it makes my skin crawl every time I walk in there. I have watched customers walk in through the main door, take one look around, turn and leave. Whole groups have left before they even ordered drinks. This is bad, and it clearly has something to do with that woman you're bringing food to."

Owen balanced the small tray of food he was about to bring down to Alice, who was still chained below. "They are fine, Clover." Even as he said the words, he knew they sounded untrue. Clover shot him a look he had little choice but to speak over. "All right, Mara and Damon are not fine, but I have seen worse between them. Everything is going to be okay. They both just need to let off some steam. Trust me, Clover, this has happened before."

"Owen, they are both so strong. A fight between the two of them would level this place. What needs to happen to fix this? Do they need to get carnal with each other or something? Because it is so uncomfortable here. I'm going insane."

Owen knew what she meant. They were all feeling it. Too much unsettled power, raw energy. It fed each person's internal itch, making it a constant, growing thing. Just thinking about it made it worse.

The signs were in everyone. Jessie ran his hand over the top of the piano when he thought no one was looking, all five fingers sliding over the smooth black top. The look in his eyes was hungry and distant, as if somehow he could bask in a memory of playing the piano.

Daphne had to be told at least five times to stop singing. One time he had practically broken down the door to the shower in order to get her to stop. As for her bass guitar, it was locked away in the truck beside his own.

Max was the worst. It seemed like every time Owen turned around, Max was doing something wrong. Whistling a tune with a tinkle of ethereal power while he swept the floor. Tapping out a rhythm with a set of wooden spoons while he was supposed to be cleaning dishes. But it was the magic tricks that were the absolute worst, as they tended to go wrong at the best of times.

Max was using ethereal power like flour in a baker's kitchen. Five times Owen had no choice but to take the cards away from him. A day might pass, and then it seemed the kid had gotten his hands on another deck.

"I know it's bad, but for Daphne, we have to endure. I can't play here, not now, maybe not ever. I'll talk to Mara. Perhaps she will allow you and Jessie to play."

It wasn't safe for the younger kids to play in a place like this without him, and they couldn't leave. There was just

too much risk. All of Miami knew the Golden Horn was har-
boring an unbound etherealist. Despite Clover's words about
people turning away, more and more We were poking their
heads in and staying put, just in case. It didn't help that word
had spread Owen was back in town. Coupling that with the
attack somehow just brought more attention to his people, and
then there was the woman he continued to bring lunch to.

"What about the old sound studio? Could we play in
there?" Clover asked.

Owen had hoped to keep that a secret. Of course, such a
thing was impossible living in a place like this for two
weeks. It had only taken Max three days to find it. Thank
the heavens the kid had gone to tell Daphne rather than play
in there by himself.

"Clover, there is a reason that door is locked. That place
belongs to Damon, and he hasn't let anyone play in there in
almost fifty years. I have never even hummed a tune in the
control room, and I spent a hell of a lot more time here than
two weeks."

"I hate feeling like this. The only person who even
seems normal anymore is that guy Cornelius, and he's just
out of place."

"You know what it will be like if you and Jessie play
here, right?" Owen couldn't help the seriousness of his tone
as he himself remembered what it felt like.

"Yeah, I know." Her voice was clean of lies and weakness, but it was her steady eyes that shouted she was ready.

"Okay, try not to burn the place down."

She punched his arm as he turned away, heading to what
was commonly referred to now as "the dungeon" by his
people. The true name, and what lay beneath, having been
kept from them.

Alice remained shackled just within the silhouette of the
single illuminated sconce. She had bedding and a plas-

tic camping bucket for necessities, along with a water bottle and two packets of wet wipes. She had considered making a fuss with such items but could not see how it might serve her except to leave her sleeping on even harder ground, with a dirty body and nothing to drink, and then nowhere to go to the bathroom. Needless to say, she had decided to refrain.

Her wrists hurt from constantly trying to free herself, and her body was sore from sleeping on hard ground, even with the bedding. But besides that, not much had changed in two weeks. Each time Damon or one of the others had come down to speak with her, she had pulled on her well of ethereal power. The shackles fought the pull, burning her wrists until she fell unconscious from the overwhelming pain.

Two weeks. Two weeks I've been a prisoner, Alice thought.

The left door opened, the light from beyond spilling in, then closed behind Owen as he came in. The first time he had come in with her meal, he had tried to speak to her. That had been at the start of her captivity. The moment he asked his question, Alice had tested the bond's strength against her own. It had ended the same way it always ended, with her blacking out from the pain.

Now when the man came in with the food, he knew better than to try for a conversation.

Owen walked in a calm, strong line as he approached, coming to a stop just shy of her reach. He had been fast in the fight, and possibly deadly with his whip made of essence. But there was no true warrior before her now. No hunter. Nothing about the man who stood before her said he was a killer, a man to be feared.

And yet she had seen him. Witnessed him during the fight. He hadn't hesitated, hadn't run when he had a chance. Instead, the opposite was true. Owen had attacked even before she had. This casual, even normal-looking facade was a lie. Plain and simple.

Alice watched Owen as she had every time before. A dangerous, deceptive pawn belonging to the demons who held her.

Even so, perhaps he is the key I might need to escape. Then again, if I really need to escape, all I have to do is peel this shroud out from beneath my skin. Kerogen will come and burn this place to the ground. Only to find me chained right here. Already a prisoner—oh, what a plan, Alice.

Owen set the tray down, and she remained seated, her back to the wall, legs crossed, looking at him.

Owen took the fresh sandwich and fries and used a square piece of cardboard like a plate, sliding them off the tray and over. All the while he watched, knowing Alice was dangerous. He had expected her to try something in the first couple of days. And here they were, two weeks later, and still she just sat and stared.

This could have been me, he thought, *or Clover or Jessie or Max and—God make it not so—Daphne.* This woman hadn't had his protection and now she was twice chained in the dark, once by Mara and Damon and once by Kerogen, and still she was refusing to give in. She deserved more than this. She deserved something better. He continued to look, unable to take his eyes off her.

Owen picked up the full bottle of water and tossed it to her, rather than like each time before, when he had slid it beside the food.

Her eyes narrowed as her hand caught the bottle without effort, the chain rattling from her wrist in the air. Whatever she was thinking wasn't given away by any expression. He watched as Alice set the water bottle down so it stood beside her.

Instinctively he knew what would happen if he tried to talk to her. She was waiting for him to break the invisible line of silence. Her only control of the space around her.

Owen shook his head once, frustrated with himself. Standing, he gave her one last glance and couldn't help but notice how wild she looked. Not in her appearance. No, she was clean and somehow still looked pristine. The bruising around the nose and eye had faded a few days back. But she was wild in spirit. A caged tiger biding her time.

And maybe that was why he continued to volunteer to come down. There was a rare honest beauty that seemed all too familiar. He walked away worried and frustrated there was no answer, nothing he could do. To get involved might pull his priorities in two different directions, and he had made a promise to Daphne, to all his people.

A hollow plastic sound howled through the air from behind him. Owen turned in time, his hands coming up to catch the empty water bottle from the day before. The plastic crinkled under his hands, and it was the first real sound shared in the room since he had asked if she needed anything else on that first day.

Alice remained sitting on her makeshift pallet, as if she hadn't moved.

He smiled as he turned away. All fight and seriousness, he could respect that. Something else crossed his mind as he finished walking to the double doors. Something personal and private, something soft and warm, and possibly very, very deadly.

The following day Owen again brought the food down into the lower chamber. There was something different this time, a small possibility that it might be better than the days before.

He made a point to stay smart, to keep his wits about him. The night before, neither Mara nor Damon had gone down to have a conversation with Alice. Damon even went so far as to declare to the club that Alice's stubbornness was on par with Mara's own, so what was the point of talking to either?

Owen opened the hidden door and walked in, hearing the muffled sound of the mechanism that shut the door behind him. Again Alice was in the same spot. How could she not be?

Owen came to a stop in the same place he had each time before. Alice watched him as he watched her.

He slid the food over, this time a burger and fries, and then placed one hand on the water bottle before tossing it to her. She caught it easily and without surprise. The exchange was nonviolent, easy. He had tossed a thousand different things to his crew the same way over the years.

Alice gently placed the water bottle beside her so it once again stood tall, as it had yesterday, and then looked at him with the same catlike stare she seemed to have for everything.

So much rage and passion and control, all behind a mask of calm. Owen couldn't help but ask with his eyes, the gesture slightly mocking in question.

He hadn't planned to do it, but something about the woman was so defiant, and so deeply insisting, it twisted a feeling inside him. All they needed was a conversation and she was refusing. All they needed was cooperation and she was refusing. All he needed was the empty water bottle and she was what? Waiting for him to turn his back?

The look Owen shot her should have pissed her off, creating a *Screw you, buddy*. But there was a gentleness in his eyes that said something else.

Two-faced. Remember, Alice, he's two-faced. Even so, he might be my only real chance out of here. Maybe this is how I get free.

Alice reached behind her back while he leaned on one hand, ready to get up and leave her once more alone in the dimly lit dungeon. Her movement brought him up short from rising to his feet as she produced the empty water bottle. A disgusting and off-putting thought climbed through her mind just as she lobbed the empty bottle over. She really hoped he wasn't the one removing her waste each night from the camping bucket.

Owen caught the empty bottle with ease, a small communication, a small bond. His face didn't show a sign of changing. But there was a small, grateful smile buried deep within she thought she could see.

I am not pitiful, she thought. *I will get out of this.* Alice almost tested the bonds again, her body inwardly bracing for the excruciating pain. Almost.

Instead, Alice was distracted as, in silence, Owen reached into his back pocket and produced a worn red box of playing cards. They gave off the impression he carried them around in his back pocket all the time.

That is not normal, but then who am I to judge? I carry a thousand-year-old relic under my skin all the time. So he likes to play cards? Didn't Father Patrick always seem to have a deck at hand?

He shook the card box in unspoken question.

If she was honest with herself, she wasn't sure what the plan was here. Each morning after waking, she checked the food laid out for her for poison or drugs. Not that she was an expert in that field, but she checked anyway. Finding nothing of note, she ate and then stretched out in a small routine she had made up. It utilized the full length of the chains and kept her in fighting form. And then she meditated. Preparing her body and mind to defeat her captivity.

After a couple hours she would stretch and repeat her modified workout routine and then meditate again. After the third time of repeating her routine, Owen normally came in with her late lunch. Checking it, she would eat, then work out again and then meditate, preparing in case the night's events included Mara or Damon coming down to question her. After two weeks, it was not the worst idea to have cards around.

She only knew three games. Solitaire; gin, a favorite of Father Patrick's; and Go Fish. A game her father had once played with her.

Carefully, she gave a single nod, holding out her hand for the deck of cards. Expecting the toss.

She watched in surprise as instead of tossing her the cards, he pulled them out of the box and settled into a full sitting position. Still behind the line of where she could reach him, but the intent to play a game together was clear.

Ballsy, very ballsy. What's the angle here?

He shuffled, and the sound echoed out into the deep room, breaking the constant silence. Fast, sure hands tossed a stack of eleven cards out in front of her and ten to himself, just across the invisible line she could comfortably travel.

Alice hesitated, thinking it through, then got up and moved to the edge of the chain's length, sitting before him and the cards.

A slowness came to him, and she could see he was asking her to trust him a little bit more. Alice watched as he gently set the rest of the deck just within the edge of her reach. She could have tried to grab the hand, pull him in and try to hold him captive. Maybe negotiate for a release when others came down to check on him. Of course, he could pull on his ethereal well, and he still held his ethereal essence while she had a plastic five-gallon camping bucket on her side. Even so, Alice didn't go for his hand. Instead she picked up the eleven cards.

As far as she was aware, only one card game was played with eleven to one side, ten to the other. Gin, Father Patrick's favorite game.

She discarded; Owen picked it up. Discarded, she drew, discarded. He picked up, discarded. Four moves later he took one of his cards from his hand and flipped it facedown and set it over the discard pile. Gin. His face was reserved but cocky. *So you're not just going to let me win. Good.*

He held up a single finger, indicating the score was one to nothing.

Owen went for the cards, but he was moving slowly, as if not to frighten her. Alice swept up the cards on her side, including the deck and the discard pile, before he could, uncaring about the chains. With a single curling finger, Alice asked for the cards he had used to show the winning hand.

Fast and nimble, Alice shuffled, the sound filling the air. In rapid succession, she added the small pile he tossed over.

She dealt, giving him the eleventh card, and the game was on again.

Owen won once more, this time quickly. Almost suspiciously so. Ethereal power could be used to bend laws of probability, it was true, but she thought she would be able to feel him using ethereal power, even with the chains on. He held up two fingers, indicating he was winning two games to zero before dealing the cards out for the third hand.

Hand three went long, but in the end, she lost again. Had his face always been so punchable, or was it just this dim lighting? Owen spoke with his eyes while a competitive edge was growing deep in her chest. *I will beat you*, she thought while dealing out the fourth hand.

Following each card Owen discarded and picked up, she was sure she knew what was in his hand. Her finger touched the top edge of one of the playing cards, noticing it was not as worn as the rest. The edge was still stiff and crisp. She breathed in as she slipped it out of her hand and, like her throwing knives she had spent years mastering, set it into position, ready to snap forward.

Owen didn't miss the implication, his eyes following her thumb as it felt the stiff edge and judged it adequate to throw. Most people had no idea how fast a card could spin in the right hands. Less than four feet away, his neck and the vein that supplied blood to his brain made an easy target. She felt his sudden pull of ethereal power but wasn't surprised.

Alice studied the change, attuned as she was, while Owen's mask fell away. No longer the soft, beautiful man who had carried in food each day. No longer a man who others could call young. No, this Owen was the real Owen. He was hard. Brutal, even. Dangerous, with the face of someone who knew the cost of taking a life and living with it. She held him in the moment, cradled his life, his soul and the fire within as if it was hers to take. There was a chance he could cover in time, but they both knew the odds of her throw succeeding were entirely in her favor.

His thick, dark eyebrows arched with a slow, daring speed—on his face, it said far more than most. Owen's chin moved up, and his head twisted ever so slightly to the right, exposing more of his neck, more of the arterial vein, in a challenge that shouted clearly, *I defy you to throw and let the cards fall where they may!*

She held the card, ready and waiting, holding the silent conversation between them longer than was necessary. *Why? Because this is real, and lets us both be damned.* They were her words and his in the same moment. She could see it as clearly as the storm within his deep green eyes.

Alice couldn't help herself. She smiled big as she flipped the card over to reveal the seven of clubs, the card he had needed to win the game. And then set it facedown over the pile. She had to fight in order not to say *gin* out loud. But despite her jubilee, she wasn't about to break the silence. Instead she allowed her smile to say it all for her.

Raw, electric chemistry mixed with adrenaline and ethereal power flooded Owen's system, the sensation coursing through his body. Alice held the card between her two front fingers, ready to throw. He didn't question her skill in such a thing. He had seen it firsthand. Stupid, giving her the equivalent of a throwing star this close. How many times had Max proven how fast a playing card could spin and cause damage? How many cards had he watched the kid dig out of a wall after throwing them from over twenty feet away?

Stupid. Just stupid.

Of course, if Alice was going to kill him, it should have been earlier. If she was going to kill him, it should have happened when he first dealt out the cards, not now. Only someone made of evil would play the game, then do the deed. She wasn't evil. She didn't feel evil. Every instinct he held said so. And he knew evil. He knew the rivers of Hell and the souls trapped there. But right now she wanted him to know she held the upper hand.

It's about control with her. Fine. I'll dance with you, but careful what you ask for.

Alice smiled wide. In that smile, Owen lost. Despite his own instinct for preservation, he couldn't breathe. She was so beautiful, so innocent and broken and strong. She lit the room with her smile. And yet, locked behind it all, there was a calling he couldn't ignore.

It took him too long to see the seven of clubs before she placed it facedown. She showed her hand, revealing she had won this round.

He smiled out of the corner of his mouth, a slight shake of his head as he forced himself to look away as he collected the cards—a moment later realizing, too late, that Alice could have grabbed his hand and pulled him into the space allowed by the chains. But she had not. She had let him go.

As he looked back, Alice's smile was gone, but she held up a single finger, indicating her win. *Okay*, he thought, *let's do this again.*

Owen got lost in the game, in her. It was small. Everything was small, and silent. The way Alice's soft hands moved delicately over the cards, then snapped quick as a hummingbird's wings while shuffling. The way her face gave nothing, then broke like the sun coming up out of the water when she won. The way her body somehow went even stiller when she lost, like a violent cat just before the pounce. The soft subtlety of refusing to speak even as her temper flared hot, the anger bright within her green eyes.

Knowing he should have left already. Knowing he should get up and walk out, having stayed too long. Owen refused. Something real was here, alive in the space between them. The connection was so clear it shined.

The score wasn't tied. He was up by a single game, having just come back from being down by three. Yet before he could make a proper decision to go, his hands dealt out the cards once more. Something in Alice's face changed, or perhaps it was just hopeful on his part, but he thought he could feel the tension soften, slow down. A gentleness compared to the hard, contemplative edge that had been there for the last hour or so.

Owen moved a little slower as he picked up a card from the pile. He watched as she drew his own discard with a little less energy. He didn't look at her as he let out his breath, instead focusing on the cards in his hand. Owen discarded.

What am I doing? he thought as she discarded. *There is something absolutely perfect about her. Oh, this is a bad idea.* He reached out, drawing from the pile, his eyes flicking up to hers by accident.

Owen stopped, his whole body refusing to take part any longer as he looked at Alice. Her eyes were soft as a sad chemistry zipped between them. It hurt, even as it pulled his focus from her eyes down to her parted lips.

Owen understood traps straight from the river of Hell itself. He knew the will, the need to break free of Heaven's touch and the Devil's grasp. But her lips and soul were far from his strength to refuse.

His heart hurt as his pulse quickened. It was all there between them, open and free. He followed her smooth, white skin back up to her eyes, as some part of his mind remembered what it had felt like to catch her just before the guns exploded. When her body had been cradled against his own. In desperation, when the space between life and death had been ever so thin.

Alice's slow movement stilled, and somehow he knew she knew what he was thinking. When their bodies were intertwined. The stilling between them shifting into a full-out pause, and he knew for the first time he was seeing Alice unsure.

The warrior set to the side and the woman beneath revealed. Every aspiration he held screamed at him to break the line, to move forward and kiss her. To sweep the pain away. At the same time, every scrap of honor he could call his own shouted out that such a thing wasn't fair. That she deserved far more than what he could ever give.

Owen's body and mind stilled as the connection between them hummed.

The silence stretched, and Owen found he came closer and closer to leaping off the ledge and allowing his soul to be damned even further.

Light, bright and blinding, sliced into the room, breaking the connection.

Like starting a race, he felt an imagined gunshot go off. Both he and Alice scrambled like teenagers to hide their activities.

He swept up Max's cards with fast hands, even as Alice tossed hers on top of the pile. Uncaring about the box, or if any cards were crushed or damaged, he forced them into a pocket and stood, taking the tray and the empty water bottle with him.

A single figure moved in the light, walking in through the doorway and continuing to move partway in.

"Ah, Owen, just making sure our little hostage hasn't

torn out your throat. Good, you're alive. Come on, then. Others are starting to worry." Cornelius's sure voice was rhythmic as he spoke.

Owen didn't know what to say. In truth, he still didn't want to speak. The last hour had given way to a type of silence as the only way to communicate with her. To do otherwise seemed like a betrayal to what had formed between them.

He gave Alice one lasting look before calmly walking away.

Cornelius just waited and watched by the single lighted sconce ahead. If there was something the man witnessed, or even felt in the air, he kept it to himself.

Owen approached, and Cornelius turned without a word to join him, moving toward the door.

Something in the air changed, and Cornelius swiveled back, his right hand snatching something out of the air aimed for his back.

With a small flourish, Cornelius straightened, revealing a red playing card, snapping it over with just his long, deft fingers. Owen made out a woman decked in red, yellow and black, surrounded on four corners with large, perfect diamonds.

Cornelius spoke up to be heard clearly at such a distance. "The queen of diamonds. It suits you, Alice." He smiled at his own joke. "Wait, my dear. I am leaving. No reason for you to continue your pointless defiance on account of little old me. After all, I have not only felt those chains before but have seen them stop someone with three times the power that you possess. And despite what you believe, I don't wish to cause you any more harm than what is absolutely necessary, of course. Now come, Owen. I think Mara wants to see you. Young Max is causing a bit of trouble once more."

Owen didn't look back. The balance that had been between them for the last hour was washed away by Cornelius and his talking. Looking back would only ruin the softer parts he had seen there in the low light.

The large door shut behind him, and Cornelius handed him back the queen of diamonds.

"Thank you," Owen said, surprised by the sound of his own voice.

"Of course. She is something, isn't she? All alone. Otherwise, we would have known about it by now, and yet she refuses to give in. Twenty-six years old and so full of fire. I can't help but wonder what her fate will be. What do you think of her?"

"She is in pain." The words came out before he even knew they were there. But hearing them, he knew it was true.

"You're not speaking of us hurting her?"

Owen had kept his eyes and ears open. He knew they weren't above torturing someone, but that wasn't the plan as of yet. Otherwise, they would have started by now. "No. I know you haven't even started anything really, just letting her wear herself out so she will talk. But she's in pain. Possibly she's been in pain ever since she was bonded."

"Nine years old," Cornelius said to the unanswered question. "She was only nine when Kerogen formed the binding, and I am afraid he has lost all kindness."

"Have you ever *hunted* down one of your kind, Cornelius?" Owen emphasized the word *hunted* so the level four understood he was implying more than just finding someone.

"Many times, Owen."

Something in the We's eyes darkened, and for a moment the We he had known most of his life changed into something far more animalistic. A very real danger, causing Owen to feel small and vulnerable. Just as fast, the sensation was washed away. "I have never wanted to. I have killed We before and will no doubt have to again. But I have never gone after someone the way she is going after this Kerogen. She acts with a single-minded focus," Owen said.

"I suspect few on this Earth have ever gone after someone the same way Alice is going after him. As for you,
you're a musician, Owen. You have your own battles to win
and wager."

"I have missed you, Cornelius. I always thought I would
look up someday and you would just be there in the crowd.
Just like when I was younger."

"You traveled a lot farther than the small bars and back-
room clubs of Miami I used to find you and David playing
in," Cornelius said with a warm smile.

CHAPTER TWENTY

Owen struggled to find sleep. His body was tired, but his mind was in a rolling chaos, slipping through aggressive thoughts and memories over and over again. He needed to play. He wanted to see Alice again. He needed to wait—just wait until Daphne turned eighteen.

He hadn't been able to go down to see her again with Damon this time. But he had heard she had challenged the chains once more. And once more passed out from the pain.

Owen wanted it to stop. He wanted it all to stop.

He felt like an old-fashioned plate spinner from a carnival who had overreached. If he didn't keep everything balanced just right and spinning, all would come tumbling down. And he had given his word, his promise to Daphne and to his people. Even walking through the doors of the Golden Horn again was its own sense of promise to Mara and the others that he would respect the unspoken rules. Mara's wishes.

Damn, once she loved to hear me play, and now, I feel like I have my own chains.

Owen climbed out of his cot, making a point not to be loud. Even knowing Jessie and Max as he did, he wasn't all that worried about waking them, but no reason to take chances. A look at his phone revealed the time as four forty-five in the morning.

I laid in bed for an hour. Now what?

Despite the time, the air was still warm, so he left his jean jacket there on his duffel bag and slipped on his boots, grabbing the keys to his truck.

Owen's mind buzzed as he moved to the only thing that grounded him when the world refused to settle. In his chest there was a note, thick and cruel, the weight of it crushing his soul.

Slipping out of the makeshift bedroom, Owen moved into the side hall just off the back of the Golden Horn. He passed David's old room, the same room he had once shared, the two beds now given over to Daphne and Clover.

Continuing on, Owen found the crisp morning air outside in the low light shading his truck. He refused to ask himself what he was doing as he unlocked the door, unlocked the secret compartment under the bench seat and moved Daphne's bass guitar out of the way.

He needed to feel, needed to let go of all that pressure and pain, and the lack of justice in the world. He needed the responsibility off his shoulders for just a breath, just a moment so he could remember what it was like to live, to fly, to burn inside. *I just need to touch her for a moment.*

Owen pulled the old case free of the hidden compartment, then reached back into the corner to grab a mostly filled bottle of bourbon he had stashed there from a month back. He didn't bother resetting the hidden compartment and Daphne's bass back into place. Instead he left it all where it was and just shut the door.

Reaching with ethereal power, he flipped up the glass to the camper, uncaring if someone could see. The tailgate crunched loud as it went flat for him to take a seat. Owen slid the case up and over the long steel grooves running the length of the bed. With fast and efficient hands, he held his guitar out, the bourbon bottle lid already set beside him as he sat on the open tailgate.

The parking lot wasn't silent. The morning sound of Miami came drifting over the buildings, but it was low and muffled.

The ethereal strings slipped from under his neck, snaking down under his shirt to slide into place over the guitar. Their movement was almost angry and agitated, matching his mood.

He pulled hard on the American-made alcohol and enjoyed the deep flavor even as it burned its way down. A gift from Jessie for turning another year older. Another year still alive.

The fingers of his left hand danced a quick little jig over the neck, enticing the strings to vibrate as he released each, only to be dampened down by his right hand. The instrument was a mustang ready to ride. But she was his as much as he was hers.

Tonight Owen just needed to feel it. Feel the power. Feel his control on the edge. His fingers danced again, running up and back, the familiar bite of the strings against his skin calming to his agitated nerves.

He needed to play, but she was an electric guitar without an amp.

Owen pushed his left hand, his right hand plucking the last few bars.

"What are you doing, man?" he said to a half-empty parking lot. "Seriously, what are you doing?"

In response Owen pulled on the bourbon, letting it wash away some of the frustration that lay in his mouth.

"You are almost there. Daphne is almost safe. Then you can take some time and regroup."

He played again, this time shifting the tune in his head to match the higher vibration of the ethereal strings. A tingling sensation ran up his arm and body. She, the guitar, was calling. Matching the itch inside him, and asking for more. The storm inside started to swirl. Owen could feel his own heart rate take a small climb. *Control and power*, he thought as he plucked and rotated his wrist to hit a difficult chord. He pushed the sound, then cradled it back in. Even without the amp he could hear it, feel it. The storm within his soul helped push some of the responsibility out of his head. This storm was familiar, wild in a way that made sense.

"She's just another pretty woman who already knows the Devil is real. Let her go." As he spoke, his fingers stopped playing.

Now stop being an appetizer when you're a main course. Clover's words came back to him.

Oh, fuck it, he responded.

He pulled hard on the bottle before setting the guitar back into its blue cradle, within the old case. The ethereal essence snaked around his wrist just before the lid over the guitar closed down, brass clips snapping firmly shut.

With the back of his hand that held the case, he pushed the tailgate back up so it clanged closed. The hand with the bottle lowered the glass of the lid.

Owen secured the guitar away, placing Daphne's bass on top and locking the secret compartment, then closed and locked the door of the truck, taking the bottle of good bourbon with him.

Passing the door to the girls' room, and slipping back into the common room he was sharing with Max and Jessie, Owen went straight to his cot. He was nothing but efficient in grabbing the acoustic guitar out from under his bed. A random thought had him snatching a couple things out of his duffel bag before leaving.

Owen moved with speed, not caring about grace and subtlety. The softer side of him was on edge, and he was too tired to care right then. So many memories were here.

Locked in the bones of this building. David, his best friend growing up and brother. Mara, and a younger version of himself. He could feel them each as if they walked the halls just ahead and behind. Now his own people were here. Daphne was so close to being safe, and now Alice, the hunter with the soft eyes and lips, was chained up below, and it was wrong. She didn't belong there, and yet he didn't have an answer to Alice.

Owen made his way to the lower chamber and opened the door. He strode in, seeing Alice was awake. Be it because of him or some other reason was anyone's guess.

Alice climbed to her feet, eyeing him like a hawk might a mouse.

"Now just wait. Give me a second to explain." He held up the bottle and the guitar as if they were self-explanatory.

She looked deadly as he went on.

"I couldn't sleep, and thought I might check and make sure you were still alive. You see, I have this bottle that a good friend of mine got me and thought, well, I thought getting drunk is a better way to go to sleep than scorching yourself against the chains until your mind shuts you down. Could be the same amount of brain cells that die, I don't know, but I like this version better myself."

Suspicion shifted to curiosity, then shifted to humor as she caught the bottle he simply tossed her way. Owen sat, before she could object, in his usual spot across from her makeshift pallet, careful not to allow the guitar to bang on the hard stone floor.

"Now don't break the bottle and stab me in the heart. That is expensive booze. We should at least finish it first. Look, I don't have words to make your life here better, but damn it, can we just be cool for an hour? I just want an hour."

He waited, having nothing left to say and starting to feel out of place.

"I might be able to wait to stab you," Alice said as she

held up the bottle to the light, presumably to judge how much work and time was required to finish the job.

"Excellent. Are you going to drink that, or am I going down this road alone?"

"You are in a mood," Alice said as she lowered herself to sit across from him.

A small part of him wanted to shake her. No, not just her. The whole fucking building. "It appears so."

"Do you have a plan to get yourself out of it?" she said, unscrewing the cap.

The way her fingers twisted, while her eyes never relented from his own, sent a shiver of pleasure down his spine. The woman before him might very well be the death of him. All her pain aside, she wasn't weak. She wasn't less, even chained and broken inside. Alice simply refused to bend.

"Like I said, I thought getting drunk with you might be a good place to start."

"Are you so hard up for a drinking partner? Am I your only option? What guys do to get a date these days," she said as she took a long pull. "Oh, how do you drink this stuff?" Alice's face squished up as her eyes went wide and then squeezed tight.

Seeing her reaction lightened the edges of what he was feeling. "Life burns. At least that drink is honest. Better than most everything else."

"Life also has sugar and spice and everything nice. I would have gone with a beer." Despite her words, she took another drink, her face flushing in reaction to the flavor and strength while clearly forcing down more than she was comfortable with. She wasn't shy about it, and he had to give her props.

"I used to think the answers to life could be found in the flames and flavors of something so tasty and complex. I was younger then," Owen said with a bite to his words.

"You didn't understand that it's just liquor left inside charred wood and that everything else is basic marketing?"

"I thought you said you were going to wait to stab me?"

She smiled and the conversation died. She was a captive, and he might not be the one holding the key, but he was on the other side of the line.

"Are you going to hog the whole bottle, or are we sharing?"

"Hold on." She reached over and took a fresh wet wipe and used it to scrub the bottle mouth clean. It was his turn to smile.

"That's alcohol. In the bottle. I don't care about germs on the rim."

"True, but if you haven't noticed, I have been without a sink for weeks now." When he didn't get it, she spoke up. "I haven't brushed my teeth, and it feels like I have a swamp living inside my mouth, you asshole."

"Oh, damn it." Owen started to reach into his back pocket.

"Relax. The alcohol helps cut the nastiness down by half at least."

"No, not that. Here. Should have given this to you already." He held up what he had grabbed from his bag. In his hand was a seminew tube of toothpaste and brand-new toothbrush still encased in plastic packaging.

He saw the recognition, and for a moment it was like he was holding an eighteen-pound turkey at Thanksgiving dinner. Before she could speak, her hand snapped out, the chain going taut, holding the hand back.

"Wow, here," he said.

"I'm sorry, it's just, bad. Here, take the bottle."

He had to lean forward, and in his hasty exchange, he forgot about the danger. The toothbrush and tube were small compared to the bottle of booze, and before he knew what he was doing, Owen touched Alice's hand.

* * *

Chemistry, raw and hungry, danced up her arm, a soft warmth heating her skin. Alice met his eyes as she took the items.

I can get lost in those eyes. She pulled away. *Oh God, get it together.*

"I need to use this, now," she said far too quickly, about the toothbrush.

"Go ahead. My guitar needs tuning."

She hesitated as she stood, turning her back on him, suddenly uncomfortable at him being able to see her. She was too old not to know about men, and yet her focus was always, always on finding Kerogen. Nothing could stand in the way of that goal. But here and now, she had to admit she was starting to feel at a loss.

"Whatever," she said. "I am going to brush my teeth, possibly three or four times, and spit in that bucket." *You're lucky it's a clean one. Oh, Heaven's gate. I hate this.* She rose in a turn.

No, I am not a gentleman, Owen thought as Alice bent over to retrieve the half-used water bottle.

Silently he admired the curve and untamed beauty of a perfectly sculpted warrior's backside. *Even if I am going to go to Hell, those curves are worth it.* He brought his lips to the mouth of the bottle, then let the bourbon pour in. Setting it aside, he pulled his acoustic guitar into his lap.

This guitar was nothing of legend, would never go down in the history books. It held tune long enough, the sound deep and clear enough not to drive him insane. For now, it was all just enough. He adjusted the second string, tightening it ever so slightly. Again he checked to make sure it was right, the vibration pitching out into the concealed vast room behind him.

Owen did his best to ignore the sounds Alice was making, content to see she was attacking the germs and not him.

The third string of the guitar needed almost nothing. The fourth was fine. The fifth was always a problem. He should change out the hardware again, he thought for the hundredth time. He tuned all six strings, then stroked the strings as one, feeling the hollow vibration against his stomach and leg.

His body swayed from the sound. *Everything is just so tight. I'm tight. I need to let some of it out.*

He took another graze over all six strings, flexing out his free hand against the desire to do something really stupid. The need to give in to the itch and power the sound with ethereal energy. Mara, Damon and Cornelius, if he was sleeping here tonight, would know in a heartbeat what he was doing. Even so, the choice was right there, just right there in the air, in Owen's skin. Down in his soul that called to be free. *How long has it been since I was in this room with a guitar? Damn, I miss you, David. The fires are calling, both above and below. And then there is Alice.*

Owen used his left hand in coordination with his right.

While he had been sitting outside in the back of his truck, he had thought to play the same tune again down here. It was unfinished, needing love and attention and, most of all, drive.

However, as he sat listening, he found he needed something more, his mind moving somewhere beyond the expected.

With gentle fingers touching strings, the darkness of a long history behind him and a chained woman with far too much pain before him, Owen had to go somewhere else. Somewhere wholesome and good. A place with roots and rules and warm sun, where the ground underneath was free and alive.

His fingers found the chord, and his hands began to play as his storm buried deep inside held his pain, calling for a solution.

Owen played light. A small thrumming that spoke of creaking porches and good people. He changed chords, keeping the rhythm of a simple life amongst people living their whole lives by the water's edge.

His song was far too delicate for words, so soft, too independent, almost shy. Owen let some of the stress out, allowing the sound to pull and tease his tension and Alice's discomfort.

His music moved from the swinging bench upon a porch down over the water where two teenage boys were fishing with gear, old and used, finding joy in the simplicity. Finding pleasure in the sound of the soft-moving current.

For a time the room disappeared as he pictured the song, pictured the slow-moving water as fish plentiful and alive jumped up out of it. And away from two boys who only wanted to escape in the summer sun.

Feeling the heat touch their faces, the warmth sink into their bones as a half-rotted-out dock creaked under their feet, both boys smiling, without a care in the world. Owen breathed the image in. Breathed it in and let it settle.

"So that is what you do for the demons. I can see why they keep you around." Alice's voice was not as hard as her words, if only by the width of a pencil.

Owen had to let the memory and the song fade before he spoke, uncaring if she could see his pain. *Let her see. David was worth more than that.*

He pulled on the bourbon bottle and set it down between them. Alice was still standing, and it felt awkward, but he didn't quite care just then.

"They are not demons. That is just what hunters call them. They call themselves the We, the people after the choice. Demons are the Devil's business. Angels belong to God almighty. Or gods, depending on your own belief. The We were given a choice and then left behind, cast out, allowed to come here."

"When you have seen one come for you as I have, there

will be no doubt. They are all demons." Alice sat down, taking up the bottle of booze.

Owen could see the fight inside her, the hard-tempered control, and with it the portion of pain that seemed to have no end. He could feel it as he could feel the depth of his own broken soul. Not the soul that had bled when David died, but the broken soul he had been born with.

He answered the only way he knew how. He played.

Owen thought of his travels, the travels after David's death. Hitting the road on his own after Mara had forced him out of Miami with the threat of death. The long highway and even longer landscape as a fresh new world opened to him. He smelled new air, as wildflowers bloomed and some of his favorite tunes played loud over the radio. Just him, the truck, the open road, the flowers in the field and the radio.

His hands formed the song his soul was calling out for, the image of his past in his mind. It was his own. A song not for unlocking doors and gates, but just to feel the open space. A song to bask in the freedom of being small in a field of something so large.

He left the words behind as his fingers started to play. Alice and he had spent two weeks without words. No reason to bring them in now.

He tried not to look at her as he played. Owen strained to stare off into the darkened shadows to his right, looking down at his guitar. Once he even looked over to the single lit sconce, though with the guitar, the movement was awkward.

Anywhere else but at her. It wasn't that she was stunning, though he couldn't deny it. There was an almost soft kindness to how tight her soul squeezed down, refusing to budge. More than strength, more than will. A pure, unbending force in a person who should have been innocent, even free.

For all Owen tried to avoid looking at her, he only made

it halfway through the song before her green eyes captured his own. Chemistry, hot and fresh, rippled through his body and set his soul on a new kind of edge.

Owen played ahead of it, accepting the truth: there was something about her that spoke to him. A connection about the pain and passion buried deep within her that matched his own.

He strummed notes, letting them brush and coat over each other, creating the feel of a wind on his face. He moved the sound, creating a picture. So the wind moved, danced and brushed softly. A gentle force, never truly ending, that continued moving on only to push through the wild fields of the valley. His sound changed as his hands came off the wheel, and he let the truck he pictured barrel down the highway completely without his guidance.

The feeling was the freedom of adventure. Of danger mixing and blending as if he were the only person around for miles. Freedom after living a life within a city. Both hands went out the window as the truck drifted over the double yellow. And yet he was a young man without a care in the world as long as he could outrun his past.

Something hot crossed her face in challenge, but that wasn't fair. She was only reacting to something that had changed with him first.

Your soul is broken, and so is mine. The words were shared without speaking, humming in the air between them. Their connection was too clear. Powerful information was being passed between them like radio waves.

Owen watched her body still, the meaning clear. Alice already had enough on her plate and could not take on another burden.

Letting out his breath, Owen moved his gaze out into the darkened room once more. His own soul was a burden. A storm. Mara knew it; Clover did as well. Everyone who spent time with him could see it. Sense it.

As in the memory, he took the wheel and straightened out the old green truck.

The song came to an end, the taillights dimming down to a single speck in the distance. The field of wildflowers, separated for all time by a single never-ending road, left once more in peace by a man all alone.

Silence returned between them.

"That was a beautiful song. I assume it is one of yours."

"That was the first song I wrote after leaving my home. It's been a while since I played it."

She handed over the bottle. It was getting low, he noticed. Taking a sip, he decided he was feeling some of the effects.

"Why did you leave?" Alice asked.

"I made a run with my best friend, my brother. He died, and I couldn't stay here anymore."

"Well, that's shitty."

Owen let out a small laugh. "Yeah, it was. Where is home for you?"

"Until I take down Kerogen, I don't have one."

"Okay." His hand started moving the strings, plucking chords soft and deep, the rhythm matching a darker part of what was within.

"I need to end him," Alice said with a simple conviction.

"I know you do," he said, meaning every word. Yet he felt like it wasn't even close to enough. "One of my people is underage and unbound. Daphne, the girl they were protecting when you attacked. In six more weeks, she turns eighteen, and we are home free. Six more weeks and she is safe. Or at least safe enough that we can leave."

"So you play for them, feed them ethereal energy, and they keep a child safe. That is the deal you made? You are being played, Owen. Demons can't be trusted. You need to know that." She picked up the bottle and took more in.

"I told you they are not demons, but it doesn't matter.

Not right now." The itch was in his chest, the need to let it out, to let the storm burn free.

He let his fingers do the talking for him. Playing two chords in contrast to each other, two sounds that should be kin but instead shocked his system before letting each fade out into the night air. His hands started to build a whisper of a sound, commanding it to come forth. Like an invading army slipping from concealment out of the brush.

He breathed in as his world narrowed to the sound, and he started to find something new. Something untouched. The song built, shifting as he played a new set of chords, building a rhythm as he went on. Everything in him hurt while he held back the storm of power that wanted to be called forth, the power and desire to infuse his song with ethereal energy. The battle of will versus creation, a living thing within his system as he played a new song for her.

It was soft and dark, driving deeper into the mysteries of the lone soul trapped within a sea of fog without hope of escape. Shackled, with sharp, raven hair and endless difficulty. A wanting that could almost match his own. His fingers plucked and held, stroking the song to be. Owen stretched out the sound into the dark spaces behind him, using the whole of sound to create.

"That is enough." Her words were soft yet unbreakable.

He let the last note he had been playing reach out into life before fading away.

"What are you?" Alice asked.

"Damon calls me a musician, and he would know. Others have called me a gatekeeper, but that was only after I received a special gift. All that I know is I can't stop playing. My spirit has never allowed it." His words hurt as he spoke true. They hurt as he heard them.

"You are very good . . . I think I could see myself, within the song."

"If you think that is good, you should see me onstage. Women love me onstage."

"Are all men as cocky as you are?" she asked.

"Only the ones who can play as well as I can," Owen said, meaning it.

"I am getting tired," Alice said, though her words rang false.

There had been something in the song she hadn't cared for, and he thought he understood what it was. "Then why don't you just leave?" His words cut deep, but he didn't care.

"Excuse me?" she asked.

"Why won't you talk to them?"

"Don't, Owen. Let it be," Alice warned.

"Look, you don't put a gun to their heads. Not here, not in this place. Look around. Hasn't it occurred to you yet that you didn't just walk into any club? How many of the We have you met, hunted or intimidated that had the strength and the resources to hold you like this? I can feel your strength, see your training. Do you think those chains around your wrist can be purchased at the local hardware store? You're a badass, Alice. Everyone here will give you that. But the only reason you are still alive is you didn't kill anyone upstairs. And right now they have a soft spot because Kerogen is an asshole and you were just a kid. But damn it, I don't know what to say to you. If you can't have a conversation with them, you're either going to be executed or left right here until you die of old age."

"You should leave. Now." Alice didn't get up. Didn't move.

"Damn it, they like honesty. Just be honest with them. Make a deal."

"They are fucking demons, Owen. You might like to let them feed off you and be their little pet, but I don't make deals with them. I break them and get what I want. Get out of here, and do not come back."

Owen came to his feet slowly despite the furnace feeding his blood. "The priests taught you how to kill, how to fight, how to hunt. But they didn't teach you what you are hunting. They just gave you a target and made you into a trigger."

"The priests didn't give me my target. They just gave me the resources to be free."

"If that is so, where the hell are they? Where are your priests, Alice? Where is your backup? This place is old and no secret. You should have come in with a rocket launcher. Possibly a tank. Your priests have tried before. Did they tell you that? Mara and Damon are still here, still standing, and you are all alone, chained to the wall."

"I am the tank. If it wasn't for you, I would have crushed them. But you and that damn essence caught me off guard. If you hadn't protected your masters like a dog on a leash, I would be halfway to Kerogen right now. Possibly already have him in my sights. You are the reason I am stuck down here. Now get out! Leave me be."

Owen took a step back. She was telling the truth. He could feel the honesty within her words, sharp and clear, resonating in the space between them. "You honestly believe I am their little puppet? You honestly do? And moreover, you believe that if I hadn't been in the room, you would have succeeded?"

"Damon's not the first level five I have taken down. Yes, if you hadn't protected your demon masters, I would be free and planning how best to kill Kerogen right now." She was furious and Owen could see it.

However, some of the heat had gone out of Owen as quickly as it had come. In all his long life, no one had ever thought he did anyone else's bidding but his own. If she couldn't see that, she couldn't see him. A different kind of pain stabbed through his body.

"They are not demons," he said with introspection. *If you can't understand me after I showed you who I am . . .* There was no finishing the thought. *Just be done with her as fast as you possibly can. It's time to leave*, a cold internal voice said to him.

"You keep thinking that, buddy, but I'm done talking to you. Now get the hell out of here."

Owen started to walk away, taking his guitar and the almost empty bottle of bourbon with him. Head up, he couldn't help but feel a sadness. Three strides, four. He came to a stop and, shaking the guitar a little, he turned back to see her standing there.

"You are right, Alice. Some of them are demons, as much a demon as any man or woman who decides to take advantage of people for their own gain. No different than a nurse who steals medication from the elderly. No different than a businessman taking advantage of a small town's ignorance. No different than anyone who has freedom of choice and chooses what is best for only themselves. Your Kerogen obviously is such a creature. But not all the We are demons. Not all of them are like him. They have free will. Same as you, same as me. Some choose good, some choose bad. The weak and the ignorant are playthings for those who choose selfishness. I can see you built yourself into someone who is strong. Too bad you also built yourself into someone who is blind."

Owen did the only thing he could do, before he left the open room. He touched the control panel, snapping the lights full on. Uncaring about the consequences, only knowing a person like Alice shouldn't spend any more time in the dark. He let the doors close behind him without a glance, knowing he was far more alone now than he had been before coming down.

Alice watched Owen as he walked away. Her anger was smashing and tearing at her self-control. *How dare he. How dare a man so closed to the world still refuse to see the truth. With his edges, soft-spoken words and storming eyes, and yet completely an asshole.* Alice thought she had seen more within him. There had been moments when it was as if she thought she knew what he was. How he was. A man with a code, doing his best to hold down the beast he was born to be. And yet. *He refuses to see the truth, and still he has the audacity to call me blind.*

Bright lights lit the room, attacking her vision in a sudden and unexpected assault.

Alice slammed her eyes closed, turning her head to the wall and covering her face. After so long in the low light, it was like tiny daggers slicing into her brain. She didn't hear the door close after him, nor could she see the outline of him leave.

"Asshole!"

Alice swore again as she fought back the pain and slowly adjusted to the light. She had to start out small, her mind and senses needing time to adjust to the new onslaught. She breathed in and breathed out.

"Oh, buddy, I am going to hurt you for that. Only a coward hits and runs away." Each word was a promise as her eyes adjusted.

Alice pried her arms away from her face, forcing her eyes to take in the new light. It burned, and she was forced to squint, but she didn't retreat. Pain was a part of who she was, and she wouldn't back down now. Particularly when she was so, so pissed off.

With effort and a touch of time, she could see down the length of the wall all the way to the large double doors. Surprise coursed through her as she made out two ornate carvings of angels flying up toward the ceiling on the back of either door. A detail she had never been able to see properly until now.

Her gaze moved slowly toward the center of the room, where the stronger light was coming from. Her anger faded as she took in the room she had been living in for weeks but had yet to really see. Alice was dumbfounded, completely and utterly perplexed as she looked on with amazement.

She wasn't in a darkened cellar, wasn't in a medieval prison. Somehow without her even suspecting, she was chained to a blackened wall within a ballroom the size of a cathedral.

A sound escaped her lips as her eyes roamed over beautiful pearl-white-and-gold inlay, all created in a sea of care and precision.

The gigantic space wouldn't have been out of place in a royal castle and was unlike anything Alice had ever seen.

The ceiling reached heavenward, climbing twenty or more feet. Bright chandeliers shone with gold, hanging with massively weighted gems. Each a work of art, as the jewels caught the light, sparkling while sending tiny colors to dance this way and that.

There were murals that even from across the long, open space she had little trouble believing were masterpieces in their own right. She followed the deep section of gold on white, white on gold. Alcoves reaching high into the sky before hexagons of gold honeycombed the ceiling, framed in with hand-carved, meticulous, intricate molding.

Alice took in the giant space, feeling small and dirty. Knowing she didn't belong here. The feeling was so strong she pulled her gaze back in, looking past the twisting pillars to where the polished tile changed to a semicircle of black stones. A deformity within the masterpiece that was the room. Her space. Her home for the last two weeks.

An island of black, unfinished stone. Like a violent scar on a pageant-worthy face.

A scent in the air had Alice shifting to the side, the chains rattling as she did so. Her head swiveled, and for a moment, all she could feel was stupid.

She was alone, despite the room's newfound reality. But then Alice smelled the odd scent again and recognized the smell as burning tobacco.

As if on cue, off to her left, Mara stepped out from behind a white pillar, a dark cigarette in one hand, a thin, long-stemmed martini glass in the other. The glass still held a cold chill to the rim, as if the drink had just been made. Mara's expression held much the same as the cold glass. A chilled frost.

"Stupid child. That man would have played for you all night. Do you have any idea what a pleasure it is to have someone with such an open heart play just for you? You can't buy tickets to such an event. And yet you sent him on his way. A shame. Owen's skill is far greater than when he left, and even then he was astounding."

Alice had to fight the sudden appearance of the woman much as she had fought the light. She needed calm to fight the chains. She needed to dig deep to take on so much pain to incapacitate herself as she had done every time either Damon or Mara had tried to speak with her before.

Yet the shock of finding herself in such a room, the shock of seeing Mara so close when she had thought she was alone, and perhaps, worst of all, after letting down some of her guard only to fight with Owen, left her unprepared for the amount of pain it would require to fight the chains to such a level.

"Even at ten years old, Owen was a one-of-a-kind boy. I knew he would cause me trouble when I took him in off the streets. That ratty hair of his and fearless smile. Do you know I once was so angry at him I threatened to cut off both his hands? I meant every word at the time, and he knew it. Even so, Owen dared me to do it. Oh, not with his words. Back then he wasn't so thick with the truth. No, with his eyes, girl, and his heart. So defiant. So strong of will. Full of life, real life. To be brash and loud. The best men always are. So too are the worst villains. A fine line, a small distinction, don't you think?"

Alice didn't respond. Instead she tried to still her mind,

find the empty space as she breathed in and out, preparing to fight the chains for the second time in only a few hours.

"Ah, planning your same, single trick? Go ahead, child, if you enjoy hurting yourself so—"

"I'm not a child anymore!" The words were ripped from her lips by a force far stronger than her control.

Mara stared at her, pulling on her cigarette, a passive, beautiful face. "No, I would say you are not. Sometimes I find it difficult to not call everyone I see children. But at least now you said something true."

Mara took a gentle sip as they eyed each other.

"Do you know, besides Owen and my son, David, you are the first human in over two hundred years to see this place? Take it all in. Take it all in." Mara's voice was distant, her mind on far more than simple things.

"Where am I?" Alice asked.

"What is this place, you mean?" Mara asked, taking a sip of her drink before speaking again. "This is my home, once a beacon, a refuge, a kingdom of a kind. A place where my kind and yours could be who we are in peace from the rabble above. Back when we dared to gather in large groups. Before we were forced to shut down. There was a time these halls ran crowded with music and laughter and love. Now they are as empty as your own heart. Just look at you, girl. Still alive because Damon believes you could be an opportunity. Cornelius believes you are more than what you seem. And Owen . . ."

Alice didn't miss the way Mara's voice wrapped around his name.

"Well, Owen is determined to burn his soul to ashes but save as many people as he can before it happens. Fool boy. But you, dear, you are an empty shell only filled with hate. I should destroy you, pull your limbs from your body as a spider might an insect. This house was once a beacon for refinement and civility, two powers that together could bend the veil that separates this world and the hereafter. You have no business here."

Alice could feel the violence building in the woman. Could feel it like a rushing wind against her face, growing with each step Mara took in her direction.

She reacted on instinct. "Where is Kerogen hiding?"

Mara stopped more than twenty feet away, staring before a smile crossed her face. "I almost forget what it is to be so young. Almost. Child, you know he doesn't hide from you. All you have to do is remove the shawl of tears from under your skin, and he will come. Because Kerogen doesn't hide from anyone. Not anyone, not anymore."

For the first time, Alice's heart grew hopeful. It bloomed in her chest. The woman before her knew how to find him. Mara actually had the answer on how to find Kerogen, other than taking off the relic. Alice had been looking for seven years on her own, and now the information she had been seeking was right before her.

"Tell me where he is. I need to know where Kerogen is."

You are tiring me with the same question." Mara turned, saddened by her individual footsteps.

After all, this room was not designed for a single set of feet to echo so, and yet she didn't have the heart to bring everyone back again. No, the time for such a place to be filled to capacity was in the past and the past alone. The danger of having such a gathering was far too high. The past had been one of honesty and openhearted good times. The future was looking more and more about shadows and staying hidden. A shame.

"No, damn you. Tell me where he is!" Alice's voice echoed off the walls as her scream touched uncaring ears.

CHAPTER TWENTY-ONE

The Golden Horn was open for business, but it was early for the Saturday lunch crowd. Mara was, for once, behind the main bar teaching Daphne how to pour drinks and doing so with a flourish she insisted Daphne needed to learn.

For all the thorns Mara contained, Owen knew her heart was wide and deep with compassion. Daphne's laughter and wonder at seeing everything for the first time was an infectious joy that Mara was clearly coming to appreciate.

Owen sipped a beer that had gone warm and flat an hour back as he held playing cards on the other side of the club at the main table. Across from him was Damon. To his right was Cornelius and to his left Jasper, one of the level fours who had come in a couple hours back, a friend of Cornelius. Jasper was friendly enough, though Owen wasn't in any mood to be jovial.

Having taken the last hand, it was his turn to play a card. Owen used quick fingers to toss the playing card so it spun in the air before landing flat in the center of the table. His card was the first, opening the latest round of the game. Jasper slid his card in so it glided with a clean, steady ease. Damon took a moment before gently tossing in a card, almost as if it were a piece of trash no longer of concern. And Cornelius? Cornelius followed Damon by dropping a higher card and taking the pile. Then he opened the next hand, rounding the turn of play back so it was Owen's turn to play once more.

Owen spun the card in the air to land beside Cornelius's opener, and Jasper slid his card in as he had done before. Damon took his time before sending in a card like trash, and then Cornelius dropped his card in. Then it was Jasper's turn to take the pile and open the next hand.

The game moved on at a quick, brisk pace. Drinks were sipped, cards were shuffled, and chips were won and lost, though at the moment, they were playing with low stakes. A warm afternoon was no time to be so serious. All the while, Owen didn't have room to speak. He hadn't slept the night before. Alice's betrayal of who he was stuck in his side like a stake being driven in, and he didn't understand why. Worse, the tension in the room between Mara and Damon was putting everyone on edge. And if he was honest, he had forgotten what it was like to just be around so much ethereal energy. Damon, Mara, Cornelius and all the others practically made the air vibrate with it. It only made the Devil's itch to play far worse.

Two hours more they played cards, his beer forgotten. Lost in his own absent thoughts, Owen tossed in his card, watching the way it spun in the air, landing perfectly in the center, faceup. His body was a lie to how he was feeling. The card toss, with an easy, fluid motion, said *control*, but it wasn't what he was feeling.

No, control was the last emotion within. A hunger to create music was eating at him. It crawled up and down his skin, raged inside his chest for release. The Devil's itch had him in its grasp, and all he could do was hold on.

Owen tossed another card. It landed soft and easy, just as all the others had. Something had him looking up. His eyes met the deeper and knowing brown eyes of Damon's own.

Information passed between them as easily as if it had been scrawled on a handwritten note.

Damon was a sax player. Damon was a fellow musician. A musician who understood the Devil's itch. In the single look they shared, Damon could read the truth.

"Holy shit, boy. You planning on setting fire to the whole city?" Damon said, drawing the game to a pause.

Owen took in the words, waiting. Absently he recognized Damon's words were the most any one person had said in the last hour. Everything else had been small gestures or small words.

Owen couldn't respond, didn't want to. Instead he just looked over to Jasper and, with a single lift of the finger, signaled the level four to play his card and continue the game.

One second passed, two, then three. Jasper slid his card in.

"Really, son?" Damon asked as they exchanged a quick glance, and then Owen settled deeper in his seat. Damon didn't wait before playing, instead tossing in his card with too much force. The card slid right under Jasper's, obscuring the card from being read easily.

Owen personally didn't care. He had seen it was the jack of hearts, and he would be damned if he was going to move more than he had to. He needed to stay still, to hold the storm inside, where it couldn't hurt anyone.

Cornelius reached over and, using long, nimble fingers, straightened out the cards, then played his own.

"You can't hide from her, Owen," Damon said, more concern and weight in his voice than Owen had ever heard from the We. Leaving no doubt Damon wasn't talking about Alice, but the locked-away guitar.

"No one is hiding." He held up his wrist, showing the leather bracelet that was not a bracelet at all.

"You aren't the first one she has broken. Why do you think she has never been given to a mortal until now? She wasn't designed for you to keep her in a cage. You have to let her out. Bleed off some of the will, or she'll roast you from the inside out."

"I remember your advice, and I appreciate the concern." Owen tried to keep his voice respectful. Yet it was false, and everyone at the table knew it.

"You have to let her out," Damon said again, this time as if the world were at risk.

Owen couldn't take much more, not from Damon. He knew it as strongly as he knew how to play. The man was a walking legend, an artist, a mentor and a friend. Owen had to change the subject. "What are you going to do with the girl?"

Damon read the move as clearly as looking at sheet music. "What do you think I should do with her?" he asked.

"Tell her where Kerogen is and send her ass packing. Get her out of here. She is far more trouble than she is worth."

"You are right, she is," Damon shot back. "Say I send her to Kerogen. Say I ask the right friend and find him. Say I give her his location, sending Alice after him. Then let's say Alice wins, she's free. Kills Kerogen and all that. What is it, Owen, you think she will do next? Remember how she has spent her whole life becoming a hunter. Now what will she do with her freedom?"

Owen could see it, hear it even. Alice honestly believed any and all We were demons. She believed it when she spoke. She was telling the truth even though it wasn't so.

"She will hunt again," Owen said grudgingly.

"That's right, she will. Musicians play, bartenders pour drinks and hunters hunt. Now let's say I send her to Kerogen, and Kerogen wins, takes her back fully under his control. What do you think happens then?"

"Kerogen will come after you for giving him up."

"Not only that, but Kerogen isn't a nice man. He's old, and since he bonded with Alice, his power has only grown. We think he wants to get past the fourth arch and try walking his soul into Heaven. Not that it's ever been done before. But that's why we think he bonded her in the first place. Even so, he will need musicians. Ethereal musicians like you and high-level guys like me."

"You're thinking of killing her?" Owen said with a cold tone that spoke of false indifference.

"We are all thinking of killing her. Just as you should be."

Owen let a breath escape louder than he wanted, the sound shaking something loose.

"She was just a kid, Damon. Forcibly bonded to a monster, and she has spent what seems her whole life trying to break the leash. By the look of things, it has not been so easy."

"And that is why we haven't killed her. But keep in mind, your damsel in distress has killed We. Our sources have been looking into her trail of dead bodies. And no, it doesn't appear she is a murdering maniac, but the bodies are out there. Anyone between her and her goal gets trampled."

"You want to play 'raise your hand if you have ever killed a We,' Damon? Because I don't have a doubt three out of the four at this table have done so, and I'm willing to push my entire stack of chips in that it will be an even four for four." Owen's gaze left Damon's hard brown eyes to snap a glance to Jasper. The only man in question.

The level four's features were smooth and younger than those of Cornelius's normal group. He looked to be around thirty, with white teeth, a strong jaw and eyes that reminded Owen of a lion's—they were yellow and speckled with dark black flakes.

Jasper pursed his lips in a way that made it clear he had killed and that he was planning on staying out of the current conversation.

"We all do what we have to do to survive, Owen," Damon said.

"And isn't that what she is doing?"

"Stop being a child," Damon snapped.

As one, they both rose up out of their chairs. Damon was a big man, with thick shoulders and arms to match. Despite his normal, easy behavior, nothing about him said *pushover.*

Right then, Owen didn't care. "A child?"

"Yes, a child," Damon said before Owen could go on. "You made your choice. Now own it. The first human to ever wield that guitar. The first human soul with the power and need to unlock the gates. And you sit there feeling helpless. Where is the fire? Where is the heat and brimstone of your soul? Where is your song right now, Owen?"

"Don't push me, Damon. Don't you fucking push me. I have been doing it right. Look around—my people are safe."

"Safe!" Damon spat the word like venom needing to leave his mouth. "You were made to take on the fires of Hell, to challenge the hard brutality of Heaven. Pay attention, son. This isn't a safe place. This is our home. Where we live and die. This is where we get to be who we are, and you come back and pretend to be something you're not!"

"That's enough, Damon. Leave the boy be." Mara's voice punched in, wrapped with ethereal force. It would have been a slam to the gut, a force that could steal free will from both Owen and Damon—that is, if either hadn't already been on the verge of throttling the other.

"No, Mara, I won't. It's bad enough I have to watch you lie about who you are. It's bad enough I have to sit here and witness fear and sorrow beating truth and honesty. You could have killed him, Mara. I wouldn't have blamed you. Hell, I half wanted you to, because at least then, you would have been true to yourself. Cornelius and I would have helped you bury his body and shared tears with you, absent of any blame."

Damon shook his head slightly from side to side, reinforcing his words.

"You gave Owen a choice, and he made his own by coming back. But you didn't kill him. You let him live and come back in here. Only you don't want Owen. Not the real Owen, not the wild kid who grew up with us now turned man. Not a man with a soul that rages inside. No, Mara, you want a watered-down version of who he is. Don't be a musician, don't play, save people. Sacrifice your gift over passion for the good of others. As if he is some fucking hero. You are not, Owen. Neither you nor I will ever be a hero. We weren't meant to be that kind of man. We were meant for more, and you're holding back now, and I can't bear to see it, to hear it, to smell it!"

The room was silent as Damon finished.

Only Owen couldn't hear the silence. His body was a vibrating mass of need, anger and frustration. His toes were dangling freely over the edge of a cliff, threatening—begging—him to let go. To jump, to fall, to do anything but hold back. "You don't know what you are talking about." He was barely able to get the words through his teeth.

"Yes, I do," Damon demanded.

Mara spoke, but Owen didn't turn from the old sax player. "Damon, I know you have never been comfortable with us closing the doors downstairs, but we barely survived last time. And look around, life isn't so bad." Mara stopped, the last words she had spoken were weak, as if they held in their center a lack of truth.

"We are fire, Mara. We weren't meant to be caged, but to burn. If you don't allow Owen to vent the heat, the fire will just burn him to ash right before your eyes."

"I'm fine, Damon. Mara," Owen said, turning away. "Really, I am fine." He directed the last comment to Mara alone. She had enough on her hands with helping him keep his people safe. She didn't need to take on his burden as well.

"Owen?" Mara said as he started to walk away.

Owen knew he didn't have a choice to stay and talk any longer. "Truly, Mara, I am fine. I can handle the itch. It's nothing I haven't had to deal with before."

She made to stop him, the softness in her eyes hurting him far more than the bullet she had fired.

Owen placed a hand up to stop her, not wanting or able to handle any contact just then. "I'm okay, just a little frustrated." Owen continued on past even while trying to reassure himself.

This place is like gasoline. It's in the air, the scent of the room, the weight of my own childhood, David and all the extra power just sitting in the air, waiting to be used for a run.

He walked into the hall, past the restrooms, heading toward the back of the building where the sleeping quarters were located.

Max was waiting for him at the corner, where the side corridor met up with the front hall, a sheepish grin coming over his features as he handed over a bottle of expensive whiskey, no doubt pilfered from the bar or stockroom.

Owen knew he should reprimand the kid. *And yet at last Max had palmed something of value.* How Max had the foresight to grab it, Owen would never know, but even so, Owen took the bottle without exchanging any words, finding himself thankful.

Owen walked farther back, turning right past the office and storage pantry. Made to make a left toward the room he shared but instead came to a halt.

He didn't know where to go.

I won't be able to sleep, not right now. I could go out to the parking lot, get some fresh air. Although, can I resist pulling out the guitar? And if so, can it be put away without making even a small run? He knew the answer. *David's old room is right there. Once, it was a safe place.*

Owen felt a pull in the air. His eyes followed it, looking past the door, down the hall to another door that led to one of the passageways that led down to Alice and the forgotten chamber.

He stared, surprised to feel a wave of anger starting to rise within. *She is obstinate. Alice is just so incredibly stubborn. You never give the We a no-win situation. Always, always give them an out. The woman deserves her fate. She won't even try and deal. What is her plan? Seriously, what is her plan? She can't break those chains, and by the time she figures that out, she won't have a choice. Damon or one of the others will have already placed a bullet in her head.*

Damon's words ran through his mind in response. *You are not a hero. We are fire.* Owen's feet started moving before he knew what he was doing. Each step, his anger flared higher and higher. *They are going to kill you, and there is nothing you are willing to do about it.*

The first door in his way opened as Owen stalked toward Alice.

Alice meditated in the shining lights. She had managed some sleep with a cloth tied over her eyes and now was forcing her will to strengthen, to grow so she might have the strength to overcome the chains and break free. So far it hadn't happened, and it was shaping into a concern. She was starting to believe she might not be able to do it.

The doors opened to Owen as he moved with ethereal power, his feet propelling him to skip over the ground as he came right at her.

Scrambling to her feet, every instinct within her screamed she was in danger even as a white-hot anger at seeing him filled her once again.

A bottle broke against the wall as Owen reached the halfway point between her and the door. Her body shook as she forced her muscles to be ready to move. He was coming in too fast, too hard. Setting her weight on the balls of her feet, she watched, evaluating even as he transferred what remained of the broken bottle to his right hand. Its remnants, sharp and deadly, catching the bright light. *Very well*, she thought as he took one long step to the side and then came in for the attack.

Owen moved in fast, making a single, long strike with the deadly glass. Alice's hands met the strike, and even without ethereal power, she was fast. Owen released the glass and relaxed his arm, practically handing her the weapon as Alice disarmed him.

And yet Owen didn't stop, only slowed his rush as she snatched the broken bottle out of his hand and brought it up to his neck.

"Go ahead. Go ahead, Alice! I'm just a dog to you anyway! Isn't that right? I'm just a dirty mutt on a leash who doesn't know my owners are monsters. Isn't that right? Come on, Alice, put me down. Slice my neck. Come on, hunter. Do what you have been taught to do. Don't think, just kill." Owen spat the name *hunter* with as much violence as he was feeling.

"What are you doing?" Alice asked in confusion.

"You can't trust me, remember? I'm the enemy. No, worse—I'm the enemy's puppet. I know, use me, hold me hostage and trade my small life for your release. Do you want me to call them? I can. Is that what you want, Alice?"

"What is wrong with you, Owen?" Alice asked. He had to be feeling the sharp edges of the glass slicing into his skin as he pushed his own body closer. She had to take a step back, and another. Together they backed up as he pushed her against the wall.

"What is wrong with *me*? You don't have a plan. As far

as I can see, you are all by yourself, and you won't leave here if you don't change that."

"I'm not afraid to die."

"We are all afraid to die. Don't believe me? Then go ahead." He pushed in farther, forcing his body closer to hers.

Knowing if Alice killed him with the broken bottle she would meet the same fate wasn't a comfort, wasn't anything at all. Owen was so tired of hiding, of being restrained.

"Hey! Back off, you're going to kill yourself."

Owen changed his voice as something in her eyes softened. "Alice, they are not demons. Yes, Kerogen is a living nightmare, but he doesn't work for the Devil and neither do any of the other We. Just as they don't all work together like one big hive! Each is an individual. Some of them are my friends, and some here are even my family. But others I have to protect against. The world just isn't as simple as you wish it to be. You have to stop and look for yourself."

"I can't stop," she said, tearing the words from deep within.

Like feeling the sun, Owen basked in the truth. "Why?" he said, demanding the answer.

"I can't ever go home until Kerogen is dead. He told me he would come for me, but I knew what he meant. Even at nine years old, I knew what he meant. If I go home, he'll find me and kill my mother and father and my new baby sister."

"Okay," Owen said, the fire inside hot to the point of boiling but suddenly still as he focused on Alice's eyes, her lips, her soft cheekbones.

I am not a hero.

Owen pushed against death's door once more as he

leaned forward, the bottle slicing in slowly until Alice was forced to pull it back or otherwise kill him.

"Owen, what are you doing?"

He came in, knowing she had nowhere else to go. But moreover, knowing he had nowhere else to go. The connection between them was an arc of electricity pulling and twisting them together. They had no more room and no more time and space but right now. He kissed her softly at first, her lips gentle and timid, then warming as they parted and accepted him.

Lost in the feel and heat of her, Owen deepened the kiss with an artist's touch that pulled her out of timid and melted her into his own heat. She was spice and honey. A drug uncapped. He pulled back, needing her to know his soul wasn't worth saving. No, it was more than that—she needed to know he couldn't be relied upon. That Damon was right. He was fire, and fire wasn't used to build but to burn.

Alice wasn't wild. Instead, she stood unflinching, with just a touch of awe.

"Burn me," he whispered as he bent again.

She met him just a moment before he reached her for another kiss. Her need was huge and wild, blending with his need to feel something real and true. Alice was all of that and more. Toxic to the point of pain as his tongue touched hers, blending of its own kind, sensation and chemistry that only intertwined, driving the kiss on.

He felt her hand grip his sides, and what remained of the broken bottle shattered behind him. He didn't miss the soft brush of chains on his side as his hand touched her cheek, rejoicing in the soft, smooth feel.

Alice didn't have anywhere to move, her smaller body caged by his larger one, and for the moment it didn't matter at all. He took, with greed and spice leading the song. Owen's hands, his kisses urging her to come in against him. Driving the need and chemistry to a new level. He could feel her rhythm, the rhythm inside her soul wanting more.

A need of something concrete within a world spinning far too fast. His lips moved to her neck.

"Owen. Owen." She said his name again, pulling, calling for a time-out.

Reluctantly he pulled back. He watched as her body gave off a small shudder. A song interrupted.

"Yes?" he said.

The single word held it all. Moving past the question to the promise of sharing something wild and forbidden, to cross barriers and for a time let it all go. Owen meant every nuance.

"We are not having sex here. Let's bypass that I am chained to a wall or the fact that I haven't showered in two weeks."

"I don't care about any of that."

"Not going to happen."

His smile was shaped into a promise that vibrated deep inside.

She looked around the empty room and, for the longest of moments, thought, *Why the hell not?* Looking at him only made the idea grow in length. But then the feel of the chains around her wrists were a soft reminder. "No," she said.

"Very well." Owen's words were a promise of bodies intermixing into a forbidden bliss.

"Okay," Alice said, needing time.

Owen sealed it with another kiss, pulling her body up against his own once more. Chemistry arced between them, and it was all he could do to keep it at bay. Even so, he wasn't chivalrous in his need. Far from it.

The kiss shifted from soft to mind-bending as he pressed for more. Her body was a beautiful combination of hard muscles and soft curves. Her hands dug in but didn't push him away as they tasted each other. Dazzling on the sensation of texture, spice and raw, living electricity.

"Nope," broke through Alice's lips, while she turned her head to the side. "I swear you could make a nun go wet."

"Wait, what was that?" Owen asked in surprise.

"Nothing. That was nothing."

"No, you just said I could make—"

"Shut up. I did no such thing." His smile grew as he watched her grow uncomfortable and . . . embarrassed? She was. He was looking at a real red flush to her cheeks.

Alice watched the smile grow, and before she knew what she was doing, she punched Owen quick in the stomach.

He hadn't been expecting it, and the air left his system before he knew what had hit him. A hard woof, driving out of his lungs. The mood shattered as Owen doubled over in pain.

"Oh no, I am so sorry," Alice said more gently than anything he had previously heard her say.

"No. I'm okay," Owen tried but didn't have the air.

"I can't believe I just punched you."

"It's fine. Really, I'm okay," he said, warding off her hands as she tried to help straighten him.

"I punched you. I didn't mean to. Honestly."

He could hear her as she tried and failed to hold back some of the joy she was feeling. He had to take a step back, his shoes grinding glass underneath. "Bloody woman. Not to say I didn't deserve it, but . . . damn."

Alice gave Owen room to catch his breath, and he took it, straightening his body as he breathed in air. "You didn't deserve to be punched," Alice said.

"I just didn't see it coming."

"You aren't afraid I am just using you to get out of here?" Alice asked.

The space between them was contained by an invisible half circle, marking the length Alice could travel while being chained to the wall. Seeing it openly now and him within the half circle changed everything.

"First, I think I am more bent on getting you out of here than you are. And second, I have spent my life around the

We. From an early age, I was taught to listen to people as they tell their truth. Now I can hear someone telling me something they don't believe from across the room."

"Really?"

"Every etherealist can. It's a passive trait that comes with the energy. Personally I think it is because back before the Earth and humans were made, lies didn't exist up there. I mean, think about it. All these angels are having a good time, hanging out in the great above. Who is going to lie, and for what reason?"

"You have given this some thought," she said, and there was something in the way her body was still that said she wanted to move to him again.

"A bit. Yeah," Owen said, wading in toward her, slowly this time. "The We can feel the truth. I think it vibrates like notes in the air. When the note is off, they instinctively don't like the sound. The general rule, the one I tell my people, is never, ever lie to a We even if it is something bad. Better for you to tell them you shot their brother in the head than to lie about it."

"Sounds like you believe in what you are saying." Her words purred with a power far stronger than his own resistance.

Burn him, the need for more of her was too high. Without asking permission, he picked her up, her legs swinging around his waist. She moved with him as he gently pinned her against the wall for a second time. Looking up, Owen found a spirit that might just be more broken than his own.

She smiled, enjoying the power of being above. "Now what in the world am I going to do with you?" she asked.

"Alice, I can promise you one thing."

"Oh, and what is that?"

"I won't ever be boring." Before she could answer, his mouth reached through the soft T-shirt and gently brushed against her left nipple. The soft sound that escaped her lips created a new craving within him. Instantly he had to wonder what other sounds he might be able to bring forth.

H aving just told Alice his plan to bring Damon and perhaps some of the others down there and work this whole thing out, Owen knew what came next wasn't going to be easy.

"Wait a minute, you did what?" Clover asked as Owen slipped on a clean black shirt.

"Yeah," Owen said, unable to believe it fully himself.

"Only you, Owen. I swear there are times I think, 'My buddy Owen, he could be a normal guy,' and then you go and make out with the girl trapped in the basement who tried to kill us all."

He didn't reply, only stood there dropping the fresh shirt down over his rib cage. The old one had gotten more than a little of the shattered whiskey over it.

"Well . . . was it hot? She was all kickass and stuff. You said she is chained to the wall. How the hell did you get a girl chained to the wall to make out with you, by the way?" Clover's expression turned from charmed and intrigued to dark and angry.

"No, it wasn't like that, I didn't force myself on her. The woman can kill me ten different ways. It's just that there is this connection between us. I have never felt anything like her, you know?" Owen paused before going on. "She was just a kid, Clover, when her whole life was screwed up. Anyone can see it. You know?" There was a deeper meaning in his words, the question about a time they didn't talk about.

"So you made out with the chained-up girl out of pity?"

"Don't you do that crap to me. No one was there to stand between her and this Kerogen. Nine years old. I wasn't there. Mara wasn't there. Damon, you weren't there. It just happened, and she is fighting to break the bond. To get back to what you and I have right now. Freedom, Clover. So, yes, I went down there and pushed her to talk to Damon and Mara, and me. The kiss . . . the kiss . . ." He faltered. "The kissing was just really hot."

Clover shook her head from side to side as if she were going back and forth over the information. "Okay, as long as I don't have to cut your dick off for forcing yourself on the girl." Her hand went up into the air and stopped. Owen gave her a sheepish grin before smacking the hand for a high five. "Making out with the hunter, bonus points," Clover said. "Very rock and roll."

A voice smooth as silk intruded behind them.

"You have been kissing the prisoner?" Cornelius asked from the open doorway.

Both Clover and Owen swiveled, like two teenagers with their hands in each other's pants.

"Cornelius, I didn't hear you come in," Owen said in confusion. His hearing was fantastic, and he could have sworn the door had been shut.

"You have been talking with the hunter Alice. What are you thinking, Owen?"

Owen responded without a second thought, as if the level four had been able to pull the answer right out of him. "We should all do what we can to help her. The right thing to do is break the bond. No one should be bonded without choice." He looked back to Clover not in support but in warning. What he had just said was a task far larger than protecting Daphne.

"I know Kerogen, as do Mara and Damon. He won't break the bond with the girl. The easiest way would be to kill him. However, there is a second option you should know about." The door shut behind Cornelius as he came farther into the room.

* * *

"You told Owen? Oh, I am going to chop off your balls, roast them on a spit and then feed them back to you, Cornelius. How dare you tell him? What were you thinking?"

Owen thought he could see the steam boiling off Mara like a teakettle already come to temperature and still over the fire. He should have been worried, and yet it reminded him too much of his childhood and the times she had been so mad at David. And just like then, this time it wasn't directed at him.

"Honestly, I was thinking a little fun sounds like a good time, Mara. Besides, read the room. Everyone wants a party. Don't you remember what it was like? I want to hear the gatekeeper play. I want to hear your voice as you sing again. I agree with Damon—I am tired of hiding. Let us dazzle once more. Let us reach for the unreachable, if only for a matter of hours, and let us remember what it is like to be alive. And now we can do so for a noble cause. For what is nobler than saving a young woman's freedom?"

"You are all trying to force my hand. In order to break the bond between the girl and Kerogen, we will need to fill the downstairs with etherealist and We. And even if we are successful, what then? We signed an agreement. And then there is the church with their hunters. You know the church will come after us. They will hear and come again. In this day and age, doing something so outlandish is just stupid. They already have hunters out there, and you want to give them a target?" She looked to Damon, who had only sat back and listened to the interaction. "Not to mention, Kerogen will come for retribution. Do any of you really want to tangle with him? This is a bad idea. We'll slit the girl's throat and be done with it." Even as she said it, her words rang false.

Mara swore under her breath.

The room was already aware—if they killed Alice, Kerogen would come anyway. The best option was to get ahold of Kerogen, let him know they had his bonded hunter, and make arrangements to give her back. Only it seemed no one was willing to do it.

Owen moved to Mara, gently coaxed her to look at him.

"When I went out into the world, when I left here, it became clear to me that I had no idea why you never bonded me or David. Neither did you ever allow anyone else to bond us. All those years, it would have been so easy. My well of power is far stronger than most, and I didn't receive the guitar until I was eighteen. Before that I was helpless. Absolutely helpless. Then I met someone who was bonded." He did his best not to look toward Clover, but the room knew who he was talking about. It had been years, but the signs were there. Faded but still easy to see. "It's wrong. It is just wrong. If we can undo it for this girl, well, I think we should."

"You're just like Damon. Just like him," Mara said. "Willing to jump with both feet into the fire with no plan on how to get out."

"I am also just like you, wanting to keep everyone under my care safe and free so they can make their own choices, for better or for worse. Alice is now under my care because she has no one else," Owen said.

"Well played," she whispered as she chewed on a thought. Owen could feel the struggle within Mara as she weighed options. "How well can you play that guitar these days?"

"I can't wait to show you," Owen said.

The weight in the air moved as her head dipped to the side, taking his measure, judging him—pride, pleasure and ego bloomed before her as Owen smiled.

"I should have shot you in the chest."

Damon spoke up from his normal plush-backed chair,

where he had stayed silent on the whole matter. "Do we have champagne on ice?"

Mara's head snapped to him in a way that said she was absolutely going to murder the old sax player before the sun could rise again.

CHAPTER TWENTY-TWO

Alice sat on her makeshift pallet, still chained to the wall, unsure for the first time in years.

What the hell am I thinking? Come on, Alice, you know that was stupid. Stupid! Hold him hostage and get free. Get free, take down Kerogen . . . return home. The last thought was weak from years of holding on to the same goal. So many years. Did her mother even still think of her? Did her father? Only through spying had she found out about her baby sister. But the spying had turned up her own head-stone too.

Am I even any closer to getting back to them? Certainly not at the moment. What the hell am I doing?

Alice swore, breaking the endless silence of the ball-room. Somehow the light had her feeling even more alone than the dark had. She didn't belong here. Even the stone around her was blackened, as if from her presence.

"What am I doing?" she asked into the vast space.

She had thought to try again to break the chains. And yet, Owen had told her he had a plan. Of course it required

her to trust him. Hormones—it was the only explanation
for why she had told him she would cooperate. Hormones
and his lips and hands. *Damn hormones.*

So that was what kissing a boy felt like. It had only taken
all of her life to experience. Only he wasn't just anyone.
There was a fire inside him, a controlled burn just on the
edge of destruction that had called to her. Even here without him in the room, she could be honest about it. For a
moment, the chains, her past, her need to kill Kerogen and
everything else in the world had simply disappeared, leaving just him and her. Never in her life had she experienced
anything like it.

How did he do that? How did we do that?

The doors opened, and Mara, Damon and Cornelius
were behind them, led by Owen. His movements were brisk
as his head nodded yes. Alice came to her feet, unwilling
to remain sitting as the others came in. She had just enough
time to brush off her legs and butt before the four of them
were standing in front of her.

"I spoke to Mara and Damon. Just be honest with them,
and we can work this all out right now." Owen reinforced
his words with a positive stare.

"Fine." The single word echoed low before fading away.

A thin, vibrating tension was in the space between the
three We, with Owen somehow in the middle. It caused her
to feel uneasy and yet not outwardly threatened.

"Mara," Damon demanded, breaking the silence. His
voice was too perfectly in between question and rebuke to
know which he meant.

"All right, all right. It seems you, little harlot, have con-
vinced Owen that you can be trusted. Somewhat. Break my
club again, and I will kill you myself. Endanger anyone
under my protection or any of my patrons, and I will snap
you like a twig. Do you believe me?"

Alice couldn't help but see the woman's rage boiling
beneath. No, she thought, Mara wasn't a creature to be

taken lightly. But then, she had already gathered that. "I believe you."

"Speak up, child. We are out of time for games."

Pushing her anger aside, Alice shot a glance to Owen, with a promise of retribution. "I said I believe you. I need information so I can leave. I am certain you have it."

"We do, but that is not what you need," Mara countered.

A lightness came to Alice's arms, causing her to look down just as the chains leading to the cuffs around her wrists dissolved to a black ash that disappeared on a breeze that didn't touch her skin. Alice raised her arms to see the cuffs still remained, but she was no longer chained to the wall.

A joy bloomed in her chest. Right then, she could attack if she wanted. Right then, she might be able to leave if things went more her way. *Freedom of a type. Progress.*

Alice looked closely at the cuffs, knowing she still could not pull on her ethereal power.

So a longer leash? At least this is something.

A changing behind her on the wall caused her to turn and look. Before her eyes, the round anchors that the chains had been connected to shimmered, the black stone beneath matching the vibration. Alice took a step back, not sure what to expect. When all the black stones that didn't belong started to shimmer, both on the wall and underfoot, Alice looked to the right and left, tracking the shimmering stones.

Like scales on a snake being flipped over, the black stone disappeared, revealing more gold-and-white polished tile.

"What are you?" she asked as she looked back toward Mara.

"I am one of the We and keeper of this house. Now, as I was saying, you do not need information. You need your bond to be severed, and we might be able to help you with this."

Alice rolled the words back and forth in her mind, unsure of what she had just heard.

The bond severed.

When nothing more was forthcoming from Mara, Alice had to ask. "What do you mean, severed?"

"Severed, child. Cut, dismantled, snapped, torn apart, undid, undone. It is one of the rules of this world. Anything made can and will be unmade. One must only have enough control, power and understanding to make it so."

Damon made a sound like a low cough. Alice could see the man's brown eyes were bright with life even as his face was placid.

"Right," Mara said. "One must also have the will to dive into the flames. Lucky for you, we have two fools here who seem willing and wanting to do just that. Now here is the agreement. My people will try and help you break your bond, and in return, you will not go against any of us. Not ever!"

"When will you try and break my bond with Kerogen?"

"Good girl. One month from today. It will take that long to get the word out and prepare for a process that will not be easy, nor without risk."

One month. One month and the connection could be broken. She flexed her hands. "And you can do this? Break the connection, and I can be free, fully free?"

Unbound, and without the relic?

Mara raised an eyebrow as if the question was insulting.

Alice defended herself. "No, I am not trying to offend you. I have never heard of anyone breaking a bond. And I have asked."

The eyebrow dropped. "Few have the tools, the power, and fewer still remember how. But it can be done, though it is not without its trials. Be warned—"

"I agree to the terms. My word on it. But I want my weapons back," Alice said.

CHAPTER TWENTY-THREE

"The shower is just in there. Use anything of mine," Daphne said to Alice.

Owen watched from the doorway of the small bedroom the girls were going to all share.

Daphne is sweet, too thin and very innocent, Alice thought.

"We are getting some of your own clothes for you—yes, they have your van—but if you need anything of mine, just ask. If I don't have it, I am sure Clover does," Daphne said as she continued to give the small tour.

"Who is Clover?" Alice asked as she looked toward the bathroom. After two weeks of being chained to a wall, she couldn't wait to be clean.

"Oh, you haven't met her yet? Clover is part of our crew," Daphne said. "She is absolutely awesome and super nice. She's been on the road with Owen the longest and plays a mean violin."

"The waitress?" Alice guessed, looking back to Owen for confirmation.

"The one you almost impaled," he responded.

"Oh, you mean, with my knives? The same knives you are refusing to give back to me?"

Daphne made a sound, but they both ignored her.

"Not really the point, is it?" Owen said.

"Don't get in a tiff. That knife I threw sidearm was meant for you. It never had a chance of touching this Clover. Besides, you're the one who almost took out her eye with that whip of yours. And what kind of man uses a whip anyway?"

"Still pissy because your plans were interrupted?" Owen shot back.

Alice took another step in his direction before it registered that she had taken the first one. Owen was no longer in the doorway but halfway into the room.

"What is with you, Owen? Why are you always trying to piss me off?" Alice said.

"With me? Alice, you're the one with the edge. I get you free and you can't even say, 'Thank you'?"

Alice moved past Daphne, who leaned against an old dresser, trying to stay out of the way. "Is that what you want from me, Owen? You want a thank-you?"

"Guys?" Daphne said.

"I don't need a thank-you, but some gratitude wouldn't be the worst thing in the world," Owen said.

There was something about his face that captured and irritated her in equal measures. "You don't want gratitude. You want to kiss me again, Owen. Admit it!"

"Guys!" Daphne hollered.

"Daphne, what?" Owen snapped.

"If you two are going to go at it again, in any way, I do not want to be in this room. I am all rock and roll, but you two are too much for me."

Go at it? Alice felt some blood rush to her cheeks. *I wasn't going to go at anything with him. I was thinking about punching him again, maybe.* "We were not going anywhere. He just needs to be punched in the face. Which, by the way, I still owe you for." Alice redirected back to Owen. "You thought I forgot about the punch to my face in the fight. I didn't."

"Alice, you put a knife into my shoulder, cut my stomach and my leg, not to mention broke at least three of my ribs when you kicked me across the room, twice."

"You punched me in the face, and that is far, far worse."

"Oh my God, I am getting out of here," Daphne said, raising up her hands in surrender. "It feels icky being in the same room with the two of you. Alice, if you take a shower, alone, I will make sure your clothing is on the bed. Otherwise, help yourself to mine in the bag right over there, but I am leaving and shutting the door."

"There is no reason for that," Owen said, backing up.

"No. No. Nope. I am out of here," Daphne said, sliding by Alice then Owen, her hip touching the blue dresser just before making the door as she hurried to move out of the room.

A warning rang in Alice's mind as the door to the room shut behind the girl. Dirty, tired and yet heart pumping in her chest as if she were ready for a real fight, she couldn't help but lock eyes with him again.

This could be bad. This could be really bad.

Owen could hardly hold back. Alice had a way of getting under his skin and just twisting his energy. No matter how cool and collected he was, it was like she had a key or a built-in secret passageway right under his defenses, and bam! No more control.

"I should go," he said, trying to keep his words to a minimum.

"Wait."

Owen paused. *We are not heroes.* Damon's words echoed once more in his mind.

"Really, Alice. We can talk, if we need to, later. After you're clean and comfortable. There is plenty of time."

"Owen." His name came out soft, more vulnerable than anything before. "Thank you for helping me get out of there."

"You are welcome. And I am sorry about punching you in the face." He held his position, trying to remain calm. The connection between them and the chemistry all mixed with the vibration in the air. Everything, each curve, each edge beneath was an enticement for Owen to be brash.

"Don't be. It was a good punch. Rang me a little. Owen?"

"Yes, Alice?"

"What's the matter with you? I can feel it like a fire in the palm of my hand. You're active." She stumbled to make the word fit. "And I don't think it is normal."

How can I possibly explain, if you don't already know what it is like to go too long without letting the pressure out? The need to do something crazy, reckless. And then there is what is between us.

Owen took the coward's way out and changed the subject. "Alice, I need to ask you something, something important. Something vital." He opened up his soul so she could feel his words as he stepped forward, crossing some of the distance that remained between them. "You're free of the chains, at least, and my people are going to do everything they can to break the bond between you and Kerogen. Invitations have already been sent out for more ethereal power, and we will prepare over the weeks to come. My word on it. But I need your word now. I need you to promise me you won't hurt or endanger any of them. I need to know I can trust you in this. I need to know that those I protect, be it We or human, that you won't harm them. That you won't betray me and mine, in this room or out there."

Alice felt the weight of the air change, could see the mask he wore slip, almost melt back to reveal the real Owen. Each word spoken pulled threads of her will within.

"You want my word?" she asked slowly.

"My people need to know—"

"Stop. I know you need to know. I can see it in you. Owen, I'll hold up your promise, and I give you my word I won't hurt any of them. I swear it to you. But if you try to break me, Owen, I will kill you." The last part just came out. She didn't know from where, and yet she meant every word.

"My battles aren't with you. I'll let you get cleaned up now."

There was pain in his eyes, a deep, raw cut into his soul that she could feel, almost touch. Not completely understanding, she moved to him. And before he could speak, she leaned in and kissed him.

Alice wanted the kiss to be soft and gentle. She wanted to help. Instead, she had little choice but to settle for non-clumsiness. Then, turning, Alice walked away and into the bathroom. The sound of Owen opening the bedroom door to leave could be heard just as she closed the door to the little bathroom.

Alice still wore the cuffs, but the water washing down her body was magnificent. Greedily she used Daphne's shampoo and conditioner, then conditioned again. The soap she used repeatedly, until her light skin held a bright red tint to it.

Oh, to be fresh again!

When her fingers were sure to begin wrinkling any second, Alice finally turned the spigot handle to the left, shutting off the water.

Almost lazily, she wrapped herself in the towel, using a second towel for her short hair, and went to look for the clothing Daphne had assured her would be on the bed.

Apparently they had found her van the first night. And had no trouble going through her things. Hence her clothing folded neatly on the corner of the bed as she went back into the small room, with its two beds across from each other, a small writing desk off to the far side.

Alice hadn't taken a single step into the room before realization hit her—she was no longer alone. Clover, the waitress, stood before her. Tall, blue eyes, long-limbed but with enough curve to give her figure a healthy shape.

"Hello. I'm Clover. I heard you will be sharing our room." Each word was in balance, in control.

"It seems that way. I'm Alice."

"The hunter, yes, everyone knows." Clover's tone shifted to cold, unfriendly.

"Do we have a problem?" Alice asked, feeling vulnerable and cornered, wet and relatively exposed. Not trusting the timing of the meeting to be accidental.

I did throw a knife close to this woman's head. Is this the issue? I also let her leave when I didn't have to. Or is this about Owen?

"I'm not sure if we do have a problem. You see, Owen has a blind spot for protecting people. Particularly when it comes to women being bonded."

"Oh, is that right?" Alice asked from beside the bed, where she stood wet and wrapped only in a towel.

"It is right. I was bonded once. It was for five long, grueling months. That's when Owen found me playing in a bar for the We. He and I don't talk about it. I don't talk about it." Her words came out as much a threat as a warning. "I am sorry for your situation. I am, Alice. But you need to know that I know the evil that can seep inside, through the bond. The darker parts that can't ever be washed clean. I remember the desperation I was in to be free. So I hope you can hear what I am telling you, because I am not saying you are not welcome here. But before you and I can be cool, you need to know if you screw with him, take advantage of him because of his soft spot, all for the sake of your own freedom, there is a whole group that will tear you apart without him ever having a say. It will happen in a blink, hunter or no hunter, raw deal or no raw deal, and I will be first in line."

Alice didn't know what to feel as she listened. Clover's words were touching too many parts of her soul she normally kept locked away. Too many places Alice would prefer were left alone. It was easy to be hard, to be a weapon. Steel didn't feel, didn't have to think about the tragedies of others.

She felt a deep sadness and compassion for the woman before her. Just as she felt a reaction to the threat. As well as internal twisting that this woman had such a strong connection to Owen. Wrapping everything together, she was struck with a respectful openness, because at least this woman wasn't all bullshit. "What are you to him?" Alice asked.

"I'm Owen's friend and bandmate. And you are about to find out any friend of his will walk into the fire, either with him or for him. However, if you're worried about anything else between him and me, don't be. There is not, nor has there ever been, any romance between us, nor will there ever be. I like to think the two of us are just travelers on the same twisting road, bonded in our own way. But knowing our destinations are not the same."

Alice took a moment, letting Clover's words settle in. "So you were bonded for five months?"

"I was. The We who fooled me, trapped me and forced the bonding is dead, along with all of his friends. That's the last I plan to say about it. Now you know something about me and I know something about you. You are going to want to get dressed." Alice listened as Clover's voice changed, slipping into something almost friendly. "Mara just gave Jessie and me permission to play onstage. The bar isn't full, but it's going to be fun. And after the last two weeks we have both just gone through, I think every one of us could use a bit of fun. I know I sure as hell can."

Alice watched as Clover slipped a violin case from under

the opposite bed. One hand took the handle as the other stroked over the case.

"You're going to play for all of them?" Alice couldn't help the question. She had been told it happened. But the only time she had ever seen a human singing or playing with power with one of *them* in attendance was when she had been forced to sing all those years ago. On the day her life had changed forever.

"Yeah, there are at least twenty strong We out there, let alone the main table. It's going to be awesome! There is so much raw energy in this building, it's going to be like surfing one of those giant waves you see on the covers of magazines. Jessie's words, not mine, and even though it wasn't my idea to come here, the musicians in this town really know what they are doing. I would say there is a better than decent chance someone will join us onstage after we get started. Don't worry—we are not making a run. Just flirting a little. Oh, it already feels good, like I can breathe again." An energetic joy spilled from the woman, a stark contrast to what had been there before.

Is everyone here two-sided? Or just bat-guano crazy? Or just broken? The last thought was soft, with a reverence that reverberated down her spine.

"Can't . . . I mean . . ." Alice had to quell the stress in her voice as she started again. *Twenty of them, plus the main table?* "Aren't you worried one of them will try and bond you again?"

Alice dropped the extra towel she had used to dry her hair on the edge of the bed, eager to get dressed in fresh clothing. At the same time, her hands itched for her weapons. Just the idea of being around so many of them was very unsettling. Now, cuffed as she was, she still couldn't pull on her remaining ethereal power. And every one of those creatures out there could.

"No, they can't bond me without my permission. I mean, there is a story out there that says it is possible, and since they can unbind you, I'm guessing the story is true. However, I am sure it would take someone like Mara or maybe Cornelius and Damon working all together, and then who gets the bond? Besides, those three gave their word to me, and to Owen."

Alice fidgeted as she tried to make sense of a world far different than her own.

"Wait, you're confused? You don't know about any of this? How can you not know about the rules? About how everything works?"

"The priests spent a lot of time on training. And, well, I separated from them before they got to the rest. I have been hunting Kerogen down ever since." *Nothing else ever mattered.*

"How long ago was that? That you separated from them?"

"About seven years, I was nineteen. Until now I never needed any other information. It's not a big deal," she lied.

"You know straight-out lies to any of us just aren't a smart idea, right? We don't all have Owen's hearing, but still."

"Owen mentioned something like that. I think I will just stay in tonight, if that's all right. I haven't slept on an actual bed in some time."

"Ouch! But no way. You can't stay in here, it's going to be awesome. You don't want to miss it. I promise. Look, Jessie is smooth. Not big and powerful like Owen, but all low and groovy-like. And with all of these high-powered We in one spot, not to mention it's like the walls are filled to the brim with essence, I promise it is going to be a show."

Alice felt fear slide deep inside her chest. She hadn't really thought about facing a room full of . . . well, maybe not demons. A panic gave her a little shake at the idea of facing them without ethereal power, without her weapons.

What am I supposed to do? I will be practically helpless out there. Absolutely helpless and at their mercy.

"No, I can't. I will just stay here." With each word spoken,

Alice felt more naked and exposed than any other time but when she had been with Kerogen.

"Why not?" Clover asked, moving forward, a look somewhere between curiosity and—could that be sympathy crossing her face?

"It doesn't matter," Alice said, bringing up her hands to ward off the woman from coming any closer. She wanted the room to change, wanted space to gather herself.

The cuffs caught the light as Clover came to a stop. Alice hated the sadness she could see in the woman's eyes.

Alice, what is going on?" Owen asked, while coming down the hall in surprise. He had been watching for her to come out of the back rooms; however, he had positioned himself by the front bar and hallway. When Clover and Alice had seen him and headed away from him, moving toward the back hall, Owen had come in pursuit.

"Owen, she forced me to get dressed, handed me this case with her violin, then told me not to worry about any We, because if anyone touched her violin case, presumably besides me, she would murder them. And then Clover forced me to follow her out here. I think she is a little crazy." Alice pointed to where Clover had stepped up toe-to-toe with none other than Cornelius.

"She needs that knife back, Cornelius. Alice. She needs it back, and I know Jones gave it to you," Clover said to the level four, who had been ordering a drink from the small side bar. Heads nearby turned in their direction.

"Clover, what's going on?" Owen called, leaving Alice just within the shelter of the hall, violin case in hand.

"Cornelius has that jeweled knife of hers, the one made out of ethereal essence. He needs to give it back to her so she can be comfortable around everyone."

"I don't think *comfortable* is what everyone else has

in mind right now, Clover. And that knife isn't just any weapon."

"Owen!" That voice was the Clover he knew onstage. "Think about it. She is here surrounded by We and trapped. It's like getting onstage without your guitar, like stepping up to the mic without your voice. Need more? It is like stepping into a ring of lions without even a chair or whip. Can you feel how that would be? She is a hunter surrounded by We, and she can't use ethereal energy, even though you and I and any of the We walking through the door can. Alice has no way to defend herself. How can she possibly feel safe here?"

"She also can't stab anyone," Cornelius said with a surprising amount of mirth.

At any other time, the We's joke might have been funny, Owen thought. However, Clover could very well burn down the house if she thought it appropriate or, in this case, in defense of a bonded woman. A situation Owen hadn't fully considered.

"She gave her word, right? And you all heard it, right?" Clover pressed. "Alice has the cuffs on. Fine. But you can't leave her defenseless. Give back her damn instrument of choice."

Cornelius started to laugh, his sound so pure and real it turned heads, even more so than Clover telling the high-power We what to do. "I love it, 'her instrument of choice.' Mara, I agree with Clover."

"You what?" Owen asked with surprise.

Mara had already turned in her chair at the main table and had followed the conversation. "It is connected with her anyway. Our agreement holds if she has the weapon or not," she said, turning back as if the conversation was no longer worthy of her consideration.

"Excellent," Clover declared, and shifted to include Jones the bartender in the conversation. "Now that that's taken care of, we will need—what?" Clover started count-ing on her fingers. "Say, ten shots of whiskey and orange slices to match."

D on't you want a seat closer?" Alice asked Owen.

"No, right here is fine," Owen said.

They weren't alone, nor were they at the main table in the corner, but instead were at one of the middle tables be-tween the main table and the small bar. Remnants of shots taken, half a bottle, along with a plate of eaten orange slices were dirtying their area. Daphne was taking a turn at the side bar with Jones inspecting her progress.

Owen watched as Max gave a high five to both Clover and Jessie, for luck, as he made his way back to the bar. The piano was no longer tucked up against the wall but instead stood ready for Jessie to play.

Owen could feel the weight of the room, the power and need for action. It all was so thick it felt as if he was chok-ing on it. He sat still, waiting, watching as two of his people smiled out to the crowd.

"Owen, what happened to the room?"

"What?" he asked. Alice was looking at the walls, tables and chairs. "What do you mean? The room is fine."

"The last time I was here, I was pretty sure I destroyed most of it."

"You did break a lot more tables and chairs than most. However, your attack was nothing out of the ordinary. Well, besides the fact they didn't kill you."

"Well, that was kind of insulting. So there is a lot of vio-lence here?"

"Sort of. Mara and Cornelius tend to handle anyone who is looking for a fight. General plan—stay out of their way, and they will sweep up any problem and get the bar run-ning back on track before the night is done."

"That's not what you did?" she said.

"Did what?" Max asked, sitting down.

"Max, cards!" Owen demanded, holding out his palm for the expected deck.

"Oh, come on, I haven't even done a trick today. Owen, it's not fair. The others get to play. What is the big deal?"

"I never said it was fair, Max, but card tricks set a vibe of being untrustworthy. That vibe and misdirection have the possibility of changing the laws we all abide by. Remember, we survive amongst the We by establishing trust. The card tricks you play are a ripple when we want the waters as calm as they can be."

"The huntress is getting back her knife, but I can't have a deck of cards. This is bollocks. Bollocks, Owen," he said, standing up and placing a new box of cards still wrapped and sealed with plastic down in Owen's outstretched hand. "Really, boss. It's like you enjoy stealing my fun. How did you even know I got another set?"

"I am just protecting you, Max." Something in the air changed, and Owen couldn't help but think Max was the cause. "Besides, you have someone new to perform for. I simply played the odds you wouldn't miss such an opportunity." To accent his point, Owen crushed down the fresh pack of cards.

To his own surprise, the box crinkled as it folded in on itself, empty.

"Ta-da!" Max said with a dazzling white smile, coming back to his feet as he directed his full attention to Alice.

"Damn it, Max! Where are the cards?"

"I don't know, boss. It must be magic."

Owen watched as the kid waved his fingers in a mocking display meant to be mysterious. "Come on, man. Don't do this."

"Why don't you have another drink, Owen?" Max said.

"Oh, there they are," Alice said with more surprise than Owen would have liked.

Sure enough, Alice was right. Beneath the bottle of

whiskey, which hadn't seemed to move, set in the center of the table, was a crisp set of cards.

Owen reached for them. Max did as well. For the smallest of moments Owen thought he had the cards, but somehow his hand came away with the bottle of booze instead.

"Here they are. Oh, but wait, they look a little thin to me." Max pinched the deck between two fingers and held them out as if he could tell just by the feel there was a card missing.

Owen couldn't help himself—he groaned as his eyes did a quick sweep of the table once more.

"No, no. It's okay. I am sure we can get to the bottom of this," Max went on. "We just need a little 'ta-da.' You know, magic."

Holding the cards with two fingers of his right hand, the kid made a show of only using two fingers on his left hand to pull the cards in half to either side as Owen watched. Smooth and graceful, the cards were cut in two, half the pile going in the left hand between two fingers, and the other half staying in the right between thumb and forefinger.

"Wait, that's not right. We need to get to the bottom of these missing cards, not separate them." Max pushed the two half decks back together, and Owen could feel something change, almost a tingling in the air. It was small and subtle, but there.

The deck re-formed but was clearly only half the size as it had been before, half the deck disappearing right before everyone's eyes.

"That is awesome," Alice said as she watched.

"Now wait, we are running out of time." As if on cue, Clover onstage started to check her strings, one by one.

Max smiled, then his face furrowed as his concentration grew. Holding half the deck between the same two fingers, he suddenly flicked the corner of the cards with his free hand, sending them all spinning in place. He flicked again, causing them to rotate even faster and faster.

"Ta-da," Max whispered as he suddenly pinched the cards tight, bringing them to an instant stop.

Only it was not cards, plural, but what looked to be a single card, facedown as before, but too thin to be any more than one—the rest of the deck having simply disappeared.

"Wow!" Alice exclaimed. "That is cool. You know I can do something similar with a throwing knife?"

Owen kept his face still. Anything less would only give Max the impression there was more wiggle room going forward.

"Now let's see what card is missing." Max shook the single card, keeping it flat to the table, then flipping it up.

Owen couldn't see what it was as Max faced the card toward Alice. "Please, madam, please tell the crowd what the card is?"

"What crowd, Max?" Owen asked.

"It's the king of diamonds," Alice answered.

"The king of diamonds, you say, a card filled with power and strength. Interesting, very interesting."

The red card went flat again and spun once more between Max's thumb and forefinger. With another snap, Max turned, and the queen of diamonds was in his hand, thrust up for Owen to see.

"And you, good sir, what card do you see?"

"It's the queen of diamonds, Max," Owen said, wanting this to be done with.

"The queen of diamonds! Now that is a ta-da. For there to be two cards missing from the deck—how intriguing, the king and the queen. And yet how could they have escaped, as they are no longer here!" Max flipped the queen so she disappeared from view, then slammed the card down on the table faceup, his hand over the top. Only it wasn't the queen or king of diamonds, as the black ace of spades could just be seen poking through his long fingers.

With a flourish, Max swiped the card, fanning out the deck in perfect order across the table for them both to see.

Only the cards weren't perfect—they only seemed that way at first. Owen leaned in, unable to help himself, as Alice did the same from the other side. He spotted the gap at roughly the same time she did. Both the king of diamonds and queen of diamonds were absent, the remaining fifty cards faceup in perfectly spaced order.

"Now where have our elusive king and queen gone off to?" Max made his fingers dance once more in the air and looked silly in doing so. "Good sir, would you mind—"

Owen cut him off. "Really, Max."

"Very well, madam, would you be so kind as to check your pocket?" Max shifted, bringing his hands together to build a steeple, then pressed his palms in like some sort of gleeful prayer.

Alice checked her right pocket. When it was clear it was empty, Max signaled she should check the other one. Alice did, again coming up empty.

"Well, that's not a good sign. Is it possible that dirty old king is in your bra? You never know what a king will do. I don't make the rules."

"Max, I swear if she finds that card in her bra, you and I are going to have a discussion outside." Owen kept his eyes on Max as Alice quickly checked.

"Not here either," Alice said.

"Are you sure?" Max asked, his voice taking on a hint of panic. It wasn't the first time Max's tricks had gone awry.

"Pretty sure," Alice said.

"Could you check again?"

"No," Alice said.

"Max!"

"That's fair, that's fair. Owen, can you check your pockets?"

Owen did, happy the attention was off Alice. "No cards, Max."

"What about your shirt pocket?" A slump came to Max's shoulders.

Owen checked, finding no card once again.

"Hey!" A patron in one of the corner booths along the wall yelled as he stood and held up a light gold glass of beer with a red card within. "Who the hell put this in my glass?"

"Quick, man!" Max said, his tone and posture shifting back to that of a performer. "Is it the queen of diamonds?"

"Max? You did this?" the patron asked.

"Hey, Sam. Is it the queen?"

"No, it's the joker," Sam said.

"Damn it. My bad, buddy," Max called out.

"You ruined my drink, Max!"

"Sam! Pal, my friend, sorry about your drink. This one is on me," Max said, turning with his hands up as if someone had just robbed the place. "No hard feelings. Right? Clover is ready to play, and I know the bartender. Let me buy your party a round. Sometimes magic is a mysterious thing, even to me."

"No," Owen said, catching Max's belt as he tried to make a break. "Max, cards!" The little ass had swept the deck up off the table, somehow.

"Damn it, here," Max said as he handed over the deck. "Sam, what was that you were drinking?"

Owen turned to regard Alice. There was a question in her expression, "Yes," Owen said in response. "That kid is going to start a fight in here. It is just a matter of time. Not everyone loves magic tricks. Particularly when they go awry, which they often do with him."

Even as they watched, Max flung an arm around Sam's big, stocky frame as if the two of them were longtime friends. Sam was human, but even so, Owen thought he would keep an eye out just in case.

"I have to say," Alice said with joy, "for a moment there I thought it was pretty awesome."

"At times he can be. However, no matter how many extra years he gains, Max is always going to push."

"You're one to talk. What instrument does he play?" Alice asked.

"Max, he plays harmonica. He's good when no one is watching. He isn't really a musician. Just has the power, not the will. Plus, I swear, whenever I think I know what he is doing, I can be sure he is doing something else. It makes playing with him wild and crazy. Great for a song or late night. Not so great for a full set. Out of the question for making a run."

"Makes sense, I guess. But you never answered my question."

"What question was that?" Owen asked.

"The bar—I can't see a trace of the fight. Not even the wallpaper looks to be damaged. Everything seems to be perfect, and I recall a pretty big explosion."

"Welcome to the Golden Horn. I have seen this place on fire, and less than a day later, Mara has it back to the way she wants it. Even the smell was the same."

"What is she, Mara? I can't tell. Her underglow marking says level five, but it blurs and almost shifts. And her power hides, like most of it is reversed. When I came in, I didn't even have her pegged as one of the strongest in the room."

It was easy for Owen to hear the question was more than casual. "She is something else, I think. Sort of like when a human with ethereal power makes a life contract with a We and opens a sanctuary. From then on, everyone calls the person a companion because the person starts to shift."

Everything about Alice said she didn't know what he was talking about.

He went on. "I have seen it firsthand. They don't age as fast, begin to be stronger, tougher, and in far better control of their emotions. As if time plays a different role. I think this has sort of happened to Mara and this place, even though she is a level five We and not an etherealist. You have seen the downstairs. I promise it is only a fraction of what she can do."

Alice responded by finishing her shot of whiskey she had only sipped on. "So she is a super badass."

"Pretty much, at least here." Owen looked at the half-full bottle that was set down before him. It took only a moment to decide it wasn't a night for drinking.

"Catch!" The call came from Cornelius as he strode in from the hall corridor.

Owen raised his hand, but the projectile wasn't aimed at him.

Alice swiveled in her chair, her hands coming up, plucking the serrated-edged knife right out of the air as if it had been practiced a thousand times.

"Well done," Cornelius said, all smiles as he took his seat at the main table.

"Is there something about me that just says, 'Hey, let's all chuck stuff at this girl'?" Alice said as she swiveled back in her seat.

Owen made to respond, distracted as the knife danced between Alice's thin fingers, much as a drummer's stick might in his own. "I can't say I see anything particular at the moment that makes me want to throw anything at you. Though you do seem to have very fast reflexes even without ethereal power."

Alice shifted the blade into raw, glowing essence, then let it slip down beneath the table. Presumably to let it form over her belt buckle as she had when she entered the club for the very first time.

But not seeing it left something uncomfortable in his gut. "Do you feel better?" Owen asked.

"Having the knife, yes. Knowing I have to spend weeks here waiting? No."

"Do you want to get out of here?" Owen asked, trying to hold back the wave of desire for her to answer in one direction.

"You don't need to stay and watch your friends play?"

"It's your voice, with those eyes, and your soul. The combination is what cracks my walls of control. I have been trying to figure it out for days. It's not one thing but all of them. No, I don't need to stay. In fact, it might be better if I get some space from here. My people are safe. Clover knows what she is doing. And Jessie is solid up there. Besides, the party is just getting started. They will be at it for hours. Come on."

Owen stood up, leaving the bottle and the mess. Suddenly he needed to be out of that space. Before Alice could object, he reached across the table and took her hand in his and helped her to her feet. Daphne, Mara, Damon and Cornelius would all see the exit. And if they had a problem with his choices, they could bloody well go burn themselves.

CHAPTER TWENTY-FOUR

Alice was led down the back hall of the Golden Horn. Owen's hand, unquestionably strong, was smooth and sure as he directed them both deeper into the building. Together they moved left, leaving the club, heading back toward the private rooms.

With each step she took, her heartbeat raced faster and faster. Excitement, risk and reward—all three were in the air between them. Her skin tingled with excitement.

This is a very bad idea. A very bad idea, and I just don't care anymore.

Of course, the intensity between them hadn't started out that way. It was just that the connection continued to shift and grow with each step taken, each stride separating the two of them from everyone else. Each moment Owen held her hand and Alice held his.

Gently she shook her shoulders, the go-tension too high not to let it out. Owen turned to her.

That wasn't very subtle, Alice thought as she met the

lightness of his eyes that seemed to belong to him and him alone.

"Outside I have my truck, and we could get some fresh air? Or we could go to your bedroom? There is a lock on the door." His voice was deeper than normal. Rough and heavy. She could appreciate she wasn't the only one feeling what lay between them.

Alice tried to answer. Found she couldn't.

Owen looked back to her once more, the sound of the bar fading behind as his world narrowed completely. Owen pulled Alice in close, lips slowing just before contact as he kissed her.

Alice wasn't surprised as Owen pulled her in. Of course this was where it was leading, where it had always been leading. The chemistry, the constant pull and push between them.

I am action and so is he. Could it really have led anywhere else?

She leaned in and kissed him back. His body was all muscle beneath his shirt. And his lips—his lips were divine as she took what she wanted, what he demanded.

Chemistry and fascination zipped through her senses, tingling her mind, and she could admit right then she wanted more. Alice twisted, shoving his body up against the wall, his head hitting a little.

Owen's laughter was short-lived, and she ignored it, kissing him as the sound cut off. Alice's free hand slipped underneath his black shirt to feel the hard and soft ripple of Owen's stomach, the feel, the texture, fascinating to the touch as she met tiny peaks and valleys of hard muscle under smooth skin.

Owen couldn't get enough as she pressed him in. How could a woman so small be so full of life? So ripe with power? Exotic to the point of pain. He wanted more, more of everything. His hips adjusted for the tension he was feeling as his hand took her behind the head, and he bent her neck to the side. Soft, white flesh was exposed as he set a trail of kisses up to her ear.

Alice felt him grow, his body shifting to make room. Fear, joy, raw energy rushed her system, flooding it as her mind went hazy with need.

Alice's hand changed direction from exploring up under his shirt to fingertips moving down, gliding over muscle until they reached his denim jeans. She had a choice, but in truth it was already made. In some ways it had been made when she had chosen not to kill him with the broken bottle. Her fingers continued over the belt, then down over the large bulge in his pants as his lips warmed her neck and tingled her mind. She felt him twitch in response, his length stretching the fabric and pressing into the palm of her hand, heavy and hard.

"Owen," she tried to say, but it came out of a dry mouth.

"Bedroom," he whispered.

Before she knew what was happening, she was in his arms, her hands going around his strong, clean neck.

Owen wanted to move fast.

No, what he wanted was to have her right here in the hallway and let the world be damned. He wanted Alice naked, to see everything she was hiding. He wanted to feel her body and will as she pushed and lost control. He wanted to drive her crazy, feel the truth and power of life as it pulsed between them.

He wanted to touch her and have her touch him as they both forgot and remembered who they were.

Owen settled for a fast walk as he took Alice in his arms and moved down toward her bed. His eyes met her own, and it was a mistake—cheeks tinted red, lips full and inviting, her eyes smoldering with desire, framed in by the hard, sharp cut of her black hair. Owen couldn't help but kiss her again. Her arms pulled him in as he leaned forward.

The kiss was hard and hot as she refused to let go. Refused to let it end. The thick bulge that drove into her hip a constant reminder this was headed for far more.

Alice wanted it to last, needing to be lost, to be grounded. She wanted to forget and live far more than the twinge of fear in her gut called for her to be careful.

Owen broke the kiss. The door to her room wasn't far off, but she wouldn't let him go. Alice's arms were steel bands around his neck, and she smiled as he had no choice but to come back in again. This time the kiss turned soft in contrast, and it melted away a touch of the frenzy.

Owen pulled ethereal power, and the door to the bedroom she was to share now opened as if on its own.

Alice let Owen have his head as he took them both through and in. Letting go of his neck with one hand, Alice used her now free hand to reach lower, squeezing between her body and his to feel his form once more.

In her mind's eye, Alice tried to picture its length, but her mind was too fuzzy to be any help. She felt him tense and had an idea of what was about to happen before it did.

Alice's hand half stroked, half groped him through his jeans, and it wasn't enough. His desire for her was too high to be settled away by half measures.

I want all of you, and I want you right now, Owen thought loud enough he was sure she could hear him, just before setting her on the bed.

Alice's laugh was pure and inviting. Owen's shoes came off before the springs beneath the bed had settled down.

"Owen, wait." Her words had him stopping, and the tension was like running a hand on the edge of a knife. It almost hurt. It seemed as if it was going to kill.

"Is there a problem?" he asked, unsure.

"Not at all, I just wanted to screw with you. Take off your pants." Alice swept off her shirt, revealing a purple bra and two perfect, pale breasts beneath.

"You just wanted to screw with me?" he asked, slipping his shirt off and tossing it over Daphne's bag of clothing.

"I did, yes. Your pants, please."

There was an innocence in her movements, even behind

her voice, which made him think she wasn't as experienced as she was letting on.

Alice's pants slipped off, revealing toned legs and matching purple lace boy shorts that enhanced far more than they concealed. Her eyes were big as she placed her jeans beside the bed. And Owen couldn't think, not a single thought. Alice was beautiful and, simply put, enticing.

Strong muscle, smooth lines and soft, mind-bending curves. But it was the will behind the body that trapped him. Held him captive as he took her in. She was a warrior, a woman who knew the long dark road and refused to break.

His buckle unsnapped, and Owen took off his underwear and socks with his jeans as he finished undressing. He knew the reaction his body sometimes elicited, but the way her eyebrows crawled high up her forehead, along with her lips parting for breath, was a delicacy. A bright pleasure blooming as he moved toward her.

You have got to be kidding me, Alice thought.

Alice had known Owen was strong, a musician in shape. But he wasn't a big guy. Sure, he was tall, but holy crap, it was like once again he had hidden part of himself from the world.

Alice forgot her fears, her mind racing to take in as much of his body as she could. Shoulders and arms were sculpted as if by a master's hand. His chest, not overly large, was trim and curved, leading down to a stomach full of lines and bumps that said he was made for long, hot nights and evenings where he wouldn't quit, wouldn't slow, wouldn't tire.

Alice's eyes braked as they moved lower, as if somehow she was spying on something sacred. His erection stole her ability to breathe. It was thick and hard, long and waiting. Her body tingled as he moved closer.

Three steps before he closed, Alice suddenly moved in a hurry, sliding her underwear off and then coming up to stand beside him.

Alice kissed Owen hard and fast, one hand gripping his shaft and pulling. Then she bit his lip just a little. "You lie down."

She thought her meaning was clear. Owen gave a small kiss, then lowered to the bed so he was sitting, his hard shaft falling out of her hand as he did so. His skilled hands wrapped around her waist and pulled her in close. Alice's breasts were practically in his face, and the idea for the first time was fascinating.

Moving on instinct, she pushed both breasts up in invitation as she ran her hands in his hair.

Owen held her hips then, reaching back, squeezing both butt cheeks at the same time. A tingling sensation zipped up her spine in response as he watched.

Everything he touched moved her, heated her. Everything about him consumed her, and yet there was a problem she needed to fix.

"Can you lie back?" she asked.

"Of course."

Alice couldn't help but drop her eyes to his hardness as Owen scooted back over the bed. *Here we go.* She climbed up on top of him, her body ready and wet.

Owen watched as Alice took her time. Gingerly even, moving up the bed.

This might be the cutest thing I have ever seen. Alice has a softer side.

It wasn't like Alice to look off-balance. And he had to admit he was loving every moment of it. *She is so beautiful, so sexy.* His hand reached for her, needing the contact as Alice swung a leg over so she was straddling him.

If he was surprised she wanted to get right to it, Owen wasn't showing it.

Leaning to her right, she reached down and stroked him slow and smooth, light dancing in her eyes as she watched the sensation rock his body in a long, growing wave.

Carefully she lowered, rubbing his tip against her wet core. Once, twice, three times. He was so big and thick.

It is like holding a . . . well, I don't have the word. But damn, he is big. And sexy, with those eyes and lips.

Owen wasn't rushing. Instead, with each back and forth he grew more and more still.

Gently she lowered, Alice's whole body and mind focused on the sensation as pain and pleasure blended too close together to separate the two. She breathed out.

Owen's mind was lost as heat covered him. Her body and hand, her spirit felt as if she was coming close to a shattering point. The sound she made was a mix of pleasure and being overwhelmed. Instinctively his hands caught her, held her.

"Are you okay?" he asked.

"Yeah, you are just, a bit, big."

"Thank you. You're breathtaking."

"Oh, I bet you say that to all the girls."

"Hey—" His objections were cut off as she raised herself off the first few inches.

His body wanted more, needed more. But there was time. If she needed to be on top for control right now, that was just fine with him. He would play in whatever position was available. For now.

Alice lowered again, this time with a little back and forth rocking motion as she slid halfway down. Her breasts, covered in purple lace, shifted as she moved. He watched as a tightness came to her lips, causing them to thin as she continued to rock down farther.

"Hey, we aren't in any rush here. I mean it," he added when she looked to him. "Why don't you come here to me?"

Alice could see what he intended. It wasn't a bad plan, to be side by side, but it wasn't her plan. "No, I'm good if you're good."

"I am very excellent, I assure you," Owen said while

Alice pulled up once more, then rocked herself halfway back down his hard shaft.

He was finding her core to be a perfect blend of silk and heat.

"Good. Besides, I heard it's better if I'm on top?"

"Wait a moment." Owen didn't move as his heart missed a beat. "What do you mean, you heard it is better?"

Alice moved a little faster, pulling her hips up almost off him, then pressing down a little faster with force. "I didn't tell you? This is my first time. Oh my." She breathed out, bearing herself down on him.

"What?" Owen asked.

"Shut up. I have just been very busy. Oh wow, okay." She let out her breath.

"Wait a minute, Alice."

"Owen, you're inside me right now, and that is sort of the way I want it, so don't screw this up."

Internally Owen thought his soul, if it hadn't been bound to Hell before, was surely secured in that direction now. Owen couldn't hold back his next words. "I think screwing it up, Alice, is kind of the whole point at this moment in time."

Her hand smacked down over his chest in a reprimand that only had him smiling.

She slowly started to rock once more. Sensation pulsed through his body as she stayed small and gentle.

"Damn, that feels good. But don't rush anything, and if you need to stop, Alice—"

His next words were cut off as her hand covered his mouth. "I am just going to sit here for a while. And you are going to remember that I can and have kicked your ass, twice."

She paused as she moved her hips slowly back and forth, the sensation building in tight little waves of pleasure. Their energy easy and euphoric.

"And you, Owen, are going to let me, because I am

about to take off my bra. So stay right there and be quiet. And damn, this feels good."

Owen smiled against her hand, staring into her beautiful eyes. The contact was raw and pure, despite the hand over his mouth. Alice wasn't scared, wasn't in real danger. He wasn't a monster, damned to the river of souls for all time. Maybe.

Owen watched as her eyes closed before she finished speaking, some part of him relaxing as she did.

Virgin? No, Owen was absolutely sure she had not said a thing about never having sex before now. Not that there had been a lot of talking. *Alice knows what she wants. You didn't force this. You're not hurting her. Not yet*, a small voice in his mind assured him.

He pushed Alice so slightly with his hips, letting her feel more length, more depth. The sound she made was exhilarating. She needed it slow, she needed this to be in her control. He could give her that. But he would be damned if Alice thought this was to be a solo act.

His hands ran up the sides of her perfect body, cresting soft skin. She was lazy and tense, but gone was the fear, the weakness. He basked in her as she opened her eyes and looked from high above him, giving a smile that curled and fed the flames. Fed his storm.

Ethereal energy answered his call as Alice's purple bra suddenly unclasped and fell free.

Owen couldn't help but smile beneath her hand again.

"How helpful of you." She had to stop talking as one of his hands settled over her right hip and Owen pushed himself deeper. Basking in pure, raw pleasure as her eyes glassed over.

Owen was transfixed as her bra fell away, and Alice removed her hand from his mouth to toss the item to the side. He didn't miss his opportunity. She was slick and hot, her body wrapped tight around his shaft.

In the low light, it was her breasts that called to him, loud and sharp, as he leaned up, careful to keep the soft, gliding rhythm. Moving forward, Owen took her nipple into his mouth. Her breasts were this side of heavenly, tight and firm. They called with a voice he couldn't refuse as his tongue danced over the pale skin.

"Damn it, Owen," she said suddenly, clamping down hard. Once, twice. A third time, breaking their rhythm and establishing a pattern as her body continued to clutch.

Owen switched to the other breast, unable to ignore it any longer. He could feel a growing rhythm within Alice, could feel her need as the pleasure and pressure grew between them both.

He was surprised as her hand came down on his chest. Alice pushed him back, the force rocking the bed and adding to the excitement.

Alice started pulling her own hips up, but Owen could feel what she really wanted. What she was trying to achieve. His hips moved slightly, gently pulling back and moving forth. It was angles and strokes. Friction and heat as he gently pressed in. Pulled back. Pressed in again. Stealing back.

Owen was mesmerized by her glow, her body and spirit, as Alice bit her own soft lip. This moment was real, full of power and life. A magic of its own kind. He wanted it to last, wanted it to go on.

Fight for me, he thought as a softness broke in her eyes. She rocked back as he pushed forward, the combination forcing him deeper. Alice's internal muscles gripped, then released as she moved forward, sliding her body away, then sliding it back as she matched and danced with him.

A rhythm formed again, this one unlike the others. This timing held an edge. A slight risk of danger on both sides.

Owen kept his side locked down. His role needed to be consistent, the base, the foundation, where she could find the room to build until she spilled over, her way. Her first way.

His body was hard and hot, and the need to take the lead was almost too intense. Almost.

Alice let herself go, her mind and body riding waves of energy and pleasure. There was a pain, but it was nothing compared with the pain she had been forced to endure already. Different, but this was her choice, and she would be damned if she wasn't going to enjoy every part of it.

She wanted to feel more of his chest, indulged as her fingers splayed wide over the hard, shaped muscle.

"Oh my, oh my." She pushed herself down, driving him deeper inside, the rhythm building until it was too big to hold back. Her body twitched, slipping out of control, but Owen refused to let her go, instead driving in again and again.

"Come for me, Alice." His voice was hypnotic, a combination of silk sheets and a log fire within a stone hearth. "Break for me. Shatter. I want to feel you."

"Yes, yes, Owen, Owen?" Alice said in desperation as her body climbed higher and higher, then explosions, wave after glorious wave, confounded her mind and body.

That was mind-bending and perfect. You were perfect in every way. I am just going to clean myself up. I'll be right back," Owen said as he made to grab a cloth from the bathroom.

"I think I will stay right here."

Despite Alice's words, he heard the change in pitch as she rolled her head over to watch him leave. Internally he smiled.

"Owen!" Alice tried to speak more, but laughter, bright and pure, shook her whole body.

Owen turned back to see what was going on but was dumbfounded as Alice was just half pointing, half smothering herself as she laughed into the thin pillow.

"What is it? What did I miss?" The line she was pointing

was now at his exposed shaft, and he couldn't help but look down, seeing nothing amiss.

"No, not that. The king of diamonds." She barely got it out. "I found it."

"What are you talking about?" Owen turned, following the line she made with her hand toward the wall and dresser beside the door.

"It's right there on your butt," Alice finally got out.

"What?" Owen scrambled, his hands running over his own ass for the edge of a card. Nothing, only smooth skin.

"Did you two plan this? Because it's a pretty good trick," she said, gaining control with each word spoken. "Really well played. Just don't tell me how many times you have played it on the different women you sleep with. I don't want to know."

Owen flipped back and forth between trying to find the card and looking at her for more information. "Alice, I can't see anything. What are you talking about?"

"Your tattoo, a small king of diamonds. I didn't expect that. It was pretty funny."

Fear dropped in his stomach like a cold stone as he tried to make sense of her words. "Alice, I don't have a tattoo. I am probably the only musician in the world who doesn't have one, but I don't. Let alone one on my butt." He turned so she could see his backside.

"Owen, it's right there. A miniature depiction of the king of diamonds. I am staring at it. Not bad work either. The detailing is crisp. It catches the light, with an almost silver texture."

Owen twisted and bent as much as he could and thought he could just make out the vague outline of what might be a tattoo. "I am going to kill him," he declared. "I am going to freaking kill him. Max is a dead man. Wait! Alice, roll over."

"What? Why?" Alice asked.

"The queen of diamonds? Where is the queen of diamonds? Roll over." Owen stood witness as Alice suddenly understood what he was talking about.

"Oh, hell no," she said, rolling and twisting her body much as he had tried to do.

Unfortunately the sheets moved with her. Owen knelt on the bed and pulled the white linen back . . . and revealed a perfect, cream-colored ass. With a cute, finely detailed one-inch playing card depicting none other than the red queen of diamonds tattooed and detailed with a metallic ink right there on Alice's right butt cheek.

Inwardly the stone in his gut dropped deeper as he thought he could actually hear Max's voice in the room calling out, "Ta-da!"

Wait, let me get this right, Owen. Max—your Max—somehow put a tattoo on both your butts while you were sitting on them? And neither of you noticed until now?" Before Mara could finish, the main table started to roar with laughter.

Cornelius and Damon both looked to be hitting the cups in a celebratory manner this night. And everyone else at the table was clearly joining in.

In the background, a drummer, a male singer and a man on horns who knew what he was doing had all joined Clover and Jessie onstage and were playing a tune that had the crowd fully enthralled.

"This isn't funny. Have you seen Max? Because I am thinking about snapping his neck," Owen said honestly.

"King and queen of diamonds? That is splendid," Cornelius said as he grabbed Owen's arm as if somehow he could pull him in on the joke.

Mara smiled, and some of the tension left her for the first time in weeks. "Well, don't be rude, son, let us see the work! I'll be proud and all that, I assure you."

"I am not showing you my butt, Mara."

"Come on, Owen. A tattoo, that's a big deal. Let's see it," she teased.

"You have a house full of people here. Where is Max?" Owen said, cutting to the bottom line.

"I haven't seen him since you and the queen of diamonds there disappeared. For a respectable time, I might add," she said to the chuckles of everyone else.

Alice felt her cheeks get a little red. Again. She needed to find a way to stop that. Somehow she had known everyone would know about Owen and her having sex, but now that she was standing around the table and everyone could see her, she felt vulnerable. Fragile, even.

Damon spoke up over the joy of the others. "Owen, I agree with Mara, and this is serious; however, the only way for us to believe this tale is for us to see your tail." The laughter grew again as the pun fell into place.

"I hate every one of you right now. Max? Where is Max? I want the tattoo off. I don't even know how he did this." Owen looked to Alice for help, but she only shook her head.

"Could it just be a fake tattoo? Did you try rubbing your butt with water?" Cornelius supplied.

"Yes, Cornelius, we tried rubbing it with water. It's real. On both of us. It's a real tattoo. It looks clean, as if it was done a month ago, instead of angry and red. But it wasn't there two hours back."

Damon spoke up again from his seat at the back of the table. "Owen, you are telling us . . . that you checked your own ass two hours ago? Why would a man do that?"

"I hate each and every one of you right now," he repeated in both his words and his voice as he continued to feel foolish.

Mara's laughter was bright and clear, and as Owen turned, he spotted Alice holding back her own humor.

"Why the hell are you laughing? Max tattooed your ass also, Queen of Diamonds," Owen reminded her.

Alice raised her hands in surrender. "Hey, I am not happy about this, but you have to admit, it was a good magic trick. Plus, you have a nice ass, so the tattoo sort of works."

The table paused as she spoke, then settled in for another round at his expense.

"Screw this. Screw all of you. I need to play." Owen froze, every muscle in his body shifting cold in reaction as he knew he had just crossed the line.

The words had just come out. And here of all places, right beside Mara.

The look she gave him was hard and sharp. But not violent. "Then what are you waiting for?"

"No, that's not what I meant."

"Yes, it is. I mean it, go play, Owen," Mara assured him.

"No, I am too close. I can wait."

Anger reacted deep in Mara's eyes at being told no. "What is it going to take for you to believe me? Go play, it's fine."

Anyone else, he thought. Or rather didn't think, as he was suddenly filled with anger himself. Fire raced in his veins. There was no way for him to take the stage without at least touching the road or the river. Her words were true and untrue.

Mara was happy to hear him play an instrument, but stepping onstage and pulling ethereal energy into the song would hurt her. It would remind her of David because she wasn't fine. It would cost her far more than the anger she currently was feeling.

"You want to know what it will take? Here it is, Mara. I will get on that stage when your lips touch champagne once more."

The world changed before him as Mara's anger rose fresh, hot and red.

Owen didn't care about her anger toward him. Or he did,

but he couldn't. Not after hearing what Damon had said. Because it was true. Damon was right—Mara too was asleep. He had known it his whole life. Had known it with each step, each laugh. This Mara was weak and asleep, the real woman caged within by bars of fear. Bars of her own making.

Owen leaned into the flames of anger as the woman who was far closer to a mother than an aunt went red with rage.

"Owen."

"No, Mara. I don't play music, I open doors. I thin the veil of this world. It is what I was born to do. You were right, I should never have taken David with me. I was young and didn't know better, and yes, I will most likely die up onstage like every other person who has ever wielded that guitar before me. However, the choice was made. It was my choice then, as it is my choice to keep going. If you want to be in my life, you have to accept my death is just part of the package. It's my life you get to celebrate now. Be a part of it or let me go forever."

Glass shattered in Mara's hand as her martini burst apart. She stood up slowly, gin running down her hand to land on the table as she took her time. "You really want it, Owen?"

Owen knew exactly what "it" Mara was referring to.

"Damon spoke the truth. We aren't meant to live forever. Whatever comes for each of us on the other side doesn't matter. We were meant to be great, to shine, to blaze. If you need me to be a watered-down version, I will, for you, in your house, because I owe you far more than that. But I can't take your stage. Not anymore. Up there, it will always be my house."

"I have kept this place safe for over nine hundred years. Nine hundred, and you want to risk it all?"

"No, I want to live." Owen didn't back away, couldn't. Her anger was true, but the passion behind it was false. "I want to be free. I want us both to be free."

Owen was prepared for a slap, for violence of any kind, as Mara's anger turned so hot it went cold. "You want to set the world on fire?" she asked.

"I want to play," Owen shot back. "I want freedom. The only kind of freedom that comes with putting everything out there."

In the background, Clover's violin picked up its rhythm as she showed off her own creative skill. Each musician onstage shifted to give her room.

"If we do this, there is no going back. None. Not for any of us. It will change everything. Is that what you want? Is that really what you want, Owen?"

"I want to see the Mara they"—he indicated the others at the table—"whisper about when you walk away. I want to see her before I die. I want to see the legend free and out of her gilded cage. I want stories to tell in the afterlife. I have faith. I have faith in you and us that when you're free, whatever the consequences that come, that whatever those might be, each of us is willing to bear them. And above all . . . Mara, I want you to shine so you can feel true happiness and not a watered-down version."

Mara breathed in and out. "And that is what you all want? Is it?" She glanced at Damon and Cornelius before shifting right back to him. "It's going to hurt, Owen." Her words slipped out, true and full of sorrow.

"It always does. It's the price for being alive. I will pay it. I will place my hand in the fire right now if it means you get to be free." Owen found he couldn't move. She was too close to the edge of a decision. To close to coming out of the cave she insisted she stay within. A cave without sun. Without light.

"Well, that's why God made champagne. It helps lift the spirit."

Shock zipped through his system as he watched a subtle change settle in and around the table.

"Are you sure?" Cornelius asked, his words low and unassuming.

"Jones," Mara called, "bring us two bottles of my personal champagne and have the OPEN sign changed to CLOSED. It's going to be an all-nighter."

CHAPTER TWENTY-FIVE

Do you have room up there for one more?" Mara called, stepping up onstage.

The man who had been singing made way like a wide-eyed fleeing mouse, removing himself in a hurry.

Owen held a glass of champagne in his hand, back at the main table. The glass was still tingling from the bubbles as they climbed to the top and broke the surface. *Free at last.*

"This is going to be a fun night. I am going for your guitar, Owen," Cornelius declared.

"Thanks. Do you need the keys?" Owen didn't question how Cornelius could find the guitar. After all, he was the one who had helped him build the secret compartment years earlier.

"You are not the only one who can get into places they don't belong."

"Are you drunk?" Owen asked in surprise.

"Maybe, but then, why the hell not? I have missed the taste of excitement." Cornelius set his empty champagne glass down, then left with a small wave of his hand.

"There is something strange about that guy," Alice said.

"He's one of a kind. So much power, and yet there are times I think it has made him go mad." Owen changed the subject. "Mara looks good up on that stage."

"She does. Owen, how come I feel like what is about to happen is far more dangerous than the first time I came into this room?"

Owen turned, dazzled by the sight of her. "Because, Alice, we are going to create. Right here, right now, in front of everyone. We are going to break the rules, splash in and have some fun. There is a danger, but not so much for the crowd. Sit back, enjoy tonight, and if you see Max, you have my permission to break his nose."

"Seriously?" she asked.

"The kid tattooed my backside and yours. Though his face isn't doing him any great favors, so maybe just break one of his ribs instead." Owen smiled. He couldn't help it. Before she could react, he kissed her lips, unable to go a moment longer without the contact.

Mara was onstage with Clover and Jessie, and he was going to play here in his home once again. Alice was here to see it, the connection between them new and bright and somehow shockingly strong. Like a missing piece he hadn't known was there.

A thought struck him, an idea he hadn't expected. "I am really glad you are here for this."

"Owen, we just met."

Before she could pull away, he kissed her again. Her lips were pure chemistry, stealing away previous thoughts and anchoring him at the same moment. A new fantasy of her body interlinked with his own, naked and active, heart and body pumping until sweat ran down Alice's spine, and the feel of smacking her perfectly tight ass as he drove into her from behind resonated. It had his blood going hot.

Alice pushed him back, but her teeth softly bit his lip before he could separate. Her posture said it all: she wanted him as much or more than he wanted her.

"There is more here than you want to give credit for," Owen said.

"Go play me a song before I punch you again."

"If you insist, but you should know that before this night is done, I am taking another look at the card you're hiding."

"Pervert."

"Rock star, baby. From my head down to my toes."

Alice found herself enchanted by Owen's smile as he turned toward the stage and started to walk away. Each step he took was like seeing another false layer fall aside. He seemed to grow in size and power, heads turning to watch as he made his way.

It is like everyone already knows he's something special. And they have been waiting all this time to see it, and now here he comes. Like a comet burning in the sky.

"Alice, why don't you join me? I think we both want a better seat for this," Damon said, climbing out of his normal chair in the back and grabbing the remaining half-open bottle of champagne. The first bottle was empty and tipped upside down in a gold leaf ice bucket with little birds sculpted into the handle.

"Are you sure that is a good idea?" Alice asked.

Damon stopped, studied her. "Are you going to break your word and start attacking everyone?"

"Wasn't planning on it," she admitted.

"Then join an old man as his friend takes the stage for the first time in years. Let our differences stay in the past. Bask in the now."

Alice thought, considered. Then signaled he should lead on.

Together they made their way toward the main room. She followed, surprised to see this side of the club held standing customers covering both walls and a thick knot of people around the bar.

Furthermore, each table was already filled with patrons who had been enjoying the show.

"When did it get so full?"

"Word went out the moment Mara gave her permission for them to play. Clover has a reputation, and anyone with Owen gets props in this city as well. Back before he turned eighteen, Owen built a reputation for only playing with the best. Musicians, like this city, never forget." The last Damon said with pride.

"I see. So Owen is good? Hey, all the tables are full," she said, unsure where to go.

"That one," Damon said, pointing to a table that was not far from the stage but remained close to the inside wall. "I wouldn't use the word *good* to describe Owen. You will see."

Strategically, Damon's choice of tables would have been her own. The wall right at their backs and the stage just ahead. With a glance, able to see into either side of the club. And yet Alice couldn't help but notice the table was already occupied, each chair already taken.

In answer, Damon placed his half-empty bottle of Mara's expensive champagne on the center of the round table as if he owned the space. Alice, only a step behind, wasn't sure what to do as Damon's words became clear.

"All right, y'all. You have had your fun, but it's time for you to get away from me now." Each word held influence backed up with ethereal energy, the force crisp and clear as it sank deep in the minds of those gathered around the table.

All three of the humans got up without a complaint and started to walk away, one going so far as to forget his jacket he had laid over the back of the cushioned chair.

Only the fourth patron at the table didn't move, the blue underglow declaring he was one of the We, and a level four at that.

"Table is taken, Damon. And that was rude."

"Only a simpleton would deny me a table here in Mara's house. Is that what you are now, Derick, a simpleton?"

Alice watched and understood it was a pissing match between heavyweights. Damon would win, but this other guy had to make a show or look weak. Inwardly she smiled.

Raw essence shaped at her will as she brought her hand across her belt buckle, the serrated knife forming in her hand as she slammed the blade flat on the center of the table. Even here she was careful not to make a scratch while locking eyes with the level four.

Alice didn't speak at first. She knew she didn't need to. The knife was made to kill We. It was the weapon's purpose. It was her purpose until a couple hours ago.

In all her time, only Owen had a weapon that could match. These things liked honesty; she could be honest. "You should go. Right now."

The level four looked between Damon and her, and then the knife. "I am sorry, Damon. The table is yours," Derick said.

When the We was no longer in earshot, Damon spoke with rumbling mirth deep in his voice as he took the vacated seat. "That was fun. In fact, I really enjoyed that. Cornelius is going to be sorry he missed it."

Alice slipped the knife away, letting it re-form over her belt as she took one of the seats facing the stage, her back to the wall.

"Out of curiosity, what would you have done if he stayed?" Damon asked.

"There was never going to be a fight. That level four just needed to show he wasn't afraid of you. Since there wasn't going to be any actual fighting, I just had to scare him. Plus, with Mara here, you have this whole 'women own the house' thing going on."

And I am a hunter through and through, even if I only have one demon left in this world to hunt. Oh, Father Patrick, I miss you. I'll check in as soon as I can.

"You determined all that in a heartbeat and then gambled on it?"

"Wasn't much of a gamble," Alice said.

Damon simply looked to her in question.

I don't owe you anything, and yet if it wasn't for some kindness on your part, I could be dead right now. After all, I attacked first.

She didn't like the way her thoughts had her feeling conflicted. "Hunting Kerogen on my own didn't allow a lot of time for second-guessing. If I couldn't read one of you"—she struggled, not wanting to call him a demon but still not comfortable with the new title—"then I never would have made it this far. You only have one chance to get it right. One chance to strike and move on."

"Fierce, strong, smart, deadly, beautiful and all wrapped in such a small package. Let me ask you this, Alice. Do you enjoy playing cards?"

"If this has something to do with my new tattoo . . ." She made a *tsk*ing sound that said there would be retribution.

Your queen of diamonds has more fire than good sense," Mara said to Owen as she watched Derick, a stubborn level four, get up and walk away from the table.

"Yeah, she does, and her fire is fantastic."

"Really, Owen?" Clover said, turning to look at him.

"Something that amazing needs to be shared, even if only by proxy."

Mara laughed, Clover shook her head and Jessie, who had been watching and listening, raised his hand for a high five from across the stage. In a relaxed five-fingered salute, Owen answered the high five and ignored the rest.

"Who wants to start?" Mara asked.

"I do," Owen said, a second before Clover said, "Owen."

He adjusted the amps in the back to the setting he would

need, then plugged in the black cable and turned, facing the crowd.

"Old times," he whispered, catching Alice's eye as he adjusted the mic stand to fit his taller height.

"New times," Mara said on his left.

Owen was attuned to the horn player on his right and behind. It was an easy thing with someone so skilled. The drummer, on the other hand, bounced in his seat in the back, a feeling of active energy zipping this way and that despite the fact he was drinking water through a straw.

Understanding the skill of each musician was easy, like seeing a menu backlit with lights. Mara was a ringer, on special. Followed by himself, then Clover, followed by the horn player. Then there was a competition on the page between the drummer and Jessie, as both had their strengths and weaknesses.

The last singer, the one who had stepped offstage, knew he didn't belong on this menu.

Damn, it is good to be back in Miami. It only took being on the run, being shot, stabbed and . . . a tattoo on my ass.

Owen gave a small nod to both Clover and Cornelius as he spotted the We with his guitar case in hand. "Hey, everyone," Owen said to the crowd through the mic. "My name is Owen, and it is really good to be back home. I hope you have enjoyed the show so far. Let's give another round for these musicians up here."

The crowd didn't disappoint as they clapped and catcalled. Jessie gave a little wave as Clover smiled like a pageant queen, giving a half bow. The drummer raised his sticks as the horn player raised his instrument, giving it a small pat on its side.

Owen directed a hand to the singer who had joined some of his friends by the wall on the right, and the crowd gave their appreciation. Owen looked back to Alice, needing to see she was safe. And there she sat, smiling as Damon said something while Daphne took the seat on Alice's right. Across the distance, their eyes met, and the connection pulled at him, anchored him as he looked to her.

So much can change in a day, Owen thought. *And what are two weeks but just a group of days?*

"Thanks, Cornelius," Owen said as he accepted the old guitar case.

Without ceremony, Owen flipped the brass clasps up and reached in, removing the guitar beneath. He was careful to angle the neck up, showing the backside to the crowd as the essence around his wrist splayed before dropping into place.

Play me a song, Alice had said. *Play me a song.*

This is the first time she will see me. He didn't finish the thought. Instead Owen's fingers started to move over the strings, and his foot started to tap out a beat as a song unknown called to him.

The power was there, a storm for the taking, and he fell into it, allowing the storm to consume his hands, his ears and his mind as he coaxed the harmony into a soft, upbeat promise. A promise of fingers and skin, of trust and new beginnings.

He had to let out a breath as he watched Alice shift in her seat. Absently he took in the crowd as they moved with his sound, several taking a step closer, needing contact. Needing to be connected. He couldn't blame them. Contact was good; contact was right. It was human and freedom. Healing and life.

Mara was the first to come in, her voice rich and textured like a tapestry too valuable for human hands. Her words were in Spanish, rolling with the sound of his guitar, combining together to be one.

He could feel where she was going, what her next words were going to be as if they were written on the wall, or possibly imprinted on his soul. He changed chords, and her voice filled with ethereal power, mesmerizing the room as it swept up their spines and into their hearts.

Owen pushed the strings, falling headfirst into the passion of the song as he felt pain and pleasure and a soft but deep, heartbreaking joy. Inside, his chest broke open. Raw and real.

Jessie with his piano and the drummer came in next. Both were soft. The drummer gave a heartbeat to the song as Jessie worked with the keys, adding another layer, another character to accompany his own playing. This character was softer than the first, lighter even. It moved around his guitar and Mara's voice. Separate but the same.

Owen shifted to catch, to combine, but Jessie shifted keys at the same time. Stealing away the connection so they circled around Mara's voice, like two lovers who couldn't keep holding hands, as they were far too busy twirling them around Mara's words, but still needed to reach.

All the while Owen watched the patrons, and Alice, as he lent life to something more than emotions and sound.

Mara's voice came to a close, and she stepped back away from her mic. The song went on, Clover rolling forward to take Mara's position and her place onstage. Clover's sound introduced a third character into the song. She was fate, a troubled mistress who swept from side to side. Interfering with the dance of the first two but loving both far more than they could love themselves.

Mara's hand touched his back, and Owen drifted to the right, giving her room to share his mic.

He could already feel the sorrow building inside his chest as she sang once again. Her Spanish, her voice, haunting and beautifully capturing the song and lifting it to a new level rarely ever experienced in his life.

Owen's hands slowed, coming to a stop as he backed away. She didn't need him to play to finish the song. Clover and Jessie fell away as one, leaving Mara's voice all but alone, captured only in the soft tick of time and beat of the drummer as they encompassed the room together.

Owen held his guitar, basking in the song being played. He was still a part of it, one with it, even as he stood still and watched. Alice looked from him back to Mara and back to him again.

A vibration started to build in his chest, an understanding, even a plan.

Mara brought the song to an end, and the crowd erupted into applause. Alice, Damon, Cornelius and Daphne all came to their feet.

Owen raised a hand to give the gratitude where it was deserved. As the crowd showed their appreciation once more, Mara gave a small bow, her action more graceful than any bow Owen had ever seen.

"Jessie, why don't you start this one?" Owen called, knowing that Jessie, for all his skill, only had so many of these types of songs in him. A night like they were just starting had an escalation to it. And even now he saw We in the crowd making calls. More were coming and with them more power, more musicians. A flame fed by its own wind.

Jessie started the next song, letting his fingers dance and slide. It was upbeat, and Mara took this one by herself. She chose Italian as she put words to his action. Owen watched, feeling the song, the happiness within them both blooming out over the crowd. Clover shot him a funny, questioning look as she came in, adding a type of zest to the atmosphere. The crowd smiled, and a few of the We even laughed with Mara's words. Cornelius even went so far as to bang his glass on Alice's table in all-out open humor.

But Owen was still, staying back, content for once to feel the storm inside and be one with the crowd as the woman who had protected him, the woman who had given him shelter and food for most of his life, let go of the steel grip she had wrapped around her own heart.

Damn, I love hearing you sing. You were born for the stage. It's too bad David isn't here to see you now. Lots of love, brother, and rest easy. I'll do what I can.

The song had three parts, and the crowd loved each one, going so far as stomping their feet as they pushed tables and chairs in the back to either side to make space for people as the room continued to fill up, despite the CLOSED sign outside.

As the song came to an end, men and women, both strangers and friends, laughed and applauded as one.

"It's time," he said as the guitar called and his spirit prepared to respond.

Ethereal power, the same power that shaped the world, demanded he move and take flight.

Owen let out his breath, watched as air fell from his lips, glancing from Alice to Mara.

Are you ready for this? Owen silently asked as he stepped forward.

They can do that? Just make up a song like that on the fly?" Alice found herself leaning toward Damon as she asked.

"There is a fresh vibration when you can create like that, a new vibration trapped in the song when done right. It's like the chemistry between all the musicians onstage and us in the crowd. Altogether, the vibrations can be wrapped up with patterns and anticipation. At least that's how the best do it," Damon said as if he were giving her a private lesson.

"Hey!" Daphne said. "Owen's not going to go under right now, is he?"

Alice registered a mix of fear and excitement in her voice. "What do you mean, 'under'?" she asked.

There was so much she didn't understand, didn't know

about any of this. She looked from Daphne's young, fresh face up to Owen, who displayed perfect white teeth as a small smile broke in her direction.

He's about to do something.

There she was. Alice, fearless and bright in a way he had never before been drawn to, sitting beside two high-powered We for the first time in her life. And to his left, onstage, was Mara. A beam of light amongst the applause even as she turned his way, asking . . .

Show me something, Owen. Mara's shoulders, her face, her eyes spoke to him. *Let's see what you have been hiding while you were away for all those years. Let me see what you have become.*

Owen shrugged off the comment as if it were a tangible thing. This wasn't for Mara or for Alice. It couldn't be.

What he was about to do was for one thing and one thing only: the stain over his soul he was born with. The reason he was doomed for life. The same reason he had been given the guitar to keep in the first place.

He needed what was to come. Needed to taste the blue water that made up the river of souls, the only substance with the power to cool the fire that could never be quenched.

A section of him held it all, contained it all. Too much fight, too much emotion, and the will born from both.

Only one place to take such a burden. It was never a wonder to him, even as a child, why Damon mostly chose only to play where he thought no one could hear him.

Where Owen was going, no living person, We or otherwise, should ever be tempted to go. If such a place could be erased and not remembered, it should be.

Owen pinched a string, feeling the essence running the length of his guitar. He touched it between two fingers, slowing his heart rate down as he focused on the feel of the instrument.

* * *

Owen is a true musician, not a singer or performer. But one touched and held by the forces that make up this world and all others. The vibration of sound. Of course he is going under. It's where we are born to go. The only question is how deep, and if, this time, he will be able to make it back out," Damon said.

"I can't believe it," Daphne said with excitement.

"I like seeing him up on our stage," Cornelius added from Damon's left.

"Wait, what is going on?" Alice asked.

"Owen is about to walk in the water! Right here in front of all these people, with his well overflowing," Daphne said, unable to sit still in her seat.

"I don't understand."

"He is a musician, a true musician. A true etherealist. Not only does he have the power to thin the veil between Heaven and here, but also the river of souls. The Devil's playground."

"You are talking about Hell! Owen can go to Hell? Is he about to go into Hell?"

"Not Hell, but the river of souls that leads to his bridge," Damon said with a reverence that bordered on worship.

"Hell is on the other side of the bridge, like Heaven is on the other side of the four arches. Really, it is not so bad. It should be fun," Cornelius said as he poured himself another glass of champagne.

Owen used his connection to the essence to do the impossible, all six strings sealing themselves to the neck of the guitar, halfway up. Each of the six strings shortened right where he wanted. The effect would be the same as if he had slid a bar over the string and then tightened it down, shifting the sound they would create.

The moment it was done, Owen's left hand came down, finding the chord he wanted, and he strummed once, twice over three strings, then shifted again. His song, a solo, a lone man leaving all others behind, low but strong as he pushed the air around him. Power crawled in his skin as he called on the ethereal energy to infuse his song, his body, his soul.

He went in, diving down through the music, thinning this plane, as the veil between this space and the space below drew closer together.

He's in." Damon breathed out the words.

Daphne whispered in Alice's ear in a rush. "It's not really going into Hell, just thinning the space between here and the entrance. It's rare, really rare. Except for musicians like him, I guess. Jessie calls it being born with the crossroads already on your back, but then he likes to be dramatic sometimes. Either way, I have never seen it."

"How dangerous is it?" Alice asked.

All three answered her question at the same time.

"It can kill him."

Alice watched as Owen changed before her eyes, only then realizing Damon hadn't said, "It can kill him," but instead had said, "It will kill him."

Blue flames coated his skin. Within heartbeats, those in the crowd who held even the smallest active well of ethereal power could see the flames and reacted as one. Much to the confusion of every normal who had no idea Owen had once more stepped back into the river of souls. The Devil's territory.

Owen's hands slid from one chord to another as the song dove lower. This wasn't a battering ram, not this time. This was a key, the perfect key for this place and this time. It was his song. He shifted it, driving deeper as the flames grew higher. Blue fire swept in from the other side, covering his hands and body. And Owen followed the river deeper as he played and opened the way.

A sound entered the room. It came in like a banshee, sweeping in from the open door and rushing over the heads of the crowd for the stage.

Damon stood up and followed the specter's path, but Owen couldn't be bothered to care. He released the essence holding the string halfway up the neck and used his talent and fire within, banishing the creature away as his hands blurred up to the top and back down again.

Gasps came from those who shared the stage, as well as from all sides, as blue flames grew, and Owen could feel the ring around his feet. As if he were standing inside a bonfire of blue.

Translucent hands coated in fire reached up through the flames, grabbing at his pants and boots. Even his cord and amp were coated in the blue of the underworld. Owen didn't care, couldn't care, not even a little.

He pulled more power, pressing the storm as the people at the front of the stage took a step back, followed by a second, mesmerized and terrified in equal measure.

Owen played on as more specters were pulled through, pulled into the room, and the call of souls broke through the veil, so even the normal humans could hear the sounds of the trapped as they moaned in harmony with his song.

Straightening legs Owen hadn't even understood he had bent, he stood tall as he came to the mic. His lips breathed blue flame as he whispered out over the crowd.

I don't belong here and neither do you.
Come for me. Come for me.
Dark one.
For God loves me far more, far more than he loves you.

Power, raw and thick, filled his voice in a challenge so it could be heard in the here and after. The souls quit their screams, and Owen shifted his song as he played a rhythm he had only ever fantasized about.

The room went silent for all but his guitar and amp, the air stilling as Owen dropped to one knee, leaning into the music as an unseen weight pushed down on his shoulders, and he fought back with power, precision and skill.

He shot a look at Alice, needing to know she could see him. The true him. The real him. To be true and honest while in the heart of the damned. That he was made to bend the rules and live in all places.

In that half second—his hands dancing over the strings and his soul wide open for all to see—time slowed.

*O*wen is chained to a different wall. The thought struck Alice square between the eyes. *This is your demon. One you were born with. A demon you will never escape. A demon you can never fire a bullet through or cut the heart out of.*

Both externally and internally, a strange, welcoming calm flowed down over Alice.

We are more the same than we should be. You and I.

*T*he connection between the warrior and the woman—both understood the message he sent. She sat in her chair as if it were a Sunday picnic. He watched for the fear, for the terror. Instead, she was calm and cool as they shared a truth neither could fully hold.

A low rumble started to shake the foundation, while hands reached up higher through the flames to grab at his waist and belt. The Devil's domain and his river of souls, always hungry for one more.

Owen shifted his song, his sound, letting the chords and power temper down. It wasn't easy, not by half, the force it took to pull back. To climb out was exponentially more

difficult. It wasn't anything like leaving the arches of
Heaven. Coming out of Hell water was far more like suc-
tion, where each step taken in a retreat held additional force
for him to stay.

Each moment of resistance threatened to distract, threatened to burn him to a crisp. Owen let his skill and power
fight for him. He didn't force it but instead teased his way
back up through the river of souls, letting the flames dim
and the hands fall while he pulled back. It took more time
than he thought it would, but he didn't rush. Instead he let
the song run its course until he was out.

When it was over, when the last note had faded away,
there was only his heavy breathing, as if he had just run up
a mountain. Owen's breath, caught by the mic, echoed out
into the room. He could smell burned clothing, and singed
hair on his arms. He could taste copper in his mouth, and
he could feel sweat coating his skin. But none of that mattered as the crowd erupted in applause.

Owen accepted the cheers, taking a portion and tucking
it away, ignoring the rest—Mara's impressed slow clap,
Clover's shake of the head, Jessie's pale face and repeated
air high fives. Damon's hard eyes and Alice's raised glass,
toasting him: *Well done.* These he tucked away. Even
Daphne and Cornelius's whistles. The rest he let flow right
by him. Glad to share in the success, but he didn't play for
them. The need was rooted deeper. Too deep.

"Owen! Max is on your right," Jessie said clearly, despite the noise of the crowd and the distance separating the
piano player and himself.

Max! The tattoos! The thought was like a bucket of cold
ice water being tossed over his head. He turned to see the
young man in the process of waving a hand in his direction,
clearly trying to get his attention.

Owen attacked with a pointed finger, locking the kid in
place. Max gave a slight shake as if he had no idea why

Owen would be upset, then held up a water bottle and a fresh rolled-up black shirt. Both looked ready to be tossed up to him.

"Come here, Max," he said.

Max hurried forward, all concerned smiles. "That was amazing and terrifying. What was that sound? All the times I have witnessed you going down into the river, I have never heard or seen anything like it. You were so deep. The room is filled with energy from the other side. You rock, Owen. Seriously rock and roll. That was fantastic!" Max spoke fast as he handed over the bottled water, the lid flying off into the crowd as Max used ethereal energy to remove it. "Here. Your shirt is in tatters, and I thought you could use some cold water."

Owen took the water, his touch sensitive to the cold of the bottle after the insanity of the river. After a long drink, finishing half the bottle in one long pull, Owen received more of his own voice back before he grasped the kid by the front of his shirt.

"Hey!" Max said in protest.

"I have a tattoo of the king of diamonds on my ass, Max. I want it off!"

"What, Owen? What are you talking about?"

"Max, this isn't funny. However you did your little trick, I want it to be gone."

"Man, wait—the card trick earlier?"

"Yes, Alice and I both have what seems to be a permanent tattoo of the cards you were trying to find right there on each of our right cheeks. I want them gone. Do you understand me?" He tried to make his voice like stone and at the same time keep it low enough those nearest him couldn't hear.

Everything about the way Max's face shifted in confusion revealed a truth that destroyed the small amount of hope Owen had been holding for a quick resolution.

"I don't know what happened. I had the cards, and they

were supposed to go in your back pocket, and then they were gone. Just gone. A tattoo? I thought they were under the table or something. I was going to go look for them after everyone cleared out," Max said.

"Yes, a bloody tattoo!" Owen had to take a deep breath to keep from hurting the kid. His hand shook, causing Max's shirt to wiggle. "Just go sit at the table. I want this undone. Figure it out, Max."

"Seriously, the card changed into a tattoo? Oh, here," Max said, holding out the rolled-up black shirt. Owen recognized the shirt from his own bag.

Owen took stock of the one he was currently wearing. To be honest, there wasn't much left. His pants too had issues, along with his boots. And that was too bad. Normally his boots held up, but this time he had gone farther down the river than ever before, and so, after tonight, the shoes would be tossed.

Rather than taking the offered shirt, Owen handed the guitar over, then peeled off the remnants of the shirt he was wearing, going bare-chested in front of the crowd. There were calls, but he ignored them. Owen gave himself a quick wipe down, using the remnants to clear some of the sweat before slipping on the fresh shirt. Taking back the guitar, he slid the strap over his shoulder and back into place.

"Go figure this out, Max."

Picking back up the half-empty plastic water bottle from the stage, Max mumbled, "Break a leg," then scurried over to Alice's table by the left wall.

N ow that was rock and roll! Did you all see the flames, the music! I should have had that recorded! What was I thinking?" Daphne said.

"Well, what did you think, hunter?" Damon asked, signaling Jones for another round of drinks before taking his seat.

Alice let her first thoughts fall from her lips. "There is so much more I need to learn."

Damon's brown eyes seemed to grow in depth and magnitude, a bright, clean connection shaped in time as she looked to him, and he looked to her. "You're a nuclear plant being used as a single kitchen appliance. Careful what you ask for."

"I am not one to be used, not by anyone or anything, and until that appliance goes lights out . . ." She let it hang, the threat and understanding clear. Until Kerogen was dead or the bond was undone, she couldn't do anything else. Years of coming to the same understanding clear in each word, each moment she held his gaze.

"Do you know that after every major war, weapons and armor were smelted down into tools to help rebuild? They took what was used to kill and remade them into tools to create."

"Do you really believe even after the bond is undone, Kerogen will leave me alone?"

Her question was interrupted as Max, tall and lanky, made his way over. "Hey, guys, can you believe him? Owen is unbelievable. I thought he might actually make it to the bridge! Then I was terrified he wouldn't be able to make it out, but he did."

"Hey, Max, come sit by me," Daphne said, slightly adjusting the remaining seat.

"Max, before you sit, you should know that unbelievable guy onstage—he gave me permission to hit you, and I think you know why." Alice had, of course, taken notice of the way Max had avoided looking at her.

"Ah, man. This sucks."

Well, that was a nice show, Owen. What do you want to do next?" Mara asked while he resumed his place onstage.

"The road," Clover said, unable to hold back. "We could touch it, Owen. Mara is wide open, Jessie is warmed up, and you and I know the way to get there like it's a path behind our house."

Clover made to say more, but Owen didn't give her a chance. He raised his hand, the waters of Hell still coursing inside his bones, then turned to look at the drummer, who hadn't missed a beat, and the horn player, who had yet to join in.

"What's your name?" he asked the horn player. The man looked to be in his late thirties, mixed race, and the way he held his horn reminded Owen of a person with only one true possession in the entire world. As if that tube of brass and valves was the greatest treasure he could hold.

"Zion. I am good to go," he said to the unasked question. He was a level three, not terribly strong, but his soul was already open and ready.

Listening, seeing and feeling, Owen nodded. "I believe you," he said. "And you?" he asked the drummer. "Your name?"

"Scotus, but everyone calls me Sco." Light skin, corded muscles beneath the shirt and over the forearms. Even as Owen took him in, it was clear the man always carried a beat within. A human with ethereal power. Another etherealist. It wasn't uncommon, but it bonded him to his group instantly in a way no other normal could be connected.

"Hello, Sco. How do you feel about getting your feet dirty on the road made for angels?"

"I was born for it."

Yeah, I can see you were. Me too.

"Okay, Mara, what say you?"

"You are just like Damon. I swear it's like you are his kid. Cut from the same cloth."

Owen felt a warmth from the words, from the acceptance behind them. "All right, let's go place our feet on the road. Stay in the pocket and stay with me. I lead, first in, last out. Everyone understand?" Owen didn't mean to direct the last question more to Mara than everybody else, but it happened.

"I was making runs before this house was even on this continent. Don't you worry about me. You lead and we follow."

"You want to start, then?" Owen challenged.

"Oh, now you're going to act like you have manners."

"You are not holding a shotgun against my chest. It's easier to be civilized."

"There is the smartass I remember."

He held his hand out to the mic, all challenge as he did so. Owen might be a professional when it came to this sort of thing, but Mara, she was a ringer. A musician on another level. It was there in the in-between, both the space that surrounded each member onstage and between heartbeats they each shared. *It's like stealing one of the greatest players throughout history for one night*, he thought as Mara glided forward.

Owen watched as all but the front row of tables were cleared out, the rest of the room shifting to standing room only. The main bar had gone from two bartenders to seven. Even the left side of the room was changing to standing room. Soon it would only be Alice's—or more to the point, Damon's—table left. It was crazy and it wasn't enough. What he had done wasn't enough. The pull of the other side didn't fade; it only grew. The majority of people coming in were We or etherealists within the city. Each one brought power to share. Each one had a portion of ethereal power just ready to be used. Like moisture in the air—simply change the pressure and everyone could drink.

Moisture from their skin, moisture coming out of every breath they took. Power. Ethereal power. The same power that granted life, granted formation and granted evolution.

Mara ran a scale, each note pitched to perfection. She filled it with power, carving her voice into the souls and toes of every person who could hear her. She didn't need a mic. Right then, he would have sworn she didn't need sound—the vibrations alone were perfection.

Owen looked back, made eye contact with Sco, and together they slowly counted off and then joined in just as Mara started to sing.

CHAPTER TWENTY-SIX

The road to Heaven was not made for the mortal, but rather those subject to immortality.

Six souls onstage made music into a living, breathing entity, a substance intangible but alive inside the rhythm and vibrating matter that separated their world and the path to Heaven. Living free, their music, their sound soared in both the club and over the path made for angels. The road to Heaven was a living snake in the minds of each musician, none more clearly than Owen. Each moment had to be handled with care and skill, the rhythm and power shifting and twisting in Owen's hands. As heartbeats and energy shifted, so too did the path. This road was wild and untamed, demanding constant attention as he led the group both onstage and in his mind, led them above.

Knowing at any moment a full mistake would burn their souls to a crisp.

Of course, it wasn't a road, not like the one outside. Not the kind of road you would drive your car over. It was a path for souls and angels to follow home. A path forward that had to be discovered from one note to another. One heartbeat at a time.

To any mortals with far too much audacity, it was a jungle of golden flames within their mind's eye, even as it lit the walls with light from the other side, as the space that separated this world and the road to Heaven thinned.

Owen lived in two places at once, while his soul called out to be free.

Clover, Mara, Zion, Sco, Jessie and he were one. One space, one heartbeat, a force of will sheltered within their song, their sound, as the path shifted with them.

Owen could feel the warmth on his skin as the world around the bar thinned to the space made for goodly souls. In his mind, Owen could see where they were going, see where they were and what was behind him.

Even without his insight, the evidence was everywhere, in the air, on the walls. In the eyes and hearts of those who listened.

They have started a run! I knew they would," Max said, practically bouncing in his seat.

"They are already on the path to Heaven. Look at the walls, kid. Feel the fresh, ethereal air just starting to leak through. Can't you smell it?" Cornelius said as he closed his eyes, tilted his head to the side.

Alice felt her heart in her chest. The music was softer. Gentle, even. But the emotion and will in the room was growing around her.

Is this what Owen meant when he said he would never be boring?

Sco's crashing force and perfect timing with the drums helped to widen the road for each of them to stand within as the walls of the Golden Horn shimmered with power from the other side.

Together they were moving up the path at a faster pace

than any other time Owen had moved. With Mara boosting the group, they were running. Running through the open flames. Ethereal power was in the air of the club already, the crowd breathing it in with each intake of air as it slipped in from the other side.

Jessie's constant calm on the piano steadied the group as they made their way closer and closer to the first of the three steps. Zion and Clover's music danced around the group, securing the walls of the small bubble of power that held back the golden flames on all sides. Both were brilliant, moving in time. Trusting each other and the group.

Owen was the driver, the engine and the steering wheel, using hands and soul to keep the snake headed in the right direction. But it was Mara who stole the show. It was like the road was a set of stones leading to her own personal cottage. A fable come to life, leaping on balanced toes.

The steps, the trail to achieve before an arch, were just ahead, though not in the plan. Just the road had been the destination, but with Mara influencing the group, it was so easy. So fast. So tempting to go deeper than they had precisely agreed. Others might take hours, some even days before reaching the first three steps. But the steps were just ahead now. Owen could feel them like a blind man approaching a bonfire. The weight in the air massive and strong, the danger climbing tenfold.

A question resonated between each of the six onstage. A question and permission.

Do we go on, or do we go back?

Men and women danced in the crowd. Others raised their hands and simply basked in the feel of fresh ethereal power and the holy bliss of the other side even as all eyes were set forward—ears, minds and hearts open to the stage.

Sco was first to answer. His sticks hit a three-beat combo, declaring he was in, ready and willing as he worked his answer into their song so smoothly it only helped to glide them farther along.

Zion went quiet and still, but after almost an hour of playing with him, everyone knew he was in. Even amongst this group, Zion stood out as a man who lived to play.

Clover, as always, stood strong, unwavering. Owen knew she was game.

Mara sang another verse, the words in a language he had never heard before but that somehow matched the light yellow flames and purer aspects of the group's soul.

Jessie answered last, but in time as the song shifted. *I am loving this. I am loving every moment*, his keys sang.

Almost too much, Owen thought in response. *Okay then, just to the steps. No more.*

Owen spoke behind the music, his words measured and quick. "We take one step at a time, no gate. After the third step, we head back down." He didn't need to add *follow me*. His lack of full attention to the song had the fires over the walls flaring before settling once more.

As one, the song shifted on his cue, while the road matched their pace. Snaking left then right, they moved forward with speed.

Owen caught a look from Damon, who sat studying him as they played. Where everyone else was happy, Damon was clearly somber. A mind not at ease.

What is it going to take for you to be free, my old friend? Owen thought.

The first steps were just ahead in the minds of each of them. Mara shifted her words, ready to make the leap.

The crowd, enthralled, couldn't look away. Each member onstage followed Owen's lead, pouring more ethereal energy into each note, each beat, so it built as a sort of platform.

Hearts slowed, time slowed as they pushed off, pushed forward. Together as one, they built their song higher and made the leap.

The crowd let out a sound as real joy poured out over them. Euphoria. The drug of choice in the hereafter splashed out like a wave throughout the Golden Horn.

The landing was all grace as Mara's voice and Owen's guitar smoothed out and anchored their footing upon the first high step in their mind's eye. On a path no feet had ever touched and yet each soul to Heaven had no choice but to climb.

The second step just ahead was fast in coming. The crowd quieted, too caught up in what was about to happen to be aware of anything else.

Owen was tuned to the crowd, to his members onstage, tuned to Alice and the others at the corner table. He was connected to everyone in the room, and they were connected to him. The music, the ethereal power in the air, all part of one world. One life. One universe.

Owen strummed chords in concert with Jessie's piano while he gave a tiny motion to Zion to go for it.

Zion and his trumpet called out into the crowd with brilliance, propelling them all forward and up. It took longer than the first step, but Zion crested, then landed, another wave of euphoria sweeping out over the crowd.

Clover looked to him, and Owen gave her permission to take the third step.

She planted her feet as her violin gathered speed. Sco's rhythm matched her work with the bow, and Owen could feel the crowd's perception of what was to come again. The club was no longer a place of disharmony but of friends and family. Of lonely souls now finding comfort and love with one another.

Owen smiled. How could he not as Clover took center stage? The rest fell in behind. Something changed as she leaped with her sound. It was subtle and broke Owen's heart to feel it, a dark feeling catching in his throat as goose bumps covered his skin in warning. Clover, with her violin, was perfect.

* * *

Alice felt the leap in the music. Some part within her mind, like a window she could almost see into, was tracking the progress of Owen and the others as they moved within a force too large for her own comprehension. She didn't understand all the points even while she felt the leap of the second stair powered by the brass of the horn.

Her own heart throbbed as they landed without death or destruction.

Alice was riveted by the sound, by the performers and the tension of what was to come. The third step before the first silver arch. She could feel wonder in her bones as a joy unlike anything she had ever experienced rushed through her system.

Clover played with her soul and spirit, spinning her sound as the music leaped forward again, over and up.

Perhaps it was Alice's own self-awareness or the way Owen started looking out over the crowd or even just the strange connection she was feeling to everyone in the room, but Alice turned her head toward the entrance. And couldn't see much of anything, as the seventy-five feet of space was packed with all sorts of adults enjoying the show in what had become standing room only but for her table. Shoulder to shoulder, men and women blocked her view of everyone but those crowded closest.

Clover landed! The shockwave of pleasure, of home and satisfaction, washed out over everyone who could hear as even more fresh ethereal power saturated the air. The golden flames on the walls danced and sparkled like small jewels in the contrasting light.

Owen felt the rush of emotion, while many in the crowd cried tears of joy in response. Owen played the guitar with his hands and heart, and continued searching the room with his eyes. Unable to shake off the sense that he was missing something.

His gaze was drawn to a section in the far corner, by the entrance, where about twenty of the crowd had at least one hand raised, swaying in time with the music. Love and joy were in each back and forth of the hands in time with Sco's rhythmic beat.

Owen locked eyes with a level two who was all smiles behind short cropped blond hair. She wore a soft blue collared shirt and long gold earrings. And a smile with full lips that said life was good and fair.

Looking, watching, Owen fought every reaction as a strong hand went over the level two's mouth. Owen fought down his shout, his warning. No one in the crowd reacted, all too caught up in the run, in the feel of the other side, while the level two with gold earrings was yanked backward and disappeared from view.

Where is she? Where did she go?

Unsure, he stared hard, his vision pushed to the side. Even so, he watched as another person, this one a man who had been standing beside the level two, was likewise pulled backward and disappeared from view.

We are under attack.

Owen watched for signs of distress in the crowd, hoping against hope he was mistaken. But no one moved. No shout or cry or scream.

Owen's heart clutched deep in his chest.

Why is no one moving? The question came even though he already had the answer. Someone was masking their presence with a reverse weave of ethereal energy. Right there in the corner of the entrance, and whoever it was, they were killing people.

And I can't stop playing, or we are all dead.

He spared a look at Mara and could see he wasn't alone in his thinking. She had seen too.

Together they spoke without words. *We are both stuck playing music until we are safely off the road.*

Who is attacking?

No We would interrupt a run, even a small one. Such a thing is too sacred to them. The only ones that would . . . Hunters are here. Hunters are here and have come to kill us all.

Owen could feel Mara's reaction, though her voice never slipped or changed, and he was thankful as he shifted the song with her. Guiding the others like a pack of running horses, he needed to turn back around so they could race home at all speed.

Flames flared on the walls as the others shifted, taken almost off guard by the sudden change. Only through his guidance and Mara's will did they stay on the path as they turned back so quickly.

This wasn't the river, where one waded in, then backstepped out, fighting the growing restriction. This was the road, where there was a beginning and an end. They had to get back to where they had started. One entrance, one exit—it was the only way to leave without risking the flames.

Until they made it out, any real mistake would mean their deaths. All of their deaths. Owen understood this down to his toes while he helplessly watched four more customers, those closest to the entrances, be silenced and pulled back. But this time he thought he spotted the gleam of a black blade as it quickly cut the throat before the images blurred and disappeared.

Something is wrong." Alice said the words as she watched the song shift. A change in both Mara and Owen had her rising to her feet.

To her surprise, Damon and Cornelius stood at the same time.

There was something in the air that wasn't right anymore. It was like oil over water. Alice could almost taste it on her tongue. She glanced to either side, then without waiting or warning, she stepped up onto her chair, looking over the heads of the wild crowd.

Searching every single face, she found eyes were all bright and alive but focused forward on the show. Smiles almost to the last as people danced and bumped with the music and the energy in the room. She followed row after unkempt row of humans and We, all the way back to the bar.

She searched the crowd, going deeper and deeper until she found . . . nothing.

Right at the space surrounding the entrance, there was nothing. No one. Moreover, as she looked deeper, her vision was forced to the left, back toward the bar. When she looked back, again her vision bounced away to the right.

Only one thing in the known world could do that. Reversed ethereal energy.

On instinct, she checked the far wall and found a second missing spot of nothing. Only this one was on the move, making its way toward the stage, just as she had done.

Mentally she cursed as Owen and Mara, working in unison, snapped hard looks her way.

She held the eye contact and then went back to watching the entrance, fear crawling up in her throat as a group of clubgoers silently disappeared from view.

"There is a large blank spot at the main door, and it's growing. More than one, several at least. I think they are killing people. There is also another, smaller spot of nothing making its way along the right wall toward the stage. They are cloaked," Alice said to the table, once again locking eyes with Owen.

He nodded slowly, confirming what she was seeing.

"The hunters have come, and they have already started killing. Max, get Daphne out the back right now." Corne-

lius's voice no longer held a trace of humor or intoxication.
Instead it held an executioner's edge.

"Owen and Mara can't stop playing, or they're dead,
along with everyone else up there and possibly half the
room with them," Damon supplied. "I'll protect the stage."

"Max, get Daphne out the back. Jasper is by the exit. Tell
him I say, 'Ring of fire,'" Cornelius ordered. "Go now!"

Hunters. Understanding, she stood on more than just
the edge of her seat. She stood on the ledge of a decision
she would never be able to walk back. While balancing, she
watched another layer of bodies closest to the entrance drop
out of sight.

"Alice?" Damon asked as if the weight of the world
hung in the one-word question.

"Are they just going to kill everyone?" Alice asked,
dropping from the chair before she could be spotted. "They
are going to kill everyone here, including those onstage?
I'm right, aren't I?"

The answer was reflected in both Cornelius's and Damon's hard looks.

"Alice, come with us," Daphne said, holding Max from
dragging her away.

"How much time do Owen and the rest need to stop
playing?" she asked quickly.

"It wasn't a long road, and the trip back will be much
faster. Three to five minutes. Maybe less, assuming there
aren't any mistakes," Damon answered.

The music was already gaining tempo, the sound of the
drums coming closer to her own heart rate as it picked up
speed. As if the vibration of the music was aware of the
violence in the room and the violence to come.

*Three minutes? Thirty seconds is too long. How many
will die in three minutes? You're talking about killing hunters. And you can't even pull on your own power. What are
you going to do?*

She felt the tension in her neck and stretched it on instinct, bending it to the side as she gave a single nod. "I need to get to the entrance, and someone else needs to take out whoever is moving down the wall." As she spoke, she heard a muffled scream in the back and then another one, the soft sound just sliding under the music.

In that soft sound, Alice found a soul-comforting peace within her decision.

She made to rush through the crowd, planning on pressing and slamming bodies out of her way. Only Cornelius raised a hand, preventing the dash before she could begin.

"No, not alone. You and me, hunter. Damon, clear her a path, protect Mara and help get the crowd clear. I'll take the one on the wall and then make my way to the entrance. You two, I said get out of here, now!"

Owen knew Damon and the others were about to do something, as Max and Daphne ran for the back rooms. He was thankful that one of Cornelius's guys left with them. He thought it was Jasper, but in the quickness of it all, he couldn't be sure.

Owen continued to build the song so it grew faster and faster, leading them all back down the path at breakneck speed while folding in the reactions of the crowd.

Stupid, just stupid. Another six men and women disappeared, the number of missing growing. *I hate being helpless. How could such a thing of beauty be shifted so terribly in such a short amount of time?* His eyes tracked back as Alice sprang forward.

"Do not stop playing." Owen tore his eyes away from the crowd, leaving the mic stand at his back, directing everything he could spare to the others onstage, his voice infused with ethereal power. "Do not stop playing!" he shouted over the amps. "No matter what happens next, you stay with me! You stay with me."

A small voice of doubt crept into his mind, where he held an image of each of them. In his heart, he shouted back. *Not again!*

Alice watched as Damon flexed his fingers in the direction of the crowd and the entrance. His lithe and sturdy hands came together, his fingers crossing past each other as thin tendrils of black ethereal essence poured forth, the vines so thin Alice could hardly believe it even after the demonstration with her guns on her very first night.

"Go," Damon said as the black strands surged thicker and started to swarm.

The black ethereal strands drove and weaved through the crowd, which had yet to understand the imminent danger they were in.

Alice, caught between her chair and table, stepped back, then forward, using the chair as a step stool to gain the table, charging the bystanders lost in the music. She followed the line Damon set, ducking under the essence as it separated in two, shoving the customers hard out of her way to either side. Her feet matched the tempest of Owen's music, which encouraged her heart to beat faster and faster.

People fell to either side like bowling pins just before her charge, being knocked down as the room cried out in full-blown disaster.

Hunters. Humans with ethereal power and weapons ready for a fight. Ready to kill. She forced the idea to the side as she chose each running step, careful not to trip over legs and feet.

Just strike and move, Alice. Strike and move as fast as you possibly can.

The crowd separated just enough, Damon's thread of power catching the last patron and tossing him safely to the side just in the nick of time, revealing a hunter's black blade simply hanging in the air. Behind the blade was a sea of blurring images—that had to be none other than the ring of hunters.

Alice knew an opening when it was before her. The enchanted blade formed in her hand as she drew her fingers over her belt buckle. The familiar feel of the rough, jeweled grip was cold and solid. Surprise was on Alice's side as she went for a three-strike kill.

If this was a fair match, there was no way she would be able to win, not with her power blocked by the cuffs. The difference between normal and ethereal-enhanced was simply far too great a thing to overcome. But surprise would win almost every fight, no matter how unbalanced the scales.

Alice swung her blade out wide with her left hand in a slashing motion. The cloaked hunter's right hand and the black knife he carried were faster, moving to intercept. As he did, the reversed weave slipped, revealing a dark-hooded man with tactical gear beneath.

Alice drove her right hand into the hunter's windpipe, crushing cartilage and forcing him to stagger back. Alice avoided a wild swing, switching her knife to her right hand, attacking under the swing and driving the blade right under the chin, angled up.

Her first kill complete.

Using her left hand, she drew the silenced forty-five from his holster as several more hunters dropped their reversed weave now that their attack was fully underway.

The hunter to her left died before Alice could see into the hood. The recoil of the weapon in her hands was familiar and welcoming.

Firing a weapon into a room full of bystanders was a terrible idea. It was why she always started with knives. But without ethereal power, Alice didn't have much of a choice. She just couldn't afford to miss, not even once, as men and women of all kinds screamed and ran for the exits.

* * *

Owen felt the moment Clover and Zion noticed the hunters. It was an icy stake to the band's shared heart as one, then the other had to fight down reactions and stay with the music. Sco and Jessie, confused with the blip, continued on, not fully aware of the violence in the back.

The group ran down the third step, heading for the exit as fast as Mara and he could get them to go. And yet it wouldn't be enough.

One more hunter on my left. Alice sidestepped to get a better angle.

The hunter, sensing or seeing what had happened to his companion, drew his own pistol with speed.

He is moving too fast. He won't be there. He won't be there by the time the bullet gets to him. Left or right? Do I shoot to his left or do I shoot to his right? Alice thought everything in less than a blink of the eye as she judged each obstacle, knowing the consequence of being wrong.

Be there, Alice willed as she squeezed the trigger, the gun aimed to the hunter's right, directly in line with the back of the head of a pretty blonde, who had no idea how close she was to death.

Owen's music filled the air with a sense of desperation that accompanied the chaos and horror of the room.

The hunter moved, and his head snapped back, blood and brains painting the woman's hair red as he fell dead.

Too close! Alice, keep moving. Keep moving.

Shifting her body, she spun in time to see the remaining three hunters between her and the entrance, each in different stages of killing customers. The closest spun his latest victim dead to the ground atop the legs of another, all while sizing Alice up.

Alice drew the gun in line, not for the hunter watching, but for the hunter just behind him. Squeezing once, feeling the recoil vibrate up her arm as she made to squeeze twice. Unsatisfied as the bullet tore into a rib cage, but from this angle, it was the best option.

A hard kick she didn't see coming launched the silenced handgun out of her hand before the hammer could fall again.

Moving on instinct, Alice dove to the side as a knife sliced where her head had been. Four attackers in total appeared out of thin air. Three dropped from the ceiling, joining the one who had kicked her gun away. The hunter who had dropped the body continued to circle in on her right, forming an open box around her.

"Alice?" An almost familiar voice called to her from beneath a deep green hood.

"Josh? Is that you?" she said as she held her knife ready to defend and attack.

The middle hunter pulled back his hood to reveal light brown hair, cut short and a bit messy. His brown eyes sparkled with life and adrenaline as he lowered the silenced weapon he held close to his chest. "Alice, you are alive? We'd hoped, but we had no way of knowing. Father Patrick sent for us when you didn't contact him. We have a truck out front. Go with Simon here while we finish God's work."

Josh, one of the stronger kids from the monastery all those years ago. Her friend once.

"Josh, you need to stop your people and get them out of here. Right now."

"No, Alice, I can't do that. Go with Simon. We know what we are doing." Josh's voice held an edge, an order and a promise of consequences if she refused.

"You are killing everyone!"

"Alice, go with Simon and leave God's work to us. You two go for the stage. You know what your orders are. I want this place burned to the foundation. Let me know when you start the clock." Josh directed the last order at the hunters on his right, just to her left.

Both held automatic rifles, but the smaller of the two held a black backpack over one shoulder, heavy with gear. Something about the way he held it said *boom* to Alice. As in, holy hell, they brought a bomb inside a place packed full of people.

You should have brought a tank. Owen's words came back to her.

I guess this time they did.

A scream to her right had the hunters' heads turning as Cornelius drove ethereal power like living tentacles of steel, cutting down the remaining two hunters who hadn't stopped in their killing of innocent bystanders.

Seeing the opportunity, she struck out toward the two who were headed for the stage as they made to pass by, going for the legs of the closest one. The one with the bomb over his shoulder.

She wanted a kneecap—she focused her strike, hard and clean. Needing to slow him down. Possibly get his rifle.

The butt of his weapon intercepted the kick, his enhanced speed far faster than her own normal muscles could supply. Josh's hands wrapped around her in a chokehold before she could recover—the knife in her right hand pinned tightly to her side.

"Now, that wasn't nice, Alice. What happened to your well of power? You were so strong, so fast. I still have to hear the stories about you."

Josh signaled for the two hunters with rifles to continue toward the stage, the meaning clear. *Go kill everyone.*

Alice tried to slam her head back, but without ethereal power, she was a child to Josh's ability.

"Hey now."

Alice calmed in a heartbeat. She understood that voice. He could snap her neck without even trying, and he had cause. She had, after all, just killed three of his men and shot a fourth in the ribs. "Let me go." Her words were stran- gled as Josh squeezed, depriving her of air.

A whistle, low and perfectly in tune, came in from behind Josh, and Alice knew it was Cornelius. A signal. An op- portunity.

Alice dropped the knife. Her left hand, mostly free, caught it in reverse grip before the blade could fully fall. Twisting just enough, she drove it into Josh's side.

She was a dead woman. She understood as her blade was buried up to the hilt. It would take less effort than tearing open a bag of chips for Josh to snap her neck with the amount of ethereal energy running through his system.

"I always thought you were something special. You shouldn't have crossed me, Alice."

She could feel his breath on her skin, and it was disgust- ing as the pressure tightened. Her world started to blacken. Even so, she twisted the blade and found herself spinning as Josh tried to use her as a shield. His left arm fell away in a spatter of blood as Cornelius's ethereal cord of energy sliced the arm holding her cleanly off so it landed with a splatter over the dirty floor.

Ethereal strands waving in the air like a great god of war, Cornelius was both a welcome sight and a frightening one.

Alice quickly withdrew the knife from Josh's side, step- ping out of his reach, and threw the weapon over Corne- lius's shoulder. The blade sliced through two of his own black strands in time to be buried in the heart of a hunter who had taken aim at Cornelius's back from inside the doorway.

"Move!" Cornelius yelled too late.

Owen's world was in two places—the song and his band staying just ahead of the flames, while he watched, helpless, as the room descended into full panic.

The crowd was in every possible shape of chaos. Damon,

with Jones, helped to guide people from coming onstage in their terror, instead ushering them out the back.

Men and women were down on the ground across the whole of the room. Others were running or trying and failing to hide, and in the distance they were still dying. All Owen could do was play one note after another. And keep the others onstage in the heart of the music. As Alice fought hunters she couldn't hope to win against.

Two hunters broke from Alice, separating as they came forward in long, even strides.

Internally he cursed, unsure if Damon had noticed the new threat as they were half the room away.

The run was almost over; they were almost out. The exit was not far away, but it might as well have been miles when it came to the two rifles that swept up in unison.

Go, Mara. His soul spoke inside, where he held each member of the band, whether they were playing or waiting to play. He forced her ahead and out of the song, knowing the consequences and hoping he could pay for them. With all the energy he could spare, he gave Mara's soul a push with everything so she might survive. So they all might survive.

Flames flared bright on the wall, and Owen could feel the heat of Heaven's wrath burning over his skin as he took the brunt of the destruction. Mara tingled orange as small flames crawled over her arms, legs and hands. Smoke rose up and over the stage while she pushed her way back out.

Through it all, Owen played. He played fast and clean, accepting the heat as his birthright as he took the brunt of the force from the other side. An easy price to accept as his power and skill fought back from the very edge of being burned alive.

Alice tried to drop away even while her hands came up to block the kick, but Josh was far faster.

His foot smashed in with the force of a truck, her arms

hardly softening the blow to her face. She smacked the ground hard, her mind dazed.

Defenseless and on the ground, she shook off the blow as Cornelius tried for the kill. Four black vines shaded with silver tips cut through the air.

Josh, with only one arm, reached for the weapon on his leg even as he disappeared from view, dodging to the side.

I am dead. Alice knew a bullet was coming for her.

Pushing off the ground, she felt Cornelius strike out over the bar, clearly tracking Josh despite the reverse weave while everything inside her said she was going to die.

O wen's lungs burned as if his head were in a kiln. Even so, he used more power from within, and at the same time forced his body to take in ethereal power from the air. Unrelenting, he pushed the sound, giving it more.

Jessie's piano went silent. Zion fell back too, followed in time by Sco's drums as the song, shifted by his command, fell more and more over his shoulders. His sound, his burden.

Clover's softer tones raced in the background as he pushed ahead even farther, the weight and heat scorching into his soul.

In his mind, Owen was the nose of the rocket, fighting to come home as the fires of Heaven grew with each string he pressed and strummed. In his mind, he let the story of the flames and him unfold as his song grew to life.

Owen played his solo for a room of violence and death as the two assailants used their rifles to kill a small group of patrons who had the misfortune to turn back and face them. Not out of heroism but out of pure fear.

Their bodies were torn apart by the bullets as Mara drew the full weight of her power.

* * *

Every muscle within Alice's body pushed to get off the ground, to move. To find some sort of shelter from death.

A clamp in her mind opened, the restrictions simply falling away. Alice both watched and felt the cuffs that held back her ethereal power release and drop to the ground.

Wrath, power and a type of euphoria that was not made for this world filled her bones, strengthening her fingertips as unrestricted ethereal power flooded her system for the first time in weeks.

In greed, she pulled as much as she was able. Both hands sticking to the floor, she pushed back and slid away. Three bullet holes tore wooden chunks where her head and heart had been.

Oh, I missed you.

The room bubbled, as in actually bubbled out as Mara stepped off the stage. The lights dimmed as she raised a hand toward the two hunters who were killing her people. The hunter on the left died brutally as seven black ethereal vines shot up from the floor and down from the ceiling, staking him in place as his gun fell lifeless.

Owen watched the tile floor roll like a small, smooth wave, knocking down each person who stood in its way.

The second gunman dodged enough to the side for his life to be spared as another set of seven spearlike vines drove up and down where he had been. The rolling tile sped toward him.

If there was fear or joy to be found in anything Owen could see, right now he couldn't feel it as the fires of Heaven wrapped his body like a living torch. Only his power and the guitar protected him as he continued to finish a song that had grown too big, too fast. And yet he refused to give in.

In his heart and onstage, the others were there, silent but with him, knowing if he didn't finish, they too would burn.

Pulling more and more power, Alice reversed a weave, likewise disappearing from view and moving to her right as another set of hot bullets tore through the air where she had been. Another dodge and she leaped up to meet Josh.

Without any but the smallest of visual distortions, Alice attacked as her feet set on top of the long, wide bar.

The hunter with the backpack over his arm rushed the stage, jumping the small rolling wave as more spikes drove down and up in his wake.

Damon's five thin vines caught the hunter midair, stabbing straight through his body and holding him off the ground like a macabre trophy.

Mara moved to Damon's side as the hunter spoke while blood started coating his teeth, Damon slowly drawing the man closer.

"Do you believe you have won? You can't win, devil scum. The light shall always cleanse the dark." Too late, his words were accented by the click of a red button strapped to the hunter's hand. "Now go back to Hell, where you belong, you evil bastards."

"The bomb is in his backpack." Damon's hand caught the hunter's head, under the chin and behind the hair, and twisted hard, the neck breaking in one clean motion.

Owen could see the exit to the road as Mara faced the right wall and shoved air to either side, sending her hands out wide.

And the right wall simply wrinkled. Like a curtain being pulled back with a string, the wall that was made of brick and mortar opened to the outside world on her command.

Suddenly the room was fully open to the night air. Owen could see the dirty sidewalk, and a large white moving truck beside a blue two-door convertible, and beyond, people were running and screaming for their lives.

A black vine of ethereal power moved up out of the floor, snatching Damon's dead hunter and the bomb he still held like a sea creature, closing over his head. And quick as lightning, wiggled and whipped the hunter thirty-five feet so his body hit hard against the white truck with a sound Owen already wanted to forget. The broken body hit the cement sidewalk as the curtain closed.

Alice moved in, blocked a kick, and dodged just to the side as another muzzle flashed, too close. With power and clarity, she hit Josh hard with her knee as she drove him off the bar top.

The front door to the club slammed shut as they sailed through the air.

The room rocked, and the building rumbled as if a Greek god had suddenly landed atop the place as the bomb outside exploded.

Focused, Alice drove her fist into Josh's face before they both hit the floor. The impact of the ground dissolved his invisibility.

Rage-filled eyes were framed by three long cuts where he hadn't fully avoided Cornelius's tentacles of steel.

An elbow tried for her, but she avoided it. Knowing he was the last of the attacking hunters, Alice chose her next move with care.

With a twisting momentum, she used her strength and power to roll and fling Josh so he tumbled across the ground into the center of the room as Owen's last note faded away.

Alice breathed as she watched the room while climbing to her feet. The fight was over, the music finally coming to an end.

She noticed the dead bodies—more than she had thought, just as there were more We who had stuck around to help. Each of the living looked to Josh as he started a slow rise, weapon still in hand.

"Alice," Cornelius said, tossing her a silenced handgun taken from one of the dead.

She caught it and oddly felt a weird sort of familiarity by doing so. Like just maybe she belonged here. "Thanks." She raised her voice and used his name. "Josh, keep that gun down."

She watched him, weapon still in hand as he came to his feet, his breathing hard. The missing arm had already stopped bleeding, a testament to Josh's power.

How has everything gotten so screwed up? Why did you have to kill everyone, and where in the world is Father Patrick?

"Damn it, Alice! You're supposed to be on our side!" Josh yelled in frustration, seeing the fight was over and his side had lost.

The others in the room gave him a wide berth.

"Just keep the gun down and we can talk about this. Where is Father Patrick?"

"Your pet priest? He asked for us to come. Begged, in fact. Now you will never see him again. I can promise you that, Alice. Not after what you did here today. You have no idea the hornet's nest you just put your foot into. Your priest is ours, and you're a dead woman. Everyone here is going to die, and there is nothing you can do about it. You think my team hurt you? This is nothing to what I have seen. What will come for you!"

"Josh," Alice said, trying to calm him down.

"Don't same my name, Judas. You betray us. Betray God."

"Where is Father Patrick and why did you bring a bomb? Why were you killing everyone? Humans and them?" Alice asked in confusion.

"He likes it," Mara said from behind Josh, causing him to turn. "You can see it on his face. It is there, written over his soul."

"Shut up, witch. You know nothing of my soul."

"We can see you, see the way your eyes light up in murder. The holy thing you claim, that's just your lie."

"A lie? There is no lie. They were in our way. Don't you see?" Josh said, turning back to Alice. "It's what we are made for. God gave us this power to kill these monsters. These agents of the Devil. It's what he wants. It is what we are born for. Our mission, our right and responsibility."

"If God wanted us dead, son, he would never have given us the choice to come here. We were his children once too."

"Shut your mouth, witch!"

"Josh, put down the gun." Alice could feel the energy building. "Josh, the fight is over. Put down the gun and we can work this out."

"Stop saying my name. No one is safe with these things around. They are a disease. They need to be eradicated from this world. Sandy—you remember Sandy? One of them killed her! Sandy is dead and it's because of them. You're on the wrong side of this. How could you betray everything you were taught?"

Alice saw the tightness in Josh's neck. She witnessed the tension transfer down his arm as the gun shifted. A bullet to the side of his head snapped him to the left an instant before her own gun took him in the heart. Blood sprayed the dead on the floor before Josh's lifeless form fell and joined them.

"You killed him?" She hadn't meant it as an accusation, but it came out that way.

"I did." Owen's eyes held sorrow and a sense of justice that was too clean for her liking. His shirt was gone and his skin glowed red as if agitated, but besides that, he was alive.

She shook with pent-up violence. And, if she was being honest, with sadness. "I didn't want it this way. I didn't want any of this. Certainly not all this," Alice said to a room full of dead bodies and blood and Owen's people. "I didn't do it this way. I never did it like this. Everyone who was between me and Kerogen could heal. I gave them a choice. I never took innocents just because . . ."

Alice wiped off the handle of the gun, not wanting her fingerprints on any of the weapons used here today. She held it out for Cornelius.

"We know, Alice. Everyone here knows," Owen said.

"You were great. A queen of diamonds when we needed you to be," Cornelius said as he accepted the firearm.

"There is too much death in the room to try for funny, Cornelius." Her voice came out worn even to her own hearing.

Cornelius's words matched hers in strength. "There is always time for humor. If you hadn't done what you did, if you hadn't killed these hunters, there would be so many more dead right now. And the outcome would have been the same for them."

Alice shrugged it off. "You saved me. You didn't have to."

"Likewise." He moved away, scanning the dead.

And yet she knew it was pointless. None of the hunters' victims would have a chance. It was, after all, what they had trained for. To be a weapon.

"Cops will be coming," Owen said to no one in particular.

"Owen, that was at least two bricks of C-4 outside. Half of Miami will be coming," Mara said. "And yet it will be fine."

"Does this count as your coming-back party?" Damon asked Mara.

"How is it no one shot you? All these people with guns, and you are still here. If I didn't know our Lord almighty, I would question his existence right about now."

Damon let out a laugh. "Oh, let's keep the big man out of it. He has a lot going on."

"Thank you for the protection," Mara said.

"Always, my dear. Always."

Silence crept into the room. Be it for loss or for honoring the dead was anyone's guess.

"I am sorry about your club," Alice said as she met eyes with Mara, remembering it was part of the deal not to mess up the place.

"It has seen worse. Might have been that way tonight if you didn't do what you did. Are you hurt?" Mara pointed to Alice's hip, where one of Josh's bullets she hadn't noticed had torn out a small section of skin.

"This must have happened on the bar. I am fine."

Owen was in motion before she had finished speaking. His hands were gentle as he pulled the shirt up a few inches to reveal the red line of torn flesh where the bullet had grazed through flesh.

"I am fine. I heal well. It's not a concern now that I have access to my well of ethereal energy. In fact, it should already be close to healing." Alice stopped talking as she looked down. The room was focused on her as she and Owen both watched the wound bleed.

"Alice, you're still bleeding."

"It should stop any second."

"It's not," Owen said.

"Oh . . ." She cursed.

"What is it?" Owen asked.

"I am out of energy. My well is empty."

Owen watched fear fill Alice's eyes, and it was terrifying to see someone so strong suddenly so vulnerable.

"The room is still full of ethereal energy. Just take it in. Pull it in. You will be fine. This is only a flesh wound—"

Mara cut in. "The shroud she wears under her skin won't allow her to refill until it takes its toll of blood and pain."

"I need to get somewhere . . ." Alice struggled to find the word. "Safe."

"Go," Mara said at the same time Owen asked, "Wait? What?"

Chapter Twenty-seven

No time! It's starting to hurt. I need to get out of here." Alice began to move away, shoulders hunching in, as if she could somehow protect herself from what was to happen.

She fast-walked past dead men and women, made it to the hall as a pain she couldn't contain ran through her body.

Absently she bounced off a wall while trying to make the corner, dealing with the pain as the shawl started to pulse faster and faster. The shawl, designed to purge evil, cut into her back and neck again and again as it vibrated free.

Soon she would be drowning in pain. Already her shirt had started absorbing small trickles of blood from a thousand small cuts, and some of the threads were being cut away as the shawl unburied itself from her skin.

Owen had her in his arms like a child before she knew he was there. "Where?" he asked.

"Somewhere safe." She let out a small scream as the pain grew too intense.

"What is going on?" Daphne asked as she, Max and Jasper made room in the hall for them to pass.

"The fight is over. Go see Clover. She is in charge."

Owen used ethereal power to open the door to the bedroom. As they passed inside, the door shut hard behind them, leaving them both in darkness for only a second before the lights overhead turned on.

"It's fine. Just put me down and get out of here." She punctuated her words with another muffled wail. Even after so many years, the pain had a way of eating her from the inside. It wasn't like any other type of pain she had ever had. And she had been shot, stabbed and experienced any number of broken bones. But this was something else. It was like her soul was burning.

Owen placed her on the bed, shocked at the sudden change. "What the hell is going on?" His right arm was coated in thick crimson.

"It's the relic under my skin. Just get out of here, Owen. I'll be—" Alice's words were cut off as another wave of pain built too high for her to keep it down.

Owen didn't know what to do as part of Alice's shirt started to fall away, the material being shredded to fiber right before his eyes. A soft white glow peeked out through each new hole in the fabric.

"Owen, move please," Mara's calm voice said behind him.

"Mara, what is this?"

"I know, son. Move to the side. Thank you. It's the shawl of tears. Alice wears it to block the bond she has with Kerogen. Right now it is demanding its payment for the protection it provides. It's okay. Go get your guitar, and we can ease some of this. Go. I'll keep her safe for you."

Mara's voice was soft and so gentle. In itself, her voice contained a promise of protection. It was nothing like the normal woman everyone else spent time with. Owen slowly moved from the bed.

As he went to the door, Mara took his spot. Her hands

were kind while stroking Alice's hair in a way he hadn't seen in a very long time. "It's okay, it is only pain. Just let it run its course and you will be fine. Owen, go get your other guitar." The power in her voice was unwavering while her eyes held a steely compassion.

The door shut behind him, cutting off Alice's ongoing agony from his ears, while the discomfort in his chest only grew.

Jessie and Clover stood waiting. Jessie was holding Owen's guitar case in front of him, his friend using two hands to hold the handle as if he feared someone might try to take it from him. Clover held her violin case in hand.

"Thanks," Owen said, reaching for the guitar case and heading for the guys' makeshift bedroom.

"Owen? What is going on with Alice?" Clover asked.

Clover and Jessie fell into line behind him as he moved farther down the hall. If they minded the brisk pace, he didn't care.

"I don't know. It looks like the relic she uses to block her connection to Kerogen is skinning her alive. Mara wants me to get my acoustic to help ease some of the pain. Where are Max and Daphne?" he said, opening the door to his room and heading to his cot.

"Daphne is throwing up outside, if she still has anything left in her stomach. Max went with her. Most likely, he is holding her hair. You sent them to see me, and there are about thirty dead bodies in the next room."

Owen cursed. "Screwed that one up. The cops?" he said as he looked at his acoustic guitar lying flat over his tightly made bed.

"Are all out front. Mara assigned Cornelius and Damon to them. I get the feeling there will be a lot of missing people by tomorrow. Cornelius's friends are picking up the dead and carrying them down a trapdoor that turns out to be right there in the middle of the main room."

"No kidding." Owen knew why the building had such a

large furnace in the basement of the bar. An oddity, in the heart of Miami. But then, this wasn't the first time it had been used to dispose of unwanted complications.

"Owen, should I be packing the van?" Jessie asked.

"No. We are fine," Owen said abruptly.

Grabbing his acoustic guitar, he thought about shoving the case in his other hand under the cot. But it was far too valuable to just leave sitting there. And yet he didn't want to go put it in his truck.

"Here. Don't let go of this," Owen said, handing back the guitar case to Jessie.

"Hey. Wow," Clover said, her hands shooting up as she blocked his path back to the door.

"Clover, I need to get back to that room."

"Just wait a moment. Owen, there are over thirty dead in the bar, and an explosion happened outside. You always say we need to stay under the radar. But cops, probably FBI, Homeland Security are going to be coming in here. What do you want us to do?"

"None of them will set foot in this club, not even for a drink. This is Miami. In all the years, no matter who claims to run this city—this space, it hasn't belonged to anyone but the We. When I told you this was the safest place for Daphne, for all of you, I meant it. Get the kids, bring them in and keep them in here. That's it. I have to go."

"Here," Jessie said, holding out a fresh T-shirt.

With nothing further to say, Owen slipped the shirt on and made his way back to the door separating the outside world from Alice's torment.

Carefully, Owen opened the door. The lights were now dim, the mood changing as he looked in on Alice. It was like stepping into a hospital. Mara held a blanket, mostly red with blood, around Alice as she held her in her arms, singing softly. A light glow from beneath the cover could just be seen, highlighting the back of Alice while she half rocked, half shook with pain.

Owen pushed the door shut behind him, blocking Jessie and Clover out, and slowly leaned his weight on the opposite bed frame, never taking his eyes off Mara and Alice.

Owen's hands started to play as if they weren't his own, the feeling inside materializing with the soft stroke of the strings.

He might as well have been playing a completely different instrument compared to his performance onstage. Together, Mara and he both poured energy into the air. Not a run, not a thinning. Just ethereal energy for Alice to take in the moment she was able.

Three minutes passed. Five. Owen honestly had no idea, as each time Alice let out a shudder of pain, it whipped away the memory of everything before. His heart was breaking, and all he could do was watch and play a dark sorrow song from inside his heart.

Mara's cheek came back bloody and red as she spared him a look while whispering words of encouragement into Alice's ear. *It's bad*, her look said.

Owen started to sing. His words were of strength. He sang private words of light shining through rolling black clouds of thunder. Peace of the open road. Words he found just for her.

The door opened, and it was Clover standing there in the hallway, sparing a look in. Compassion was in every line of her face, open and on display.

Daphne, Max, they were all behind her. She gave a little nod his way while looking in on the room. Carefully backing out, having taken her fill, Clover shut the door, stopping just shy, leaving a two-inch opening. A gap in the safety of the walls.

Owen stopped singing, his hands finishing the song, taking the guitar as he rose up off the end of the opposite bed.

His intention was to use his foot to kick the door shut the rest of the way, sealing the breach.

As he neared the door, however, Daphne's low bass guitar

came in, matching his last chord. A second later, Clover was there too, along with the small electronic keyboard Jessie always had close at hand. A sound of someone blowing into an empty bottle told him Max wasn't staying out this time.

He shot a glance to Alice as she turned her head for the first time so he could see her tears.

For almost an hour, ethereal power from his crew poured into the room on the wings of compassion. Mara's perfectly pitched voice sang softly, other times whispering words of encouragement as Alice's body and her soul continued to be racked with pain.

"Hey, Owen," Damon whispered, leaning in, "I am sorry to interrupt, but I need Mara out here. It is vital."

Mara gave a knowing nod, then started to rise.

Cops and authorities, Owen thought.

"You're okay now, hon. Your skin has already started to heal. The worst is over. I am just going to place a clean blanket around you now. I know it still hurts. Owen, come take over for me."

Owen set his guitar to the side without a second thought as Mara got up off the bed, removing the bloody blanket with her. He followed her signal and switched positions, a question between them as they passed.

"She is fine now, just needs to finish healing. And she needs to rest."

The music stopped outside as Mara exited, her free hand shutting the door firmly behind her. In the low light, Owen was careful not to touch Alice, and yet he was torn. There had been so much pain, so much blood and too many tears.

"Just hold me, Owen." Alice's voice was so soft, so vulnerable, it was all he could do to speak.

"Of course," he said as he put his arms around her. As if the warrior was a porcelain doll, he held still as she leaned back against him.

Together they heard the others leave. And he was grateful. His people were good. Great, even. The best.

Time disappeared as they sat, mostly in the dark.

Later, by some unknown signal, Alice shifted, then climbed off the bed, gaining her feet, the blanket wrapped tightly around her body.

"I want to be clean. Will you be here when I get out?" Alice asked.

It wasn't a real question.

"I will be right here," Owen said.

Alice didn't respond as she took the blanket with her, disappearing from view into the bathroom.

Owen sat in silence, only moving his leg that had gone to sleep hours ago. Not wanting to disturb her, he hadn't moved. His own discomfort insignificant.

He heard a small moan of pain coming from behind the thin door to the bathroom. Compared to what he'd witnessed, the sound was nothing. And yet it too cut into him.

"I am going to kill you," Owen whispered to Kerogen, hoping wherever the monster was, he could hear the promise.

The shower water turned on, and it was everything he could do to just sit and wait for her.

The bathroom door finally opened again, Alice's shower completed. She stood like an angel in a tightly tucked white towel. Owen couldn't sit any longer. Standing, he was so close, it hurt not to go to her and take her in his arms.

"Don't leave." Alice's hands covered his as her body pulled in tight against his own.

There was something soft and inviting, and yet her pain, although gone, was still there, covering her skin, her soul. Owen squeezed her hand. "I wasn't going to leave."

"You weren't?" Alice asked.

"No, Alice. You are the only thing in the world that could

get me out of this room right now." He watched as his words landed, were consumed.

"Can we just lie down?"

"Yeah. We can do that," he assured her.

Carefully he lay on the bed, giving her enough room to squeeze in beside him. His eyes glanced at her fresh, newly made skin, which had regrown perfectly over the relic once again, leaving her shoulders and neck a pinkish white. But when he looked closer, he could see thin little lines beneath.

Before laying his head down fully on the pillow, Owen waited. Alice pulled back the light bedcover and sheet, sliding in. Alice gave him one final glance before rolling over, her back to him as she faced away.

Alice felt Owen settle and was oddly grateful as his hand gently fell over her upraised hip. She wasn't used to sharing a bed, wasn't used to sharing anything, and yet . . . having him there wasn't bad. She didn't want to think, didn't have the capacity. She didn't really have anything left.

She shifted once, her back and body curving into his. All the while she stared out at the light blue paint on the wall as her own ethereal power continued to heal her wounds.

Her mind drifted, so she spent time at the monastery with the other kids. With Josh and Sandy and Father Patrick. Then drifted to her mom and dad. And a little sister she had never met.

But it was Owen's scent and warmth that called to her as the hours grew. He smelled of orange and spice, which was a constant anchor, bringing her mind back to him. The heat of his body filtered through the towel and covers, stealing the memory of pain.

And his hand was still but weighted over her hip, a focus point in the swirling thoughts.

Alice knew Owen was awake, knew it by his breathing, in the tension between them. For another hour she lay still in the silence, mind thinking, rolling over memories as she tried to let go of the pain still clinging inside. So much pain. So many years of pushing herself to be a warrior. So much time by herself, refusing to let go. Refusing to give up the dream of going home. Free of danger.

Alice flipped over, faster than she had planned, needing to move away from her thoughts even more than she wanted to see him. It was a mistake—not moving quickly but moving at all. She knew it the moment she turned.

He was there, right there, the shadows of the room catching his face and holding him in focus. Owen, with his eyes that always promised sin and adventure. His calm demeanor wrapped all nice and neat, but every instinct she had said Owen was wild, untamable and dangerous. The set of his jaw, the kindness that shouted his soul was far more broken than her own. He was all right there. Almost nose to nose. Mouth to mouth.

She thought he would speak, thought he would move.

Owen held still.

The hours of lying motionless were the least he could give her. The most he would take for himself.

Hunger started to build in her eyes. He could feel it. Driving it was far more honest.

"Owen?" she asked with a wanting that melted what remained of his broken heart.

"I think I am going to Hell," Owen said to Alice's need.

"Do you think I am worth it?"

"Yes. A hundred times yes."

Her kiss was gentle, but her eyes said she wanted to forget. Wanted to make new memories, ones that didn't have anything to do with dead bodies and pain.

Alice's hand left his face, then reached for his shirt.

* * *

The room had turned into a quiet place. They came together with the smooth glide of hips, as his thumb ran over the tattooed queen of diamonds. His other hand sliding down her back as she turned to look at him. No position lasted for very long.

The energy in the room, the energy between them, wouldn't allow for it. It was like there was some unseen lock, and only the right combination of their bodies would grant release. Neither minded as sweat started to build.

Alice shifted, rolling over, her hands running over his chest, and down the sides of his well-muscled ribs while she pushed the rhythm over and over again. The orgasms that came were small, tightening her body, but she clearly held greater need.

Owen's body was harder than anything he had ever experienced. But he knew he wouldn't be satisfied until she was back. Until Alice was once more fully in control. That was what she really wanted here. What they both really wanted.

All he had to do was be here, be in each moment with her. Each touch of skin, each rise of sensation.

Some of the darkness in her eyes cleared away as they switched position once again.

Her legs curled under his as she ground herself down on his hard shaft, something clicking as her eyes went wide, and the note of tension in her body finally stilled. Together they breathed out. Then started a growing race.

Alice couldn't think. Mind, heart and body needed something real, and good.

He's holding back. Even while he drives into me, he is keeping something. I want more than this. I want more. Her mind tingled with a truth she couldn't deny. Her nails scratched his skin.

Her efforts were rewarded as surprise crossed his controlled face at the same time his body crushed harder over her own. Danger hissed to life in his eyes.

I am not broken. I won't ever be broken. Nor fragile, nor timid. I will not hide.

"Come for me, Owen." It was supposed to be spoken sexily. It was supposed to be spoken in control. Instead, Alice spoke in a challenge.

"You first," Owen said, a dark lust present within each syllable.

"You're holding back." Alice tightened her leg around his, trying to force the issue. Looking into his eyes, she knew it was true. He was holding back.

"Alice."

"Owen." She challenged again, knowing it was the right thing to say. She felt his thigh tighten and his body move around hers as her legs somehow corkscrewed farther around his own.

"Woman."

"That's right. Now shut up."

Their bodies twisted and fit, just fit together as the tempest quickened.

As one, they moved together, racing as something almost terrible inside built within.

"Owen."

"Come for me, Alice. Come for me right now."

His body was all muscles and torque, but she could feel how close he was, and it was like a drug as she pushed his body to break free. She felt her world start to shatter, her only comfort Owen's control cracking.

Every nerve ending in her body went from playing fireworks to holding still, until together they both shattered and clutched.

* * *

N ot bad, Owen," Alice said beside him.

"Not bad?"

They lay there panting, bodies intertwined. She could feel his seed sliding down her leg and inner thigh and found an odd sort of satisfaction in knowing it was there. "You realize I will need to take another shower now."

His laughter tickled her insides as the bed shook a little. "You're not the only one. Are you okay?" His question was clear. Owen wasn't asking about the sex but what had happened before.

"Yeah, I'm good. It's not the first time I have gone through that." *Hopefully the last.*

"How often? How many times?"

"I stopped counting. As to how often, it depends on how quickly I run out of ethereal magic."

"How come I get the feeling this isn't a once-a-year sort of thing? Your ethereal energy really doesn't just slowly build back up inside like—"

"Like a normal ethaerealist? Like a normal hunter?" She shook her head from side to side. "It used to. There was another relic that blocked the connection and didn't restrict me, but it couldn't do the job anymore. For the last seven years this has been with me, give or take." Her finger brushed over the crisscrossing lines, almost unnoticeable but for the way they lay over her collarbone.

Owen's hands caught her fingers. Carefully he brought her fingertips away from the buried shroud and up to his lips.

The moment stretched and sealed as she held his gaze.

Before Alice knew what she was doing, she used her free hand and ran her fingers over his chest. They came back slightly salty. "I kind of like you working up a sweat. It reminds me of when you were up onstage."

"I kind of like you naked. It reminds me of when you were naked."

"Is that so?" Alice asked.

"It is. My eyes are fascinated by you."

"Are you getting hard again?" she asked.

"Seems that way."

"I need to clean myself up." Alice rose up off the bed.

"A shower sounds nice," Owen added.

"Stay down, rock star."

O wen watched her walk back into the bathroom.

"She's okay," he whispered when the door was securely shut and he was sure Alice couldn't hear.

Owen used the time Alice needed to untangle the towel from the sheets and remake the bed. What remained of Alice's shirt from before, he tossed in a trash bin beside the small desk in the corner.

The shower water turned on and Owen smiled.

He was three steps from the bathroom door, and it opened to his surprise. Alice smiled, greeting him as if she were in the middle of catching him in the act of doing something wrong. He watched as her eyes tracked his body, from up to down and back again.

"You were going to come in?" she asked.

"We have unfinished business, you and I."

It was her turn to let out a chuckle. "Well, perhaps we do. Get your naked ass in here, King of Diamonds."

W hat was I thinking?" Alice asked herself out loud as she balanced half in the water, half out. Owen was kneeling beneath her standing form.

"You thought we should get to know each other better. Perhaps now would be the right time to thank you for this opportunity?"

"Ha, ha," she said. But was interrupted as his mouth once more found sin and desire, his tongue stimulating as the texture of his lips teased sensation through her body in a rippling wave. The hot water spraying her back was forgotten as a shuddering within started to spread over and over again.

Owen's hand squeezed her butt as he pushed his mouth in deeper. All the while, he built a rhythm within her body.

"Oh my, Owen, Owen?"

His mouth refused to stop, gentle but insistent, pulling and touching. She made the mistake of looking down. Hungry green eyes swallowed all thought as sensation within took over.

"Shut up," she said to the depth of his stare. "Oh, God." Her body pulsed once, pulsed twice, then clamped down, and all she could do was hold on, riding the wave that swept her mind into white bliss and splashing beyond.

Owen's tongue and mouth stilled as his hands helped keep Alice balanced. She had to force her hand to uncurl from the cold water knob.

Rising, Owen's mood was that of a man satisfied while at the same time knowing he was just getting started.

Climbing to his feet, he was aware of the tension and energy in her body. Alice had more to give. His fingers couldn't stop from running over her soft, slick skin. "I can't get enough of you, Alice. I just can't."

"I don't like just words, Owen."

"I plan to give both action and words."

He kissed her breast, slow and full. The soft, round curves were like God's divine raindrops. Each calling for his attention, demanding he drink. Surprise mixed with a growing need as he himself made a sound he hadn't expected.

The need to see her, to read her face and know she was safe, was too great for any other position but face-to-face, and yet . . . a single devilish thought solidified.

Standing to his full height, Owen lowered his head and

couldn't help kissing Alice again. "Now give me your foot," he said as he broke the kiss.

"My foot?"

"Come on, Alice." He placed his hand out flat. "This is no time for words."

Alice's face flushed with more wonder than fear. Owen caught the foot and gently raised it higher.

What is the point of having sex with a warrior woman if you can't have warrior-worthy sex?

The thought had him smiling as he watched her body bend, glistening with warm water and smooth, gentle skin. She smiled as her calf slipped up over his shoulder.

"This isn't going to work," she said.

"Watch me make it happen."

Alice moved with him, taking his hard length and positioning it just in front of her. With a firm grip, she squeezed, stroking him once, twice, enjoying his eyes as he adjusted to each wave of sensation.

"Be careful with me," she said almost as a joke, but it missed.

Owen couldn't answer. He wasn't the hero. He couldn't promise not to hurt her. Instead he eased himself in. Gently, slowly, watching the way her eyes too changed, glazing over as more and more of him pressed in and went farther.

"Okay, this isn't going to work. You're too deep."

"Maybe I should try covering your mouth as you did mine," he said.

Before her response could come, Owen shifted his hip ever so slightly.

Alice was forced to pause before speaking. "You are welcome to try covering my mouth. But the last time I punched you, you dropped like a sack of potatoes." Her voice alone was a drug, driving his need to new heights.

"Is it always going to be like this between us?" Owen let the words fall, unashamed about how much he wanted the answer to be yes.

Alice contemplated, then a small, quiet smile pulled at the side of her lips. "I sure as hell hope so. You have beautiful, expressive eyes, Owen, and I like to see them change."

His focus was distracted as she pulled her hips back, curling her spine ever so, causing a few lone droplets of water to run down and over her perfect breast. The combination pulled him like a man on a string.

"Just for that"—*and everything else*—"I am going to make you come so hard, it'll be as if your mind ran away."

"I dare you to try."

Knowing she couldn't take him all the way out, as he had moved too close, sent an odd sort of exhilaration down to her toes. It left only one more place to go.

Closer. Tighter. Deeper.

His eyes held a wild, untamed streak Alice wanted to see more of as she pushed down again, grinding over his shaft, the sensation dazzling to her body and mind.

Alice matched push for push as they found a gliding, slow rhythm.

Owen needed more contact. Needing to take more of her, needing to give. His kiss shifted the bond, stealing the sensation from individual to more than alone. Connected. Her tongue echoed his own demands.

Owen's hips moved with a building rhythm, once, twice, three times. Long and slow, connecting their hearts and forcing their blood to pump faster.

Owen could feel Alice's want. Her body was the perfect race car, all power and curves. His hands held, pulling her in, coaxing her in tight as she rode his hard shaft.

"I want more of you," he said.

"Not sure how much more I can give."

Owen couldn't help but rejoice in the truth of her words. She was being honest, perhaps more so than he was right then. The thoughts he held inside were dark and twisted, but then too was his own soul. He wanted Alice in a different position; he wanted her hair in his hand. He wanted to hear her sing out in ecstasy. And yet more than everything else, he wanted to push her over the edge. So she could be free, free to fall and tumble in pure pleasure. "I want to hear you, Alice. I want to hear you."

"Oh, shut up," she said as her left hand unwrapped from his arm to grab tight behind his neck.

Their bodies shared everything, moving with a rhythm that only had room to rise.

CHAPTER TWENTY-EIGHT

"You know, Owen, we have to leave this bed sometime. We can't just stay here. I have been in this room for over twenty-four hours. It's getting kind of ridiculous, and I have to eat again."

"I don't think I see it that way. Besides, I brought you a sandwich." Owen's lips were the Devil's mistress, as they warmed and soothed her skin as he curved kisses over her hip bones in equal measure.

"That was over five hours ago, Owen. It's starting to feel like you have me chained to a wall again."

"I thought tying you up might be too soon, but if you're ready, I'm game."

She knew she shouldn't encourage him, but the laughter that came out was real, and she enjoyed how relaxed her body and mind felt with him. Alice gave a small pat to Owen's naked shoulder.

The sheet was twisted around their feet, as much of a symbol of how they had spent the last number of hours as any other.

"Owen, I can't stay here with you. I have never felt like this with anyone in my life. Not ever, but I can't."

His kisses settled away, but if anything, his confidence glowed brighter. "I know," Owen whispered.

She turned, curling in as she shifted to face him. "You have the most beautiful eyes on a face that no man should have."

"Alice?"

She couldn't respond with words, only leaned and let her lips brush his for a small delicate kiss.

"Thank you," Owen said as Alice rested back into place only inches away. "What's going on in that mind of yours? Whatever is bothering you, we can work it out. You're not alone anymore. You can tell me."

She felt the pull of his words down through her spirit and could feel his sincerity. "Josh, the hunter we killed at the end."

"You mean the one I killed," Owen corrected.

"Sure, whatever. Josh said Father Patrick is being held or kept by someone in their organization. I need to find him and free him. The only reason Father Patrick isn't safe anymore is because of me. He was trying to help me. Has always tried to help me."

"Cornelius always warned me about women. I should have listened. First, you needed to be rescued from the basement. I did that. Then you wanted me to help you break your bond with Kerogen. Then you wanted a sandwich, which I made with these hands of mine just for you. And now you want a priest. I should have listened to him— nothing but trouble."

She punched his arm. "Hey, I am serious. I need to find Father Patrick and make sure he is safe."

"Who is he to you?"

Alice held still as something inside turned over. She fought back a couple tears as they started to free-fall. "He is sort of like my godfather." Alice slowly took a breath.

"Maybe more like a partner. He was there before I knew I was an etherealist. Back when I was just a little girl who loved to sing, particularly in Grace Cathedral on Sundays. Father Patrick served there. It's also where Kerogen bonded my soul." Alice gently moved; the feel of that day was like black oil over her skin. "Um, Kerogen used his magic to force Father Patrick to play the organ as he forced me to sing with him." Alice rubbed her fingertips together in the same way she had seen Father Patrick do a thousand times. "Most people don't know it takes hours to bond a soul. I assume the ivory keys are stained red, because Father Patrick had to have skin grafts over eight of his ten fingers because of that day."

"How did you get away? It's not very common that people do," Owen asked.

"Mostly luck. The other priest had been taking a nap in the back, and when he came out, it distracted Kerogen, just as the bond was complete. Father Patrick picked me up and ran out into the street. It's because of him and the other priest, Father Jacob. From there, the church hid me, trained me and Father Patrick never left my side. He could have. Could have gone back to his old life, but he refused. Even when I decided to stop trusting the church and go at Kerogen alone, he stayed by me. I need to get him back. I need to make sure he is safe."

"I understand."

"I am not sure anyone can understand." Alice sat up because she had to.

"I know what it's like to have people in my life I would do anything for. People who have done the impossible for me. The debt, the responsibility. I understand those things. And, Alice, I too have never felt like this with anyone else. I know this world we live in is crazy and at times upside down, but I don't want to be anywhere else but by your side. If this Father Patrick is part of your family, we will get him back. It's that simple."

"Why do you care about me?"

"You know why."

"Owen, it's just not enough—our connection. Our chemistry. I have Kerogen and now Father Patrick, and all of this?" She wiggled a hand between them, indicating what they had together. "It's just not enough for the amount of trouble I am causing. That attack was because of me. You need to let me go. I need you to help convince the others to let me go."

"Not in a million lifetimes." Owen's lips went flat as if he knew something she did not.

"I need to find Father Patrick and make sure he is safe. I owe him that much, and I want to do it now."

"And what about Kerogen?"

"We have four weeks until they can break the bond. I know they need time to prepare and need more We to lend their power. I can be back by then." She sat up, unable to lie still any longer. The guilt over the attack and knowing the good father was in jeopardy was too much to stay still now that she was rested, healed and held a full well of ethereal power.

"You gave your word, Alice. If for no other reason, that is why you need to stay here. Wait until we break the bond, and then together, we can go find your priest."

"But, Owen, he is in danger because of me. He already lost the life he was supposed to have, and I believed Josh when he said Father Patrick is in danger. I need to make sure he is safe. If I have to find another way to deal with Kerogen, I will, but I have no choice. I owe him."

She made to rise off the bed, but Owen caught her hand.

"Alice, you're not alone anymore. Let's just go talk to the others and see if they can help. But before we go out there, you cannot mention breaking your deal with Mara. You can ask her to consider releasing you from the deal at most. But even then, only as a last resort."

"So I am still a prisoner, only without chains."

"You made a deal with them. In their world, when you give your word, it means everything. As it does in mine."

With a soft twist of her wrist, his hand fell away. Alice turned, needing to look anywhere but at Owen. *I know.* She didn't say the words.

Only the faint sound of rustling sheets and springs signaled Owen climbing up out of bed from the far side as the room filled in with silence.

What is the plan? Alice thought for the hundredth time. *I can't just go track down a cardinal and beat the crap out of him until he tells me where Father Patrick is being held, can I?*

That is what you would do if the cardinal was a We.

And look where that got you. Seven years of following a failed plan. And a cardinal is only human. He won't be able to heal like me.

Slowly she looked from side to side as if the answer were somewhere to be found.

Four weeks and the bond with Kerogen will be severed. Freedom at last. One month and I am free of the shroud, free to go home. Free to see my mother and father and little sister.

But I won't sacrifice the only person who stood by my side. Father Patrick saved me twice. Once in the church, then at the monastery. And even now he is only in danger because he wanted to save me a third time. If I hadn't been caught, he never would have gone to the hunters for help.

I have to save him. I have to find him.

"Alice?" Owen asked.

"Your people are already helping me. Do you really believe they would help me save a priest on top of it all?"

"The funny thing about demons is you never know what they will do until you ask them."

"This isn't funny, Owen."

"My God, Alice, we just survived a full-out attack from hunters. I was almost burned to a crisp while bullets flew at my head. And yet I would do it all over again because I was able to spend twenty-four hours with you in this room. With you. I know, I know, you don't like words. But this time you're going to hear mine."

Owen's lips found her own, and chemistry, real and raw, danced between them.

"I am fascinated by you, by your will, your mind. I can't get enough of your skin or the sight of you. I know you're a little bit broken. I am broken to the core. I was born broken and will always be that way. It's the cracks within that make me who I am, and even so, you protected my people. You, Alice, didn't run or hide. Even without ethereal energy, you stood between everything in my world and those who came to destroy it. I feel joy in my heart when I look at you. I feel joy in my hands when I touch you. We had something from the very first moment. We had something in the silence and shadows when you were a prisoner here. We have something now. Sure, it's new, and maybe you can say it's untested. But I say give it a chance. Give my people a chance to decide, because like you, they are the best this world has to offer, and I think they will surprise you."

"Owen?" she pleaded. Trust, or rather relying on others wasn't something she did—besides, he was too much. Too true and sweet and good. And there was nothing within her that deserved it.

Together they turned a corner and traveled down a flight of wide stairs.

"So we're going back down into the weird room again? The one where Mara can change the walls on a whim. The same room it took two weeks and some chemistry between us before I could leave?" Alice asked.

"Not your favorite place?" Owen said, shifting his body closer to hers. Alice's arm fit nicely inside his, the connection warm and comforting.

"I can't say that it is," Alice responded.

"Not for nothing, but I think by now you understand Mara can shift any wall in her home with just the wave of her hand and probably do a lot more besides."

"I put that together during the fight upstairs. You pointing it out is not making me feel more comfortable here."

"Nothing bad will happen to you this time. I am sure. Mostly sure," he finished saying as her look of apprehension set in.

"Any idea why everyone is down here?" Alice asked.

"You heard Jones just now. The club is closed for a few days while the attention from the attack settles down, and Mara left word for us to come on down. Maybe she wants to redecorate for the big party and wants everyone's opinion?"

"Don't take this the wrong way, but Mara is not one of those women who want other people's opinions."

"You're probably right." Owen walked toward the two large doors, and Alice matched his gait, knowing they would open as they neared.

Sure enough, the large, ornate doors decorated with angels in flight opened, smooth and graceful, and her body was at odds as she entered into the room that had held her captive.

"Wow, look at this," Owen said.

Dazzling purple and red balloons held by gold string floated from almost every surface. They hung in groups of five to fifty, depending on the placement. Fresh roses of every shade of red filled the room while light shined clean and elegant, illuminating the pristine hall.

"There must be over five thousand balloons in here," Owen said, his voice matching her own thoughts.

"And five thousand roses. Did you know about this?" she asked as they slowed their pace to take it all in.

Together they shifted toward the center of the room, where a long, square table held cascading desserts of every type displayed over white linen. To its side, or rather the middle, only a few strides away, was a round table with gilded gold chairs. And just past both a gleaming portable bar.

"No idea," he answered in awe.

One by one, each of Owen's people turned to watch as they came in. Clover held a napkin folded over a pastry she had been eating while talking to Cornelius and Daphne.

Jessie sat at the long table talking to Damon and Jasper. An old, dark, musky bottle sat upright on the table between them. Mara stood in a long purple dress that shined like tiny stars while she waited across from Max, who was in the process of pouring three martinis at the bar.

They are all here, but what is going on? Alice thought. *Are they going to try to break the bond now?*

Alice raised a hand to Daphne, who had raised a hand in kind.

"You two finally made it down. It's about time. We are celebrating Daphne's birthday early!" Clover said as she and Daphne made their way over.

Owen took a pause to do the math; Daphne's birthday wasn't for another two weeks.

"Here, Owen, try this." Alice watched as Clover shoved a small pink macaron into Owen's mouth before he could speak. Clover's tall frame turned in her direction as Owen made to swallow. "Alice."

"Yes?" As the word was leaving her lips, Clover came in, wrapping her long arms around her in a tight but awkward hug. Body stiff, she felt each word Clover whispered.

"You saved us. I know it was hard, but you saved us, and I will never forget it."

Clover pulled away; however, as she did, Alice noticed there was something soft and fragile caught in the crystal strength of Clover's deep blue eyes.

"You would have done the same," Alice mumbled while preparing for another hug.

Despite a small, wiry, thin frame, Daphne's hug was all

soft and yet equally heartfelt. "Thank you for saving everyone. Cornelius has been telling us all about it. You were amazing."

"It was nothing. And happy birthday!" Alice said.

"Your birthday isn't for another two weeks. I thought we would combine it with the big show or something. Why are we doing it now?" Owen asked.

"Mara said we could all use a relaxation day," Daphne said in answer. "And what is a relaxation day without cake? Her words. Besides, I like knowing it's just us. Reminds me a bit of home. And look at this place. All this time it was right here, right under our feet. I have never been in any place like this. It belongs in a fairy tale."

"Beautiful, isn't it?" Owen asked.

"*Beautiful* doesn't begin to describe it," Daphne said as she gave him an awkward hug.

"Happy birthday, Daphne."

Together Owen and Alice made the rounds until finally settling in at the long table as Clover, Daphne, Jessie and Max were still walking the room with Jasper, who was giving Clover more attention than the rest.

"You open up some of your favorite gin?" Owen asked as he took Jessie's seat beside Damon. He was talking about the dark old bottle that stood upright in the center of the table, covered with age.

"Take a pull and tell me what you think," Damon said. "Let's find out if you can drink as well as you can play these days."

Owen settled into his seat before picking up the bottle, giving it a sniff. His eyebrows rose, and he couldn't help the hard look he shot Damon's way. "This isn't gin. It's bourbon."

"Good nose," Damon said with his normal frumpy-framed face. "Glad you didn't waste all your time while you were away."

"I thought you only drink the dark when you're about to do something stupid?"

"You mean like pushing Mara out of a run and taking on the brunt of Heaven's fury while we were all under attack? Or are you talking about before, when you went so deep into the waters of the river I thought you were going to knock on the bridge by accident?"

"I wasn't anywhere near the bridge." Owen took a pull of the bourbon that was made before the Civil War. It was smooth and layered as it burned going down.

"You were a lot closer than you think."

"What are you two talking about?" Alice asked.

"It's a myth, or rather a legend," Owen said.

"The hell it is," Damon said, indicating Owen could take another pull from the bottle if he wanted. "The bridge is as real as you or me, perhaps more so, and it's a damn terrifying place to find yourself by accident, I can assure you."

Owen obliged in the bottle, knowing such an opportunity wasn't likely to ever come again. The flavor of caramel and spice with just a faint touch of vanilla fed his soul and cleaned out some of the webbing inside his mind as he set the bottle down.

"I don't know anything about it. One of you want to fill me in?" Alice said as she tried one of the macarons on her plate, a green one.

"The legend says if you go deep enough into the river of souls, you can find the Devil's bridge," Owen supplied.

"Ascend to the bridge," Damon corrected.

"Right, ascend to the bridge. And while you are there, if you knock three times, he'll show up and possibly let you in or let you make a deal. Not that I have any intention of going in that far," Owen said with a shake of the head. "He's not who I play for."

"Is that what you were doing onstage as the blue flames covered your legs?" Alice asked.

"Something like that."

Damon pointed a finger for Alice to try the bottle next before speaking. "Go ahead and give her a try. You sure as hell earned it. The way Cornelius is talking, you killed seventeen hunters and a giant with only your pinky. But we both know you saved a lot of our people too."

"I'm not much of a bourbon fan."

"You are today." Mara's voice broke in from behind as she pulled up a chair beside Alice. "Go ahead, hunter, you did earn it."

"You know they came here because of me? A friend sent those hunters to get me out?"

"We heard. We know. But then, that doesn't really matter, does it? Actions over words and all that. Drink up, girl. That spirit is one of a kind and can't be bought off any shelf. Call it an old tradition. We are alive, as our hearts still beat, so we toast the dead and celebrate the dawn." Mara flicked her finger toward the dark bottle that sat lifeless on the table.

Alice held her gaze and felt an odd understanding falling into place as she brought the old bottle up and drank. The smell hit her a moment before the booze burned, a complex intertwining of flavors coating her tongue as she drank more than she planned.

"Good girl. Now share," Mara said, taking the bottle right out of her hand.

"Haven't any of you heard of using a glass?" Alice asked as she forced her throat to accept the fire of the booze. Only soft grins answered her question.

"I thought you had Max make you a martini?" Owen asked.

Mara set the bottle down and slid it back to Alice with a nod to take another pull. "Hardly. Those were for your piano man and the two girls. You think I would have Max make me anything? I could see it now—I take a drink and find a tattoo on my ass."

Cornelius and Damon both let out a chuckle.

"Funny. You realize Daphne isn't even eighteen yet?" Owen said with a touch of concern.

"She's an etherealist in my house, under my protection. She will be fine. Like you, not all rules are designed for her to follow."

"Wait a minute. The bridge—you're talking about summoning the Devil?" Alice broke into the conversation. "That is who comes when you knock on the bridge three times, right?" Each word spoken asked the same question: *What is wrong with you people?*

Owen took the bottle, took a swig and passed it over to Damon's waiting hand. "Don't worry, it's only a legend."

"No, it's not. And you were close, boy. The guitar and your soul are one hell of a combination. Trust in it. When everything else seems dark, you trust in it." Damon took a pull and passed it over to Cornelius's waiting hand.

Owen felt an edge to the group despite the cake, the pretty balloons and bright lights. "Very well. We have another problem I was hoping for some guidance on."

"Ha. The last time you asked me for guidance, you had already broken Damon's saxophone and were trying to buy time until the replacement part showed up. What have you done?"

"It isn't him. It's me." Alice had to swallow the word *again*. All heads in the vicinity turned her way. "The man who called the hunters here for me is in danger. I think he has been taken, and I need to find out where he is so I can save him."

"Father Patrick is a priest held by other priests. I am sure he will be fine," Cornelius said.

"I don't believe that. You heard what Josh said. Father Patrick is in trouble because he tried to save me again."

"He's a priest, dear," Mara said, though not unkindly.

"He's more than that. He's a good man who only ever tried to do his best by me. You don't understand. He saved me from Kerogen at the end of the bonding, then saved me again when Kerogen came for me years later. He's never abandoned me. I need to find him. He had no idea about any of this, about ethereal energy, about any of you. And he never would have if it wasn't for me. There is no reason to hate him. He's just good."

"Of course we don't hate him." It was Cornelius who spoke with a smile that soothed. "Hunters and the secret order that trains them are just a small hidden faction sheltered within the extremely large and old religion. We don't hate priests or even the church, for that matter. Never have, in fact. They have their place and the majority of it is, just as you say, good."

Mara drew attention away from Cornelius. "They help build towns and cities, pulling people together, and help to provide roots and community. They stand sentinel for those who have fallen and as a beacon for those who remain. Nothing wrong with that," she said in somber tones.

"They help you mortals find your place with the hereafter, both above and below. Pretty big shoes to fill, if you ask me," Damon said, taking another pull from the bourbon bottle and passing it over to Owen.

"It's the factions within that we have to worry about. Not only those that trained you but another that is even perhaps more dangerous, as they are determined to have as much information and power as they can. But don't worry about any of that right now. Let's relax, have a drink to the dead for being alive. I'll find your priest and see what can be done. My word on it," Cornelius said.

Owen pulled and passed the bottle.

"You can do that? You will do that?" Alice found the bottle in her hand, but she held Cornelius's gaze, needing to know.

"When you have been around as long as we have, the church is far less of a mystery. And everyone likes to barter. You just need to know who and how much."

"True or false, if I would have come straight to you seven years ago, you could have found Kerogen for me?"

"True, but the price would have been too high. And you wouldn't be the woman you are today."

Alice forced down a choking sensation before she knew what she was doing. American-made bourbon, rich and bright, burned inside her mouth. She hadn't planned on drinking again. It had just sort of happened.

Owen tilted his head to the side. Something was off. He looked to see his people circling toward the double doors of the main entrance, but they weren't alone. Jones had come in and joined their group. Suddenly his seat felt too tight around him. Damon didn't seem to be as relaxed as he wanted the room to think he was, but then neither did Mara.

"What is going on?"

Three of those he considered family held steady eyes as he checked in with each.

Damon reached over and took the bottle out of Alice's hands and pushed it into his. "Take a big pull, son. You're going to thank me for it."

The lights dimmed and a soft breeze shifted through the room, followed by a maniacal laughter that sent his heart racing and his skin crawling as it curled through the air.

"He's here," Alice said beside him.

"You son of a bitch! How?"

Those at the table rose as one out of their seats. Damon, Mara and Cornelius held his accusing gaze while Alice searched the room.

"Jasper, Jones, remove them, please," Mara called out toward the group in a voice that said she had been expecting this.

Not that it was necessary, as both Jasper and Jones were

already herding Max, Jessie, Daphne and Clover toward the main doors.

"Owen? What's going on?" Clover called, her body blocked by Jasper's upraised hand.

"Go, Clover. Just do what they say. Get out of here now," Owen called.

A door in the opposite corner from the main doors flung open, slamming hard against the wall.

"Will you look at this place? Hasn't changed in a hundred years. The balloons are a nice touch, Mara. I hear you have something of mine? I am here to take it back."

Kerogen wore a black suit like a nightmare wore evil, radiating destruction and violence as he stepped into the room. Ethereal tentacles swarmed in behind him as if he were part sea creature come to life.

A level six, Owen thought. *And a big one at that.* He turned to face Alice as power began to radiate off her in massive waves as she drew energy out of her well, ready to attack.

Before Alice could move, Mara's hands caught her wrist. Alice let out a small scream as the cuffs from before clinked tight. The wave of power radiating off and over Alice just as suddenly ended.

Owen couldn't believe what was happening.

"Hush, child, and play your part!" Mara said to Alice before turning her attention to Kerogen. "I see you got our invitation. The party isn't for four more weeks. You came early. What a very naughty boy," Mara said.

"Mara?" Owen asked, but Damon's hand came hard down over his shoulder, halting him in place.

Two black vines shot up from the floor and connected to Alice's cuffs, binding her once more in place just in front of the table. Even so, Mara didn't take her hands off the hunter.

"Oh, my doe, how long have you run? What a waste of my time." Kerogen held out his hand as if for the end of a leash. Behind him, a swarm of tendrils swirled and gyrated in anticipation.

"Now, now, Kerogen. I have something that you want. It is only fair you trade something in kind for her."

To accent the rage swimming over his face, Kerogen's vines twisted, then slammed the floor in a violent, rhythmic pattern. The tile floor beneath cracked, then shattered altogether as he took a stalking step forward. "She is mine and mine alone. Give her to me, or I shall tear down this house, if I have to do it one stone, one bone at a time."

"Manners, old friend. Where are your manners?" Cornelius chided as he stepped farther to the side and away from the table.

"I will not hear a word you speak, meddler. If you open your mouth to me again, I will tear your jaw from your head and shove it down your throat. One word."

"Kerogen. Oh, Kerogen. Have the years really left you so un-"—Mara paused as if searching for the right word—"flirtatious? There was a time when the world was fun for you. No reason not to have a moment. You are here, we are here, and look, there is cake."

To Owen's continual surprise, Kerogen did seem to settle. Or at least the swarming mass of tentacles finally stopped crushing floor tiles.

"Very well. If a moment is all you require, that I can give you in payment for what belongs to me."

"Owen?" Alice asked in desperation.

Mara, who still held Alice's wrist, gave a nasty yank. "Quiet, hunter."

"Isn't my doe magnificent? She chased me all through the lands, and here she is. How ever did you acquire her?"

"She came right in through the front door. Looking for you, if you will believe it. Been a bit of trouble, but we kept her in hand."

"And the boy? There is something odd about him."

"Oh, now, that's the fun part. You heard rumors a few

years back that I was protecting not one but two etherealists here?"

"Of course. One died, the other . . ." Kerogen's words drifted off as he put the pieces together. "Had received a key. This is him?"

Through boiling anger, Owen felt Kerogen's hard, inspecting stare while he took notice for the first time.

"You might have more for me than just the girl after all, Mara."

Owen felt Kerogen's eyes leave him to search the room. It was as if a heavy wind was no longer trying to push him over.

Damon moved, breaking the stillness of the room and drawing his eye. "I told you, Mara. Kerogen wants to go back on up. Didn't I say it? He has that look, but then that's the only real reason why someone like him would have the need to bond a child." Damon spoke, then tipped the bottle of bourbon up to his mouth and took a drink.

"Damon, the musician. I have never liked you."

"You like it when I play, and that is all that really matters for someone like me. So let's stop screwing around. We have your girl and the boy here. As you can see, the room is primed for a run. Mara is even all dressed up. We could take you on a trip right now."

"You think we are a simpleton," Kerogen said with an edge. "I do want back in, and yet to go through the fourth gate, even you will need to prepare."

"Nah. Come on, Kerogen. Tell the truth. You don't want God to take you back into his embrace, to reshape you into one of his angels. I doubt you even truly believe he would. Long ago you made your choice to come down here, as each of us did. No, old man, you don't wish to be an angel. You don't want to go up, but down once again. And that's where I come in."

"What are you saying?" Kerogen's eyes flashed with hot fury.

Damon pressed the bottle into Owen's chest and gave it a small shake until Owen had little choice but to accept it. Damon stepped forward to confront the level six all alone. "I too am tired. Tired of games, tired of waiting. With your power, with your help, I can get us both to his bridge. I know the path, the names of the souls on the way. Mara owes me. She will use her house to help guide us there. Everything is set."

"Why in all the universe would I trust you to take me to him?"

"Because I want to see it. I want to know what he looks like after all this time. Both in spirit and reality. A wonder of the ever after. I want to taste the air, feel the weight on my chest. I want to smell the water and see what lies both beneath the bridge and above it. I have spent my life splashing into the river. I want to see the end of it, and you want to make a deal with the Devil. I say this—make a deal with me first, and let's go do what we were always born to do."

Kerogen's tentacles of ethereal power slowed, coming to a full stop, his entire body pausing as if frozen in time. And to Owen, it was as if the entire room paused, waiting for his answer.

Owen's heart pumped double time while he simply stood watching, waiting inside a storm of betrayal. Clearly Mara, Cornelius and Damon had known—known Kerogen was coming early. They had planned this! Planned this whole show. Even Jones and Jasper were in on it, and all this after he had given his little speech to Alice to trust his people, to trust his family.

He looked at her. Alice's pale skin and sharp eyes held both rage and fear as she looked back.

The essence over his wrists hummed, and his skin itched with all the power soaking into the room.

"We will take the girl and your gatekeeper with us. Stand aside, Damon. I will not make a deal with the likes of you," Kerogen ordered, having clearly made up his mind.

"You are turning down my offer to see the bridge? Why? It is what you wish more than anything else. You cannot deny it."

"I do not trust you, nor her." He indicated Mara. "My plan is set. I have no reason to change it."

"You are a fool, Kerogen. I might be the only one of us alive who can get you there, and you are turning me down because of trust. How human of you!" Damon said.

"You sound pitiful, musician, and weak. Step aside or I shall crush you."

Damon turned away and slowly locked eyes with Owen.

Alice held the rage boiling inside, enough rage to burn the world as Mara's hands held her clamped down like a vise she had no chance to break. Cuffed and chained, her well of power blocked unless she wanted to pass out from pain again. And that simply wasn't an option with Kerogen in the room.

The world was upside down, twisted and inside out. From cake to betrayal. The only consolation was that Owen seemed to be taken completely off guard as well.

She heard Damon's offer, heard Kerogen's refusal.

Alice didn't miss the way Damon locked eyes with Owen, but it was the way his three fingers brushed his pants pocket before settling partly in, partly out that said she was missing something. Something important.

It's too casual, too simple, too relaxed. Why would anyone place their hands in their pockets with Kerogen in the room? You always want your hands free. Why? Three fingers? It's a sign.

What the hell is going on? Owen's mind raced to play catch-up. This was too big. Never would he have thought his people would have betrayed him. And here he stood, frozen with a bottle of Damon's booze against his chest, with Alice's monster across from him.

Kerogen needed to die, but his power was absolutely crazy high and a level six.

Always leave an out. The thought was as much a statement as a question. Part of the teaching Damon and Cornelius had given him on countless nights. *What out did they leave?*

Damon's deep eyes continued to drill holes with their intensity as he brought his hand into his pocket.

Three fingers.

And it clicked in.

"Give me the girl, Mara. I won't ask again." Kerogen's words moved the air. Clothing rippled and the balloons all moved around the room.

Owen cursed aloud as the full weight of the plan settled in. With more ease than common sense, most of the tension washed away. Kerogen didn't even bother to look his way, and the simple fact of it had Owen smiling.

Without further guidance, Owen lifted the bottle to his lips and took two big chugs, letting the heat and fire burn his throat.

"Kerogen, you don't like Damon. It's easy to see why. I don't really like him right now either. But I'll make you a deal, *asshole*." Owen added that for Alice. "I can take you. I can take you into the river. Build a temporary bond with me, and I can take you to see the bridge. Knock three times, and the Devil will come to make a deal, right? That's what you want. I'll take you."

"You're a mortal."

Owen cut Kerogen off, seeing him clearly. "And so are you."

"Arrogant child! I have seen kingdoms rise and fall, and you interrupt me! I shall crush your body into pulp."

"Wake up. You don't trust Damon, and why would you? But then, he's not the only one who can take you there. I can, and I will if you make a deal with me instead. I know you can hear the truth of my words, just as I can see you have no business in Heaven."

"Don't be ridiculous."

"You really believe Heaven is where you will be happy, where peace will find your soul? Do you even want peace? I don't. Peace isn't who I am. I am the storm and the never-ending question to find new answers. I can see you, Kerogen. You and I both know you don't belong up. So let's go down. Make a deal with me, and I will take you where you want to go."

"The last time I trusted a human, I was betrayed. Why would I possibly do so now?"

"Because even more than I want to see the bridge today, I want to see the girl free of you. I have given her my word to help, so you see, you have me two ways. I want her to be free of you, and I want to see him. I want to know what he looks like, what being there feels like. All my life, I have wanted to know."

"I don't believe you can take me there. Why are we listening to this?" His swarm of tentacles thrashed more of the tile floor to dust.

Owen knew he was losing him. He tossed the bottle to the ground, shattering it as he moved forward as Damon had. "Hey, dickhead, you're not looking! See me. All of me. There is a reason I was given the guitar. There was a reason I was given that damn guitar when no other ethereaslist has ever been granted her. See my soul, see the truth of my words, and stop being an asshole so we can go see the Devil." Owen didn't stop moving until he was before the We, standing face-to-face.

Time ticked by as they stood eye-to-eye, Owen hiding nothing.

"Mara, can the boy get me to the bridge?" Kerogen asked.

"He's my boy. Of course he can," Mara said.

"And you will lend us the power of your home to reach the bridge?"

"I will."

"Very well." Kerogen's hand caught around Owen's throat, squeezing tight, depriving him of air. "You listen to me, gatekeeper. If you try to betray me in any way, I will destroy everything you hold dear. Do you understand me? Mara, Damon, those who left—yes, I took notice. They will die terribly by my hand. Do you understand?"

Owen was just able to move his chin up and down to signal he understood.

"Good. Now take me to see him."

Air slipped back into Owen's lungs as Kerogen's hand released and slid down over his shoulder. Gasping, Owen did his best to force his body to settle.

"We have a deal." Kerogen's forehead touched his own as the level six leaned in.

For the briefest of moments, Owen thought of trying for an attack. But the truth of being overmatched was ever present within Kerogen's knowing, cold eyes.

He wants me to try to use the essence on my wrist.

Seeing no other option and trusting not only those in the room but some preordained piece of his will, Owen leaned in.

The bond took less than three seconds to form. The shock of it not only had Owen's skin crawling but his heart racing. Kerogen was so strong, even without Alice's well of ethereal power.

"There is one more thing we need to get out of the way before I take you there," Owen said as they leaned back from contact.

"Oh, and what is that?" Kerogen asked.

"For . . . the . . . girl." Owen punctuated his words by slamming his head forward as hard as he could. Kerogen, caught off guard, took the impact like a mountain accepting a thrown stone.

His nose cracked to the side, but no blood fountained free. No other part of Kerogen's body even gave off the impression of being hurt. "Do such a thing again, and I will send you to meet the Devil on your own. Do we have an understanding?"

"We do. Now, will someone please get me my guitar!"

What the hell is going on?" Alice asked from the same spot where she stood tethered to the floor. Only Mara wasn't standing guard any longer, and Cornelius had traded places with her.

"Keep your voice low, and don't look at me when you speak. Kerogen would prefer I fade away. He really doesn't like me," Cornelius said.

Alice fought her temper. Fought every instinct that called for her to attack him. "You betrayed me."

"Did I? To whom did I do such a thing? Pay attention, Alice," Cornelius said as he watched a stage in the corner of the room slide out of the wall at Mara's command.

"To whom? To Kerogen, you asshole."

"Pay attention," he repeated.

Owen watched a circular stage glide out of the wall, forming like frosting being poured over a baker's cake.

"Here is your guitar," Damon said, having come back from retrieving it from the truck. "Now, you understand what happens when you ascend to the bridge, right? When you get there, when the music stops, you are no longer here and neither is he."

"How do I get back if I am no longer here?"

"Same way all great musicians get there in the first place."

"Pay the Devil?"

"Just give him his due. You'll understand when the time is right. I believe in you."

"I am ready, gatekeeper. Get up here, and let us be on our way," Kerogen said.

Owen took the case out of Damon's hands and stepped up onto the stage even as it continued to rotate forward out of the wall.

"If anyone here tries to interfere, I will kill him and then the rest of you."

"Anything else?" Mara asked as the stage settled into place.

"I could use a stool for this one. Along with an amp of some kind," Owen said, slipping his guitar's strap over his shoulder and into place.

"You got it, and the cord you are looking for is already by your feet, just like when you were younger."

"Sure beats carrying an amp and extension cord from upstairs," Owen said, remembering the first time he and David had snuck down here. "I'm set. Kerogen?" He reached down and connected the guitar without any flair, the weight of what he was about to try settling deep into his chest.

Owen felt more than noticed the floor move behind him as a black box melted up out of the stage. It gleamed as if freshly polished, coming to the height of a stool.

"Thank you," he said to Mara, doing his best not to look at Alice. For some unknown reason, Kerogen wasn't focused on her anymore, and that was for the best.

Owen took in a breath, feeling the caramel and burn of the bourbon still on his tongue. *They planned this. Trust them. And trust the sound.*

Fingers tested the strings in a familiar set of chords as he let his body relax. *This is different than before*, he thought as Kerogen's hand dropped down onto his right shoulder. "Less pressure, asshole, and if I stand, you need to move with me."

"Please, child. This isn't my first time. Not even my hundredth. Now begin. I am losing patience."

"Careful, I hear patience is a virtue." Pain radiated down his arm as Kerogen's hand squeezed hard enough to bruise before releasing.

Chapter Twenty-nine

Owen's body relaxed, his eyes closing, going dark to the room as he began to play. In his mind he held the image of Alice once again chained.

Kerogen's hand weighed down on Owen's shoulder while Owen thought words that he refused to let fall from his lips.

You deserve to be free. You deserve to have a different life than me.

Through each stroke of the strings, ethereal power filled his skin and bones in the greatest way he knew how. The internal call of wilderness and wild drove his body and soul deeper and deeper as the blue flames rose up once more from the great river of souls below.

The combination of icy heat crisped the air he breathed with determination while he drove deeper, needing this to be done, needing her to be free.

The house and stage were like a focused beam for his power and sound, granting control and stable footing as he opened his heart to the instrument that belonged in his hands.

Kerogen's power added magnitude, but it was passion and skill, the storm of his soul, that opened the familiar way wider and wider.

The screams and rhythm of the other side filled his chest, and Owen inlaid their pain into his song. Shifting notes calmed and soothed those trapped souls he moved past as he carried Kerogen deeper and deeper into the water.

I always wanted this life of mine. Fighting for peace and freedom of another kind. I won't stop, break or fall.

Owen's mind shifted as he played. He thought about Mara, who was trusting him, even as she hadn't trusted him enough to let him in on the plan. He thought about her struggle to be free. Her struggle to live in this world as a woman with conflicting needs. The need to be whole and broken at the same time. He thought of David, and the loss of his brother that still weighed tightly within his heart.

Owen thought of his past as he played.

But mostly, always rounding back, he thought of Alice and the monster who stood at his back.

The river took its toll as the flames danced over and up from below. Owen only pressed in farther. Not a heated comet needing to outrun the stars, but instead a single-minded engine, driven with purpose. To go deeper and deeper. In this, he leaned on Alice's conviction, so she was there with him in each stroke of the strings, each press of the blue flames.

The world fell away as he played, the call of the other side mixing with the vibration of his strings and the opening of his heart.

I am not afraid. I was not meant to cower and hide. Fear me, asshole. Fear my heart and my pride.

Blue flames consumed his mind and his skin as he played notes over notes, dancing with the unheard rhymes of his heart and soul as the flames climbed up from below, higher and higher. Dead hands clung to his pants and shirt.

Owen didn't fear them, couldn't fear them. No matter the cold of the blue flames or the demands of the damned. This was his place. This was his first home. The one place no one could take from him.

Cornelius, is she ready?" Damon asked through gritted teeth as he stepped up and slipped a hand around Alice's left bicep, securing her even more in place, now from either side.

Owen continued to play alone in the rising blue flames.

"She's calm enough to hold still for a while."

"Cornelius?" Mara asked, disguising her words by picking up one of the macarons Daphne had set on the table.

"What is going on?" Alice whispered, trying to match the others' voices.

"I will explain to you what Owen and Kerogen are doing while you stand there, very still." Alice didn't miss the emphasis on *very still* as Cornelius spoke loud enough to see the wrath of Kerogen's hate fill his eyes.

"You see, the river of souls, unlike the road above, does not require an etherealist to play. But it does require a special type of soul."

"A soul in kind," Damon added.

Alice held still as she felt a cold liquid move over her shoes and up under her pants. Whatever was happening, its touch was foreign and extremely creepy.

Be it in understanding of what was happening or simply in sensing her discomfort, Damon gave a hard squeeze, and she took it as a reminder to hold still as Cornelius continued to explain.

"Right, a soul in kind. Damon and Mara, and yes, even I recognized it in Owen from the very first. But Kerogen doesn't have it. He is made of a different sort. No matter how angry he feels inside, he could never make this trip down into the river on his own."

"It's not for everyone," Damon said.

Alice thought his voice held a stiffness, but it was nothing compared to the odd sensation of a cold liquid gliding up her calves, similar to wet paint.

"No, it's not for everyone. And yet, like all rules, even this one has a back door. Or maybe a bottom door, so to speak. You see, if a being, be it a We or an etherealist, can build a short-term bond with someone who is going down, then as long as the two keep contact, they can go together. Therefore, a person who has no business in the Devil's river can get there, as Owen and Kerogen are doing now."

"And don't say baptism. Not even our kind like the perversion of the reference," Damon said. The tightness in his voice was clear this time.

Damon is struggling to speak. Cold ran up her thighs. She held her breath as the wet substance she couldn't name climbed higher.

"It's true no one likes the commonality, and yet there it is. Now, to make it to the bridge is not something that most can do on their own. But Mara's sacred hall can be used to help focus the will and the ethereal energy. With Mara's permission, of course. Think of it as a lens for ethereal energy. Yet even so, getting to the bridge isn't just about power. The cost has always required the will, the storm and the heat of the soul coupled with the skill, and then add in enough power, and you have a chance of getting there."

Alice could feel Cornelius's pure confidence.

"Now, here is the secret we don't normally share. Unlike the road to Heaven, the blue river wants people to come in and stay. So watch carefully for when Owen and Kerogen get to the bridge. You will see them shift—no longer here, they will have slid through to the other side, leaving an odd gray-like outline to hold their place. Until it too dissipates, or they return."

Alice listened, knowing this was not only information she didn't have but sensing it was vital to why she had to hold still. There was a plan, and this was all somehow a part of it.

Trust my people. Owen's words slipped over and over again through her mind.

Listening, it took everything she had to hold still, giving away nothing, as whatever was climbing up her skin continued to climb higher.

"And you are just going to let Owen go to Hell up there?" Alice said despite her orders to hold.

"You heard Damon. He made the offer to take Kerogen. It wasn't enough, or rather Kerogen didn't trust that Damon wouldn't just stop halfway to the bridge. He is old, after all. Very old, and Kerogen can sense in Owen what we can, what you can. That he wants more. Wants to know the other side. Be a part of both spaces. That deep within is a need to push on."

The cold covered her feet, legs, belly button and lower back, and continued to climb higher.

Damon's hand squeezed tight and held pressure. *Hold still*, his hand said like a parent forcing a child.

Owen went deeper, relaxing the ties on his soul and the sound he hadn't known he had been holding tight. Creativity mixing with skill, soaring higher and higher, Kerogen's power through the bond and Mara's house focusing his will and clearing out parts of his mind that stood in the way as the shape of sound danced to the rhythm of his soul and the souls of the damned.

It wasn't fair, but it was right. The way the sound could stretch out into eternity and blend, mingle and touch. Music couldn't be contained, couldn't be restricted. Not a substance in time could pull back the edges, could tie down the freedom of sound. Not God, not Heaven, not Hell. Not now.

Owen let go as he played deeper and deeper, the blue flames crawling higher and higher.

"Burn me," he whispered as understanding of what was required to ascend became clear.

Alice felt the cold slide over, encompassing her chest and spreading higher. A feeling as if she was being entombed sent fear, real and alive, driving through her nervous system. And yet Owen's music raced skyward, challenging the unseen but ever-present stars above, an awe-inspiring distraction that lent will to her challenge.

"I myself never have felt the need to partake of the waters that lead to Hell, but then, they can be quite addicting, and the cost ever so high on the soul. I find I have more than enough faults of my own here and now. You can trust me in this," Cornelius said.

Despite the order to hold still, despite that something was clearly happening that the others didn't want Kerogen to know about, she couldn't stop herself from angling her eyes down toward her bare arms as the sensation reached up her neck. She had to see, had to know what was going on.

And there it was.

A ripple so minute, so thin it could be a layer of nail polish, running over my skin. What is it? She watched it run down her arms, blending over, matching the color and contrast of her own skin.

Damon's hand tightened even deeper, like a vise, coming close to real pain.

It's going to cover my mouth, Alice thought as the substance climbed up over her chin. With little time to spare, she shut her lips, sealing them closed.

The feeling of being smothered to death climbed exponentially higher as the cold, wet liquid ran over her lips and up over her nose.

But the worst was the feeling as it crawled up over her eyes. It took all of her hardened will to accept the feeling and keep them open and still.

* * *

A new sound—a sound he had never heard nor felt and yet still didn't fear even while it vibrated through the air—swarmed like a hum of a million insect wings, and Owen felt the hair on the back of his neck stick up as every survival instinct he had within said he was passing the point of no return.

Owen felt the force of vibrating wings growing in strength and magnitude, and so he stood to meet what was coming, all while shifting chords.

Kerogen's hand never left his shoulder as the stool drifted back down into the stage. "We are almost there," Kerogen said.

But Owen refused to care, knowing each stroke of the song he took forward was another step toward a place made of forsaken ground. Owen opened his eyes and looked to Damon, Mara, Cornelius and Alice. Holding the image of each of them, he closed his eyes once more.

With a freedom of the soul, he let his song go. Let his fingers dance and accepted the weight of freedom. His freedom.

Hands danced over and up, pressing into strings with a rhythm and honesty that tied his heart and breath into the hereafter as the swarm of sound crashed into his mind and body. Owen weathered the blast and felt a twisted ray of euphoria. For a heartbeat, his soul rejoiced.

Then the world cracked blue, and Owen and Kerogen both hit the floor of the stage as a force great and unbending slammed them to the ground.

M ara shot the top of a champagne bottle, creating a loud distraction. At precisely the same moment, working together, Cornelius and Damon peeled Alice back. The motion was fast and dirty, and Alice had just enough time to see a copy of herself still chained to the floor, standing between them.

Alice turned her head as Damon spoke from behind, right into her ear. "Stay down. We need to get you out of here right now."

Owen's hands were over ice that threatened to crack beneath him. Kerogen was likewise beside him, all dignity gone, with a loud unrhythmic choking filling the air. Owen felt the burn in his own throat and finally understood the full implication of Damon's words.

Carefully he stood with his guitar in hand and took a look around.

A thin, circular wall of blue ice encased the stage, trapping him. Both below and above, it held him as if he were inside a giant blue ice cube.

I'm in another world. No, just a space inside a space. Like a run but physical.

Owen turned to see Mara standing frozen by the pastry table, a bottle of champagne in hand lifted halfway up to her lips. A half smile was on Cornelius's face as he looked straight ahead, one hand over Alice's shackled wrist.

Damon stood beside her, and looking through the ice wall, be it some fluke or simply a twist of luck, or simply the old sax player's never-ending disposition, a crack within the ice blocked his lips from view, leaving the man to look far more serious than all the others combined.

"You did it. We are here." Kerogen's words were harsh, as if he had lost his voice only an hour ago.

Here? The bridge? Through some of the fog in his mind, Owen pivoted, looking around.

"Where is it?" Owen asked, the words slipping out.

"It's everywhere. Just feel it, gatekeeper. Can't you feel his touch is all around you?"

Owen's eyes tracked the ice and the room on the other

side. He tracked up and down as Kerogen's evil laugh rolled out and around the enclosed space. Owen took a single slippery step, and a second later he heard the ice crack under his feet, and it had him holding still.

"Don't move, fool." To accent his point, Kerogen slammed his foot down with the force of a mountain. Cracks splintered out ten feet in all directions, including up the wall nearest the We. "This is my time, and I will not suffer stupidity now."

"Or what? I brought you to the bridge. That was the deal. It's time for me to go."

"Keep your mouth shut!" Kerogen's ethereal energy pulsed bright, a fist forming out of his hand as he spun, slamming hard against the nearest wall with a thunderous force.

Owen watched as cracks formed up and down. Across and deep.

Kerogen is knocking on the ice. And he has already done so twice. Fear radiated up Owen's spine. It was one thing to reach this space, another thing to summon the Devil.

"Witness, it's been over a thousand years since last I heard of anyone completing this. A thousand years. Witness my rise."

Owen felt the energy climb in the room as Kerogen pulled more and more of his power to bear. His hands formed two fists that he raised over his head to slam down. If so, it would mark the third knock, summoning the Devil.

Owen watched but couldn't stay still. The strings over the guitar shifted at his will, forming once more into raw essence that dropped down into his waiting hand. His own ethereal power filled his skin and bones.

One chance. One chance to shut Kerogen down. If Owen could just get the essence around some portion of Kerogen's body, his power would be locked within.

Focused, Owen lashed out, going for the body, striking with the glowing whip.

As fast as lightning, Kerogen dropped one hand from

over his head, catching the whip with a feral smile. "Fool. Now your life is mine." His words were interrupted when a hard force jolted his head forward.

An odd, twisting, surprised look crossed Kerogen's downward-angled face as he let go of the whip and dropped hard to his knees.

Owen snapped the whip back as Alice's black hair and beautiful face appeared over Kerogen's shoulder. Her expression was clean as she twisted the handle of the blade that she had jammed in the back of Kerogen's head. Owen watched, mesmerized, as more of Alice came into view.

"How?" Owen asked as Alice pulled the blade free.

Kerogen's body balanced over his knees.

Damon and his brass saxophone shifted out of a reverse weave and came into view just behind Alice, answering who had brought her.

"Me, son. I know the way far better than most. Plus, Mara inserted a trap door. Come on, we need to go. Take hands, and I'll get us out of here."

"I can't move. If I do, I'll break the ice."

"Don't worry, there is a trick. We will come to you," Damon said.

"He really is dead?" Alice said over the top of Kerogen's lifeless body.

"Yeah, he's dead," Owen said.

"The connection inside is just gone. Gone." With power, she pulled the knife free and kicked the body forward.

"Wait!" Owen said in warning. Too late—

Kerogen's body flew ahead, his one outstretched fist whipping forward to smash down on the ice.

Damon cursed as the ice around Kerogen's hand cracked once, then twice. A long, uneven crack spread back toward the floor where Kerogen's foot had made the first crack. Then up the wall to where he had made the second. Both pressure and sound drove into the room through the crack as a hot wind blew through the air.

He's coming, Owen thought.

"To me now!" Damon said, his saxophone coming up to his lips.

Owen shared a look with Alice as they both turned to go for Damon.

Owen leaped the long crack with guitar in hand, wanting nothing to do with what was going to happen next. Midair, he tripped, something solid catching his right foot and sending him headfirst.

He fell hard even while sliding over the ice, keeping the guitar in the air.

The pressure in the room doubled, and it felt as if his skin were being pressed back into his bones. His feet and free hand struggled to grip the ice, slipping and sliding on its slick surface.

Alice's hand reached out, taking his own while her other hand touched Damon's shoulder. Instantly his feet found traction. Scrambling forward, Owen moved closer as Damon's first notes started to play.

Owen noticed an opened trapdoor leading down below the stage, and he didn't pause as he descended. Alice came in behind him, one hand helping to guide Damon back out.

The room below was blacked out and felt small. Owen was careful to keep close to Alice and make enough room for Damon to come down the set of stairs.

The sound of Damon's playing grew with intensity as he stepped off the last step. The trapdoor snapped shut above, locking the room in darkness as Damon finished his last note.

"Is he dead?" Cornelius asked from within the darkness, his voice as emotionless as a steel beam.

"He's dead. Alice drove her knife into the back of his head," Damon said as soft orange light glowed from all four corners.

The room was familiar, and yet Owen's mind pulled hard at what he was seeing, thinking it impossible. They were in Damon's studio. Only Damon's studio shouldn't have been right under the stage. It was upstairs, down the long hallway just behind the room he shared with Jessie and Max.

"Are you okay?" he asked Alice.

"Is it over? I can't believe it's over."

Owen turned fully to see her. Her face was a mask of heavy contemplation, eyebrows slightly furrowed.

Sensing his attention, she looked up. "It's over. I can feel him gone. All this time, and now I can feel him out of me! I am free." Her eyes held such intensity it melted a stone within Owen he hadn't even understood he had.

"It's over. You're free, Alice. Kerogen is dead," Owen said.

"I get to go home." Her expression changed. "Get it off, get it out. Cut it out of me!" Enchanted bloody knife in hand, Alice suddenly went frantic as she started to cut into her own shoulder.

"Wait!" Owen said, jumping for the knife as fear and panic drove his actions.

Damon was right behind him.

With effort and struggle, Owen caught the wrist holding the blade, Damon catching her other free hand. But it was Cornelius who stopped Alice from cutting out the shroud of tears.

He snapped his fingers right before her eyes, and she paused as if frozen.

"If you will allow me, Alice, I can get it out in a different way. A way with far less pain and brutality." Cornelius's voice took on a rhythm that snared the ears and mind they were attached to.

"I want it out. I don't care all that much about how. I'll use up every scrap of power inside me right now if that is what it will take," she declared to the three of them.

"What if I told you I could do it with a flower? A simple white flower." Cornelius's voice built in power and rhythmic tone, pulling Owen in, and yet it was directed at Alice.

"Do you know about the white flower? Over the ages, a white flower has moved men and women. It has moved ideas and opened doors. The white flower has so much power it has helped build nations, and it has stopped wars. And today, with your permission? In fact, right now the white flower will do one more trick. One more deed for good."

Cornelius slipped from inside his lapel a pure white rose.

"See, Alice? Look." The stem was lush green and absent of any thorns. "Beautiful, isn't it? See the crisp lines and soft tips."

Cornelius held the flower closer, and even Owen couldn't help but stare.

It is beautiful and pure. It reminds me of her. A soft peace, straight from the breast of Mother Nature.

Cornelius twisted the flower ever so delicately. The petals seemed to breathe with a subtle life. To almost dance, to be just on the verge of speaking.

"It's a wild thing, the white flower. A wild thing, to be sure. But one for good, for life, for love of a different kind."

Cornelius sent it spinning, and Owen thought he noticed Alice's skin glowing where the shroud could be seen peeking through the gaps in her clothing, and yet Owen found he couldn't look away from the flower.

"In all time, there is a balance. Something given, something received. Always a balance. Can you see the balance, Alice? Can you see it inside the white rose? Look carefully."

The rose shifted or blended—Owen couldn't be sure if the motion had changed—from moving in a slow back-and-forth to a soft spinning. The glow in the room changed, brighter and brighter.

Owen jolted as Cornelius's hand crushed the rose, breaking the spell.

Alice let out a shock of breath, her hand flying up to touch the skin over her collarbone.

"It's gone! The shroud is gone. It's not in my head. It's not under my skin anymore."

"Of course it is gone," Cornelius said as he opened up his hand, revealing crushed black petals, falling from his hand as ash. As if it had been a dried, dead thing for some time rather than the beautiful plucked flower it had been.

"What the hell was that?" Owen asked.

"It was magic, Owen. God-loving magic."

"I don't care, it's gone. And Kerogen is gone. I am free!" Alice said to Owen.

"I don't understand. And why the hell didn't you tell me the plan?" Owen said as he gently released Alice's arm, having partly forgotten he had been holding it the whole time.

"We couldn't, Owen," Cornelius said in a normal voice. "Kerogen needed to see it, to feel your words. To feel the betrayal, it had to be real and not real. Damon knew you were ready for your next step, to go all the way to the bridge. Mara, though she hated it, did too. Even before the attack the other night, when you almost did it without our help. All three of us agreed you were ready."

"It doesn't matter," Alice said. "None of this matters anymore. I am free. Completely free."

Owen caught Alice in a hug as she flung her arms tight around him in celebration. Her lips stole his as she shared a pure, raw joy that didn't match the small set of tears as they glided down her smooth skin and touched his own. "Alice?"

"I am free, Owen, finally free. I can go home. I can go home, and that thing is out of me. Father Patrick?" Alice turned to look at Cornelius, needing to see if what he had said before was still true.

"As promised, I will find your priest and see what can be done. Now, let's go back upstairs where Mara and the others are all waiting to celebrate Alice's freedom and the

demise of—as Owen so eagerly put it—an asshole. Along
with Daphne's early birthday, of course. As you can imagine, Mara doesn't like to be kept waiting, and she can be a
little bit prickly when she is concerned over Owen."

"I'm free," Alice whispered low, though everyone in the
room could clearly hear it.

It took a moment for Damon to reach up and pull the trapdoor back down. The four of them climbed back up the stairs
to something far different than the ice-covered entrance to
Hell that they had left.

The air was clean, as if a fresh breeze had just passed
through the enormous hall. They stood on the black polished stage with bouncing balloons, shiny lights and their
people eager for their return.

Mara's smiling face was the first to greet them as she
stood with a champagne glass in hand. To Owen, it looked
as if she were standing first guard before Clover and Jessie,
Daphne and Max. Jasper and Jones hung back by the bar.

But what was completely odd were the three lifelike
imitations of Cornelius and Damon holding a chained-to-
the-floor Alice. A perfect full-sized replica of the three, so
lifelike it was enough for Owen to spare a questioning look
to Alice.

"I believe they didn't want Kerogen to see me coming.
Just another reason going in alone is a better plan than
working with others. Far less surprises."

"No. You're not alone anymore."

"Owen, I was just making light of it," Alice said as they
walked forward.

"I don't care. You're not alone anymore." Owen paused
as a buried feeling so solid it seemed to scrape his insides
clean bubbled up from inside his chest. Harder than facing
Kerogen. Scarier than the idea of meeting the Devil. And
more responsibility than leading a run through the gates of
Heaven. Owen was caught between Alice's deep green eyes

and perfect face, and a stone of truth as it bubbled up from within. "I don't want to be without you."

The world paused while she looked at him.
I am finally free, and he wants me to tie myself to him. Home is within my grasp. I am free. And yet . . .
"I don't want to be without you either."

CHAPTER THIRTY

John Legend played over the radio as Owen's old green truck rolled down a quiet suburb in the heart of Denver, Colorado. Normal, everyday houses with small, tidy little lawns and the occasional apple tree or oak dotted the planned neighborhood. It was everything his life wasn't: safe, organized, a perfect place to raise a normal family.

A quiet anticipation sat with tension within the edges of the cab as the truck rolled over a small speed bump that to Owen's mind was just silly.

Alice sat still, watching out the window, hands in her lap while her mind was deep in thought. All the while the music bathed the air with rhythm and soul.

"There it is," Alice said, sitting up. "The third one on the right. You can see the red mailbox and the large window."

Owen took notice of the house with the blue door and gray trim with an immaculate lawn before a large square window. He didn't speak as he checked his mirrors, seeing Jessie's van right behind him and spotting Alice's van behind

Jessie's, which Max was driving. He let his old truck slow, Alice's childhood home coming closer and closer.

"Would you like me to go in with you?" Owen asked.

"I don't know. I don't know what I want," Alice spoke as he pulled the truck to a stop just shy of the house. "I am not a little girl anymore. I am not what I was when I left this place. I am not sure I belong anymore."

"Sure you are, Alice. We are all little boys and girls when we go back home. Just hold my hand, and everything will be fine, I promise you. Besides, I have never seen you back down from anything. You won't start now. Now get out of my truck before I kick your ass."

"You think you can just say anything and there won't be consequences?" Alice's voice held an edge, but it was false, and they both knew it.

"Come on. You're almost home. Let's get you the rest of the way."

Together they climbed out of the cab, if not fast then at least together. They walked down the rest of the sidewalk, making their way toward the front door.

Owen didn't look back to check on the others. He didn't need to as Alice's soft green eyes both melted his heart and confirmed he was on the right path. Her hand was cold but a pure comfort as it slipped into his own.

Together, Alice and Owen walked down the long cement path toward the simple house neither understood. Owen gave a small kiss to the side of Alice's cheek before reaching up, ignoring the gold knocker and knocking three times on the Davises' door. Tension overlapped as they waited and listened.

A child's voice started to shout that there was someone at the door. At the same time, a woman's voice said, "No, honey, you stay. I'm closer. I'll get it. Please see she finishes her green beans this time before she gets down from the table."

Alice squeezed Owen's hand with force, and he leaned

over so her shoulder ran up against his arm. The contact was a soft comfort of love and support as the door opened.

"Hello, can I help you?"

Owen waited for Alice to speak as he looked clearly at Dede Davis. The shape of the face, the indenting around the nose, even the sparkling eyes all claimed this woman as Alice's mother.

Alice didn't speak, just stood there. And Owen felt a slight shake in her hand even as it was squeezing his own.

"Hi," he said awkwardly into the silence.

"Hi. Can I help you—"

Owen watched as Dede's gaze tracked to Alice and held. Held.

He bore witness as reflection and a slow bridge of clarity vibrated between mother and daughter.

"Alice?" Dede's voice was soft and thin. A single thread of hope for the impossible.

"Mom?" Alice squeezed out the word.

Dede shook with emotion, then suddenly, almost violently, wrapped her arms around Alice in a fierce hold.

ACKNOWLEDGMENTS

I have worked for years to become a writer, and this is my first published work. Behind each word, each sentence, was barrel after barrel of support from family, friends and even strangers.

I want to thank each of you, for my journey here was long and meant everything to my family and me. We did it together, and I wouldn't have it any other way.

Michelle Greene, for the unending support and being my guiding light, my first advisor. My mother, Christine Feehan, for supporting my path. Domini, Chris and Denise for always being there. Michael Greene and Gayle Greene for always having my back.

My reading group, The League of Awesome (they did not choose the name). Sco, Abel, Rachel and JoCarol, Peggy, Erin, Judith and Gayle, Manda, Renee and Dian. You came through for me when I needed you the most, and you told me the truth.

The starfish writing group. Christine, C.L., Sheila, Kathie, Karen and Susan. It has been a crazy, out-of-this-world ride!

Steven Axelrod at the Axelrod Agency took a chance on me and my writing. I will never forget the kind words. Julia Gains edited my work, helping clean the novel from a rough stone into something readable. Your skill is unreal.

And lastly, to my editor, Cindy Hwang. You saved this story and gave me perspective when I was in the dark.

Thank you all so much. I know I did not get here on my own. I hope you each rejoice in this Alice & Owen as much as I do. Go Team.

Keep reading for an excerpt from the next book
in the Alice & Owen series by Brian Feehan,

HARMONY OF LIES

Available spring 2023

Owen Brown sat on an old wood round, his legs stretched out toward the large steel-ringed fire on an old farm in Denver, Colorado. For the last couple hours, the cool wind of autumn had done battle with the heat of the tall fire as Owen silently pressed and released the strings on the neck of his old acoustic guitar with one hand, while his free hand held a warm beer he had forgotten about.

Around Owen were his people and Alice. They were all laughing and drinking and smiling up at the moon while he mostly held still but for the drifting finger of one hand over the guitar, and he let his mind sing with the chords of music. This time, as it had been the last few nights, he held a secret. A secret he wasn't prepared to share. It would be foolish to share, knowing Alice as he did, and knowing what he knew.

This time, as with those other times he had created music just in his head, Alice was singing with him. In his mind, her voice was strong and rich and had the ability to curve around words as easily as a dancer could move around a room. In his mind, where it was safe and he was entirely in control, they rode the sound together as it poured out of him into the night, his fingers digging into the strings of his acoustic, moving and tucking and pressing as the music in his mind reshaped and charged forth. He did this all deep within himself, while the others talked, joked and drank beer, leaving him alone with his secret.

"Hey! Hello! Why is nobody listening? I am trying to perform here," Max said from across the fire with enough force that the music was pulled back into Owen's body and away from his eyes and fingertips.

"Max," Clover said with a warning, "you don't need to be rude about it."

"I was listening. Don't bunch me in with the two of them," Daphne said, referring to Jessie and Clover.

Owen knew if he needed to, he could pull back the conversation, but he didn't bother after this many hours around a fire under the night sky. It was about letting the stress out. Letting go and letting the magic of the stars above sink into your soul.

"Daphne? I wasn't sure you were even in your own body, the way you have been staring into the fire for the last five minutes. Something on your mind? Something you need to get off your chest?" Jessie asked with genuine concern.

"Hey, leave her chest alone; she's only eighteen," Clover shot back with a grin. "Pervert!"

"Not cool, Clover," Jessie said quickly, pointing a finger off his beer bottle in accusation.

"No, nothing is on my mind!" Daphne called out, ignoring Clover and the attention she was bringing. "Nothing I need to talk about. I just like the fire tonight. It's pretty and sort of alive as it dances in the air, and I'm not sure those veggie tacos were all veggie." Just then, a small burp slipped out of Daphne's mouth, and everyone chuckled as her face turned a little red and she apologized.

These were his people. His people who lived outside the

rules of normal humans. Clover with her sass and spice. Jessie, his best mate, smooth and handsome. Max, tall and always able to find trouble. And Daphne, new and far too skinny, but bright and intelligent. And then there was Alice. Her left hand was in his hair and on the back of his head, her strong but gentle fingers moving over his scalp. A slow rhythm as her fingers moved this way and that. Her other hand held an almost-empty beer. She, too, seemed to simply be basking in the night air.

Alice was something altogether different. Her soul was broken, but it didn't stop her from burning bright. Owen could feel her, sense her in the deepest fog, the blackest night. Sure, she was an etherealist like everyone else around the fire, with an incredible well of power, but it was the fight within her that made them a match. Their love was new but genuine, a tangible force between them. She had been quiet the last half hour, the pressure of being reunited with her family three weeks ago slowly easing with each passing star.

"I am not rude," Max defended. "You are rude. I will say it again and again—musicians make the worst audience members. It's not cats, and it's not children. It's you people."

"No one says it's children. Besides, the worst are politicians. I think that's right. Politicians make the worst audience members," Daphne repeated.

"Not true. I used to think that, but it turns out politicians make for a great audience because they assume everyone is looking at them, and they play the part. What about A-list actors, like Matt Damon or Will Smith or Will Smith's daughter . . . what's her name?" Jessie continued. "But I might be wrong. Now that I am thinking about it, a comedian once told me the worst audience she ever went onstage for was at a corporate retreat. The retreat was in Atlanta at one of those big places. Anyway, she said she would give her left eye never to have to perform for any of them ever again. So there you go."

"How drunk are you?" Clover asked.

"About the same as you. Why?" Jessie said with a grin that lit up his eyes.

"Because first, don't screw with Will Smith or any part of his family. I think his wife is classy," Clover said. "Second, which female comedian were you quoting? Was that the short woman in Michigan who wasn't funny and who you flirted with for like four hours and got nowhere? Or the tall blonde with that lazy eye you went down on inside the coat closet at that bar in DC, who also wasn't funny?"

"Thanks for that, Clover. And neither, you asshole." He added, "And I wasn't ripping on Matt or Will. Though Matt Damon did screw up the Martian movie when he didn't have a beer with the girl at the end."

"Not his worst crime." Both Daphne and Clover said it at the same time.

"One, two, three, jinx," they both called before falling into laughter.

The song inside Owen's mind was calling, a relentless pull to be both finished and played aloud. He had seven songs already stored in the back of his mind with Alice at the microphone; he could hear or play them at a moment's notice. Alice and the others didn't know about any of them. There was a balance, a fine line with people—with a band. Press too hard, twist the knob too tight, and the string breaks.

You can only break a string so many times before you have to start all over, he thought. *I don't want to start over with them, and I'm about to twist the knob again.* His last thought held regret and concern.

A chilling air swept around the six people, and the fire's flame, hot and fierce, climbed higher into the night sky. Owen understood this couldn't last. In fact, it was over. He had stretched out the relaxing time around the fire for as long as he could without being reckless. Soon Daphne or Jessie or one of the others would head off to bed. Or Alice would tap him on the back of the head and say, "Let's take a walk."

"Hey, that's enough. Everyone shut up and give me your attention. It's time for my magic trick. Alice, you want to kick Owen and wake him up or something?" Max said.

"I can hear you, Max," Owen said, and shifted the guitar to the empty camping chair on his left.

"That's good, Owen, because we all thought you were going to start drooling if you played in your head any longer," Clover said.

Owen felt the laughter as much as he heard it from the others. But it was Alice who held the spotlight. Her skin held the glow of the firelight, and her internal strength never seemed to dim. His chest moved, and he drank her in. The smooth skin, her sharply cut hair and her deep green eyes captivated his mind and soul.

She was a punch he couldn't defend against, and he didn't want to try. A single contact from her was like water in the desert. A natural force to worship over.

How can I walk away from you? His thoughts drove a spike into his chest, and for a single perfect moment he wondered if he would feel real blood pouring out of his body.

"We will settle down and give you the stage. You tall, lanky, oddly dashing man-diva," Clover added, opening up the ice cooler and taking out a set of beers. One she took for herself and the other she passed to Jessie, who took it and tapped glass.

Everyone else seemed to settle for the first time in about an hour. But Owen couldn't feel the comfort. He looked toward the fire, the golden orange-and-black embers moving with an alien life that refused to be bound.

I can't hold still any longer.

Max moved from sitting forward to standing, the orange light of the campfire shading the stubble around his jaw, and for a moment he held everyone's attention.

Behind him the dark night swallowed the world, so it seemed as if Max's face and body could command the unnatural world between light and dark.

"All right, now that I finally have your attention, I have been working on a magic trick, and tonight, with each of you here as witness, I would like to perform for you." The voice that spoke was different, aged perhaps.

"Max, is one of your tricks tonight removing the tattoos you placed on Owen and me? Because that's the only trick I really want to see," Alice said.

Once more they laughed, and Owen tried to smile, but his face felt two-dimensional instead of natural. Laughter wasn't inside him right then. A phone call had come earlier, and he hadn't shared it with the others or with Alice. And they all needed to know. He had pushed the clock as far as he could.

"No, it is not," Max said. "I told you—I told everyone—I'm working on finding a way to remove your tattoos, but it's been difficult. I am still not sure what went wrong with that magic trick, and every time I ask for help, no one here, not one of you," Max accused, "is willing to be my volunteer."

"He has a fair point," Alice defended. "I am not going to volunteer."

Everyone laughed again. And Owen could see the defeat on Max's face.

Owen understood completely. Max used ethereal magic to perform magic tricks. It was incredibly subtle work, using the tiniest, thinnest cords of magic. No one else in his group even attempted such a thing. But Max seemed to be obsessed with his tricks. Only, every once in a while, they went wrong, and that was how Owen wound up with a king of diamonds tattoo on his butt cheek, while Alice had the queen of diamonds on hers. Of course, now, with the connection between Alice and him, Owen wasn't sure he wanted the tattoo of a playing card removed, but nobody needed to know that tonight.

"Okay, again, everyone shut up. I love you all, but can you please just shut it? Tonight, to break the tension, for my first magic trick—"

"Hold it!" Owen said, raising his flat beer high into the air and climbing up onto his feet.

"Owen?" Max asked. Then he swore with a knowing grace.

"I love you, Max, but I have no idea what your next trick or tricks are going to do, and I have something to say before we all start diving into chaos or for cover."

"Why are there so many days in my life that I can't understand why I bother with any of you?" Max sat back down. Jessie was there with an arm around Max's left shoulder.

"It's all good, buddy. Owen's just building some anticipation for the next time you do your thing. Let's hear what our fearless leader has to say. Go ahead, boss. We're all listening. We are all ears, just like Clover."

Clover reached over and good-heartedly punched Jessie, and Owen ignored the byplay.

"Thanks, Jessie. You're too kind," Owen said. Unable to help himself, he looked back and down toward Alice, some deep part of his soul needing to hold on to her.

Together, Alice's and Owen's eyes met, and the world became so simple, and then overwhelming. What he was about to say was going to change everything.

I have to go, and you have to stay.

Internally he swore as she broke the contact with a questioning look crossing her face. Not sorrow, but perhaps a sense of what was about to come.

"Boss, is this where you tell us we aren't working hard enough with our instruments?" Clover interrupted. "Or is this . . . is this where you tell us we aren't pushing ourselves as artists? Oh, I know—you're about to tell us we need to anticipate one another, to think and feel and move like one heartbeat when we are up onstage or we will all burn to death." She and everyone else gave a small chuckle.

And this time, when Owen smiled, he thought he could feel humor on the outskirts of his emotion. And then his will for what needed to be done hardened over his heart.

The road is a brutal place to call home. Tell them the truth.

"I received a call a couple of hours ago. Mara is asking for our help." Owen was shaking his head *no* before Alice could ask.

"Does this have to do with Father Patrick and me getting him back? Cornelius said just a couple of days ago that everything is on track with negotiations."

"No. This call had nothing to do with Father Patrick or the negotiations to get him back. No, this was just a request to do a thing for Mara and the Golden Horn—do them a solid by hand delivering some personal invitations in San Francisco." Owen turned to include the rest of his people. "We all know Mara's secret ballroom under her club was a special, important place for our kind and the We population before Mara shut the doors years ago. I don't have the details, but it's been alluded to me that reopening the space is a big deal in the We world, and Mara needs the right We to sign off on it. I said yes to hand delivering some invitations. I plan for us to be on the road by no later than eleven tomorrow morning. If we drive all night, we should arrive in San Francisco around the time the invitations show up."

Jessie said, "Do we have to be on the road that early? I have been working hard on getting a solid hangover by tomorrow. It would be nice to sleep most of it off."

"Sorry, Jessie, eleven it is," Owen said with a smile for his friend. "Unless you all want to stay. I can go alone."

"I think I can pull myself out of bed, but you are on notice, Owen. No more of these early-hour leaving ideas."

"Sure, Jessie. Clover?"

"You think I am going to let you go to San Francisco on your own? I missed the last time you went. I'm going this time. Do we know who the invitations are for? And how many are there?" Clover asked. "Must be some important people if Mara wants you to hand deliver them."

"I have no idea, I just know that the invitations will be at the Grand Hotel around noon the day after tomorrow, and I need to make the deliveries right away. Then I figure we can hit some shops, take in a club. There's an old friend I want to see too. Might have a line on some musicians."

"Sounds good to me," Clover said. "I have never been. You?" she directed her question toward Jessie.

"No, never. I'm an East Coast man."

"Of course you are."

Owen didn't sit, didn't let go of the spotlight, but he waited.

"Road trip?" Max said. "It's about time. If I have to spend another week here with all of you in a barn, I am going to go join the circus. No offense, Alice."

"None taken," she said.

"San Francisco," Daphne said to Clover, low under her breath. Owen thought he could actually see her spirit rise at the idea. "I have always wanted to see the Golden Gate Bridge. And Alcatraz, I hear it's haunted. Will you go with me?"

"Hold on," Owen said. "Daphne, you aren't going with us." Owen paused, letting his words sink in and over the group.

"I'm sorry, what? Did I do something wrong?"

"Not at all. Our group is just too dangerous a place for anyone not in the band."

"Wait, what? What do you mean, she isn't coming with us?" Jessie said.

Ignoring Jessie and the reaction of the others, Owen pressed on. "We told you we would do our best to keep you safe and unbound until you turned eighteen. You're unbound and relatively safe now. When we head out tomorrow, we will drop you off at the Denver airport. It's not very far from here. We'll cover a ticket back to your home in North Carolina. I am sure your parents will be happy to see you. After all, the holidays are only a few months away."

Each word broke her inside. He could see it. Read it on her too-young face and soft frame. *You want to stay. You thought you were part of the band.*

He watched as she held in the pain. Held back tears that were even now pushing against her control.

Show me the fire. Let it burn out the lie.

"Owen," Clover said with a reprimand.

"Ah man," Max added from the side.

To his surprise, it was Alice who stayed silent. He had thought she might interfere.

Jessie stood up. "Hold on a second. You can't just make that decision and tell us how it is. Daphne has done everything we've asked her to. She belongs with us. If she wants."

"Of course I can. It was the deal, Jessie. You asked if we could take her in and keep her safe until she turned eighteen. Well, we did that. And now with Mara and all the trouble we have at our backs—not to mention I want to put a band together—she belongs at home with her family. Daphne will be safe there. She's eighteen now and isn't in danger of being bonded by a high-level We. She knows what to look out for, and we can give her some names and numbers to call in her area if she gets into trouble."

"You didn't even ask, and you can't possibly know she will be safe there. Why didn't you talk to us about it?" Jessie said.

"Hey, I get it; she's a nice girl, and she hasn't stepped wrong this whole time, but you know what we do, how we live. She's made it clear this isn't her place. I'm not a baby-sitting service, but if you want to be, you go ahead. No one is stopping you."

"You're being an asshole, Owen," Jessie shot back.

"You're right, Jessie, me getting Daphne out of harm's way and sending her back to her parents is me being terrible.

Grow up. Does everyone else forget the world we live in and the crap at our feet? Not all the We out there are happy with us, and there's an unfinished payback with hunters that could show up at any moment. You know what we are about; we aren't a safe place for her now that we aren't hiding."

"You didn't give Daphne a chance. You just made up your mind without talking to us, and now you are sending her off just like that. That's not fair, Owen. Fuck you, man," Jessie said.

Owen held still as the last words vibrated inside him. His skin started to itch, and the flames dancing between Jessie and him seemed a minor inconvenience as he looked at his best friend in the world.

Is this where you leave me? Is this the place and time, old friend? Owen wondered, not for the first time.

Owen breathed, and as he did, he felt the heat of the fire mix with the cool night sky.

"Give her a chance? Wake up. We are musicians; every moment is our chance. She spent three weeks inside the Golden Horn. Three weeks. Surrounded by some of the best musicians in all of Miami, and that includes you. She never took the stage. Not even when it was closed. Not even in the morning when the bar wasn't open. We were in Chicago, and she didn't step up there or at Tim's. She plays in the van with the door closed, where no one can hear her. She doesn't fight for the stage, for the moment. Did she hit up any one of you to jam with? No. She listens to each of us then goes and plays all by herself. At the same time, we took her to stage after stage after stage. And you know what, kid? There is nothing wrong with that. But we don't force people to play, and we don't ask them. Shit, the best thing I can do to keep you safe is to send you home. If that makes me a terrible guy, I'll own that scar over my soul. God knows I have far, far worse." Owen felt her pain, her crushed heart, as his eyes locked onto her big browns. He held her pain, tucked it inside where it flared bright and real inside his own chest, the sensation multiplying as Daphne's first tears started to fall. But his face held, unchanged.

Quick and nimble as only the young can be, Daphne got up and ran from the firelight. The sound of her muffled cries flowed behind her.

"Clover, go with her," Owen commanded.

"Why are you such a dick sometimes? She's just eighteen. Not everything is about Heaven and Hell and you."

"Clover, she went out into the farmer's field, and there could always be some barbed wire out there. She might not see it in the dark."

"I'll stay. Max?" Clover said, quick and cool.

"Yeah, I'll go." Max got up quickly, tapping Jessie on the shoulder and giving a nod Owen's way at the same time.

"I can't believe your hubris. You are worried about wire? You just crushed Daphne's soul. You broke her heart in front of everyone she looks up to. And you're worried she might bleed a little. You do know she is one of us. She is not just an eighteen-year-old, she is an etherealist. She is a musician, and you treat her like she is less than you are," Jessie said.

"I'm aware," Owen replied.

"You and your rules. You never think. Not everyone is like you. And that's a very good thing. I get that you didn't grow up with a family, and so no one taught you how to ask permission. You weren't taught about the advantage of being nice. But you just broke her heart and you didn't have to. She would be safe with us. We've kept her safe so far, and now she's an adult. What's wrong with that?"

"Do I really need to spell it out for you, Jessie? Are you going to make me hold your hand? I know you like her, and she's a good kid. But this isn't a safe place. Next to me isn't a safe place. And if you were being honest with yourself, you'd know it's true. Now, I'm not talking about this anymore. We all have to be packed and leaving by eleven. Alice, you want to take a walk with me?"

"Just like that you're walking. Walking away."

"Yeah, Jessie, I am. Before we both do something we can't take back."

"Really, but I'm not done talking about this."

Owen felt his fist tighten. And one of the rules he lived by onstage crawled up his leg and bit into his spine. "There can only be one leader."

To his surprise, Alice's cool hand caught his forearm and slid down, opening his fist until her fingers were locked with his own as they started to walk away.

"Jessie, let him go. You know how Owen can be."

Owen continued to walk, hand in hand with Alice, back toward the barn as Clover finished speaking.

"I know. No, Jessie, stay here. I know how Owen can be, but let's talk it out. You've been drinking. Let him go," Clover continued.

Ready to find
your next great read?

Let us help.

Visit prh.com/nextread

Penguin
Random
House